FANDANGO AND OTHER STORIES

RUSSIAN LIBRARY

R

■ □ ■

For a list of books in the series, see page 301

FANDANGO & OTHER STORIES

ALEXANDER GRIN

Translated by Bryan Karetnyk

Columbia University Press / *New York*

Published with the support of Read Russia, Inc.,
    and the Institute of Literary Translation, Russia
Columbia University Press
Publishers Since 1893
New York   Chichester, West Sussex
cup.columbia.edu

Library of Congress Cataloging-in-Publication Data
Names: Grin, A. (Aleksandr), 1880–1932, author. | Karetnyk, Bryan,
    translator.
Title: Fandango and other stories / Alexander Grin ; translated by
    Bryan Karetnyk.
Description: New York : Columbia University Press, 2020. |
    Series: Russian library
Identifiers: LCCN 2019016190 (print) | LCCN 2019980628 (e-book) |
    ISBN 9780231189767 (cloth) | ISBN 9780231189774 (paperback) |
    ISBN 9780231548502 (e-book)
Subjects: LCSH: Short stories, Russian—20th century—Translations
    into English.
Classification: LCC PG3476.G68 A2 2020 (print) |
    LCC PG3476.G68 (e-book) | DDC 891.73/5—dc23
LC record available at https://lccn.loc.gov/2019016190
LC e-book record available at https://lccn.loc.gov/2019980628

Columbia University Press books are printed on permanent
    and durable acid-free paper.
Printed in the United States of America

Cover design: Roberto de Vicq de Cumptich
Book design: Lisa Hamm

CONTENTS

INTRODUCTION: THE MAN FROM GRINLANDIA

BARRY P. SCHERR

I t is easy to understand why some of Alexander Grin's contemporaries within Russia assumed that he was a foreign writer. The surname is not only very unusual for a Russian but also pronounced like (and in the Cyrillic alphabet serves as the transliteration for) the English Green or Greene. Similarly, many of his characters have names that are not typically Russian. In a few instances these, too, sound English (Hart, Steel, Grey), some resemble names found among other nationalities (the German Braun, the French Dupleix, the Italian Garducci), and still others (Bam-Gran, Scorrey, Egl) simply seem invented. The influences on Grin, whether cited by himself or others—including Rudyard Kipling, Robert Louis Stevenson, James Fenimore Cooper, Jules Verne, Mayne Reid, and Edgar Allan Poe—were almost exclusively foreign and often authors who wrote in English. Some even suspected him of plagiarism: one of the many legends that swirled around the reclusive Grin held that, as a sailor, he had murdered an English sea captain, stolen a suitcase full of manuscripts, and was gradually translating them into Russian, passing them off as his own.

Grin's style no doubt played into the rumor that his works had been rendered into Russian from another language. He frequently resorts to convoluted syntax that requires careful parsing, devises odd phrasings and similes that impress with their originality but can resist ready interpretation, and employs italics with a frequency rarely found among Russian writers. Readers of this volume will find that Bryan Karetnyk's fine translations have met the challenge of dealing with Grin's sometimes difficult manner. While remaining admirably close to the Russian and conveying the sense of Grin's style, he has managed to find ideal equivalents for even the more obscure Russian phrasings and to put the whole into highly readable English. The settings of Grin's stories also set him apart. Some take place in Russia, whereas in others the action occurs abroad, often in exotic regions. And many of his major writings refer, either entirely or in part, to places that are not found on the globe at all: Zurbagan, Liss, and Gel-Giu are among the place names that recur from work to work, so that more than one attempt has been made to create a map of this nonexistent territory. Shortly after Grin's death, a Soviet critic labeled it "Grinlandia," a term reminiscent of the Russian name for an actual exotic locale, Greenland ("Grenlandia"). Grinlandia has since become synonymous with the world that found expression in Grin's work, yet again emphasizing the so-called foreignness that distinguishes so much of his writing.

And yet Grin was very much a Russian. Born in 1880 as Alexander Stepanovich Grinevsky, he died in 1932, with his literary career, which began in 1906, bisected by the Bolshevik Revolution, an event that was to prove fateful for him personally and for his reputation as a writer. His early years were spent far from the political and literary centers of Russia. When he was two, his family moved twenty miles from his birthplace in the town of Slobodskoy to what was then the small city of Vyatka. Today, renamed Kirov to honor an assassinated Bolshevik leader, that city has some 500,000 inhabitants and is a major manufacturing center. But in Grin's youth, Vyatka was a relatively quiet place, with a population of perhaps 25,000 that a few decades earlier had served as a place of political exile, thanks in no small part to its relatively remote location nearly 600 miles northeast of Moscow. Among those sent there was the famous political activist and writer Alexander Herzen. Grin's own father, Stepan Grinevsky, had ended up in the area because of his exile to Russia after involvement in the Polish rebellion of 1863.

Most of what we know about Grin's early life comes from his unfinished *Autobiographical Tale*, which he wrote near the end of his life and breaks off abruptly in 1910. Like many autobiographies, it should be approached with caution: comparison of the published text with early drafts indicates that he occasionally rearranged or embellished events for literary effect. That said, some collaborating evidence exists for its latter portions and suggests that he remained broadly faithful to his experiences. Grin describes reading voraciously as a child, drawn to adventure stories that described distant lands and the romance of sailing ships, all of which contrasted with the drab milieu of Vyatka.

The growing allure of the sea—abetted by the oppressiveness of life in his hometown and a lack of desire to continue his schooling—caused Grin to set off for the port city of Odessa, 1,400 miles away, shortly before his sixteenth birthday in 1896. There his dreams quickly clashed with reality. His lack of experience and frail build made it difficult to find work as a sailor, and his money soon ran out. He managed to find a few temporary jobs on ships that sailed the coast of the Black Sea, and in 1897, he served on a cargo ship to Alexandria—the only time he ever ventured abroad. But he was fired during the return voyage and that July returned to Vyatka. The following year Grin again headed for a southern port, this time Baku on the Caspian Sea, but found only occasional employment, his one enduring remembrance of that time the malaria that would plague him off and on for the rest of his life. His subsequent efforts to establish himself included odd jobs back in Vyatka, brief work mining for gold, lumberjacking, and sailing on a river barge.

In 1902, still unsettled, Grin volunteered for the army, but he chafed against its discipline. His first attempt to desert, only a few months after he enlisted, ended with his swift capture. Later that year, assisted by a cell of Socialist Revolutionaries (SRs) with whom he made contact, he succeeded. The SRs, along with the Bolsheviks and other groups, were agitating for the overthrow of the tsarist regime and conducting a campaign of terrorism, assassinating numerous individuals associated with the government. Grin proved a poor terrorist but was an effective propagandist until his November 1903 arrest in the Crimean seaport of Sevastopol. He spent nearly two years in jail, thus missing the violent events of 1905, which began in January with the shooting of demonstrators in St. Petersburg on what came to be known as "Bloody Sunday" and continued with strikes and riots throughout Russia for much of that year. Freed by a general amnesty for political prisoners, Grin went to St. Petersburg under an assumed name but was again arrested early in 1906 and sentenced to four years' exile in Siberia. He soon escaped from the city to which he had been sent and by July was back in St. Petersburg, where he spent the next four years under a different false identity, living with Vera Abramova, who would become his first wife. The authorities only discovered his identity in 1910, when he received a less severe sentence: a two-year exile to the northern province of Arkhangelsk. This time Grin served out his term. After six years of wandering about Russia and failing to find a calling, he spent ten years living either illegally, in jail, or in exile. These early experiences are reflective of his character: unwilling to submit to discipline or to social norms, motivated by a youthful idealism, and drawn to adventure and to following his own path.

Grin's literary career began in 1906, first with stories that served as propaganda pamphlets for the SRs—toward whom he soon cooled—and then with a series of tales largely based on his experiences with that movement, sometimes depicting individual adherents favorably but for the most part reflecting antipathy toward the SR program. He signed his first published story with the initials of the false name under which he was living but soon settled on "A. S. Grin," the name by which he was thenceforth to be known and which for several years proved sufficient to conceal his true identity from the authorities.

Grin's signature technique developed rapidly: the first manifestations of Grinlandia appeared in his prose as early as 1909. During these years, he also enthusiastically embraced the bohemian life of the capital, spending hours in various drinking establishments where he especially associated with other writers. Among these, his closest friend was Alexander Kuprin, at the time among the most popular Russian prose writers. Grin, though, never became associated with any literary school, and his mode of writing—with its frequently non-Russian characters, imaginary settings, adventure-filled plots, and excursions into the improbable or unreal—remained very much his own.

On returning from exile, Grin quickly resumed the unruly life he had led prior to his arrest. Although he was to look back on this time fondly, his years of wandering had left him with an unsociable manner, so that even those to whom he felt close found him to be reserved and melancholy. Arkady Averchenko, a prominent satirist and editor of *Novyi satirikon*, to which Grin began to contribute in 1914, called him "Mr. Inveterate Pessimist." Another writer recalled that Grin impressed him as a person who did not know how to smile. Meanwhile, Grin's heavy drinking, dating from the pre-exile period, helped bring about the end of his marriage to Vera Abramova and was to remain a near-constant habit.

The writing, though, continued apace. Grin's first volume of stories had appeared as early as 1908; by 1913, he had written enough that a three-volume collection of his works appeared that year. When World War I started, he was found unfit to serve in the army, but he began to write frequently about the war. Grin found a ready market for stories on that topic in the popular magazines that served as the chief outlet for his work. Their publishers wanted brief tales, preferably exhibiting a patriotic view of the conflict, and were not much concerned with literary quality. The pay was poor, so that to earn enough to survive, Grin wrote scores of short pieces: in 1915 alone, he published more than 100 stories and poems. Many were eminently forgettable and not republished for many decades; only in 2017 did an edition of his stories gather nearly all the previously uncollected writing. However, alongside this work Grin managed to produce several excellent tales, including this volume's "The Poisoned Island."

In the summer of 1916, Grin was banished from Petrograd (as St. Petersburg was called at this time) to a Finnish village some 40 miles away after being overheard making disdainful remarks about the tsar. However, he was able to return after the February Revolution of 1917, the event that led to the establishment of the Provisional Government. In general Grin wrote little about politics, but a nonfiction piece titled "To the Revolution on Foot," describing his journey back to the capital, indicates that he was excited about the fall of the regime that had jailed and exiled him. He appears, though, to have been less enthusiastic about the Bolshevik takeover: through the first six months of 1918, until strict censorship was established, he published regularly in several satirical journals that were hostile to the new government.

From mid-1918 Grin's life in postrevolutionary Petrograd became increasingly difficult. With many of his usual publishing outlets closed, he found his options becoming limited and frequently went hungry. Although in 1919 he managed to publish several stories in *Plamia*, a journal edited by Anatoly Lunacharsky, a prominent Bolshevik and first head of the People's Commissariat for Education, Grin's financial situation remained precarious. That same year he was drafted into the Red Army, where, thanks to his age and physical condition, he was assigned a noncombat role. Nonetheless, he soon fell ill, was eventually given leave, and then returned to Petrograd. With the assistance of the influential Maxim Gorky, he was able to get into one of the city's overcrowded hospitals, where he was diagnosed with typhus. Lacking any means of support after his discharge, he again turned to Gorky, who saw to it that Grin was allocated a food ration and a room in the House of Arts, one of several institutions that Gorky helped to establish in order to assist Petrograd's cultural elite during this harsh period.

The House of Arts, which occupied a large building in the heart of Petrograd, became a center for intellectual and cultural life during the several years of its existence, serving as both a refuge and a focus of intellectual ferment for its inhabitants. Leading literary figures either lived there or came to give readings; the swirl of activities included seminars, concerts, and painting exhibitions. Friendships and literary alliances were forged, and the House became a hotbed for nurturing younger writers. However, Grin's personality had not changed. Although he became friendly with a few of his fellow residents, for the most part he was remembered as a taciturn and morose individual who kept largely to himself. The poet Vladislav Khodasevich, who also lived in the House, described him as "an author of adventure tales, a gloomy and tubercular man. . . acquainted with almost no one and, it was said, engaged in the training of cockroaches."

Despite Grin's relative uninvolvement in the life of the House, the months that he spent there proved crucial for both his professional and personal life. He completed *Scarlet Sails*, the novella that was to establish his subsequent reputation and remains, to this day, his most beloved work; he began writing what would become his first novel, *The Shining World*; he composed several fine stories; and he found inspiration for both "The Rat-Catcher" and "Fandango." During this time, too, he renewed an acquaintance with and then married Nina Nikolaevna Mironova, who was to remain his companion for the rest of his life.

The three years after Grin left the House of Arts in the spring of 1921 and lived elsewhere in Petrograd brought a revival of the publishing industry. He began to earn a reasonable income and saw his modest reputation grow. Granted, his works were sparsely reviewed, and even at the beginning of the 1920s, some had little patience for literature that did not deal with the realities of the postrevolutionary era. However, through the middle of that decade, some critics would express at least a degree of admiration for the romantic and imaginative elements that characterized many of his works, as well as for his psychological acuity.

In the spring of 1924, Grin and his wife moved to the Crimea, where the warm weather and proximity to the sea had long been attractions. They settled in the port of Feodosia, and for a few years Grin's career was at its height, necessitating occasional trips to Moscow and Leningrad regarding publishing matters. Although he remained essentially a literary outsider and was rarely able to place his writings in the most highly respected journals of his day, Grin did not lack readers or opportunities to see his work in print. He published many stories in *Krasnaia niva*, a biweekly for which Lunacharsky again was an editor, and in the highly popular *Ogonyok*. Collections of his tales came out regularly, and, by 1930, he had published six novels as well. Thus the mid-1920s in particular were relatively happy years for Grin, though his wife later remarked that he was still his reserved and solitary self, with the couple having a narrow social circle in Feodosia.

As the decade wore on, negative assessments of Grin's works became dominant, with sharp attacks for their Western influences, fantastic elements, and seeming indifference toward contemporary Soviet life. A publication that made recommendations to libraries summarily described his books as "not needed." By the late 1920s he was thus finding it increasingly difficult to place his work. The years 1929 and 1930 witnessed the publication of his last two completed novels, but Grin had been left with relatively little time to write new stories, and reprints of his previous work had virtually stopped. The honoraria for his writing were such that his finances had never been secure; now he and his wife began to endure genuine hardship. Furthermore, his health, thanks in part to his continued drinking, was beginning to decline.

In 1930 Grin and his wife left Feodosia for Stary Krym, about 15 miles inland, in part to live more economically and in part because the higher elevation at their new home was reputed to have health benefits for those experiencing respiratory problems. With his fiction not in demand, he reluctantly began his *Autobiographical Tale*, which was serialized in a major journal, *Zvezda*, the following year, but that was to be his only publication of 1931. In August that year he fell seriously ill, apparently suffering from a recurrence of tuberculosis, and two months later was diagnosed with pneumonia. He continued to weaken as the months passed, then in June 1932 was found to have stomach cancer. Grin died on July 8, already, it seemed, largely forgotten by the wider literary community.

Oddly enough, Grin's reputation underwent a mild revival shortly after his death. During the final years of his life, the powerful Russian Association of Proletarian Writers, popularly known by its Russian acronym, RAPP, had strongly advocated for a proletarian literature and railed against those it deemed insufficiently wedded to the revolutionary cause. RAPP was dissolved a few months before Grin's death, to be replaced in 1934 by the Writers' Union.

Although socialist realism then became the officially sanctioned mode for writers, the harsh attacks on Grin ceased. Several collections of his stories were published during the years leading up to World War II, and, if the few critical articles on him still expressed reservations, they could at least praise his originality and see his works as having a place in Soviet literature.

Grin's standing thus survived the purges of the 1930s, only to run afoul of another Stalinist campaign shortly after World War II. A pair of vicious articles attacked Grin as a "rootless cosmopolitan," a label more typically applied to Jews whose loyalty to the Soviet Union was being questioned, and for some years his works were no longer published. However, the thaw that followed Stalin's death brought a rapid change.

In 1956, a collection of his work appeared, containing a preface by the popular writer Konstantin Paustovsky, who did much over the years to promote Grin's reputation. From then on, Grin's renown grew rapidly, and his best-known works have been republished many times. In 1965, a six-volume collection of his writings came out in an edition of nearly half a million copies, making a wide selection of his works readily available. Other multivolume editions have followed since. Although only a handful of scholars outside Russia have devoted extensive attention to Grin, within Russia, the body of research on his work has become substantial. Although information about his life remained scattered and, in some cases, unpublished into the twenty-first century, a publishing house in Feodosia issued a series of volumes that were extensively annotated by associates of the Grin museum in that city and that contained memoirs, biographical materials, and Grin's modest epistolary heritage.

Many of Grin's writings are widely known today, but none other matches the prominence of his signature work, *Scarlet Sails*, which has been adapted for film and stage (including an opera and a ballet).

The title has become ubiquitous, appearing as the name of not only restaurants and hotels but also enterprises ranging from a trucking company in St. Petersburg to a sauna in Nizhny Novgorod and an apartment complex in Moscow. Perhaps most famously, it serves as the name of an all-night festival in St. Petersburg that marks the end of the school year; a highlight of the celebration is the appearance on the Neva River of a ship rigged with scarlet sails. The fame of this single work has assured Grin's lasting renown, though in a way it also has sometimes served—at least among the broader public—to limit a full appreciation of his achievement.

While Grin was being reintroduced to Soviet readers in the post-Stalin era, an attempt was made to see the elements of Romanticism in his work as implying an underlying optimism and belief in the ability of people to achieve a bright future—thereby aligning him with one of socialist realism's goals, even if realism was not always present in his mature work and socialism, hardly at all.

Scarlet Sails certainly can be seen as in keeping with the official agenda. Its impoverished heroine, Assol, has endured the mockery of the local village inhabitants for having believed since childhood in a prophecy by a collector of tales named Egl, who had foretold that a handsome man on a ship with scarlet sails would one day carry her away to find happiness. Meanwhile, the tale's hero, Grey, has grown up wealthy and privileged but stifled by his environment. Drawn to the sea, he has become captain of his own ship. Reaching the shore where Assol lives and learning of the prophecy, he has scarlet sails stitched for his vessel and, as predicted, carries her away to happiness. The action takes place in the indeterminate realm of Grinlandia, as is true of almost all Grin's novels. The narrative shares certain similarities with fairy tales: the emphatically happy ending, a clear-cut conflict between good and evil, and seemingly miraculous happenings. However, *Scarlet Sails* in fact contains no outright fantasy but only some unlikely coincidences and the presence of a character who has both the means and the will to fulfill his own dream and that of another.

Among the works in this volume, "The Heart of the Wilderness" is thematically closest to *Scarlet Sails*. Again, a single individual endures the taunting of others: as a cruel prank, several men try to convince the protagonist to search for a wondrous settlement supposedly hidden in the jungle. Their made-up tale fulfills the role of Egl's prophecy by serving as a vision that one person manages to transform into reality through the strength of his own efforts: the seemingly duped hero goes on to create the village that was described to him. The notion that a single individual would possess the means and ability to create the ideal jungle colony described in the tale may strain the bounds of credibility, but, as in *Scarlet Sails*, nothing beyond the realm of the possible actually occurs. It is, finally, a work filled with optimism, in which the power of the human spirit prevails, enabling good to overcome evil. The 1956 collection that reintroduced Grin to Soviet readers included both these works, along with several others featuring a clearly positive outcome. This volume established a trend of seeing Grin as essentially an upbeat writer of adventure stories, some with fantastic elements, that appeal largely to a young adult audience.

Grin's work as a whole, however, tends to be darker and more probing of the human psyche than such stories suggest. Granted, the salient features of *Scarlet Sails* and "The Heart of the Wilderness" also appear in many of his other works: the foreign and often imaginary settings; events that are implausible, if not unreal; a sense of adventure; clear-cut distinctions between good and evil characters; and central figures possessed of enormous capabilities. But often his protagonists' struggles with the surrounding world are less readily resolved and the conclusions not necessarily so auspicious. The inner lives of characters frequently come to the fore, with readers plunged into the world of dream, delusion, or delirium. Grin essentially wrote fables in which the components of the work are harnessed to illustrate some central point and the verisimilitude of events or settings is of secondary importance. Indeed, his imaginary or at least unusual locales serve to isolate his figures from the usual trappings of civilization and bring into sharp relief their unusual traits that serve to convey Grin's central ideas.

Grinlandia thus emerges as a favored setting for Grin's fables. Granted, its exotic features—the tropical locale, the curious mix of figures who inhabit it, a sense of adventure and peril—can be seen as the author's creating in his imagination the world that he was never able to reach during his youthful wanderings. Indeed, many of the protagonists inhabiting that world, lone figures who reject or are rejected by society but who are motivated by a vision of an ideal, bear resemblances to Grin himself. More important, however, Grinlandia facilitated his unique manner. Grin claimed that he had a concrete picture of his nonexistent land and described in detail to at least one acquaintance a journey from one imaginary city to another. The made-up names of places and people put it outside any real-world geography, and yet it is a world much like ours, containing all kinds of people: rich and poor (money or its lack often plays a major role in his works), good and bad, cowardly and brave. Actual historical events, though, only occasionally penetrated Grinlandia, with, for instance, the Bolshevik Revolution being essentially absent from his novels. Some of the works set there contain phenomena not seen in the real world—thus in *The Shining World*, the hero is a man with the ability to fly—but at other times the narratives are entirely realistic. The key point is that Grinlandia is a world of expanded possibilities, where the improbable or even the impossible is on an equal footing with the everyday, thus allowing Grin to create fables in which the focus can be on the psychology of his heroes and what their struggles represented rather than on the specifics of a place or time.

■ □ ■

The stories in this volume together represent the greater portion of Grin's literary career and convey a sense of how his concerns and technique evolved over the years. The first two, "Quarantine" and "'She,'" are from the pre-Grinlandia period. The former is based on an episode in Grin's own life. When he joined the Socialist Revolutionaries, he was considered a suitable candidate for terrorist activities. Those recruited for such deeds were sometimes placed in a sort of quarantine, spending a length of time in another town in order to learn whether they were under police surveillance. If they were not, they would be dispatched to the location where a terrorist act was to be carried out. While Grin was with the SR branch in Nizhny Novgorod, he was sent to Tver, more than 350 miles away, to sit out his quarantine. During that time he came to the conclusion that he did not wish to kill anybody, and upon his return to Nizhny Novgorod, he refused to undertake the attack to which he had agreed. The story, one of Grin's earliest psychological studies, explores in depth the thought processes by which its protagonist comes to the realization that he lacks the soul of a terrorist.

"'She,'" unlike many of Grin's early stories, does not deal with either army life or revolutionaries but anticipates some of the qualities that recur in his later work. The anguished state of the tale's protagonist recalls Poe's writings, a likely influence that was to become even more evident in years to come and that was noted by critics even in the prerevolutionary era. Although the geography in the story is not imaginary, it is also strikingly unspecific: the events occur in a European country that uses the franc as currency, but even that much is not evident until toward the end. The not entirely benign role of the then–new cinema prefigures Grin's general suspicion of modern technology: movies, automobiles, airplanes, and the implements of modern warfare are treated with misgivings, if not outright hostility, in subsequent works.

Although "Reno Island," of 1909, is generally considered to be the first work set in Grinlandia, the considerably longer "Lanphier Colony," published just a few months later, at the beginning of 1910, offers the sharper presentation of iconic elements for such works: the self-reliant hero, who is in conflict with his surrounding society and often bears a name similar to that of Grin himself (Horn [Gorn in Russian], Grey, etc.); a stark distinction between good and evil figures; adventurous action in a warm clime on a sea or by the coast; odd names for both places and people; and the threat of or actual violence. Particularly important is the characterization of Horn, who, like Steel in "The Heart of the Wilderness," attempts to create his ideal community, but with far less felicitous results.

"The Devil of the Orange Waters" notably suggests that Grinlandia is located somewhere on the sea route between Australia and China. (San Riol, the port city for which Bangok and Baranov are heading, is one of the imaginary cities that recur in Grin's writings.) The story is of most interest, though, for Baranov, who is specifically Russian—and hence something of an alien presence in Grinlandia—as well as a political exile. Is he meant to be a former SR, with his despair and unfitness for life once again reflecting Grin's disillusionment with the movement and its members? In any case, Grin seems to hold this character at a distance, having him observed mostly through the eyes of Bangok, and not probing the inner person to the extent that Grin does with Horn and Steel, who are Baranov's antithesis.

Evidence of Grin's ability to write fine work even at the height of World War I, when he was busily turning out the short pieces that consumed much of his time, is provided by "The Poisoned Island," a finely wrought exploration of the fear that can be caused by the horrors of war, even when they are perceived only indirectly.

Narratively, this is one of Grin's more elaborately structured works. He allows information about what took place on the island to be revealed only gradually, with the initial findings by the crew of the *Viola*, the fragmentary account by one of the surviving children, and the contrasting newspaper speculations that only lead readers astray from the facts.

Grin sets "The Poisoned Island" several years in the future, as though predicting that the war would continue for some time. He is concerned, however, less with prognosis than with diagnosis, examining the causes of the mass hysteria that strikes the island's inhabitants. Their way of life—the kind envisioned in both "The Heart of the Wilderness" and "Lanphier Colony"—as well as their distance from the rest of civilization not only fail to protect them but make them even more vulnerable to the ravages of the modern world.

The final two stories in this collection, "The Rat-Catcher" and "Fandango," are among Grin's most enigmatic—and among his highest achievements. Atypically, he has his narrators living in a real city, Petrograd, at very specific times, just a few years after the Bolshevik Revolution (which goes essentially unmentioned). Both stories make use of Grin's own experiences, and both freely mix fantasy and reality, with the reader's perspective confined to that of their first-person narrator. If "Fandango," the later of the two, seems the stuff of dreams, then "The Rat-Catcher" is more the stuff of nightmare. The latter begins on March 22, 1920, just two days after the ailing Grin returned to Petrograd from his service in the Red Army. Like the narrator, Grin suffered from typhus and, like the character, found refuge in the huge structure that had once included the "Central Bank"—which had become the House of Arts in 1919. Some of the House's occupants lived in a number of the sixty-three rooms on the building's upper floors, which had comprised the living quarters of the wealthy Eliseev family, who owned the building before fleeing Russia in 1917. Grin's room, though, was in a different section, on a dank corridor lower down and once used for servants' quarters. The abandoned bank, with its labyrinth of empty rooms, created an eerie attraction for the House's inhabitants, who scavenged the piles of papers described in "The Rat-Catcher" for fuel as well as writing material. (Thus Grin used letterhead stationery from the "Central Bank of the Mutual Credit Society" when writing *The Shining World*.) This very real locale inspires haunting phantasmagoria, amid which the narrator, whether as the result of delirium or because he actually comes face to face with the uncanny, confronts his inner demons and sense of loss. Grin's qualms about modern technology appear once again, this time through the somewhat ambiguous role of the telephone.

"Fandango" centers on a visit to the House of Scholars, another real-life enterprise set up to aid the country's intellectual elite during the harsh aftermath of the Bolshevik Revolution. Grin went there regularly to receive the food ration to which he was entitled. This is a narrative in which time and space have been cut loose from their moorings, with the disjunction between the date of the main action and that at the end of the tale never fully resolved, and with the narrator magically transported to Zurbagan, the Grinlandian city that appears most often in Grin's works. (Bam-Gran, the agent involved in his going there, appears in at least one other story as well.) Although this work, too, has its dark moments, it is ultimately about the power of art and beauty. Unlike the music the narrator hears in a restaurant, the melody of the "Fandango" is transportive—as, literally, is the great work of art, in opposition to the more ordinary paintings that are described. Meanwhile, Ershov, a statistician, has no use for beauty. His material needs are quite real, but by insisting on their primacy, he causes the fine items brought by Bam-Gran to disappear. The narrator's sojourn in Grinlandia signifies the need to transcend the everyday, to believe in an ideal despite the realities of cold, hunger, and want. It is the assertion of such an ideal that makes "Fandango" one of Grin's most memorable stories, as well as a fitting conclusion to this collection.

TRANSLATOR'S NOTE

The twenty-six years spanning Alexander Grin's literary debut and his death in 1932 were some of the most tumultuous in not only Russian political history but also literary style and taste. When Grin began to publish in 1906, the decadent and fanciful phoenix of the Russian Silver Age was emerging from the ashes of sober nineteenth-century realism, ushering in an era of renewed interest in stylistic innovation and experimentation, a penchant for the symbolic and mysterious (both sacred and profane), and a thematic preoccupation with the metaphysical and transcendental. It was altogether a more subjective mode of writing. The rupture wrought subsequently by the Great War and the events and repercussions of 1917 would cause yet more reverberations throughout the world of Russian *belles lettres* for years to come as literature gained further in political immediacy. Although the ever-romantic Grin often stood outside the major trends of mainstream Russian literature, his writing, as this collection shows, nevertheless underwent its own distinct development, never quite losing track of those profoundly changing worlds—real and literary—around him. From his almost Turgenevian treatment of prerevolutionary political radicalism ("Quarantine") and his modernist appropriation of the cinematic vernacular ("She") to the worlds of pure imagination ("Lanphier Colony" and "Heart of the Wilderness") and their bridges with historical reality ("The Rat-Catcher" and "Fandango"), the stories presented here take in the broadest possible range of Grin's writing, from his accomplished early work to the masterpieces of his mature fiction.

Details of the works' original Russian publications are, in chronological order, as follows. "Quarantine" (*"Karantin"*) was included in the short story collection *The Magic Hat* (*Shapka-nevidimka*), which was published in 1907; " 'She' " (*"Ona"*) originally appeared in abridged form under the title "Trick of Light" (*"Igra sveta"*) in the newspaper *Nash den'* on February 18 (March 2), 1908, and was first published in its entirety in Priboi's *Literaturno-khudozhestvennyi al'manakh* of 1909; "Lanphier Colony" (*"Koloniia Lanfier"*) was first published in the journal *Novyi zhurnal dlia vsekh* (Issue 15) in January 1910; "The Devil of the Orange Waters" (*"D'iavol oranzhevykh vod"*) originally appeared in Soiuz's *Pervyi al'manakh* of 1913; "The Poisoned Island" (*"Otravlennyi ostrov"*) was first published under the title "A Tale of a Far-Distant Ocean" (*"Skazka dalekogo okeana"*) in the magazine *Ogonek* (Issue 36) in 1916; "The Heart of the Wilderness" (*"Serdtse pustyni"*) was first published in the journal *Krasnaia niva* (Issue 14) in 1923; "The Rat-Catcher" (*"Krysolov"*) was first published in the journal *Rossiia* (Issue 3) in 1924; and "Fandango" was first published in the literary almanac *Voina zolotom: al'manakh prikliuchenii* in 1927.

The translations that follow have been made from the versions of the texts presented in the authoritative Soviet six-volume collected works, *Sobranie sochinenii v shesti tomakh*, which was prepared under the editorship of Vladimir Rossels and published in Moscow in 1965.

It has been the greatest of pleasures to work with Christine Dunbar and the Russian Library team at Columbia University Press. I should also like to thank Dzmitry Suslau, whose sparkling wit and encouraging feedback bolstered me when my own confidence faltered, and both Irina Steinberg and Julia Sutton-Mattocks, whose sharp eyes and pitch-perfect ears caught more lapses of literary taste than I should care to admit to. I owe a further debt of gratitude to Professor Barry Scherr, without whose invaluable input and thoughtful commentaries this collection would not be the testament to Grin's remarkable life and career that it is. It is with profound gratitude that I thank each of them, and state that any remaining error or inadequacy in the translation is, of course, mine and mine alone.

FANDANGO AND OTHER STORIES

QUARANTINE

I.

The garden glittered dazzlingly, dusted all over, from the roots to the treetops, with a transparent, fragrant snow. A green lake of tender young grass stood beneath, penetrated by the hot brilliance burning in the pale-blue sky. Like a cloudburst, this light scattered down, bathing the transparent apple-blossom snow, falling upon its curving features like gold silk on the body of a beauty. White and pink petals, unable to withstand the hot, golden weight, slowly broke away from their cups, floating down, graciously twirling in the crystalline ripples of air. As they fell, they fluttered like moths, silently dappling the serene, tender grass with dots of white.

The air—heady, hot, and pure—luxuriated, basking in the rays of light. The apple and bird cherry trees stood as if spellbound, sleeping under the burden of their white, virgin color. The downy, velvety bumblebees hummed in a low bass, besieging the sweet-scented fortress. Fussing honeybees glistened with dusty bellies, buzzing through the grass, and, darting off suddenly, faded away, a swift black speck amid the pale-blue air. Sparrows called noisily and throatily, as loud as they could, concealed by the dark verdure of the rowans.

The little garden bubbled like a mountain spring, broken by flashes of red-gold in the granite ledges, and, like a web of shadows and light, the reflection of this cheerful triumph flitted over Sergei's face as he lay there beneath a tree in the pose of a mortally wounded man. His arms and legs were stretched out as widely and freely as possible, his dark hair mingled with the grass, his eyes looked up, and when he closed them, the light penetrated his lashes, casting a reddish shadow that touched his eyelids. Sweet insouciance, full of languid abstraction, entered through every pore in his skin, dandling and enervating him. Not a single identifiable, troubling thought had wormed its way into his head, and he wanted to lie there for a long time, serene, until the red sunset rose behind the black angles of the roofs and made everything dark, damp, and cold.

It was difficult to say where his body ended and the earth began. To himself, he seemed to be the very green of the grass, which plunged white threads of roots far down into the intoxicated, friable earth. Twisting and turning, these roots escaped into its very depths, into the cramped, damp darkness of that underground kingdom of worms, beetles, and the gnarled, brown and pink roots of ancient trees that imbibed the vernal moisture. Melting, merging with the greenery and the amber light, Sergei broke into beatific laughter, tightly, concentratedly screwing up his eyes before suddenly opening them again. A blue swell washed directly over them, hot and bright, and in its midst, green, trembling leaves stretched out, upturned.

He turned over onto his side and began to look at the dense, mysterious thicket of brushwood, last year's brown leaves, and the miscellaneous dross of flora. Trouble was brewing there. Long black beetles resembling cathedral choristers were gadding around all over the place, tumbling over impetuously. Ants being lured into a glass would drag something along, give up, and drag it again, working their hindquarters. A butterfly took a turn around before perching. Wearing a businesslike frown, Sergei stretched out his fingers and took aim at the slowly flickering white wings.

"Oh, pshaw! You're only little! . . ."

There came a clap of hands and the grass rustled. Sergei raised his eyebrows and looked around.

"What are you playing at, Dunya? Where's the little thing gone?"

"I've frightened away your butterfly!" the girl explained, and laughing creases twitched across her delicate forehead and the lines of her lips. "I was looking for you, and lo, here you are . . . Every bit the little boy, Sergei Ivanych . . . Have you really nothing better to do?"

"Oh, very well, then!" Sergei smiled, still frowning. "Anyway . . . I'd only have caught it and let it go again, for isn't it said, 'Let every thing that hath breath praise the Lord'?"

Dunya reached up, clutched a gnarled black branch, and lifted her delicate, classically proportioned face, which was adorned with a light, ruddy tan. And her inquiring black eyes reflected the flutter of the light, and the wind, and the verdure.

"But you thought perhaps it wouldn't? To be sure, it would praise Him," she drawled. "It's so hot. I've left a letter for you on the table; the postman just called."

"Did he indeed?" Sergei found himself asking.

He stood up, reluctantly and sweetly stretching out. The girl's slight, colorful figure stood before him, as the bended branch trembled and scattered little pieces of white over her head. There were no women like that where he had come from, naive in the natural simplicity of their movements, as simple and strong as the earth. Sergei lowered his eyes toward her delicate round breasts and immediately averted his gaze. Where had this letter come from?

A vague, piercing sensation, strangely reminiscent of toothache, began to throb in him, and suddenly a dreary gray shadow fell over the colors of the green day. With thousands of unseeing glass eyes, a stone city glowered at him, while a motley din assaulted his ears. Dunya smiled, and he smiled back at her out of habit, with the corner of his lips. The sparrows chirped in agitation. The girl let go of the branch, which made a terrific noise as it rushed up.

"I'm going on an outing today," she announced cheerfully. "There'll be me, Lina Gorshkova, too, the carpenter's wife, and even the clerk himself, Dmitry Ivanych . . . We'll have a rollicking time of it. Only we've no one to row us. But for that, we'd go a long way! . . ."

"Marvelous," said Sergei, lost in thought. "What a fine thing, to go for a boat ride . . ."

"Oh . . ."

Dunya opened her mouth slightly, intending to say something more, but only placed her hands to her head and smiled inquiringly.

" 'Oh' what?" echoed Sergei.

"I dare say you won't care to . . . But then if all of us . . . 'Mitry 'Vanych is going to play for us . . . Bought himself a new accordion just before the spring. With three rows, a lovely deep bass . . . Just makes you sigh when you hear it . . ."

The unpleasant feeling of alarm was quickly replaced by the thought that the letter could well be insignificant and not in the least dreadful. Yet he hesitated to go to his room, preferring to talk.

"You're as kind, Dunya," said Sergei with a bow, "as you are tall. And yet . . ."

The girl snorted. Her teeth flashed boldly; dimples fleetingly appeared on her swarthy cheeks.

"And yet," Sergei continued, "I couldn't possibly. Much to my regret . . . I'll be writing letters, this and that . . . So thank you for the invitation but, all the same, my apologies."

"Oh well, as you wish. I only meant the rowing . . . Our gallant gentlemen are so unconscionably lazy . . . We'll have to row them, these devils! . . ."

She smiled crossly, and her pretty face grew stiff and awkward.

"Shall I really not go?" thought Sergei. "Why shouldn't I? They'll be squealing, splashing water around, singing and pinching each other. 'Mitry 'Vanych will provide the music. Still, you'll likely feel awkward. No, truly . . ."

At this point, however, he envisaged the boat, the girl sitting beside him, and mentally sensed the close proximity of her slender, tantalizing body.

"No, it would be awkward," he told himself again, anxiously recalling the letter. And with that, his desire for something youthful and lighthearted was extinguished.

"Come!" said Dunya. "I'll put on the samovar and carve up some meat . . ."

The girl turned and nimbly floated off. Between a gap in an old gray fence, which served as a garden gate, she turned and disappeared. A minute later, from a little white log cabin, her shriek came flying out, accompanied by spanking and the desperate crying of a child.

II.

Sergei climbed the porch stairs and stepped into the twilight cool of the vestibule. Just outside the low, worn doors leading to his room, blocking it with her body and bent over, Dunya was holding her little five-year-old sister Sanka by the arm as the latter tried desperately to sit down on the floor. The child was giving out a piercing scream and kicking its filthy little bare feet in every direction; its dress was bespattered with fresh wet mud. Noticing Sergei, Sanka immediately calmed down, sobbing and hostilely examining "uncle's" figure with her puffy red eyes. Dunya stepped aside, lifting her tense, perspiring face.

"Look! Just look what she's done! Do you see this? You're my torment of torments! I've never seen anything like it . . . It's a punishment sent from God! . . ."

Hurriedly tucking in her skirt, which had come undone, she shot a glance at Sergei and again set about dealing with Sanka, who had begun to wail even more loudly and desperately. The young man opened the door and entered his room.

After the humid heat of spring and its dappled brilliance, it was pleasant for the eyes to rest as they met the walls; it was easier to breathe, too. A billowing white curtain covered the window; through its patterned net could be glimpsed the vague outline of a dusty, lighted street and little buildings with brickwork on the ground floor and gray roofs that looked like hats. Here and there the cheap, variegated wallpaper was hidden by lurid oleographs under glass in narrow black frames. Atop the ragged green baize of an open gaming table lay several books brought by Sergei and a writing set speckled with ink stains. Four canary-painted chairs stuck out around the table and a dresser, while on the floor there trailed a grimy canvas runner.

Sitting in its broad envelope, the letter loomed blue on the table. Sergei picked it up and, for some while, with an unsettled feeling of vexed impatience, examined the jagged, undistinguished handwriting of the address. An old desire to clarify both to himself and to others the result of these two months of voluntary banishment flared up again, only to be broken by a feeling of vague, halting fear. Somewhat alarmed, as if this simple blue envelope had borne and hurled in his face those old, fiery thoughts that he had left behind in the city and, in so doing, broken the uncomplicated sequence of spring days, Sergei tore open the letter and extracted the slim, crisp leaf of paper. Having impatiently skimmed through the inevitable, conventional text, the mask of its true meaning, he lit a candle in a green copper candleholder and brought the paper to the flame, heating its clean, uninscribed side. It curled up, yellowed, and disintegrated in parts, but it remained stubbornly silent, like a man unwilling to betray a secret entrusted to him. And only then, when Sergei's fingers had begun to ache from the heat of the flame and he wanted to take them away, did brown marks begin to appear on the paper. They snaked and twisted, and, before the last letter had been dressed in flesh and blood, Sergei already knew that tomorrow some fateful person would arrive, and after that he would have to go off and die.

To begin with, he read the solid, even letters with absolute dispassion, registering them automatically in his mind and assembling them into words. When, however, they came to an end and stopped in the whole formidable nakedness of their significance, he braced himself and gritted his teeth, ready to repel an imminent blow. Only now did Sergei realize with absolute clarity and certainty that this could not and must not take place. There, where the brain, stupefied and ablaze, makes promises, and the border between life and death dissolves in the fierce heat of fitful struggle—that is where there is a truth, a logic all of its own. While there, where you want to live, where you want to eat, drink, kiss life, gathering up its littlest crumbs like precious stones—there, perhaps, there is no truth, no logic, but the sun, the body, and joy.

In a corner, where the tattered wallpaper was beginning to peel, a distant road drew into view, with people, street lamps, and shop signs. Horses and carriages thronged the street. Someone was coming . . . Someone pale, with a clammy, cold sweat on his brow and a tempest in his heart, raised his hand, while everything around him roared with thundering, terrible laughter and collapsed . . .

Outside, sparrows were chirping in greedy, importunate bursts. Hurtling carts clattered, and an axe was chopping. A distant city rose up before his eyes, surrounded by a forest of chimneys and flocks of carriages. Noisy, breathing heavily, it laughed in Sergei's face—a ringing, metallic laugh, pervaded by a dark, fantastical flight of burning thought.

There, in the middle of this seething, frenzied fever of nerves, an enormous weblike mechanism of living tissue forged tirelessly in hundreds and thousands of hearts waves of feelings and emotions, surrounding Sergei with the mysterious, mute force of impulse. But just as then, his exhausted soul had been keen to reckon with the executioners of life, so now it was plain and simple that he had no intention of dying—he did not want it, nor could he bring himself to want it.

Never had he forgotten the bright, human side of life, and his lust for it had grown as his weary, overwrought body, full of hot, powerful blood, ate its fill and relaxed. The days passed—and he lived. The sun rose—and he washed himself and smiled at the sun. He inhaled the fresh, intoxicating air, himself growing intoxicated, and everything seemed heady and gay. The earth revealed itself to him day after day, fragrant, mighty, and green. His body grew big and heavy, full of vague desires.

It was so simple and good, and he wanted it to remain like this forever: plain to see, good, and simple.

Friends and acquaintances—or those whom he took to be friends and acquaintances—now reminded him of those droll, vocal little sparrows. While they just hopped around, making noise, trying to shout down life, life resounded all around them, quivering and resplendent. Alongside this picture flashed pale, haggard, harassed faces, hungry eyes, brains eternally starving, hearts turned everlastingly to stone in pain and suffering. Now he could clearly see hoards of heads, mountains of books, and sparse, uncomfortable rooms that recalled the faces of old maids. He set the past on rickety, feeble legs and looked on. The colors washed away, the shades faded, but the contours remained the same, sharp and angular. They had been inscribed in blood—both in his own and in that of others. Only the figures of women and girls—vibrant and bright—softened the background, as flowers do the iconostasis of a church. Thus also do the lines of a great poet, taken as an epigraph for a scholarly work, leave their fragrant trace in those terse, heavy pages . . .

And so the tireless, angry zeal he bore for his faith heaved, ready to collapse under the whole arsenal of sharpened, stinging, and wounding arguments. While farther on, in gloom-covered corners, vermin crept and a melancholy wailing droned out, fusing into one single stream tears of impotence, the sighing of a slave, dull, swinish malice, and a bloody, childish absence of comprehension . . .

All of a sudden, Sergei felt crushed, disgusted, and wretched. Worried, listening to the hurried, enigmatic whisper of blood, he stood there, hesitating for a long while, unconsciously ready to break his train of thought with a decision. And finally it occurred to him, what was hidden inside, perhaps there, where a strong body in the prime of life indignantly refused the chill of death. This brief thought was expressed in three words: "Under no circumstances!"

And although after this he felt calmer and more carefree, he was still annoyed at himself and regretted something. Annoyed because he too, like so many others, had turned out to be capable of constructing beautiful, brave deeds in his mind. In times of acute, nervous enthusiasm for an imaginary exploit, how pleasant it is to die a hero and at the same time rejoice that you are alive.

Outside, the sparrows continued their restless, relentless call, and in their cries Sergei could hear:

"Here's a sparrow! Me! Chir-r-rup! . . ."

Sergei sighed, opened his eyes, and rose from his chair. He grinned, narrowed his eyes sweetly, yawned, and, recollecting himself, quickly burnt the letter. It burst into flames and fell to the floor as a light, gray ash. He proceeded to turn on his heel, removed from the wall a little old single-barreled rifle, and went out.

By the gate he met Dunya's inquiring black eyes. She was sitting on a bench with her legs tucked under her as she quickly, deftly husked seeds. Her glossy raven hair had been done in a long, taut plait and was adorned with a yellow ribbon, while her rosy face against the background of a gray, decrepit fence looked like a flower pinned to a shopkeeper's coat.

"Off hunting, Sergei Ivanovich?" she asked, spitting out the husks. "What a pity Mitya Spiridonov isn't here. Oh, he could show you some spots! Used to go himself and come back all draped with birds. What didn't he hunt! . . ."

"Splendid," said Sergei as he examined the colorful calico of Dunya's blouse, which snugly fitted her delicate, round shoulders. "Where has he gone?"

"Somewhere far away—you won't spot him from here!" the girl said, laughing. "He's with the army, in Kostroma."

"Splendid," Sergei repeated with a smile. For some reason he found it amusing that Mitya Spiridonov had gone off to be a soldier and now, hair cropped, arms and legs contorted by training, would be performing all manner of acrobatic tumbles.

"Why don't you come with me, Dunya?" he joked. "With you there, I think we'd bag a fair amount, you and I."

"Me?" said Dunya coolly, before adding after a pause: "I can't, in any case. My aunt's asked me to keep house for a while. Her children are terrors: you look away for only a second and they'll burn the whole place down . . . The very thought!"

"I thought you were going on an outing?"

"Yes, an outing, but not across the marshes, hitching up my skirt, wading through the grassy bog," the girl objected vividly. "How funny you are, Sergei Ivanovich, really!"

And, gaily laughing, she flashed her even rows of white teeth. Sergei stood there, smiling at her cheerfulness, her health, and at the sun, which cast hot shadows in the corners of the fences, which were overgrown with a multitude of dark-green nettles.

"Well, goodbye!"

"Will you be back for dinner?"

"I don't know . . . Will you leave me something—in case I don't make it back in time?"

He set off slowly, his heavy boots raising a thick cloud of dust from the road; he could feel her intent feminine gaze on his back but could not bring himself to look around.

"What a lot of nonsense!" he yawned, smiling to himself, before turning at the corner and heading toward the river.

III.

Sergei had walked quite a distance, almost five miles, trudging to the point of stupefaction. As he crossed an undulating green meadow, unevenly cut by the shady zigzagging of a little river bordered with tufty clusters of willows, he recalled April. Back then this place had been cold, damp, and inhospitable. His feet had squelched nastily in the sodden, waterlogged earth, which was covered over in last year's faded grass and rotten twigs. The slush nested in pits, traitorously covering puddles and ruts, into whose cold water frozen feet would unexpectedly plunge. Hidden by rising mist, the sun would shine diffusely. A willow had stood naked and tattered, its boughs twisted outlandishly. The river had still slept, and the ice on its decaying black banks had swelled with a filthy white crest and was marked all over with a network of animal and bird tracks. By the banks, where dirty pools of spring water had glinted meanly, early sandpipers would sway despondently and, catching sight of a man, fly off with a frightened chirp.

Now nature seemed like an elegant woman, refreshed after a long, intoxicated night. There was a trilling in the grass, which blended its wild, monotonous melody with the cries of birds. Greens and blues, dappled with the lilac-pink pattern of blossoms, flickered in the eyes. Air streamed over a flushed face now with the dryness of heat, now in cool, balsam waves.

Far, far away, beyond a dove-gray strip of forest, the weak, plaintive whistle of a locomotive sounded, and again the enormous, thousand-eyed city flapped its sooty iron wings before Sergei's eyes. But now the apparition lost its acuity and flitted off into the transparent, crystalline distance. Among the flowers and hillocks, densely overgrown with redheaded haircap moss and bushes of rosehip and raspberry, it seemed wan and lifeless, like a dream of long ago. It had no place here. The curly sorrel and the lacquered green of cowberries had taken Sergei under their aegis. He adjusted the belt of his shotgun and slyly, youthfully grinned at something hiding in the depths of the bushes.

Yellow wagtails were hopping about, coquettishly shaking their long, straight tails. Somewhere a corncrake twitched lazily. Thirst tormented Sergei, and, ducking into the splintered bushes, he made his way down a steep, rocky bank toward the shallow-flowing river. By the bank the water pooled serenely, riddled with sedge and seaweed, and a large pebble glittered in the riverbed. Crouching down and soaking his knees, Sergei saw in the water's dusky mirror a bright, pale-blue sky, leading off somewhere below, far beneath the bank, as well as his dark face, his tangle of hair, and the swollen veins on his forehead. Having drunk from the river, he looked at himself again, a little disappointed. In the courageous, handsome face of his watery double, there was not so much as a trace of struggle. It looked calm, carefree, weary, and, as usual, a little sardonic.

He wiped his wet lips with a handkerchief, donned his cap, and, lazily grasping at tufts of grass, clambered up, feeling the sticky, cloying anxiety travel with him, following him, clinging to him, not letting him out of its sight, and poisoning the air with its breath. It was like someone else's bothersome cargo, which could not be unloaded until it had been dragged to a certain point. All his annoyance and bewilderment found expression in the realization of tomorrow's inescapability. At the same time, it seemed outrageous that people whom, in the recesses of his soul, he had somehow always ranked below himself, should now very likely despise and mock him, even though now he was no worse than they. But most vexing of all was that they, these people, seemed to have been granted the right to treat him in whatever manner they pleased. Moreover—a fact that was quite ironic and absurd, though this is truly how it seemed to have come about—it was he who had granted them this right.

This disturbing thought thrashed about and squirmed anxiously for a while, upturning a whole heap of dirty laundry that had accumulated in his soul. Other thoughts followed, indolently flaring up and plaguing him, hostile to the green, thousand-eyed life that had amassed all around. Gray and uniform, having been re-examined so many times and at such length, worn down like old coins, they lingered intrusively, lumbering and sleepy. Fragments of them, forming words about freedom, heroism, and tyranny, crawled about like pathetic, legless cripples.

Twilight was setting in, but still he kept walking, fingering the rosary of his past, until the time came when he desired to go home. His thoughts needed walls: there, free of the open air and exhaustion, simple and unadorned, long-familiar and tired of one another, they could flow by sonorously until morning, when the broad blade of an invisible axe would fall between him and them and reveal him, Sergei, to himself.

IV.

By the time he reached the outskirts of town, it was already dark, depressing, and sedate. Cattle were lowing in the yards; angry women's voices leapt out. Somewhere there were drunkards shouting. Windows were lit here and there. His weary feet burned, as though having been scalded with boiling water. He wanted to eat, then to lie down and enjoy sweet repose. Sergei pushed open the clattering gate and entered the yard.

He was unable to see any windows through the darkness and decided at first that everyone must already be asleep. However, as he went up the creaking porch steps, he heard amid the blackness of the slumbering, humid air the muffled sounds of conversation and a woman's gentle laugh. Sergei pricked up his ears. A man's voice, contented and at the same time dreamy, slowly floated across the depths of the little garden:

"Now look here, you aren't in the right frame of mind to grasp this . . . But, upon my soul, it's true . . . It's like a burst of light, a revelation. It's even described so in many works of philosophy."

"I shouldn't agree to such a thing," Dunya's feminine voice quickly rejoined. "Just think about it! You'll be eaten up by worms . . . You can stand there like a fool your whole life. And what if all of a sudden everything goes flying out the window?"

"Like a fool?" the man objected, taking offense. "You've got it all wrong. It's the opposite—the soul receives unto itself a special gift and then everything is revealed to it . . . For instance . . . I forget what his name was . . . but there was once an old man who stood on a post for thirty years and three months, and by the end he reached a point where he could understand how animals think."

"So stand, then," the girl continued, her barely concealed laughter quivering in her chesty, singsong voice. "Stand right there; you can pray and pray, wrack your mind about the divine, go hungry and cold—but what if you should suddenly sin in your thoughts, then to hell with all your merits. It's awfully harsh."

After a brief pause, she added:

"No. I, for one, am going to roast in hell, so it's all the same to me. Do you suppose it's boring there, in hell? I think the people there must be rather jolly. I'll take you there with me, 'Mitry 'Vanych! Ha-ha!"

Sergei stood on the porch, listening and smiling. He wanted to go into the garden, to have a peaceful, fanciful conversation, seeing neither eyes nor faces and breathing in the warm, soporific murk. But he decided not to go, for in his soul he discerned a vague, reliable presentiment that his arrival would interrupt the conversation, and everyone would suddenly feel flat and awkward.

"Dunechka," Dmitry Ivanych retorted in a sweet, didactic tone of voice, "although I am of course ready to follow you to the very end of the earth, to the farthest shores of Tauris—forgive me, but I have no desire to boil my soul in tar, he-he ... How can you talk like that, as if you've stacked up some great pile of sins?!"

An accordion let out a few spasmodic fragments.

"I'm a terrible sinner," the girl laughingly announced. "Oh, there'll be no redemption for me! I sin all the time. Here you are, talking of the divine, and all I can do is laugh. I'm just sitting here with you—and for what? That's also a sin."

"If you knew," Dmitry Ivanych sighed, "the feelings ... that ..."

"Please, don't. You haven't any feelings ... Why don't you play a little something?"

"Oh, you cruel ... umm ... siren! For you, though, I'd play anything at the drop of a hat! What shall it be? There's a good waltz I learned yesterday—it's Mexican."

"N-no," the girl drawled thoughtfully. "I'd rather that other one ... 'Fragrant Verdure.'"

There was a silence lasting several seconds, and suddenly the accordion began to speak, powerfully and melodiously. The player's lively fingers rapidly poured over sad, sonorous trills, growled out basses, and trembled with deep, long sighs. The tremor of the night and the warm murk disintegrated and reverberated with soft, rounded phrases, and the sounds of the waltz sounded neither trite nor alien to this backwater of life. After around five minutes, Dmitry Ivanych lustily played out a few bass notes and fell silent.

"Wonderful!" the girl said after a pause. "Teach me to waltz, 'Mitry 'Vanych."

"It would be my pleasure to be of service to you," the cavalry officer replied gallantly. "It's the simplest thing, as it happens . . . How's your lodger, by the way?"

"My lodger?" Dunya drawled reluctantly. "He's fine . . . he's alive."

"He's a conspicuous chap," Dmitry Ivanych continued. "And so haughty, too . . . He's got a ruble's worth of ambition for every half-copeck of ammunition. Just the other day I met him here . . . Well, you know how it is . . . a little chitchat, this and that . . . But no! 'Goodbye,' he says, 'I haven't the time . . .' Though he is, as they say, a man of erudition."

"You're a fine one to talk!" the girl objected, displeased. "He's actually very polite and quite modest. Just last night he was playing with Sanka, like a little boy."

"Well, yes," Dmitry Ivanych, now insulted, remarked tetchily. "Of course, for you he probably plays at being a fine fellow . . . since he's been staying with you for two months . . . naturally—"

"Oh, please!" Dunya pointedly interrupted. "Don't make insinuations! So he's staying with us—what of it? . . ."

There was a tense silence before the accordion indignantly struck up a merry, skipping polka. Sergei smiled conceitedly and, passing through the vestibule, opened the door to his room. A muggy, black void breathed in his face. After groping for his matches, he lit a lamp, gobbled down his cold dinner, changed, and, now weary, relished stretching out on the bed as he lit a cigarette. Drowsiness and fatigue had made him absolutely indifferent as to whether somebody came tomorrow or not; all that he wanted now was to sleep.

He extinguished the lamp, rolled onto his side, and opened his eyes wide, trying to imagine that the darkness was death and that he, Sergei, had thrown the bomb and died. But nothing came of it, and even the word "death" seemed to him like an empty, meaningless sound.

And, already falling asleep, he envisaged the strong, slender body of a girl. Perhaps it was Dunya; perhaps it was somebody else. Whoever she was, she radiated the stirring, palpitating heat of blood. And all night long he dreamt of women's delicate, supple hands.

V.

When—later, after much time—Sergei came to recall everything that took place between him and his comrade, who arrived the very next day to make the final arrangements, it always seemed to him as if it had all come out "amiss somehow," and as if there had been some sort of mistake. What this was exactly, he himself could not say. However, one thing was beyond all doubt: that the reason for this mistake lay not with him, Sergei, and not with his comrade, Valerian, but somewhere else, beyond the realm of clear, detailed analysis. It was as if each man felt awkward before the other, not on account of his attitude toward himself and others generally, but on account of that enormous, blind thing whose name is Life, which jealously guarded each of them from a simple, dispassionate understanding of someone else's soul. This realization was also hard and unpleasant to bear because the same thing might conceivably happen again in future and once more leave in the soul the trace of painful suffering and shuddering grief.

Sergei had not known that it would be Valerian who would come. When, next morning, the shifty, swarthy, shrill revolutionary barged into his room and began to embrace and kiss Sergei, who was still drowsy and brooding over what was to come, the latter sensed right away that their interview would be pained and unpleasant. The sudden, jerking movements of the diminutive, ebullient man betrayed so much certainty in himself and in his knowledge of people that in the first instance it seemed inadmissible to back out of a decision that had been taken long ago, clearly and decisively. But this was immediately followed by the cold, fixed obduracy of desperation, whereupon he found that he could move more freely and breathe more easily.

Along with this, a sour, mind-numbing feeling burdened his soul, yawning and wincing like a weary cat. Everything seemed astonishingly flat, absurd, and utterly devoid of sense. While Sergei was washing and dressing, Valerian bustled about, making absent-minded remarks apropos of nothing, sat down, jumped to his feet, and kept talking and talking without pause, laughing and shrieking—about "the current situation," about Liberationists and Social Democrats, about *Revolutionary Russia* and the *Spark*,* polemics and agitation. He spoke rapidly, piercingly, without end.

---

* *Liberationists . . . Spark*: The Union of Liberation was a clandestine liberal political group founded in St. Petersburg in 1904 under the aegis of Pyotr Struve (1870–1944), a former Marxist who advocated, among other things, for a constitutional monarchy and the granting of full civil rights to citizens across the Russian Empire. The Russian Social Democratic Labor Party, a revolutionary socialist political party, was formed in 1898 with the aim of uniting disparate revolutionary organizations extant throughout Russia. Its newspaper, the *Spark*, founded by Vladimir Lenin (1870–1924), was published abroad, variously in Leipzig, Munich, Geneva, and London, due to censorship, and smuggled back into Russia. *Revolutionary Russia* was a similar clandestine periodical, published in Geneva as an organ of the Socialist Revolutionary Party.

Black-haired, shaggy, and hawk-nosed, wearing a *pince-nez* that covered his bulging, myopic eyes, impetuous and agitated, he seemed like a ball of nerves hastily wedged into a frail, sinuous body. Fidgeting on a chair, tilting back his head and adjusting his *pince-nez* every minute, taking Sergei by the hands and buttons, he would rapidly, trilling with smug, childish laughter, scatter sharp, nervous phrases. Even his clothing, intentionally garish, somewhat in the style of a southern shop assistant, roundly eclipsed Sergei's usual string of impressions and seemingly brought with it all the echoes and excitement of far-flung provinical centers. He had known Sergei for a long time and always treated him with an air of hurried, businesslike condescension.

When at last Sergei was ready and walked out with his comrade into the garden, where the laughing sun shone golden, scintillating among the greenery like a fine wine, where the sparrows tweeted deafeningly, and where the downy snow of the apple blossom smelled sweet, he felt his anger and alarm give way to an influx of morning cheer and an expectant indifference toward everything that Valerian might say or do. And yet, at the same time, he understood that from those very first words on the matter, it would be difficult and painful.

They sat down on the grass, where a dense rowan bush hid the corner of a fence that flanked an old shed. Catching his breath a little and distractedly casting around his myopic eyes, Valerian was first to begin:

"You weren't expecting me, were you, my fine fellow? So, tell me the how and what of it, and so on and so forth. Is everything ready? Hmm? Well, tell me."

"The thing is . . ." Sergei forced a smile. "As you can see, I've come here, settled down, and I live . . . well, as you can see . . . in a healthy climate."

"Yes! Yes?! Hmm? Well?"

"Well, it's just . . . I eat, I'm putting on weight . . . food here is cheap. Since being here, I've had a hearty appetite. You might say I've been resurrected. You yourself saw how I was when I left—like a lemon . . ."

"Like a squeezed lemon, ha-ha! Now, as for that matter . . . Have you covered your tracks here? Is anyone watching you?"

"Not so loud . . ." Sergei looked around. "Of course no one's watching me. How could they out here? When I first arrived . . . I thought I might say I was looking to take lessons, but I rejected that idea later; I mean, this isn't even a town—it's really more of a large village."

"Yes, yes! . . . Well?"

"Well, what's there to say? . . . I've set myself up here—under the simple guise of a convalescent. And there you have it. I haven't any acquaintances, and seeing as there isn't anyone to . . . Anyway, enough of that . . ."

"Yes, yes, yes! . . . And do you realize that you, my fine fellow, are living in clover? . . . Others"—he lowered his voice—"are kept in quarantine for five or six or even nine months before the deed! There's nothing to be done about it! It has to be this way. It has to, you understand? You've got to clean yourself so that there's no trace of black powder and no root can be pulled up . . . Do you know, frankly speaking, I doubted you had it in you to stay in this . . . ha-ha! . . . this cell under a fir tree. But here you are, in the flesh. Hmm . . ."

He dropped his *pince-nez*, picked it up, saddled it on his nose, and enigmatically asked:

"Who's putting you up? Eh?"

"The head of the family and the owner of this little house works as a blacksmith at the railway depot. A gentle sort and, as they say, God-fearing. When he comes home from work in the evenings, sighing long and heavily, he takes tea, and on Sundays he gets blind drunk and says the sweetest little things. He cries and starts to repent of something . . . And then his wife's a whole bazaar: pock-marked, stout, and coarse, with a voice like brass. From dawn till dusk, she curses everything under the sun. They have two daughters: one's a little crybaby, but the older one isn't half bad . . ."

The diminutive man listened, chuckling with approval and slapping Sergei on the shoulder as he adjusted his *pince-nez*.

"Well, well? Yes?" he repeated incessantly, thinking of something else all the while. And when Sergei had finished, Valerian looked him in the eyes pointedly, full of emotion and melancholy.

"Well, what's it to be?" he said quietly. "When do you expect you'll be going, eh?"

And, as though fearing that he had posed the cutting question much too soon and too bluntly, he quickly put in:

"I suppose you've been dreadfully bored here, yes?"

The noose gripping Sergei's throat slowly loosened, and, trying to be cool-headed and firm, he said:

"N-no . . . not very . . . I've been hunting, reading . . . I'm terribly fond of nature."

"Nature, yes . . ." said Valerian distractedly, and a tense concentration descended over the muscles of his sallow, swarthy face. "Well . . . it's . . . are you ready?"

He lowered his voice and looked Sergei straight in the eye with a thoughtful, measuring gaze. All at once everything amusing in his mannerisms and appearance inexplicably faded. He went on, as though arguing with himself:

"I think that the time has probably come for you to get a move on . . . I brought the goods with me. I put *it* in your dresser. Now, listen—be careful, and watch what you're doing! . . . So long as you don't drop it or have a game of skittles with it, you could happily take it all the way to Kamchatka. That's the first thing. Next up is money. How much do you have? . . ."

The question lingered in the air, and even after it had died away, it continued to ring in Sergei's ears. He began to feel painfully ashamed and sorry for himself on account of all the deception of this conversation, which was futile from first to last and disguised miserably by an air of nonchalance and the calm of a friendly chat. He grinned inanely, whistled dramatically through his teeth, and said in a devious, subtle voice:

"Oh, Valerian! I feel just wretched ... Essentially, what you've ... quite in vain, that is ... I mean to say ... You see, I've ... reconsidered. Only ..."

With a crushing, loathsome feeling, Sergei turned his head. Those myopic black, bewilderedly blinking eyes were staring right at him. Valerian gave a crooked grin and, raising his eyebrows, adjusted his *pince-nez* with an inquiring look. Something quivered in his thin, sallow throat, which rose and fell as though it were trying to swallow solid food. He said merely:

"What?! Get out of my sight! ..."

The tone of his voice, curiously unfamiliar and dry, rendered any explanation unnecessary. He sat there, firmly biting his lower lip, and wiped his bulbous, perspiring forehead with the palm of his hand. So confident and restless only a moment ago, he now seemed weary and pitiful.

"Valerian!" Sergei said after a pause. "Be that as it may ... Valerian, are you listening?"

However, as he watched him intently, he marked with astonishment that Valerian was weeping. Great, implacable tears were streaming down his swarthy cheeks from those rapidly blinking myopic eyes, while the nervous convulsions of a grin flashed at the corners of his mouth. And it was so difficult to see this hardened, grown man look pitiful and bemused that Sergei was in the first instance taken aback and at a total loss.

"Now see here, what's all this?" he said helplessly after a brief, awkward silence. "Come, where's the good in this?"

"Oh, leave me! Leave me! I said, leave me!" Valerian shrieked angrily, feeling Sergei's hand on his shoulder. "Please, leave me . . ."

But then, with a quick effort of will, he suppressed the momentary emotion and dried his eyes. He jumped to his feet, fixed his *pince-nez* in place before rattling off in a halting, subdued voice:

"Here's what we need to do: come on! Do you hear? You and I need to have a little chat! Where shall we go, eh? Do you know a good spot? Or shall we just head into the field? Into the field seems like the best option . . ."

They went into the yard, which felt hot after the cool of the little green garden with its white perimeter of log buildings. Dunya was standing on the porch, dressed in tattered blue-striped calico; beside her stood Glafira, her mother, a fat, fleshy woman. They were feeding the chickens. On seeing Sergei, Glafira broke into a broad smile and bent double, bowing deeply to the youth.

"Good day to you, Sergei Ivanych!" she sang. "You look as though you're about to set out on a walk! Won't you have some tea? You should at least give some tea to your guest! I say, you're so undomesticated, so restless."

"Later," Sergei said, as he smiled distractedly at Dunya, who was watching him from under her round, plump hand. "Do put the samovar on, though. We'll be back later . . ."

Something was stirring, bubbling in his chest: confused, agitated thoughts thrashed about incoherently, seeking clear, sure words of comfort. Yet everything that met his eyes distracted and diverted him. With cries and clattering, peasants rode by, goats bleated, the tolling of bells rang out before fading away, and gates rattled. Valerian walked beside him, dark and diminutive, clutching Sergei by the elbow and wildly gesticulating with his free hand. Tired and on edge, fingering his *pince-nez*, he kept repeating, scornfully and plaintively:

"But how could you, eh? How? What? What have you done? Isn't this the height of piggery and childishness, hmm? Really, you aren't a child anymore, are you? Oh, oh! . . ."

He groaned and smacked his lips. So very rapidly he was turning something over in his mind, and was barely keeping pace with his comrade's long strides. Judging by the tone of his voice, which was calmer now, and by his slight, plaintive, malevolent grin, Sergei saw that the worst of it was already over, and now all that remained was talk—pointless and unnecessary though it was.

"Well, what will you do now, hmm? Well?"

All of a sudden, Sergei wanted this impetuous man, this good man whom he had deeply offended, to understand and feel his, Sergei's, words, thoughts, and wishes—as he himself understood and felt them. And, forgetting the vast gulf that separated his inner world from that of the clear, grimly logical conclusions that constituted the center, the sense, the nucleus of this dark, diminutive man's life, this man who was walking beside him, he shuddered from head to toe and grew impatient with the desire to express himself simply, justly, and powerfully.

"Valerian, listen to me! . . ."

Sergei took a deep breath and paused to choose his words. Inside him, everything was clean-cut and sure, but this was because the simplicity of his feelings stemmed from an incalculable complexity of impressions and thoughts—he had yet to grasp the principal, central theme of his emotions.

"Well?" Valerian drawled wearily. "Speak! What do you have to say?"

"Here's what," Sergei began. "Of course, not for anything should I ever be able to divulge this to another soul . . . But this is what it comes down to. This is the example I wanted to give you . . . So-o . . .

here it is: have you ever walked past shop windows, and . . . well . . . looked . . . at . . . bronze statuettes? of women?"

"I have . . . Go on! . . ."

"Well, when I look at these elliptical, harmonious . . . distinct . . . lines . . . lines that are frozen forever in the form . . . that the artist has given them . . . dead, and yet soft and animate . . . I always think— now what do I think?—that this is how the soul of a revolutionary ought to be . . . Soft and yet like metal, definitive . . . Bright, cast from bronze, strong . . . and—feminine . . . Feminine because . . . well, in any case . . . Well now . . . Now see here . . . I've never considered myself one of them at all, and I still don't . . . Of course, that would be ridiculous . . . Only because I'm not like that, but I wanted to live among such people . . . Their metal is altruism—and their lines the idea . . . Do you see? Whereas this isn't altruism alone, but—"

"Yes, of course," Valerian interrupted distractedly. "But what of it?"

" . . . but perhaps it's turned out just the same for me," Sergei added quietly.

His excitement suddenly waned. It seemed as if his true, sincere thoughts were still wasting away deep within him, and he was not saying what he thought. Valerian said nothing.

"Yes . . ." Sergei slowly continued. "Everything's the same, everything as it is: ambition, the desire for intense emotions, and, ultimately, often simply the thrill alone . . . But if that's so, then I can no longer be like metal . . . And so I don't want to die an effigy of vanity . . ."

"Remarkable!" Valerian sneered. "Oh, you fool! Of course, all people are human, and nothing human is alien to them! So what? Are you disillusioned?"

"By no means! . . ." Sergei dryly cut in.

And with a fleeting, sly smile, his other, secret thoughts slipped out, along with his desire for a great, romantic life, one that was beautiful, whole, unrestrained, and devoid of suffering. What he had just told Valerian was sincere enough, but it bore little relation to what he wanted right then. Instead of all this complex labyrinth of petty disappointments, stale devotion, and dissatisfaction with people, the powerful, irrepressible voice of young blood cried out: "I don't want to die; I want to live. It's as simple as that."

"It's a remarkable thing," said Valerian, tilting his head back farther, adjusting his *pince-nez*, and curiously examining his comrade's face. "You reason like a woman. You know, there's a decadence about you . . . You haven't been reading Max Stirner,* have you? Or, ha! . . . Ha! . . . Nietzsche? No? Well, let's leave it. Do you have money?"

"No, Valerian, you've got it all wrong," Sergei began again, angry at himself for wanting and being unable to express the simple essence of what was and would continue to be inside him, as it would in any other person. "You know, I left prison broken, feeling spiteful, my nerves in tatters . . . I was like a drunkard . . . I was drunk on ideas— and so my plan ripened . . . My nerves reacted with painful speed . . . But as I've already told you, I cannot be a hero, and I do not want to be a cog in the machine . . ."

"No!" Valerian laughed. "You haven't told me anything yet! . . . Hmm? It's only natural that you want to live, just like any other man, but what's all this about bronze statues? these revelations of yours? And why did you . . . Ach! You know, I'd never doubted you for a second! . . ."

He raised his eyebrows in surprise and slowed his pace. The field exuded heat; in the distance the town was dappled with gray, red, and green roofs.

---

* *Max Stirner*: Johann Kaspar Schmidt (1806–1856), better known as Max Stirner, was a German philosopher, often regarded as a forerunner of, among other things, nihilism, individualism, existentialism, and anarchism.

"The Central Committee has had quite enough of you! You talked their ears off about this! Very nearly with tears in your eyes you begged and badgered them . . . Do you think there weren't others? Shame on you! All that prancing and jumping around . . . So now what? . . . You might have written! Hmm?"

Sergei said nothing. His irritation was growing and bubbling to the surface.

"For a start, I hadn't expected that the moment would come so soon . . ." he said brusquely. "But now . . . I just told you . . . Do as you will."

"Come, come . . . So, what do you intend to do now?"

"I don't know . . . In any case, it's of no consequence."

"Yes-s . . . Perhaps that's so . . . It's your affair . . . Very well, then. Farewell!"

"Where are you going?" Sergei was astonished.

"There, of course!" Valerian waved his hand in the direction where, far beyond the thicket, stood the red brick structure of the railway station. "I can still catch my train; I've deposited my luggage . . . Well, all the best."

He firmly shook Sergei's hand, while his quick, black eyes fixed their gaze on him through the convex lens of his *pince-nez*.

"Yes!" He started. "I left it in your room. It's of no use to me now . . . You can dispose of it somewhere—in the woods, perhaps, or in some out-of-the-way spot . . ."

"All right," Sergei said dejectedly. He felt sorry for Valerian and wanted to say something heartfelt and touching, but he hadn't the words—only a sense of alarm and alienation.

The dark, diminutive man hurried to the station, swinging his arms as he went. For a long time Sergei watched him go, until the scrawny little figure had turned into nothing but a crawling black speck. A moment later it appeared as though Valerian had turned around, and Sergei rushed to wave his handkerchief as he peered into the green emptiness. But no response came.

The black speck rose up once again as it crossed a hillock before vanishing. The sun mercilessly cast its arid amber light, and the green of the young grass glittered and basked in it. In the distance the air quivered and shimmered, disturbing the outlines of fences, like lines on notepaper. Beyond the thicket, white puffs of smoke rose up, and a locomotive cried out in alarm.

As Sergei walked home, he recalled everything he had said to Valerian. With an obscure, vague sorrow, he lamented the past.

VI.

He had grown weary of pacing back and forth in the small room, brushing against the corner of the table and slowly turning around when he reached the low, yellowing door. With each turn, Sergei listened to the springy squeak of his toe cap before setting off again, marking the sound of his footsteps without thinking. It was easier to think on his feet. He had been used to this since his days spent in a prison cell, of which this room somehow—probably in its dimensions—reminded him.

His feeling of excitement had long since passed, and he was left instead with that of a man who goes to see a matinee: the evening light, the music, the acting . . . For several hours he watches and listens to a tidy, poetic slice of life . . . Only then for the shrill white light of day to rule and thunder once again, and for him to crave anew the deceitful, golden evening light.

The flat, smug wallpaper flaunted a motley array of colors around a few grimy, painted flowers. The curtain billowed in the wind and rippled gently over the table, disturbing some scraps of paper and a gnawed pencil. Titles of books assaulted his eyes, provoking a sense of dreariness and disgust. Grim, cold, and unbearably tedious, they engendered visions of monotonous life in an industrial world, innumerable rows of figures, hemp, sugar, and iron, visions of everything that is and yet should not be.

The light faded, fleeing the town with smooth, colossal steps, its sorry shadow creeping behind it. From somewhere came the rich, steady sound of an axe at work; a hammer quickly came to interrupt it, and for a long time two strikes, one heavy, the other light, chased one another in the quiet air. Sergei yawned sweetly, fitfully, cracked his knuckles, and came to a halt opposite the table.

Between the books and the writing set stood a little metallic box that, in form and its dusky gray color, looked more like a soap dish than a bomb. There was something comic and at the same time tragic in its shunned, redundant danger, and it seemed as if it might avenge itself, suddenly, terribly, and without warning.

He remembered now that he had immediately felt some foreign presence, an almost living entity, as he entered the room. This entity had peered at him craftily, probing him with its gaze, with one eye through the side of the dresser, docile and yet threatening, like a quick-tempered slave ready to cast off his submission. Now it lay there on the table, and Sergei observed this oblong steel box with an eerie curiosity, as when one observes an animal roaming outside the thick bars of its cage. He wanted to know what would happen if he were to take this object, so boring to look at, and lob it against the wall. An acute, alarming chill ran through him as he thought this, a ringing developed in his ears, and the building began to seem as if it were made of paper.

The gray shadows of twilight entered the room unheard. Tedium tormented Sergei, and his body was afflicted with an impatient itch. In an attempt to banish it, he thought of the impending expanse of life, his youth, and the brilliance of a spring day. But turbid darkness blackened the window, and his thought, paralyzed by this, trembled in the embrace of dull, dreary uncertainty. This gave rise to irritation and timorous, quiet meditation. And all of a sudden, at first slowly, but then quickly and more distinctly, the antique melody of a naive children's song appeared and sang out in his brain:

> The tsa-a-ar, tsa-a-ar, tsa-a-ar's son,
> Trod upon her toe-sies, the tsa-a-ar, tsa-a-ar,
> Tsa-a-ar's son,
> Take her to your heart-ie, the tsa-a-ar, tsa-a-ar,
> Tsa-a-ar's son.

This faint recollection of childhood flickered like a vague, ancient dream, only to be obscured suddenly by Valerian's dark, bounding back. The image faded away. Sergei clenched his teeth and stared blankly at the wall. And the wall, decked in twilight, looked back at him, silently and sleepily.

"I feel so dismal," he thought. "It comes and goes, in waves. It will pass. Then everything will be fine again and I'll regain my zest for life. In point of fact—what do I have to fear?"

"Sergei, what do you have to fear?" he said in a hushed voice.

But his brain gave no reply, nor did it spark any thoughts, and only slowly and ponderously did it roll over the stones of the past. There were all sorts there—big and small, dark and light. The dark ones were wet and slippery; hurriedly they fell back into their resting places, and he was loath to disturb them again.

He would live. Every day he would see the sky and the empty body of air. The roofs, the dove-gray smoke, the animals. Every day he would eat, drink, and make merry. Breathe, move, talk, and think. Fall asleep while pondering the coming day. Someone else, and not he, would have to go to the appointed spot, pale with dread, and throw a cold, grey box just like this, resembling a soap dish. Throw it and die. But not him; he would live and hear of the death of this other man and what was said about his death.

In the next room they were taking tea; someone was twisting and turning in a chair, which was groaning heavily. There was a rattle of crockery; the indistinct hum of conversation invaded his ears. The door in the hallway slammed and there came a quiet knock at the door to his room.

Shaken, Sergei roused himself. "Yes?"

A woman's voice on the other side of the door asked:

"Shall I light your lamp?"

"Please, Dunya. Come in."

The girl entered unhurriedly, and her dark, lively shadow came to a halt. Sergei brightened up a little, as if the sounds of this youthful, sonorous voice were wresting his soul from the talons of limp, meaningless despair.

"I can't see a thing in here," said Dunya as she fumbled in the darkness. "Where's the lamp?"

"It's out of kerosene. Here, take it!"

Carefully he handed her the cheap lamp in its cast-iron stand, and, as he did so, his fingers came into contact with Dunya's, slender and warm that they were.

"I'll fill it up," she said. "I won't be a moment."

"Take your time . . . Say, Dunya, how was your outing yesterday?"

"We didn't go," the girl drawled dejectedly. "There were no boats. They'd all been taken. It was such a disappointment . . . And our own needs a caulker . . . I'll be back in just a moment . . ."

She slipped silently into the darkness of the hallway, slamming the door behind her. Sergei began pacing about the room, whistling the old ditty about the tsar and his son, and envisaged the curly head of a hot-tempered little boy drowsily moving his plump lips. Was that what he had looked like? How strange. But already he felt happier and more convinced in his soul, and he wanted a cozy light, some tea, and an interesting book. What Valerian thought belonged to him and others like him; what Sergei thought was his own affair. And that was just it. One shouldn't let oneself succumb to ideas.

Like a faint, isolated blemish, the distant specter of the stone city swept over him once more before vanishing, frightened by the footfalls of passers-by. These heavy, uneven steps echoed indistinctly beneath the window and stopped there, having startled the silence.

VII.

Dunya came in, and the yellow light leapt into the room, exposing the walls and the furniture, which had been shrouded in darkness. The room looked relaxed and cheerful. The girl placed the lamp on the dresser and turned down the flame ever so slightly.

"There we are," she said. "Hmm, what's that?"

"I didn't say a thing." Sergei smiled as he got to his feet. Thrusting his hands in his trouser pockets, he stopped in front of Dunya.

"There we are indeed," he said. "So, how are you?"

He wanted to talk, to joke and appear as people had always seen him: gentle, attentive, and straightforward. This had never cost him any effort, but to realize his qualities was both pleasant and reassuring.

The girl stood by the door in a languid, unaffected pose, the hair on her wearily inclining head touching the door post. Sergei observed her strong, slender body with the covetous feeling of a sick man watching street life from the window of a dull, drab ward.

"What did you get up to today?" he asked, gazing at her dark, shy eyes.

"I must be off to bed soon!" The girl laughed and yawned, covering her mouth with a quick movement of her hand. "Can I really be so tired? All my joints are aching."

"Did you go somewhere?"

"I did ... To the woods to look for cones." Dunya gave another long yawn and stretched out languidly and wearily. "Pine cones for the samovar ... I collected a whole bag of them ..."

"Beautiful ..." thought Sergei. "She'll marry a tailor or some shopkeeper. She'll sew, cook, nurse, sleep a lot, grow fat, and curse, just like Glafira."

"And I suppose you've been sitting with your books again?" Dunya put in quickly. "If only you'd bring me a novel ... I do awfully like reading the interesting ones ... And Pushkin too! ..."

"Dunya-a-a! Da-a-amn it!" Glafira shouted from the hallway in her usual angry voice. "Go and see to Sanka! ..."

"Oh, away with you!" the girl said quietly, listening as she watched Sergei. "I'll be right there!" she shouted in a loud, agitated voice and, slamming the door loudly behind her, flew out of the room, a swift-moving blur of color. In the quiet that followed her departure, the rustle of her calico skirt could still be heard for a time, and in the air, by the doorframe, her pink smile still shimmered.

Suddenly, as happens in the street when a passer-by stares at someone from behind and the person instinctively turns around, sensing this gaze, Sergei quite unexpectedly, recalling something, turned to the table. The eyeless little metal object that looked like a soap dish was watching him dimly in the gray reflection of its facets. Gathered in its steel walls were the fruits of centuries of thought and sleepless nights, a fiery ball of yet-unborn lightning, with the unsuspecting look of a child and the poisonous body of a rattlesnake—it gleamed with a silent, malevolent reproach, like the look of a woman scorned. Sergei fixed his gaze upon it; it was as if two enemies, lying in wait with bated breath, were gathering their strength. And the man sneered with a sense of malicious triumph.

"You're powerless," he said quietly and mockingly. "You may conceal the terrible, blind power of destruction ... The wrath of a

dozen generations may be compressed within you. But what's that
to me? You'll remain silent so long as I please . . . Here, let me pick
you up . . . I'll pick you up just as easily and calmly as I would a
turnip. Somewhere in the forest, where the human voice cannot be
heard, you can bark and shatter the dry, rotten stumps . . . But you
won't tear off my skin, you won't burn my eyes, you won't crush my
skull like shattered glass . . . You won't char me or make of my body
a red pulp . . .

He picked it up—it was heavy, cold, and smooth. Then he took
a towel, carefully and meticulously wrapped the bomb in it, put on
his hat, placed a ball of twine in his pocket, extinguished the lamp,
and walked out of the room.

VIII.

The night spread itself triumphantly, filled with hush and faint,
furtive sounds. Stars set the black expanse ablaze. The earth was lost
in darkness, and a pair of feet trod cautiously though wet, unseen
grass. A smooth, calm wind was blowing, abating every now and
then, whereupon the air would exude a warmth. The hillocks and
ditches were hidden and slowly emerged as dark, dormant outlines.
On the horizon, like a distant fire, a thin sliver of moon showed red.

Step by step, carefully advancing, trying not to stumble, Sergei
navigated the hummocks and ruts. He came across silent black
bushes in dense, uneven rows, and as he drew nearer to them,
narrow, winding passages slowly unveiled themselves, filled with
a damp, leafy rustle. They seemed to sleep by day, blinded by the
light, and only now awoke to think secret, ancient thoughts. The
grass rose up, taller and denser, and his feet trod through it with a
gentle, moist squelch. As Sergei parted the bushes with his hands,
their branches would stubbornly and quickly straighten again, lashing his face with their cold, wet leaves.

He felt as though he were sleepwalking, carrying a heavy, fearsome metal in his breast, one that guarded his every step and every palpitation of his body, ready to abduct him and whisk him away, lonely, lost in a sleepy plain replete with mystery and silence. What had gone before this now appeared as a long, endless dream, and everything around him—the night, the darkness, the damp, and the bushes—seemed like a continuation of this same, eternal, alternatingly bright and vague dream.

The night went on, silently moving in the heavens, and he went on too, tense and alert. Death seemed to vanish for him, while he, Sergei, would live forever, always conscious of himself, his body, and his thoughts. The sun would continue to rise and set; forests would rot and turn to dust; animals and birds would disappear; mountains would crumble; the sea would escape into the bowels of the earth; and he would never die but see eternally the bright blue sky, the gold of the sun, and listen to the nocturnal murk . . .

There was a crack and a snap somewhere off to one side, and the faint cheeping of an invisible bird slipped through the bushes like a dreamy lament. The murk ahead rose up like a jagged black maw breathing a chill air. The forest was drawing near; its enormous sleeping body droned mournfully and whispered among the treetops. Another few steps and the trees stretched out ahead, faintly outlined, revealing row upon row of mysterious black corridors. The bushes yielded and then closed ranks behind him.

Sergei entered under the drooping vaults of conifers. Brushwood snapped underfoot; ahead, like a dark crowd, trees emerged and parted. Up above, something creaked and sighed, as if someone enormous and covered in moss were rolling over, shedding cones that fell to the ground with a distinct, gentle rustle.

A nervous sense of dread, not unlike the timidity felt by a thief, began to grip him as the twigs snapped, broken by his foot, and the silence seemed to quiver. Everything around was damp, vast, dormant. The fir trees' shaggy paws hung down, brushing his head, while gnarled stumps stuck up like freakish gnomes out for a stroll. The roots of deadfall wrenched up from the earth loomed black like knotted, crooked shields, behind every one of which lurked some wild being. Somewhere there was a gasp and a groan. From time to time came the fluttering of some nocturnal bird moving noisily to a higher perch before settling down again.

He found his way out into a clearing where it was even more desolate and somber because of the approaching dark storm clouds. He paused. Having placed his parcel carefully on the ground, he unwrapped the towel and tightly wrapped the twine in a crisscross formation around the metal object. Next, he selected a tree with high dried-out branches and, holding his breath, stood on tiptoe, looping the twine from the bomb around a branch as high up as his arms could reach. Having tied to that same branch the end of another piece of twine, a thicker one, he began to unwind it as he backed away toward the other side of the clearing.

There was enough twine to cover a distance of about thirty paces. When it came to an end, Sergei lay down behind an enormous, tall stump, where, drawing his head tightly into his shoulders, and paralyzed with anticipation, he slowly tugged on the end. The twine stretched elastically, shaking, and Sergei, having suddenly lost his nerve, let it go, his heart now pounding.

But the tree stump was reliable and the distance sufficient. So he closed his eyes and, with a chill, pulled with all his might.

There was a painful ringing in his ears. The silence burst with a colossal, panicked rumble, and the murk leapt up, as the wooded depths were blinded and unveiled by the ringing blaze. The explosion rang with the sound of a thousand bells, a crash and prolonged, cackling screams. The noise danced in a frenzy all around, radiating out in fleeting, fading circles. Its echo began to sigh with a frail, polyphonous lament before dying away in the distance.

Deafened and blinded by the milk-bright brilliance, Sergei staggered to his feet, his heart beating convulsively. The green corner of the forest, wrested from the murk by the shock of the explosion, still floated in his eyes. His ears ached, while a distinct, modulating ringing fractured inside them. It seemed that another moment would pass, and the secret of the darkness, outraged by this sacrilege, would rush at him with all the terror of the forest's sly dread.

He let out a deep sigh and straightened up. Fragments of branches, clods of earth, and sticks were still raining down from above, striking his clothes and hands. Sergei pricked up his ears. But all was quiet, as if nothing had disturbed the solitude.

He raced over to the spot where only a minute ago a smooth, heavy box had been hanging from a branch. The tree lay there, shattered at the roots, while turf and damp churned-up earth had piled up all around. At the epicenter of the explosion, there was an uneven, elongated pit. He paused there for a moment, composed himself, and set off homeward.

Once again the avid darkness came after him, dashing on ahead, while his feet now stepped lightly and quickly. Once again trees came rushing to meet him, parting to form narrow, twisting passageways. A silence embraced this space, reaching upward and beckoning with a dark, ambiguous swell.

IX.

The distant church bell gently tolled eleven times when, exhausted and overwrought, Sergei opened the gate and slipped under its clattering chain. He did not wish to sleep, and for several seconds he stood by the porch lost in thought, mopping his damp, perspiring forehead with the palm of his hand.

The warm, starry sky exuded a calm, and in its black abyss the undulating clusters of trees in the garden grew still, like a chain of storm clouds that had come down to earth. Fading amid the silence, the sound of footfalls rang out; they seemed to be engendered by the dark, empty air itself. The watchman's stick rattled with a gentle wooden vibration. The grass rustled faintly underfoot. Sergei entered the garden, which was enveloped by the spicy, aromatic sultriness of the floral grounds. The leaves were silent, as though cast in iron, and suddenly, coming to life with a soft, sorrowful sigh, they rustled with a quivering, lilting ripple. And it seemed to Sergei as if the curly, leafy waves were closing in all around in a dark embrace, trying to enfold his weary, exhausted body. In the trees' black depths, the lighted windows of a neighboring house formed a red pattern, like hot coals smoldering among ashes.

Somewhere, it must have been in the yard, there was a faint sound, a door creaking. Sergei automatically pricked up his ears; he thought he could hear the sound of footsteps. Perhaps it was Dunya. But everything was quiet, and the lights were all out. His thoughts ran to the daughter of the house, to the room where she was probably now sleeping, tossing and turning her white, lithe body in a hot bed. Thus he mused unconsciously and therefore pleasantly. The next moment, however, he felt an urge to speak and reveal the hidden seething of his soul, which was agitated and somehow both dolorous and happy. Damp, heavy perfumes emanated from the earth, swirling about his head like an intoxicating vapor. There was a smell of bird cherry, apple blossom, caraway, and damp, rotten tree stumps.

The bushes rustled and, with a faint elastic snap, fell silent again. Someone alive and breathing was standing in the darkness, obscured by the garden's black shadows. Alert now, Sergei started.

"Who is it?!" he ventured quietly, straining his eyes.

"Who's there?!" a thin, frightened cry quivered in response.

Sergei recognized it and smiled.

"Dunya, is that you? Why aren't you asleep?" he drawled encouragingly. "Surely you've collected enough pine cones for one day? You must be exhausted!"

"Oh, Lord! You gave me such a fright just then, my heart's pounding! . . . I don't have to explain to you why I wasn't asleep, you aren't my keeper." The girl had calmed down, and already a note of mockery was clear in her voice. "And what are you doing up at this hour? Hunting for buried treasure?"

She broke into a quiet, quivering laugh. And it struck Sergei that here, probably, shrouded in darkness, she felt more assured and freer than when she came in with the lamp or swept the floor, awkwardly drawing out fragments of conversation.

"I can't sleep . . ." he said. "I'm not tired. I'm just taking a walk and thinking. It's so lovely here in your little garden."

"I ought to be asleep," the girl answered languidly, "but somehow I don't quite feel like it . . ."

She paused for a moment and, as she sat down on the ground, inquired suddenly:

"You're an educated man . . . Why do people sleep? . . ."

"Because sleep restores the strength you lose during the day," Sergei said in his habitual didactic tone of voice. "It's essential . . ."

"I see-e-e . . ." Dunya drawled thoughtfully. "I'm not sleepy. So my head must be as empty as a pail . . . I'll just sit here until sleep comes . . ."

Sergei drew nearer to the girl. He could hear her breathing—long and uneven—amid the darkness.

"Shall I bring you some Pushkin?" he asked, lowering himself onto the grass beside her. His hand brushed her recoiling foot and sent a shiver through his body. "Why do you want Pushkin in particular, anyway?"

"He writes poetry," the girl sighed. "I do love a good poem . . . Don't you?"

"Yes, I do," Sergei said distractedly.

A silence fell. And the longer it continued, the more intense became the sweet, aching excitement in Sergei's soul, constricting his breath and thought. The blood flowed slowly to his head. In the darkness he could see only the hazy white of her face and her hands resting on her knees. Dunya sat with her head slightly raised. The silence grew, and it felt both luscious and chilling to break it.

"Dunya!" Sergei barked all of a sudden; his voice, constrained and faltering, sounded alien to him. His anxious dread had grown into a hot, languorous agitation that made his body feel light and his breathing heavy and quick.

"Yes?" the girl quickly replied. She immediately carried on in an affectedly carefree tone of voice: "Oh, look, how many stars there are! See how they just float there in the sky!"

Another keen, tense silence ensued. Its invisible thread stretched tremulously between them, hindering their thoughts and speech.

"Dunya!" Sergei repeated. He reached out his hand gropingly and touched her fingers, quivering as he felt her soft, hot body. A heavy lump grew in his chest, which respired with short, deep contractions. The girl sat stock-still, as though slumbering. He proceeded to clasp her hand firmly, and, blushing in the darkness, he clumsily pulled her to himself. Her hand stubbornly resisted, trembling under his hot, powerful fingers. A feeble, bashful, feverish whisper flew out:

"Stop that, please . . . Stop . . . Whatever are you doing?!"

She tried to jerk her hand away, but, seeing that Sergei was relenting, she suddenly squeezed his palm with her moist, slender fingers. A wave of intoxication rushed to his face. He seized the girl by the arm, just above her elbow, while with his other hand he embraced her from the front, squeezing her pert breast and feverishly kissing her fragrant, fluffy hair. Dunya sighed feebly and, with a shudder, fell silent. With greedy, clumsy movements, Sergei rushed fumblingly to unbutton her blouse and thrilled at the touch of her hot, dewy body.

All of a sudden she leapt up, desperately breaking free and reaching out her hands. Her crumpled white chemise fluttered against the dark curve of her figure. In a fog of confusion, Sergei threw himself at her, but two slender, feminine arms struck his chest, forcefully repelling it.

"Dunya . . . darling—come, now . . . what are you doing?!"

"No, no, no!" the girl hastened in a desolate, imploring whisper, staggering and breathing heavily. "No, no! . . . Sergei Ivanych, darling, you mustn't! . . . Tomorrow . . . I'll tell you tomorrow! . . ."

Like birds, her words flitted past Sergei as a series of empty, meaningless sounds. And again, alarmed and rushing, he pulled her toward him, wringing her delicate, slender hand.

Dunya wrenched herself away with one final, decisive movement, and after a crack and the sound of rapid steps, the bushes fell quiet. A moment later, in the depths of the yard, a door slammed and everything was silent, but to Sergei it still seemed as if in the dark, damp air the girl's frightened heart was still beating loudly and rapidly. The illusion was so powerful that he instinctively reached out his hand. The hand touched the void before lowering again. It was his own heart that was beating so anxiously.

He sat down on the ground, and, trembling all over from an unrelenting sense of excitement, he pressed damp, cold leaves to his burning face. His heart was still beating, but more quietly and evenly now. A hush filled the garden.

Dunya, Valerian, the steel box, the explosion, the false passport, Dunya again—it all flashed by and became jumbled in his head, like a kaleidoscope of irregular images. Tomorrow he would leave this quiet, sleepy town—leave to lead another, uncertain life.

"To live!" he said in a hushed voice, pricking up his ears. "How good it is to live . . ."

"SHE"

I.

He had just one prayer, only one. There had been a time when he never prayed at all, even as life wrenched cries of impotence and rage from his distraught soul. But now, sitting of an evening by an open window as the city switched on its countless silent lights, or on the deck of a ship when the approaching dawn wore a rosy haze, or in the compartment of a railway carriage, casting weary glances over the velvet and gilt of the fittings—now he prayed, and with his prayer concluded a rumbling, restless day full of anguish. His lips would whisper:

"I don't know whether I believe in You. I don't know whether You exist. I know nothing, nothing at all. But please, help me find her. Her, only her. I won't plague You with tears or entreaties for my happiness. I won't lay a finger on her if she's happy; she won't even know I'm there. But let me see her just once—only once. I'll kiss the ground she walks on. I'll unveil a vast ocean of tenderness and anguish before her very eyes. Are You listening, O Lord? Return her, give her back to me!"

But the night would preserve its silence, and carriages with fiery eyes would fly by in a clatter of hooves, and the street would dance on in sinister nocturnal merriment, growing ever more intoxicated. And the ship would course through the rosy haze toward the fiery light gilding the horizon. And the locomotive would rumble on in its iron armor, rhythmically striking the rails. And no answer would come to his prayer.

He would fly into a rage and stamp his feet, silently cry, and purse his blanched lips. And again, in anguish, trembling with rage, he would cry out:

"Aren't You listening? Can't You hear me? Give her back to me!"

In his youth he had trampled over the faith of others and scoffed heartily at idols that were as powerless as the men who made them. But now, in the temple of his soul, he was creating divinity, creating diligently and jealously, crafting the gentle, merciful image of an omnipotent being. It was from the remnants of his childhood memories, from the moments of tenderness in the face of eternity scattered throughout his life, from the church crosses and chants that he built his dark, merciful image, and he prayed to it.

Millions of people walked past him, but he had no need of these millions. They were strangers to him, just as he was to them— a sound, a number, a name, an empty room. There was only one person he needed, only one person he desired. But that person was missing. That great array of faces, gaits, hearts, and glances did not exist for him. What he needed was one glance, one face, and one heart. But that person, that woman, was missing.

From one day to the next, his face, eyes closed, was graced by twilight's sorrowful caress, and his head would slump down onto his arms. The evening shadows would crowd around, watching and listening to inexpressible thoughts, nameless feelings, and colorless visions.

His eyes would open and question the darkness and the shapes he saw, while the inexpressible thoughts crowded in his soul.

Then he would say something, and as he spoke he would listen to his voice, but his voice would sound forlorn. And those shapes and inexpressible thoughts would forestall his words, bringing a lump to his throat and constricting his breath. Looming darkly, the burgeoning twilight shadows would hear his complaint.

"I'm alone, my darling, all alone. But where are you? I don't know. Every day I see the lights of railway carriage windows go hurtling by—the people in these windows are singing, laughing, and eating. But you aren't among them, my darling!

"Ships, giants with countless eyes, call in at the harbor every day, where the electric lights are blinding, and a dense, black crowd throngs. People in their hundreds go up and down the gangways, in joy and sorrow, but you are not among them, my darling!

"The streets rumble, restaurant signs flash like diadems, and the delirious city spills out wave upon wave of people. Young and old, men and women, schoolboys and streetwalkers, beauties and beggars—they all walk past me, jostling me and staring, but you are not among them, my darling!

"I seek and I want you. I want to feel your caresses, I want to be happy. I no longer remember the sound of your laugh. I've forgotten the smell of your hair, the play of your lips. I'll find you. I'll run after every woman who looks like you, and when I catch up with her, I'll rain curses on her. I'm tormented by thirst, and my breast has run dry, but you're missing. I summon you! Appear! Come, sit on my lap, press your cheek to my face and laugh as you used to laugh, with the gold of the sun and a zest for life. I'll rock you, cradle you in my arms, let your tresses down and kiss each individual hair. I'll sing you to sleep with a lullaby."

The minutes and hours passed to the sonorous ticking of a pendulum that beat out the seconds in a charged, excruciating silence. Yet still he sat there, transfixed by his suffering, swaying from side to side. Then, from the terrible black depths of his soul, somebody began to hoist up, on chains and pulleys, a load of untold weight. These furtive labors sent the blood rushing to his temples, where it throbbed and spoke in a rapid, crazed whisper. Anguish thrashed about, beating its sharp wings within his heart, and with each stroke of its wings, his heart wanted to cry out, let out a low groan—his heart, which was ready to burst like a gutta-percha ball. Yet the weight was hoisted higher still, creaking as it went and slowly pressing his chest, forcing the air from his lungs, and there it tossed around with its sharp edges.

He would clutch his head in his hands and, tensing his shaking body, drive out that inhuman weight. But the load—the burden of memory—went on growing, gaining momentum like an avalanche, and ringing with forgotten words, rosy laughter, and the delight of lowered eyelashes.

He would cry out:

"I don't want this! This cannot be!"

But each time, exhausted and powerless, he would realize over and over again the enormity of what happens only once, never to repeat itself, not for him, not for someone else, not for anyone, never . . .

II.

The garden was dark, damp, and beautiful. He had not seen her for three days, and now he came, trembling, satisfied, and bashful. The sand crunched beneath their feet; she seemed to be smiling in the dark, mocking his love, watching it and plotting. The excitement of it tormented him further still, and the silence grew painful.

They sat down; he recoiled from her knees, fearing that their touch would inflame his love and that incoherent, serious words would break free. Then he would have to go. It would all be over and he would never see her again. So ran his thoughts during the five minutes before the happiest moments of his life.

"I waited for you yesterday," the girl said, "and the day before, and today. Is that really the way to treat a friend?"

Her voice betrayed a tender expectation, but to him it seemed like mockery, and this feeling of bitter insult made it hard to breathe. Overcoming his emotion, he asked her abruptly and irritably:

"Why did you wait? What do you care?"

Amid the dark he sensed the girl's face blanch and shrink from his abruptness, her eyes become deep and sad. After a brief silence, she said falteringly:

"If you . . . I don't know. If you don't care, then naturally . . . Why don't we go for a stroll? Sitting's such a bore."

But already he was gripped by a sense of pity for both himself and her, by remorse and a feeling of tenderness for the object of his love. Without even realizing it, he took her hands in his—those dainty little fingers were so warm and infinitely sweet—and said, first mentally and then aloud:

"Darling! Darling! Forgive me!"

Silence fell. It seemed as though it would never end. Yet vigorous palpitations of joy were already nearing. Was music playing then, was there someone singing? He no longer recalled. The scene seemed to brighten and become excruciatingly sweet. She held her hands in his; it was he who carefully and reverently let go of her fingers. Was his heart pounding, was there someone singing? He no longer recalled.

The girl—his beloved, his joy—got up, and without a word, understanding her every move, he went after her, following her into her room, where for a long time, with tears in his eyes, he watched, watched her blushing face, which had suddenly become closer than close and so utterly artless and kind. She laughed and talked, while the lace on her breast fluttered like a butterfly:

"Tell me you love me!"

He repeated the words with shame and embarrassment:

"I love you! I love you! Or rather—it's *you* I love! . . ."

She turned away, laughing; he watched her shoulders quiver with mirth and the edge of her little pink ear, which was enwreathed by a little lock of chestnut hair. He walked over to her, embraced her from behind, around her shoulders and neck, and shivered from the touch of her warm, trembling body. She nuzzled her little round chin into his arm, staring straight ahead at the wall, her eyes happy and shining nervously. He asked:

"May I hold you in my arms?"

Her fitful, inaudible laughter intensified. She laughed because he was so absurd: first to take her in his arms and only then to ask her permission . . .

III.

Thus he would sit for hours, yet the terrible burden lingered on in his soul, a burden with a pale face and a playful, affectionate glance. Eventually he would get up and make his way to the dark, winding backstreets of the city, where the drunken flickering of red streetlamps through their broken glass illuminates the filthy cobblestones before sinking in the shimmering, foul-smelling puddles. At tables where sailors and their sweethearts carouse and peals of hoarse laughter drown out swearing and women's tears, he, too, would sit himself down, drink wine, watch and listen as the terrible burden sank lower, while the face of the girl with chestnut hair drowned in clouds of acrid tobacco smoke.

High above, the night would drag slowly on, the stars would describe a semicircle stretching from east to west, and the rosy dawn would draw its sleepy face up to the broken, purblind windows of the tavern. The surrounding hum would grow quieter, the intoxicated bodies slump lower over the tables, and disheveled russet heads rest on the shoulders of their sweethearts. Whereas he felt estranged from his body, as though his head were living separately from the rest, casting crumbs of consciousness into the pale half-light.

Or else he would go to restaurants, where beautiful glittering mirrors tirelessly imitated the movements of a gray man with a youthful tanned face. On top of the little marble tables were virgin-white tablecloths, their snowy folds gleaming; a blush of fruit turned crystal bowls damask, and a fiery sea of bright light punctuated the scene, glimmering and floating amid the sound of wanton melodies. Women wearing enormous gaily colored hats and brazen smiles tottered around, while those in black kissed their hands, their red lips, their full shoulders, intoxicated and aquiver with delight.

And again the sleepy dawn would draw its rosy face up to the frosted, patterned windows, shrouding the peoples' faces in waxen, deathly shadows. In the light of the dawning day, they looked like ghosts, fragments of dreams, freakish and pitiful. The last gold would glitter; the last customers—shirtfronts crumpled and hats askew—would settle up and leave, while he just sat there, and the dawning day seemed empty to him, empty and unwanted, like the bottles standing on the table. His every breath was suffering, and his anguish an act of prayer.

IV.

Five years have passed since then.

Five years since the day when he embraced her for the first time and said: "May I hold you in my arms?" Five years.

He had emerged from the fortress gray. During the three years he spent inside, he had received no letter, no word of greeting, nothing.

He had been charged with crimes against the state, and not a single shred of news about her came to set his heart alight. His gaolers cared nothing for his suffering; they were serving the fatherland.

Later he was always afraid to remember what his life had been like during those three years, and with the terror of one condemned to die, he would leap out of his bed whenever he dreamed that he was again behind bars. He remembered only daydreaming forlornly of the bodily torture that had existed back in the good old days, and how he had lamented that his abused, bloodied body could not buy a meeting with her. Such things had once been possible—back in those good old days.

After he was acquitted and released, he began to look for her. The enormity of the task was no impediment to him. But all trace of her had vanished, and nobody could tell him where she was. Among the figures who populated his world, bonds and acquaintances were erratic, like the very lives of the people themselves. Some came along and disappeared, then more arrived before vanishing again without trace amid the noise and cold of life. They disappeared like the morning dew.

But persistently, relentlessly, as a martyr would death, as a scholar would a great idea, he searched for her, day after day, month after month, journeying from one town to the next, across borders, everywhere he might expect to find her. But that person, that woman, was missing.

He asked for her everywhere, in guesthouses, hotels, registry offices, and clubs, in libraries and unions. Waiters, kellners, garçons, and cicerones would politely hear him out as he asked, in fear and anguish, feigning calm and aloofness while limb and bone strained in anticipation of their answer:

"Tell me, has Vera N—stayed here? From Russia? She's a Russian, from Russia."

A worried, businesslike expression would flash across the faces of the people listening to him. They would dash off somewhere, rifle through large books with gilt edging, through stacks of paper and registers, and every time, running their eyes over his tanned face and gray hair, they would declare in a guiltily fawning voice:

"Vera N—? No, sir. We've had no lady by that name."

The more he asked, the more difficult it became to utter this sacred name to these indifferent strangers. And so it began to seem that his secret was a secret no more, that it had crawled out from its hiding place and, like a silent shadow, was creeping about the earth, from mouth to mouth, mind to mind, broadcasting his torment, his love. He looked at his face in the mirror with loathing, cursing its exhausted, morose features, mistrusting them, as a miser does his servants who guard a treasure. It would have been easier for him to bear had his face been turned into a stone mask; then no muscle, no trembling eyelid would have betrayed his anguish. It was all the more difficult for him to inquire about her when laughter seemed to quiver in the eyes of those answering him, when they seemed to know his secret and went carrying it from house to house, snatching at it with their grubby fingers—his treasure, his love, his prayer.

Time passed—spring dappled the earth with flowers, summer arrived, long and blue, weeping autumn turned the land yellow, and winter cooled and shone like silver. But that person, that woman, was missing.

"Where are you? Where are you? I'll let your tresses down and I'll bathe them in tears. In tears as pure as love, as pure as my anguish. I'll kiss the imprints left by your feet..."

V.

Sometimes he would bring a woman home and lock himself away with her. Servants would appear and place on the table everything that she—often hungry and inebriated—requested, before timidly retreating with soft, inaudible, well-trained footsteps. He would drink, making himself insensible, while the woman would sit opposite him, preening herself and baring her elbows. She would take off her hat, decorated with beautiful, colored feathers, tap it on her cheek, and say:

"Let's drink a toast. You seem upset, darling. Whatever for?"

But no reply would come, and so the woman would give an exaggeratedly loud laugh, thinking he no longer cared for her. She would sit on his lap and move her body, trying to put fire in his blood. She would pour out more for herself and for him; he would drink from his glass and listen to the raindrops falling outside. Sometimes he would look at her and say:

"Why did you take off your hat? It suits you."

"I do love fish with a béchamel sauce," the woman would say. "Shouldn't I take off my galoshes, dearest? I don't wear hats indoors."

Then he would take her by the arms and for a long time kiss them silently. She would sit there quietly, but all of a sudden, breaking free, she would cry out in an offended, shrill voice:

"Tears! You fool!"

"Don't . . ." he would mumble, shaking his head, which was full of nightmarish delirium. "Please, don't. Are you . . . her?"

Minutes and hours would go by. Drunk now, the woman would press herself closer and closer to him, chatting incessantly, roaring with laughter, and kicking up her fat legs in fishnet stockings. He would kneel before her and, in a timid, plaintive whisper, beg:

"Look at me . . . Won't you please look at me? . . . Caress me . . . Hold me closer, closer. Like that. Closer still. I'm your darling, aren't I? . . ."

She would break into peals of uncontrollable laughter, her teeth flashing, and torment this man with a tanned face, hauling at his neck with her fat, bare hands. Her loud, wild words would bounce around the room, rebounding off his consciousness:

"Oh, you old boy! You dear soul! Who knew there were men like you in the world, my God! . . ."

Someone would turn out the light, darkness would enfold them, and in this darkness he would lavish kisses that were frantic and tender, like happiness, upon her naked, burning body. He would hold himself close to her. Trembling in pain and anguish, he would press his face against hers. He would bury his face in her dark, fragrant tresses and imagine that it was she, his beloved, his joy.

The night would stretch on, covering the drunken figure's bereft soul in a shroud of shame and bringing repose to the beautiful lady of pleasure. And again the rosy dawn would draw its sleepy face up to the curtains, arraying the sleeping figures in a deathly light.

Indifferent and noisy, the day passes. Day after day is born and dies, but she is still missing. That person, that woman is missing.

VI.

The streets were growing more deserted, more desolate; the hurried footfalls of solitary passers-by rang out. From somewhere, as if from every direction, came the distant clatter of carriages rolling down crowded streets. Shadows of people flitted across windows glinting with a mean light, while the world concealed by the glass, wretched within, seemed rich and mysterious from without.

An hour had probably passed since he stepped out of the enormous, cheerful entrance. Moving in all directions, cutting across squares and open spaces, patiently traversing long streets and gloomy alleyways, he would occasionally pause, realizing that he had lost his way, then he would lower his head and, instantly forgetting where he was, walk on without a definite plan, without an aim, immersed in deep thought. Pedestrians gave way to him, since he gave way to nobody, even to women, for he did not see them. His legs grew weary, the soles of his feet and the joints of his knees ached; he felt all this but was not conscious of it. A beggar asking him for charity received the reply:

"I don't know. I left my watch at home."

Suddenly, as he turned a corner, amid the dark hush of a nocturnal street, he spotted a group of people crowding around a brightly lit pavement, only to forget about them immediately. After several paces, a hoarse, importunate voice shouted right in his face:

"I invite the gentleman to take a ticket! A franc, a franc, one franc only! The latest news from America and Paris!"

Like a man brought to his senses by a sudden rude jolt, he sighed, lifted his head, and looked around.

Directly in front of him, on poles adorned with flags and ribbons, hung a canvas signboard illuminated by an electric light. The word "Theater" was written on it in fancy red lettering against a white background. On both sides of this word were crudely drawn manicules, their index fingers pointing toward the letters on the sign. By the wide, open doors of the makeshift building, covered in fragments of playbills, there hung a sheet of white paper. He walked over to it and began to read.

"Surprising adventure"—"Marble mines in Carrara"—"Cowboys and Indians" . . .

Some young lads crowded around him, jostling him and peering into his face. Fatigue overwhelmed him. Blind in one eye, a man wearing a red bowler and a chequered scarf was traipsing along the rain-soaked pavement, shouting in his hoarse, monotonous voice:

"One franc! One franc only! It's about to begin! Step this way and be amazed! The latest news, all the very latest! A franc!"

The bell in his fingers tirelessly let out its tinny, feeble ringing. The man with the tanned face approached the counter and bought a ticket from a plump, drowsy woman with powdered shoulders. Pushing the drapery aside, he stepped inside and took a seat.

About a dozen people were sitting around him—mostly hawkers and laborers. They sat hunched over, yawning and scrutinizing the gaily colored posters hanging on the walls, which were decorated in green and red strips of material. A pianist—an old man with a ruddy nose and artistically long gray hair—sat in front of the screen. His spindly figure, arrayed in a threadbare frock coat, shook with each stroke of the keys as he elicited the pathetic, skipping strains of a dance.

The little bell rang once again behind the wall, and all of a sudden the lights went out. A little girl with enormous eyes loudly, and with an air of mystery, asked her mother:

"Mummy, are these people going to sleep?"

"Shhh!" said the sickly woman who was apparently her mother. "Sit quietly."

"Roosters," said the little girl as she saw the studio logo appear on the screen. "Roosters, Mummy!"

But the roosters disappeared. A gray street with gray buildings and a gray sky rose up before the audience's eyes. A silent, tenebrous, gray life slithered along the street. In the distance there were carriages and streetcars that grew to enormous proportions and then vanished. People were going about carrying baskets, groceries, smiling gray smiles, nodding and glancing over their shoulders. Dogs were running about, barking silently. The sudden deafness seemed to astound the audience. Life was in motion, but it was silent and dead, like shadows from beyond the grave.

A young boy came out of a sweetshop and, skipping merrily, carrying a basket full of tarts, made his way over to his young chimney sweep friend. They walk along, happy and satisfied, greedily devouring someone else's tarts.

A motorcar drives past. The chauffeur has failed to spot a young rogue perching on the back of the car, between the wheels, happily swinging his bare feet, kicking up the dust.

"He's gone for a ride," said the little girl, prodding her mother on the shoulder. "Mama, that boy's gone for a ride! ..."

"Shut up," said the woman. "Or else the chimney sweep will come and take you away."

The people walk on, watching the vanishing rogue and laughing. A woman in a large straw hat, clutching a handbag, pauses, looks back, and watches as the camera, unseen by the audience, records the beating of life.

VII.

He leaped up, began to sob, cried out, and, forgetting himself, lunged forward.

"It's her!"

She—his sun, his life. His darling! Her sweet, melancholy smile. Her delicate face, a little thinner now. Her movements! Everything!

She—captured by the play of light. Her eyes peering straight into his soul, into his shaken, gasping soul. The shadow of her hat falling across her face. She pauses! She's leaving!

A long, chilling scream rent the silence and shook the very walls of the theater. He hurried, made a dash for her, dropping his hat and pushing aside the audience members, running, gasping, his face moist with tears. A distance of ten, maybe fifteen, paces ...

"Vera! Vera!"

The woman rounded the railings of a garden and halted in astonishment at the scream. He caught her up, convulsing with sobs, took her in his arms, picked her up like a child, kissed her ...

She took fright, and the color drained from her face . . . She knows! She knows! She presses herself close to him. A frenzy of happiness, searing like unbearable pain, unfurled its wings, shrouding them both. Everything drowned and disappeared. They were all that remained—just the two of them ...

Somebody gripped him from behind and hauled him off. He turned around and, with a blind, startled gaze, took in the street and the other frightened people who had torn him away from his miracle, his treasure, his prayer.

Fiery snow now reeled before his eyes, and somebody struck his heart with an enormous, heavy weight. Everything went dark. Two little red roosters jumped out from each side, their eyes glinting red, and then vanished. A long, heavy ringing sounded and grew louder before fading and dying away.

When they dragged out the body, which had suddenly become an enigma, an object of hostility to all those frightened, living people, a young hook-nosed fellow sporting black eyes and a soiled tie said to the man who had been ringing the little bell:

"I spotted him before . . . Just imagine, he didn't take his change from five francs! . . ."

LANPHIER COLONY

Like a sailor
Traversing the Yura Strait,
I do not know where I shall arrive
Across the depths of love.

Sone no Yoshitada[*]

---

[*] *Like a sailor ... love*: Grin here offers a rather free translation of a Japanese *waka* poem by Sone no Yoshitada (fl. ca. 975). The original Heian-period poem was reproduced in Fujiwara no Teika's (1162–1241) anthology *Ogura Hyakunin Isshu*, and appeared in a Russian translation of the anthology prepared by Nikolai Bakhtin as early as 1905, although this is not the version that Grin quotes. A more literal rendering is as follows:

> *A boatman,*
> *Crossing the Strait of Yura,*
> *Loses his oar*
> *And does not know where he is headed.*
> *Is not the course of love like this?*

I.

Three index fingers stretched out in the direction of the roadstead. A Dutch barque had arrived that evening. The night obscured its hull; the masts' colorful lights and the little shining discs of the portholes were doubled in the black mirror of the sea; a thick, lingering mist smacked of tar, rotting algae, and salt.

"Six thousand tons," said Dribb, lowering his finger. "Palm wood and ebony. Say, Guppy, do you need any ebony?"

"No," returned the farmer, deceived by Dribb's serious tone. "I haven't any use for it."

"Well, what about a satinwood pole? You could make a club to beat your future heir, provided his back can take it."

"Knock it off," said Guppy. "I don't need any wood. Even if there were variegated or raspberry wood, I still wouldn't be interested."

"Dribb," said the third colonist, "was there something you wanted to say?"

"Me? Oh, nothing in particular. Only, it seemed odd to me that the barque, whose cargo our right honorable Guppy doesn't need, has dropped anchor here. What do you make of it, Astis?"

Astis sniffed the air thoughtfully, as if the smell of the sea concealed the necessary explanation.

"He's made a detour, albeit a minor one," he said. "The Dutchman's route lay farther to the south. All the same, that's his affair. Perhaps the barque met with some accident. Then again, maybe the captain had his own reasons for taking this strange course of action."

"A pound to a penny," said Dribb, "he'll have taken a hit in the Archipelago. Unless they're planning to open a furniture factory here. That's my guess."

"You'll lose that penny," Astis rejoined. "We haven't had a storm in these parts for over a month."

"You see, I don't keep tabs on trivia," said Dribb after a pause. "And I don't dirty my hands for less than ten pounds."

"Agreed."

"What are you agreeing to?"

"Nothing. I only mean to say that you're wrong."

"Never in a thousand years, Astis."

"Case in point, Dribb, case in point."

"Here's my hand."

"And here's mine."

"Guppy," said Dribb, "you shall be a witness to this. But here's a quandary: how are we to prove that I'm right?"

"What confidence!" Astis scoffed. "You'd do better asking how we're to prove that you're mistaken."

After a brief silence, Dribb announced:

"When it comes down to it, there's nothing simpler. We'll go aboard the barque ourselves."

"What, now?"

"Why not?"

"Hang on!" shouted Guppy. "Either I'm hearing things, or that's the sound of rowing. Keep your mouth shut for just a minute."

Amid the deep, concentrated silence they could hear a continual splashing sound that was growing stronger, rebounding, and steadily vanishing into the sea's velvety abyss.

Dribb started. His intense curiosity had been piqued. He hovered there on the very edge, vainly trying to make anything out.

Unable to bear it any longer, Astis called out:

"Hey! Ahoy there! Hey!"

"You are insufferable," Guppy said, affronted. "For some strange reason you think you're cleverer than everyone else. God alone knows which of us is cleverest."

"They're close," said Dribb.

Indeed, a rowboat had come so near that one could distinguish the splashing of water as it dripped off the oars. They heard the crunching of gravel, slow steps, and hushed voices. Somebody was climbing the path leading from the shallows up to the ledge of the escarpment. Dribb shouted:

"Ahoy there!"

"Hello!" came the response from below, in a strong foreign accent. "Who goes there?"

"You're from the Dutch ship?"

The colonist was still waiting for an answer when, very close to him, a booming, unfamiliar voice asked in turn:

"Are you the one who's making so much noise, my friend? I'll satisfy your legitimate curiosity: a rowboat from the Dutch ship, yes."

Dribb turned around, somewhat taken aback, and gawped at the black silhouette of the man standing beside him. Through the darkness Dribb could make out that this unknown figure was of average height, with broad shoulders and a beard.

"Who are you?" he asked. "Have you really come from the ship?"

"We have," said the silhouette, setting a sizable bundle on the ground. "Four sailors and I."

His manner of speaking, without haste, pronouncing each word in a distinct, piercing voice, made quite an impression. All three men waited, silently beholding the still black figure. Finally, Dribb, concerned with the outcome of the bet, asked:

"A question for you, sir. Did the barque meet with an accident?"

"Nothing of the kind," the unknown figure replied. "It's trim and strong—just like you and I, I should hope. At the first wind it will set sail and be on its way."

"I'm glad to hear it," said Astis delightedly. "Pay up, Dribb."

"I don't understand it!" cried Dribb, whom Astis's delight had cut to the quick. "Thunderation! A barque isn't a pleasure yacht that can call in at any out-of-the-way place . . . What is it doing here, I wonder? . . ."

"If you please. I convinced the captain to put me ashore here."

Astis shrugged incredulously.

"What a cock-and-bull story!" he said half-questioningly as he drew closer. "That isn't as easy as you think. The route to Europe lies about a hundred miles south of here."

"I know that," said the visitor impatiently. "I have no cause to lie."

"Perhaps the captain is a relative of yours?" asked Guppy.

"The captain is a Dutchman; for that reason alone it would be difficult for him to be any relative of mine."

"And your name?"

"Horn."

"Astonishing!" said Dribb. "And he agreed to your request?"

"As you can see."

His voice sounded more weary than self-assured. A hundred questions were on the tip of Dribb's tongue, but he held them back, sensing instinctively that his curiosity had reached its limits and would no longer be satisfied. Astis said:

"There aren't any hotels here, but you'll find lodgings for the night and food for a very fair price with Szabó. Shall I take you there?"

"Much obliged."

"Dribb . . ." began Astis.

"Very well," Dribb snapped. "You'll have your ten pounds tomorrow morning, at eight o'clock. Goodbye, Mr. Horn. I wish you the very best in getting settled here. Let's go, Guppy."

Dribb turned and set off in the opposite direction, accompanied by the pig farmer.

"Now I'll wager that I'll get my money from Dribb only after some very harsh words. Mr. Horn, I'm at your service."

Astis extended his hand, turned, and clicked his tongue in surprise. He was alone.

"Horn!" Astis called.

But there was nobody there.

II.

The blossoming dwarf shrubs of the southern hills were giving off a fine mist. The sun's molten disc stood directly over the forest. The sky looked like the vast pale-blue interior of an enormous sphere filled with a crystalline liquid. Dew glittered in the dark verdure; fanciful birdsong seemed to emanate from beneath the ground; in their warbling there was a note of languid, lazy awakening.

Horn was traveling westward, trying to skirt a chain of ravines that filled the area between the colony and the northern part of the forest. An old Colt rifle was slung over his shoulder, swaying as he went. His clothes were crumpled—the vestige of a night spent in the forest. He trod with large, even steps, carefully observing his surroundings, examining the environs and the ground with the look of a master who has returned after a long absence.

The young tropical morning embraced Horn with the rich breath of lush, succulent verdure. Almost happy, he mused that living here would offer the particular delight of wildness and seclusion, of repose for the troubled, which was impossible back there, where every square inch of land was coveted by thousands—nay, hundreds of thousands of eyes.

He passed the ravines, the ridge of basalt cliffs, which resembled enormous piles of coal, the meandering copse girding the hills, and came out, heading in the direction of the lake. The places he had just seen did not gratify him enough. They lacked a concentration, that essential and harmonious union of forest and open space, mountain, and water. He was drawn to the comfort, the bounty, the hospitality of nature, to its shady and whimsical corners. Ever since the future stopped existing for him, he had come to be hard on the present.

The heat grew more intense. The silence of the wilderness listened to the man as he walked; amid the day's quiet charm, Horn's thoughts slowly gave way one to another, and he, as though reading a book, followed them, full of rapt sorrow and an unshakable readiness to live in silence, within himself. Now, as never before, he perceived the full extent of his isolation from everything that he saw; sometimes, lost in thought and roused rudely to consciousness by the voice of a monkey or the murmur of a passing lyrebird, Horn would lift his head with a drear curiosity—like one finding himself on another planet—and examine the most ordinary things: a stone, a piece of wood, a pit filled with water. He was insensible to fatigue; his legs moved automatically and grew more numb with every impact of his soles against the hard soil. He reached the lake by the time the sun, having climbed to its highest point, had burned away every shadow, flooding the earth with the angry, unbearable heat of its zenith.

Mossy, swollen tree trunks, crowned by enormous dappled canopies, created intertwining arches from which hung ferns, with their delicate, graceful lacework of fretted leaves, and garlands of vines that draped down as far as the gnarled roots resembling a gnome's fingers that had been bunched together by some underground paroxysm. Around the trunks, hoisted up like sheaves of green rockets, drooped fans, umbrellas, elongated ovals, and needles. Farther along, toward the water, the angular stalks of bamboo interlaced, like straw viewed through a magnifying glass. Through the chinks in the leaves, full of thick, dark-green shadows and golden sunspots, little blue fragments of a lake glimmered.

Pushing apart the reeds, Horn made his way down to the shallows. Directly in front of him, the opposing shore stretched out in a narrow, misty strip; the steel-blue surface of the lake appeared smoky, as though it were enshrouded in finest gossamer. To the left and the right, the shore grew into steep hills; Horn found himself in a miniature valley, blanketed by forest.

As he contemplated and contrasted, Horn threw his leather bag on the sand and sat on it, surrendering to the diffuse calm. This seemed like a suitable spot, and, what was more, his eagerness to begin work decided the matter in favor of the shore. He spotted a square clearing and a makeshift structure, hidden from the lake by a wall of bamboo. With nothing but an axe and a supreme effort of will, he hoped to build a home, free from the unbearable proximity of people and the cloying eyes of strangers, which made you want to take a bath.

In the midst of these contemplations, erasing the scene of impending work, an old and, for the present moment, dull pain flared up, transporting his imagination back to the titanic cities of the north. The thousand-mile distance snapped like a rubber band; as he cradled his knees in his red, sunburnt arms, Horn saw with a dreadful clarity scenes and events whose focal point was his inflamed, tormented soul. His darkened gaze paused upon the features of faces frozen in a single expression, the matted gleam of parquet, window curtains billowing in the wind, and thousands of inanimate objects that recalled a suffering deeper than the very source of his own. A bright, bronze candelabrum with guttering candles shone before him, snatching from the darkness a little hand with a lace cuff reaching out toward the flame, and again, as several years before, there came a knock at the door—a loud and at the same time mute demand . . .

Horn shook his head. For an instant he was repulsed by himself, like an amputee who pulls off a bandage in order to inspect the necrotic cross-section. The languorous silence of the shore resembled that of the hospital ward, which provokes in those of a nervous disposition the urge to scream and squirm. To distract himself, he set down to work. He felt a genuine longing in his muscles, a desire to make himself weary, to lift great weights, to chop, to hammer.

And from the very first blow of blue-tinged British steel into the yielding stalk of bamboo, Horn found himself ablaze with a surge of energy, the frenzied exertion that thirsts to subjugate matter with a continual shower of efforts, following one after another amid the growing voluptuousness of exhaustion. Without pausing, he felled trunk after trunk, stripped off leaves, chopped, measured, dug pits, hammered in stakes; with eyes filled with the green mottle of the forest, with a soul that seemed insensible to the sounds he was making, he lost himself in the chaos of physical sensations. His chest ached from his quickened breathing, the stinging sweat made his skin itch, the palms of his hands burned and were covered in water blisters, his legs were swollen with heavy venous blood, a sharp pain in his back prevented him from straightening up, his entire body trembled, driven on by a feverish thirst to kill off all thought. It was intoxication, an orgy of exhaustion, a frenzy of haste, a delight in brute force. Hunger, suppressed by fatigue, acted like a narcotic. From time to time, tormented by thirst, Horn would throw down his axe and drink the cold, brackish water of the lake.

When the shadows were cast and the evening clamor of the monkeys announced the approach of night, a little wild goat, which had come to the watering spot, cowered among the bulrushes and was shot by one of Horn's bullets. A fire did the cooking. The smoking, half-burnt pieces of meat smelled of grass and bloody juices. Horn ate heartily, working his pocketknife with the same dexterity with which he had once handled a dessert spoon.

Sated, enveloped in the growing darkness, which was permeated by a red glimmer from the dimming blue-gray coals of the fire, Horn remembered the barque. From the deck of the ship, his future existence had seemed to him a mysterious succession of days, full of uncertainty and monotony, the vegetive anticipation of death, replaced occasionally by severe bouts of ennui. It was as if he were watching himself, a tiny human speck with an enormous world imprisoned inside; a speck that colored with its own mood everything its consciousness perceived.

The heady humidity condensed in the air, the melody of the rustling forest wove a fine lace of guarded hush, the putrid, sweet smell of the hothouse encouraged stimulation. Thoughts flitted around the unfinished structure, returning both to the ocean and to flashes of the past, which had lost its keenness amid a feeling of complete exhaustion. A heavy, deathly sleep was approaching; its breath touched Horn's eyelashes, muddled his thoughts, and penetrated his limbs with an invisible weight.

The last coal crackled and flared up for a single moment, taking on the color of incandescent iron and illuminating the nearest stalks that were curling from the heat, before fading away. And with it into the velvety blackness flew the Fire spirit, the happy, dancing spirit of the flame.

From a hill came the alarming cry of a lynx, which abated and, growing louder again, sounded like a long, rueful threat. But Horn did not hear it, for he was sound asleep, like the dead—a true blessing from the earth and the realm of tortures.

■ □ ■

Five days later, set amid a flat, square clearing, neatly packed down and fenced in, a little house stood with a sloped reed roof and an unglazed window overlooking the lake. The sturdy, homemade furniture consisted of a cot, a table, and benches. In the corner towered a massive earthen stove.

His work done, Horn, emaciated and hunched over, staggering with exhaustion, made his way along the narrow strip of shallow water toward the foot of the hill, climbed to the summit, and looked back.

To the north loomed a forest, like an unmoving green herd, skirting as far as the horizon a chain of chalk cliffs that were flecked with crevasses and blurs of scrawny shrubs. To the east, beyond the lake, twisted the white thread of a road leading to the town; dotted along its edge were trees that seemed minute from afar, like salad shoots. To the west, surrounding a plain pitted with ravines and hills, stretched the dark-blue expanse of the distant ocean, scintillating with white sparks.

While to the south, away from the center of a gently sloping crater, with a bright array of houses and farms, surrounded by unkempt greenery, stretched the slanting squares of the plantations and ploughed fields of Lanphier Colony.

III.

A two-wheeled native cart crossed the road mere steps from where Guppy was standing. Having passed through a cloud of acrid dust, Guppy spotted a stranger walking toward him, and unintentionally stopped. He had no recollection of the man, but, at the same time, it was if he had met him before. A vague memory of the Dutch barque piqued Guppy's natural curiosity; he removed his hat and bowed.

"Hey . . ." said Guppy, squinting. "Are you on your way from town?"

"I haven't visited the town yet," replied Horn, suppressing the desire to walk on, "and I'm not likely to, either."

"Ah, yes, I see!" said Guppy with a broad grin. "Just as I suspected. I recognize your voice. You landed a week ago, didn't you, in that little bay?"

"I landed in a little bay, that's sure enough," said Horn, weighing his words, "but I don't believe we've met."

Guppy laughed and winked at him.

"Astis and Dribb had a bet," he said, a little calmer now. "I went off with Dribb. Astis kept telling everyone that you'd been swallowed up by the earth. I'll be damned, you certainly played a trick on him, didn't you!"

"I seem to remember something of the sort," said Horn. "Yes, I definitely sensed your presence there in the dark."

"There you have it!" Guppy nodded, in a sweat from the pleasure of jawing. "Why didn't you go with Astis?"

"To tell the truth," said Horn with a grin, "frankly speaking, I felt ashamed to bother such respectable people. Another man would have lied and told you that you seemed stupid, talkative, and much too curious, but as for me—well, that's another matter. I like you, so I won't lie."

He said this with an entirely placid expression on his face, and Guppy, taking this masked affront at face value, creased into a smug smile.

"Come, come!" he objected condescendingly. "Was it really such a bother? You're a fine fellow, upon my honor, and I do like you. My farm's half a mile from here; how about some roast pork and a glass of beer, eh? What do you say?"

"Very well," said Horn, after a pause. The confident manner of the colonist amused him. He inquired: "How many inhabitants are there?"

"A lot," panted Guppy, throwing a hand up in the air. "Ever since the ferry route connecting us to the mainland opened up, all sorts of adventurers have come ashore, gadding about here, taking plots of land. After a year they all flee to the town, where there are women and everything that's difficult to give up."

A labyrinth of green hedgerows, full of dry dust, snaked its way along the rising incline. Horn's legs were covered in reddish sand up to his ankles; the dust tickled his nostrils. Guppy continued:

"You meet more snakes than women in these parts. Last year they put on an actual auction for a washerwoman who had traveled over a hundred miles here. If only you'd seen how she stood there, arms akimbo, up on the counter of The Green Conch! Three men tried to filch her from one another, and in the end they came to some sort of arrangement: they found one of them in a well . . . while the other two live with her to this day."

Guppy took a breath before carrying on. According to him, no more than half the colonists had families and lived with white women; the rest made do with native women, who were seduced by the prospect of idleness and colorful rags, while their fathers lolled nearby with bottles left around by their sharp-witted bridegrooms.

The old population, almost all of them former exiles or their children, fugitives from far-flung colonies, people who were ashamed of their previous name, servants caught red-handed—this is what had flocked in, totaling one hundred smoking chimneys around the original village, which had been founded by two former convicts. One of them had died, while the other still hauled his decrepit, disease-worn body from house to house, breakfasting here, dining there, and everywhere sniveling about the property he had gambled away over the course of a single night to some luckier miscreant.

"Here we are," said Guppy, reaching out his stiff farmer's palm toward a tall, tower-like building. "This is my house," he added. A shadow of obtuse self-importance fell across his face. "It's a fine, solid home. Fit for a governor."

A tall hedgerow stretched from two corners of the building, enclosing an area that was invisible from the outside. Thrusting his hands into his pockets and looking up, Guppy passed through the gate.

Horn looked around, struck by the peculiar grandeur of the pig trough that reigned there. The scorching heat of the yard produced an unbearable stench as myriad gleaming flies hovered in the air; a greenish muck stuck to the soles of the feet, the squeals, the hurried grunting, the pungent smell of swine—all this smacked of filthy live meat, packed into the space of a single acre. The fat yellow masses moved around in all directions, trembling under their own bulk. The yard teemed with them; enormous boars with black coats; ungainly, tottering yearlings; grubby pink piglets; swollen, pregnant sows exhausted by the milk held in their monstrously hanging teats— thousands of rodent-like tails, snouts, glinting teeth, polyphonous, rasping squeals, the rustle of bodies rubbing together—all this provoked a yearning for soap and cold water. Guppy said:

"And here are my piggies! How do you like them?"

"Not bad," replied Horn.

"Every month I sell around two dozen," said Guppy, coming alive, his nostrils flaring with pleasure. "They're really the most peaceable beasts. They give me hardly any trouble at all. Only sometimes they do savage their young—so look sharp. I love my work. You look and think: here is lazy, fat gold; if you just clean it up a little, your pocket will burst from all the money they bring in. I do relish that thought."

"Fine pigs," said Horn.

Guppy wiped his forehead and peered at Horn. This man was irritating him; he wore a look that seemed to say he had seen the pigs and Guppy many times over.

"I was about to be on my way," Horn said suddenly, "but thinking about it, I wouldn't mind a drink. If you have some wine, that would be just the thing, but no matter if not."

"I have some *sahha*, the native beer." Guppy motioned toward the house. "They make it from sago. You haven't tried it? You must. It will make your head spin, just like Esther."

The cramped, almost bare room that Horn entered was softened by the dazzling brilliance of the sky, which flooded in through the window; the square blue aperture was crowded with jagged leaves and the feathery tops of the grove. Guppy picked up a stick and whacked it loudly against the table.

A seminaked creature, with hair resembling a bishop's miter, appeared from a side door. It was a woman. Her shoulders were covered with a cotton kerchief. Her dark face with thick, as if swollen, lips motionlessly observed the men.

"Bring us some beer," Guppy ordered brusquely, taking a seat at the table.

Horn sat down next to him. The woman with the dark body brought a pitcher and tankards and remained in the room. Her quick almond eyes skimmed over Horn's hands, his apparel, and his head. She could be no more than eighteen; a shiny tin band that passed through her ear severely spoilt the rough beauty of her flat face.

"What are you waiting for?" said Guppy. "Go."

The girl's upper lip rose ever so slightly, flashing a strip of teeth. She left, drowsily shuffling her feet.

"She lives with me," Guppy explained, draining his tankard. "The idiot. They're all idiots, worse than negroes."

"I thought you didn't have a . . . woman," said Horn.

"I don't," said Guppy. "I'm not married and I won't take a lover."

"But there was a woman just here." Horn fixed his gaze on Guppy. "Perhaps I'm mistaken . . ."

Guppy roared with laughter.

"When I say 'women,' I mean only whites," he proudly rejoined, composing himself and adopting a somewhat disdainful tone. "As for that . . . well, I'm no old man . . . if you catch my meaning?"

"Indeed," said Horn.

He sat there vacantly, without a thought in his head; his surroundings seemed as sharp and acidic as the taste of *sahha*. Guppy struggled to stop himself belching, comically distending his cheeks and staring goggle-eyed.

The beer made his head spin, as the cold weight flowed into his stomach. The blue quadrant of sky smacked of sadness. Horn said:

"It goes straight to your head, just like Esther . . . Isn't that what you said?"

"Quite so." Guppy nodded. "Only you can't drink Esther, as you can the contents of this tankard. Astis's daughter. What bad luck the chaps have in these parts. When young Dribb marries, he'll make more enemies than you and I have. It's Friday today, and she'll come. If you see her, don't make a fool of yourself, like all the rest of them; she's well used to it."

"We'll see about that," said Horn. "People still fascinate me."

"There you go," said Guppy, looking askance at Horn, "I like you. Though you scarcely say a word, good God! What do you plan to live on?"

Horn slowly finished his drink.

"There's plenty of food in the forest," he smiled, examining the bridge of Guppy's nose. "I'll get by."

"All the same," Guppy continued. "Playing around with a rifle and catching indigenous fevers . . . I swear by that boar outside, you'll waste away within a month."

Horn shrugged impatiently.

"That's neither here nor there," he said. "In any case, I must be on my way. Coffee and gunpowder await me, and I've been sitting here too long."

"What's the rush!" cried Guppy, flushing with embarrassment at the idea that Horn should leave without having told him anything. "Would you really be happier on your own?"

Before Horn had the time to reply, there came a knock at the door, and Guppy, pulling the sweetest face, turned to face it with a look of impatient expectation.

"Take a look, Horn," he said, his little eyes flashing. "The head-turner has arrived—come now, don't drag your heels!"

Horn's ironic smile melted, and, with a serious face, with the blood slowly flowing back to his heart, he looked upon the girl. The idea that she might be beautiful had not even occurred to him. He felt a heavy, painful sense of unease, just as he had done before, when music presented him with unexpected melodies, after which he would want to spend the whole day in silence or else get drunk.

"Guppy, you'll have to wait a little longer," said Esther, glancing at Horn. This outsider made her feel uncomfortable, causing her to lend her voice an involuntarily grand tone. "My father hasn't any money."

Guppy turned green.

"You jest, my beauty!" he hissed, smiling unnaturally. "Just cough up what you've hidden there . . . Come now!"

"I haven't time for joking." Esther went over to the table and leaned her palms on its edge. "No and no! You'll have to wait a month or so."

In that brief moment, while Guppy took a deep breath, preparing to curse or shout, the girl smiled. This was the final straw.

"Gloat then!" Guppy shouted, jumping up and running about. "You may laugh! But will your father give me a brass farthing while I die of hunger? I shelled out thousands, and now I have to wait? I swear on my grandmother's head, I'm sick of this! I'll drag you through the courts, do you hear, you minx?"

Horn got to his feet.

"I'm disturbing you," he said.

"Esther," Guppy said, "here is a man from a land of honest people. Why don't you ask him whether it's not possible to keep one's word?"

The girl scrutinized Horn's face. Embarrassed, he turned his head away; those lusterless black eyes seemed to bear down on him. Guppy ran his hands through his hair.

"Farewell," said Horn, holding out his hand.

"Drop by sometime," Guppy muttered, "even if you do get on my nerves. Ah, money, money!" He made an effort and continued: "I hope you'll be more talkative in future. If only you'd take a plot of land!"

Horn went out into the yard and, pausing, listened. Heated voices were coming from above. He went on his way, stepping through puddles of water and mud riddled with hoofprints.

The sound of rapid breathing made him turn around. Esther appeared at his side, slightly hitching up her short striped skirt and animatedly waving her free hand. Horn tried to find the words, but she anticipated him.

"Are you the man who came ashore a week ago?"

She had a pure and lingering voice, the sound of which seemed to suffuse her entire body; her face and gaze seemed to express exactly what her mouth was saying.

"The very same," Horn confirmed. "And you're Astis's daughter?"

"Yes." Esther fixed her braids, which had become tangled under her peaked native hat. "But living here won't suit you."

Horn smiled, as adults do when they hear clever children talk.

"And why not?"

"People work here." The girl knitted her high eyebrows thoughtfully. "You have hands like mine."

She stretched out her swarthy little hands, which were decorated with rings, and immediately lowered them again. She was comparing this man with the strapping youngsters who worked on the farms.

"There isn't anything for you to do here," she said categorically. "You're a city type, and you look like a gentleman. There's nothing for you here."

"But there is," Horn replied seriously. "The lake. And my house there."

His words stopped her in her tracks.

"Your house? Five years ago people lived in that house, but it all burned to the ground."

"Esther," said Horn, "now you'll see that I can work. I rebuilt it in six days, as God created the heaven and the earth."

As they crossed the hedgerow on their way out, a deafening grunting bid them farewell; they walked side by side, their feet engulfed by the hot red sand. Esther burst into a laughter that was as slow as her voice.

"City folk like to joke."

"Really, I'm telling the truth." Horn turned his head and glanced at the girl's radiant face. "Yes, I'll live here. Idly."

He saw her mouth, half-open with respect, and her astonished eyes, and sensed that he would not be bored here. There was a pause.

A cloud of dust, resplendent with bare feet and a bronze body, rushed to cut across their path. Horn stopped in his tracks. The dust settled down; something unimaginably dirty and ragged stood before him, stamping its feet and waving its long, monkey-like arms. These strange gestures were accompanied by gruff yelps and sighs that were like a sort of wailing.

"Bekeko," the girl said. "Don't be afraid, it's Bekeko. He's half-witted, but a gentle lad . . . What's the matter, Bekeko?"

Bulbous, with bald patches, his head nuzzled into the girl's skirt. Bekeko was enjoying himself, halting his caresses every now and then to fix his staring, off-white eyes on Horn. He was repugnant and aroused a feeling of cold pity. Horn retreated to the hedgerow.

"Bekeko, go home, you beast!" Esther cried, having spotted that the halfwit was trying to bite her hand.

Bekeko stood up, laughing and yapping like a dog.

"Esther," he said, continuing to stamp his feet, "I want to get a lot of striped skirts and bring them all to you. It hurts in my jaw!"

Esther put on a frightened face.

"Fire!" she shouted. "Bekeko, fire!"

The effect of these words was deadly. Doubling over, Bekeko fell, clutching his head in his hands and trembling. His back heaved up and down.

"What's all this?" asked Horn, studying the man on the ground.

"You see," said Esther. "He's impossible. He attaches himself to you, like a dog, and he'll follow you around until you say one word: 'Fire.' His brother used to feed him, but he burned to death a while back, the drunkard. The halfwit's afraid of fire more than he is of beatings. I don't see him all that often; he prefers to hang around the swampland and eat God only knows what."

Horn lit his pipe.

"I learned of your existence," he said, knocking down the ash, "before you arrived."

The girl flashed a smile.

"From Guppy," she drawled. "He calls me 'the head-turner.'"

"Yes," Horn echoed. "You are a head-turner."

He looked at her again: not a shadow of embarrassment. Her face expressed neither coquetry nor gratitude, while he himself felt a certain awkwardness and inhaled the tobacco deeper than he ordinarily would.

"I live over there," the girl said, pointing to the left. "Do you see that yellow roof? My father loves visitors. Where are you going now?"

"Coffee, tobacco, and gunpowder," said Horn, raising three fingers. "That's what I'm after."

"You're going to see Szabó," the girl corrected him. "You have a rifle?"

"Yes."

Esther motioned with her eyes.

"I have a carbine," she said. "But it's difficult to get cartridges here, so we have to go to town. I shoot from the hip and never miss a shot."

"What you mean to say is that you aren't sure that I could do the same," said Horn. "Well, I'm not shy. Step a little to the right."

He drew his revolver and, with a chuckle, bowed to the girl.

"Why don't you go over there? Do you see, about thirty paces from here, that slender tree trunk? Walk past it, stop, and, if you find a bullet in it, come back."

He watched Esther's back, the retreating crown of her raven-haired head, and, as he took aim, the sunlight playing on the polished steel of his revolver almost made him sneeze. A shot rang out and he lowered his arm. Esther was still walking, swaying gently, and stopped at the tree.

Turning around, she gave a cheerful wave of the hand, and again Horn thought he saw her eyes, separate from her body, floating in the air.

IV.

Nobody woke Horn; he would get up by himself, suddenly and with complete clarity of consciousness, without feeling the body's drowsy inertia, without yawning—as though he had not slept but lain there in wait with his eyes closed.

Calm, slightly puzzled, he tried to imagine the reasons that had returned him to consciousness so completely. Through the window, the rose-colored haze of the morning exhaled a dewy mist, the brackish rot of the shallow waters, and a murmuring hush, which was as elusive as a train of thoughts belonging a man on the verge of sleep. A fog hung over the lake. The undulating vapors spread out over the water's surface, unveiling bright little blue pools of still water by the shores.

Horn stood by the window, lost in the melodious quiet of the sleeping air. The shimmering edge of the sun's disc flashed over the bright face of the dawn with its closed eyes; mountains of clouds drifted over the horizon, the web-like thread of forest stretched over to the other bank, and Horn mused that this could be a throng of green knights, sleeping while standing up. The lances upon which they leaned were decorated with still, green feathers.

All of a sudden everything changed. Myriad rays, like a hail of gold coins, scattered down upon the earth; the water began to glitter, and several of the rays—transparent, forged from light and air—fell at Horn's feet. The verdure, glassy with dew, dried before Horn's eyes. Clumps of brown flowers plumped up and flushed with color, straightening out like a child's trembling fingers reaching for a toy. The thick smell of the earth tickled his nostrils. Green, blue, brown, and rose hues drenched the stalks of bamboo, quivering in a tangle of shadows among the fabric of foliage, and somewhere not far off, the throat of a forest bird emitted a low call, broken and uncertain, like the sound of an instrument being tuned.

Horn stood there like an empty bottle being filled to the brim with the young, green wine of the earth, which was stretching out as it awoke. Milk, spraying from the tender, overflowing breast of some invisible woman, imperceptibly fell on his lips, and he imagined her, caught the smile that she had directed heavenward, and narrowed his eyes because of the golden web covering the world. His soul was cleft in two: he could have laughed but did not want to; he was ready to believe in green knights but made an effort and interrupted their quiet voices with persistent memories.

The dispute between Horn and Horn came to a quick and abrupt end as the door creaked open slowly from the outside. The gap widened, and the man pulling it stood there, nearer to the corner and not yet visible.

Horn waited, uncertain whether somebody was really there. The door had opened of its own accord before; this happened because of the slight crookedness of the hinges. Instinctively, rather from curiosity than wariness, he fixed his eyes on the spot where he most expected to meet a man's eyes.

But the very next moment he was forced to lower his gaze. An eye and a section of forehead covered with a tangle of white hair appeared four feet above the ground; somebody peered in while bending over, darted behind the door, and appeared almost immediately again.

Unsteady on his feet, the man came in through the door, closed it, and, with an ungainly shake of the head, fixed Horn's face with his eyes, which were dappled with wrinkles and red veins. He was manifestly drunk.

As erect as a pole, with the dull, motionless gleam of faded eyes, barefooted and dressed in rags, he could have passed for a devil pretending to be a beggar. At a distance of several paces, his arms looked a deep blue, like those of a cadaver, but as he drew closer, it was possible to discern the solid pattern of a tattoo that covered his whole body, from his neck to his waist. Snakes, Japanese dragons, flags, ships, inscriptions, indecent scenes, and cynical images jostled against one another on his chest and arms, mixing with the whitish marks of scarring. Around his neck there hung a scarf that had been turned into a piece of rope by grime and time. The tattered crown of a hat covered his pointed, lupine ears and his face, which was the color of verdigris. His nose, which had been broken by the blow of a stick, curved sullenly down. His jacket, which had lost its sleeves, was open at the chest. His entire figure smacked of a suspicious past, the heart's dark inner recesses, dive bars, the glint of knives, rasping malice, and human fur, which could be more awe-inspiring than a tiger's coat. The old man had, as the saying goes, seen a thing or two.

"What do you want?" asked Horn. He was somewhat puzzled. This figure did not inspire trust. Strange, like a fragment of a dream, it shifted from one foot to the other.

"What do you want?" the wretch muttered back, winking and making an effort to hold himself straight. "If you ask me who I am, I'll tell you openly and honestly. But have it your way: I was curious to see a man living as you do. I myself once lived like this . . . I did . . . about thirty years ago I hid myself away on a deserted atoll, fleeing from some diabolically curious kepi. True, they did get the better of me . . . but, ah! that was later—after much time had passed."

Spittle spumed from the old man's mouth, and a lump rolled around in his dry, almost strangled throat. Horn asked:

"What's your name?"

"Lanphier," the guest croaked. "Lanphier, if you please."

Horn nodded his head thoughtfully. The old man amused him; the sense of self-importance with which he named himself concealed his devious and cunning expectation. Horn said:

"Well, I'm Horn."

Lanphier roared with laughter.

"Horn?" he repeated, winking his left eye, while the right one darkened, its pupil gleaming. "Well, yes—Horn, naturally, who else could you be?"

Horn frowned. The convict's undue familiarity stirred a slight impatience in him.

"I," he said, "could be someone else. Someone who isn't used to getting up early. While you, quite apart from being Lanphier, could be someone who only by accident found me as I am—not asleep."

Lanphier silently bared his teeth. He made no reply; his drunken thoughts, crawling around on all fours, slipped into a desire to show off with unashamed presumptuousness and arrogance.

"I was the first person to live in this hellhole," he said provocatively, taking a seat on Horn's firm bed. "Devil and beast cursed this colony before my shovel first took a bite out of the topsoil. I'd like us to get acquainted. People say an awful lot of things about me, but, upon my word of honor, I was sent down an innocent man!"

Horn said nothing.

"I've always respected hard work," said Lanphier with an obvious disgust for what his lips were saying. "You don't believe me? If only you'd seen me forty years or so ago . . ."

An ambiguous smile crossed his dry mouth.

"I relish the demise of fine young men," the convict went on. "You've come here, found yourself this out-of-the-way corner, as an independent man, without asking for anything or anyone's advice. You're on your own. I also respect people like this; indeed, I'd give you a pat on the back if I knew you wouldn't take offense at it. I'll wager that you could crush a man's skull with your fist and not give yourself over to remorse. There's no other way in these parts; bear that in mind . . . If there's anyone on the colony who hasn't smelled blood, it's harmless me; I give you my word, I'm the most upstanding chap in the world."

"Get to the point," said Horn, losing his patience. "If you need something, then say so."

Lanphier's pupils contracted and dimmed. He was pondering something. His drink-soaked brain was searching for something, no matter how small, to hook another's soul.

"I," he began with a scowl, "have nothing, even if you were to throw me out. There's only one road for a poor wretch, and that's contempt. By fire and water, I swear I only wanted to look out for you and so I stopped by to see how you were getting on. I'm not a policeman, damn it. I'm not here to interrogate you, to see whether you haven't left someone behind leering after you . . . somewhere over there, beyond this pool of brackish water. What do I care! To each his own, I say. I only want to warn you to be more careful. You see, there's a lot of talk about you. Setting aside fools' gossip, the people here will reach the following instantaneous conclusion: 'He didn't come here with empty hands.' You see, when you buy coffee or tobacco, bandages, gunpowder, you have to pay in sterling.

It's best to change money on the mainland. The sun is hot here, and blood boils quickly, much quicker than butter in a frying pan. Oh! I don't mean to frighten you, not in the least; there are some very good people here and half of them don't have a prejudiced bone in their body. But what can you do? Not everyone can have so respectable an upbringing."

Horn's eyes were fixed right on the convict's face. Unsteady on his feet, in a rattling, leisurely voice, Lanphier issued phrase after phrase, and they, correctly divided by invisible punctuation marks, evaporated into the air, like clouds of smoke released methodically by an inveterate smoker. His gaze, directed off to one side, wandered and jumped, restlessly groping for objects, while his other, internal gaze held Horn with invisible pincers, in a state of impatient irritation the whole time. Horn asked:

"Why didn't you come in at once?"

The old man looked directly at his host.

"I was afraid I might wake you," he said impressively, "and the door is devilishly stiff. Had I found you asleep, I should have gone off to sweat in the surrounding countryside till you'd had your fill of sleep."

His face took on an unexpectedly maudlin expression.

"My God!" he groaned, blinking his dry eyelids intensely. "Life has become an ordeal. No respect, none of the local simpletons cares to remember that I, outcast and despised, laid the foundations of all this laborious life. Who knows, maybe a city will one day grow here, while my bones, gnawed by dogs, will rest in the mud, and no one will say: here lie the bones of old man Lanphier, who was innocently condemned by the court of man."

"I should be ashamed," said Horn dryly, "to recall that thanks to your accidental visit to these parts, the peninsula has been infested with humans. I dislike talking to you now. I should prefer it if you, these roofs, and these plantations had never been here. As for the good people with their wretched upbringing, tell them that any unexpected courtesy on their part will meet with the proper reception."

"Wolf's talk," said the convict. "Not bad for a first meeting. Despise me all you like, but I need all the people I can get here. I keep accounts with the lot of them. With some, you see, I have a very good memory—it's a profitable string to my bow. Others, how shall I put it, are stupid and graze peacefully in their own fields. I pinch from these ones without any trouble—well, it's easy— bread, tobacco, small change for something to drink every now and then. Then there are some very cocky louts—the sort who can bleed and then lick it up, like a child eating a spoonful of jam. They all talk soberly and in hushed tones, walk slowly, and their nostrils are always flared . . ."

Lanphier lowered his voice and, hunching over, as if he had a pain in his stomach, smiled broadly, while his eyes fell completely still and narrowed.

"A boat!" he cried. "Where did that boat come from?"

Horn looked out the window. The radiant, limpid lake, full of drowned clouds, was so obviously deserted that at that very moment he turned all the more quickly, with pounding heart, to the convict who had jumped up. A false slash of a knife tore his smock. Horn thrust his hand into his pocket and in a flash was holding out the muzzle of a revolver to Lanphier's bloodless, twitching face.

The old man pressed himself to the wall, cradling his head in his wizened hands; then, after a flurry of movement, he ended up by the window ledge, jumped out, and ducked into a thicket. Three of Horn's bullets cracked among the foliage. With a nervous laugh, he listened intently to the rustle of reeds and fired once more. All of a sudden the silence that had set in was filled with the sound of blood pounding in his temples. His legs lost their agility, his thoughts started spinning and were borne away like wood chippings cast into a stream. The morning that had seduced Horn now suddenly seemed like a hideous, cheap oleograph.

Lost in thought and without lowering his revolver, he sat down on a poorly fashioned bench, feeling, as never before, the total darkness of the future and the fragility of the peace that had lasted fourteen days. His life was drawing closer to the grueling existence of the wary four-legged creatures that are turned into hearing and sight by the suspicious silence of the wilds, and he himself had to become some kind of thinking wolf. He was aware of this necessity: this consciousness concealed a heavy weight and, in a way, the sorrowful joy of a man bereft of choice.

It was now his ardent desire that the woman with the gentle face, the one who had fashioned his soul according to her will, like making a dress that became her, would pass by these hills, and this forest, and his gaze, sink her expensive boots into the soft silt of the shore, lose her way, and knock on the door of his house. Vaguely, in flashes, Horn glimpsed her morning routine among the clay anthills, and this absurd combination of images seemed quite feasible to him. His vision of life allowed for everything, bar miracles, for which he felt an instinctive aversion, holding the desire for some supernatural sign a weakness.

Lanphier's thin raised arm flashed before Horn's eyes, sending a shudder through his body. The colony, which for some unknown reason had been named after the man who had just tried to hunt him, appeared to him now in the form of the patchwork wretch who had peeped out from behind the hedgerow. As he left, he carefully locked the door.

V.

As he walked toward the open plain at the very edge of the forest, Horn was overtaken by the quick pace of a little gray horse. Esther was riding it; her concentrated face, which exuded a quiet joy, glanced down at Horn from under the shady brim of her hat. The sight cheered Horn, and with a satisfied smile he waited while the girl jumped off and fixed the saddle, turning to him without a word. The loneliness did not oppress him but gave free rein to the most frantic explosion of yearning, and now that a lightning rod had appeared in the image of another person, Horn was only too glad to seize this opportunity to talk. They walked side by side, and as they did so the little gray horse, slowly moving its ears as though it were eavesdropping on their conversation, craned its neck behind the girl's back.

"I'm pleased to see you," said Horn. "It was so funny, the way we parted last time, that I laugh even now whenever I remember that shot."

Esther raised her eyebrows.

"Why funny?" she asked suspiciously. "People often shoot at targets here, and so do I."

Horn did not venture a reply.

"My father sent me to you," said the girl, peering at the horizon. "He said: 'Take the horse and go to him. The man hasn't been seen for some time. There are fevers, and swarms of snakes.' "

"Thank you," said Horn, astonished. "He saw me once, at night. How strange that he should think to look out for me. I'm touched."

"Look out for you!" said the girl scornfully. "Him? Look out! He looks out for no one. You just don't give him any peace. Wherever you go, everyone is talking about you. Just last week someone claimed that you were a fugitive from the mainland, pure and simple. But no one will ask you that, rest assured. That's just how they are here."

Horn shrugged indignantly.

"That's the way of it," he said coldly. "When a man asks nothing of others and doesn't wish to see them, he's a criminal. That's half the trouble: if he's hated, they can beat and abuse him."

Esther turned and carefully surveyed Horn's figure—as though contemplating whether or not to let this man beat himself.

"No, not you," she said resolutely. "You seem strong, even if you are a little pale. Soon you'll be swarthy, like everyone here."

"I hope so!" said Horn.

He fell silent and narrowed his eyes, recalling Lanphier's attack. He did not relish telling the story, for he had a vague suspicion that this episode could stoke rumors of the gold that he had supposedly hidden away. Something occurred to Esther; stopping the horse, she went over to the saddle and extracted from a leather bag something prickly and round, like an apple studded with nails.

"Eat this," she said. "It's a local durian. They've begun to rot, but this only makes them taste better."

They both stood on the low plateau, surrounded by uneven terraces. Embarrassed by the repugnant smell of rotten garlic, Horn hesitantly turned the fruit over in his hands.

"You'll get used to it," she said blithely. "Hold your nose. Really, it isn't so bad."

Horn picked away the durian's tough skin and saw a gelatinous white flesh. Having tried it, he paused for a second and then proceeded to eat this astonishing fruit until it was gone. Its creamy, indescribably complex taste made him want to go on eating without end. Esther watched Horn anxiously, unconsciously moving her lips, imitating his chewing mouth.

"Well?" she asked.

"Marvelous," Horn said.

"I'll give you some more." She turned to the horse and deftly placed several pieces into Horn's pocket. "They're plentiful here, you can pick them yourself."

She paused, her mouth agape, about to say something, but she stopped herself and, with a frown, childishly cast her eyes over Horn's face, as if asking an unspoken question.

"Is there something you wanted to ask?" he said. "Well, then? Ask away."

"It's nothing," Esther quickly replied. "I did want to ask you something, it's true, but how could you know that? I wanted to ask whether my company bored you. I don't know how to hold a conversation. We're all a little uncultured here. Life must have been better for you there."

"There?"

"Well, yes—there, where you're from. They say they have all sorts of things there."

She moved her hand as if trying to envisage more vividly the city's glittering mass.

"That's neither here nor there," Horn reflected calmly. "It's only good if you like those sorts of things."

"So you didn't like them?" she cried triumphantly. "Tell me."

"Tell you?" Horn drawled in surprise.

Only now did he fully appreciate and feel the excruciating, if pent-up, curiosity that he must have aroused in her. The indelible stamp of culture, effaced, disfigured by a half-savage existence, the profile of a complex spiritual world filtered through him and, like a coin corroded by acid, spoke, albeit in approximate terms, of his worth. He reflected. Her demand was so legitimate and, in its frankness, constituted the simple desire to know with whom she was dealing. Yet he was ready to fill himself with indignation at the very thought of turning himself inside out before this simple girl.

It did not occur to him to lie; feeling abashed and not knowing how to change the topic of conversation, he cast his gaze up into the blue depths of the air.

And the emptiness of the sky settled in his soul as a cold yearning for freedom, to which every roadside leaf would henceforth attest. The harsh face of the past beamed with a sardonic grimace, and Horn's jealous tact in regard to her seemed strange and even like a distant importunity devoid of self-respect. The past had graciously freed him of all obligations.

And he longed to look at himself from without, eavesdropping on the words of his own story, to check, thousands of times over, a verified account of his life. The girl may well interpret it differently, but then all she wanted to know was the general outline, while the rest would slip past her ears, like the indistinct voices of the forest.

"My life," said Horn, "is very simple. I was a student; some ill-fated speculations ruined my father. He shot himself and made a cemetery his home. My cousin found me a position; I worked there for three years. Let's sit down, Esther. Getting lost in the ravines doesn't seem so very enjoyable."

Without letting go of the bridle, the girl quickly sat down where Horn's words had stayed her. His momentum took him a step farther, whereupon he turned around and sat down beside her, chewing on a stalk of grass that he had plucked.

"Three years," she repeated.

"After that," Horn continued, trying to speak as plainly as possible, "I became a tramp because I was fed up sitting in the same place; what's more, my luck had run out: the owners of the company where I worked died of the plague. So there you have it . . . I went from city to city, and at last I was happy. Quite recently a friend of mine died; I loved him more than anything in the world."

"I have no friends," Esther slowly enounced. "A friend—that's good."

Horn smiled.

"Yes," he said. "He was a great friend, and dying on his part was a swinish thing to do. This is how he lived: he loved a woman who very likely reciprocated his love, though to this day I've never been certain of it. He chose her from among all the people in the world and he put his faith in her—that is, he considered her to be the finest human being in existence. In his eyes, this woman was God's most perfect creation.

"The time came when she was faced with a choice—either to go hand in hand with my friend, whose worldly possessions consisted in the four walls of his small room, or to live like a river during the spring flood, beautifully and freely, satisfying her most fanciful whims. At the time she was quite sad and pensive, and her eyes flashed with a special brilliance. Finally they had it out with one another.

"It then became apparent to my friend that the covetous soul of this woman was insatiable and lusted after everything. And for her, he was merely a part of this, and not even the biggest one.

"But he, too, came from that same breed of predators with velvet claws, who thrill at the sounds of life, at the sight of its glittering pedestals. The difference between them consisted in the fact that one of them wanted everything for herself, while the other wanted everything for her.

"He had thought he was entering into a covenant with her for the rest of his life, but he was mistaken. This woman had set her sights on something ready-made, something being dangled in front of her by another man. This something was money.

"He understood her and himself, but he burned himself out in a matter of days and became an old man before his time. The blow was too much; not every man can bear such things. Everything continued on its course, and after a month, as he planned to leave, he wrote this woman, now the wife of another, a letter. In it he asked her to tell him for the last agonizing time that she still loved him.

"He did not wait for her reply. Yearning drove him into the street, and, unconsciously, unable to restrain his desire, he arrived at her door. He was announced under a fictitious name.

"He passed through a series of rooms, moving as though in a dream. Seized by excruciating tenderness, the weeping anguish of the past, his countenance was moist and submissive.

"Their meeting took place in the boudoir. She seemed alarmed. Her face was that of a stranger, a poor simulacrum of what had once been his.

" 'If you love me,' this woman said, 'you won't stay here a moment longer. Please, leave!' "

" 'Your husband?' he asked.

" 'Yes,' she said, 'my husband. He's expected here any minute.'

"My friend walked over to the lamp and extinguished it. Darkness fell. She cried out in alarm, fearing death.

" 'Don't be afraid,' he whispered. 'Your husband won't see me if he comes in. The carpet has a deep pile; I can slip out under cover of darkness without posing any danger to you. Now give me the answer to what I asked in the letter.'

" 'I do,' the darkness whispered. And he, without hearing how these words were uttered, shrank like a child, kissed her legs, and beat the carpet at her feet with his fists, before she pushed him away.

" 'Leave,' she said, alarmed and annoyed. 'Leave me!'

"But he didn't leave. The woman got to her feet, lit a candle, and, having extracted my friend's letter from her escritoire, she burned it. He watched as though turned to stone, unable to understand what he saw—was this an insult or a caprice? She said:

" 'For me, the past is no different than this ash. It is not for me to revive it. Farewell.'

"Her last word was accompanied by a loud knock at the door. The candle was extinguished. The door opened, and a dark silhouette obscured its bright oblong. My friend and this woman's husband came face to face. An inviolable silence descended—the sort when a single word would be enough to ruin a life. My friend left, and on the following day he found himself on the deck of a ship. A month later he shot himself.

"As for me, I came here on board a Dutch trading ship. I decided to make a life for myself here, far away from people—people among whom my friend died. His death came as great shock to me. I'll stay here a year—maybe more."

While Horn was telling his story, the girl's face maintained an expression of unswerving seriousness and concentration. Several turns of phrase had been incomprehensible to her, but Horn's restrained emotion touched her woman's intuition.

"It was you who loved her!" she cried, leaping to her feet while Horn fell silent. "You're trying to trick me. Yes, and I don't think you did have a friend. But that's all the same to me."

Her eyes began to sparkle ever so slightly. Until now it had been impossible to judge whether his tale had left any impression on her unyielding mind. Horn was slow to reply.

"No, it was my friend," he said.

"There's no point in trying to trick me," Esther protested angrily. "Why did you tell me that story?"

"Whether it was or wasn't me," said Horn with a shrug of the shoulders, "let's forget about it. Today I've met an exceptional number of people and animals. Look, here comes someone else."

"Young Dribb," said Esther. "Dribb, what's the matter?"

"Nothing's the matter!" the giant shouted, reining in the bay mare before Horn's very face. "I've been practicing following tracks, and I must have stumbled upon yours. It means I've succeeded, in any case. And who's this?"

He seemed not to have noticed Horn, though the latter was standing no more than a meter from his stirrups. Horn curiously examined the enormous lumbering mass—a great torso, crowned by a little head, with a round face that looked as though it had been forged from brown iron; an open white smock with pink stripes revealed a hairy chest covered in perspiration. Taken together, all this bespoke a peasant and a bandit; the broad, amiable grin disposed Horn if not agreeably, then at least indifferently.

"As if you don't know," said Esther scornfully.

"Ah!" The giant let out a heavy sigh. "Will you ride?"

Esther mounted the horse.

Dribb turned to Horn. "Farewell, sir," he said, awkwardly fixing his round eyes on him and stroking his chin.

"Horn," said Esther, "don't go near the swamp. If you do, be sure to drink a lot of vodka. Otherwise you might find yourself ill for a month or two."

In the saddle, swaying supplely from side to side atop the horse's undulating back, she unwittingly cast her radiant beauty into Horn's line of sight. Perhaps for the first time he looked upon her immaculate figure and her face, so full of life, with a man's gaze. This couple now riding away pricked him with something like the surprise of disappointment.

"Hallo! Hop! Hop!" Dribb bellowed, urging the horse on as he bobbed up and down heavily in the saddle.

"Goodbye, Esther!" Horn called after her.

She turned around quickly; her face, softened by a fleeting smile, expressed something more than this.

The pale reflection of youth stirred within Horn's soul; he took his hat and, with a low bow, threw it in the direction of the retreating figures. Esther, smiling silently, nodded and disappeared among the undergrowth. The giant never once looked around, and when his broad, rounded back vanished along with Esther, Horn thought that young Dribb had been more impolite than was necessary for a savage.

The day unfolded, ablaze with a torrid blue heat; the sultriness, pregnant with resinous vapors, was dizzying. Again a feeling of profound indifference welled up in Horn; as he absentmindedly stroked the stock of his rifle, he reached the conclusion that the virgin land had lost the charm it once held for the complex apparatus of a soul nurtured on thought. A land that is too mighty and rich wearies the nerves, as bright light does vision. Cleared and disciplined, no more than a pretty view, it could be a wondrous comfort, a lover that never wearied of caresses, a sweet-perfumed bath for those struck ill, frozen by the very thought of the river's vastness.

"What about me?" Horn asked of the sky and the earth. "Me?" He recalled his hunting and the trembling of wild bodies, the feeling of self-possession in the midst of danger, the dark flight of the night, the sleep-clouded eyes of the dawn, the gloomy bliss of the forest—and triumphantly he straightened up. Within his self, he was not yet a dead man, nor was he a castrato, nor a beggar in a strange garden. His detachment was founded on reflection. He was himself—Horn.

■ □ ■

In a voice that sounded as though he were dying, the stout fellow groaned—"Oof!"—every time the entrance door flew open, its pulley squealing, and an explosive column of light flashed down on the earthen floor of the little inn. As an innkeeper, he was grateful for the guests; as a man, he cursed them with his each and every thought.

Yet the guests preferred to see in this stout fellow only an innkeeper and ruthlessly demanded their peach schnapps, beer, rum, and palm wine. Suffering all the while, the stout fellow would clamber down into the cellar, climb up ladders, and, damp with perspiration, retake his place atop his high wicker stool.

A game was going on in one corner, clouds of tobacco smoke hovered over a pile of wide-brimmed hats; the characteristic rattle of dice mixed with profanity and the clicking of purses. It was relatively quiet; the walls of this serai, which bore the name The Green Conch, had seen real fights, blood, and games of knives whose stakes were life and death. From time to time young strangers would appear with tight leather belts, suspiciously clean hands, and a pile of trinkets; they would coolly and politely play for any sum and would leave the colonists scratching their heads and spitting.

Lanphier came in unnoticed; his bony body seemed capable of crawling through the gap under the door. More drunk than he had been that morning, holding his pipe between his teeth, he slumped himself onto the gamblers' table and burst into peals of silent laughter. For a moment the dice stopped clattering against the table; with a look of bemusement, their faces turned to the new arrival.

"Now, here's a thing!" the convict wheezed after he stopped laughing, having sensed that the gamblers' patience was at the end of its tether. "He told the truth: and such a fine young lad, too!"

"Who?" inquired the stout man on the stool.

"The new master of the lake." Lanphier lowered his voice and began to speak slowly. "You see, I paid him a visit today. He's a fine fellow, to be sure. 'Were I the governor,' he said, 'I'd set fire to this colony from the middle and all four corners.' He said, 'They're all swine and swindlers, and those a little better are fools—as stupid as a thousand crocodiles.'"

"You're a master of tall tales," said the owner of a coffee plantation, breathing heavily. "You're lying."

Lanphier's eyes glimmered darkly.

"I should be dead now," he shouted, "if this man's aim were a hair's breadth better! I accused him of being arrogant and he threw a bullet my way just as cold-bloodedly as if it were a pellet of bread. I jumped out the window quicker than a lizard."

"Admit it, you're lying," the innkeeper yawned.

The old man said nothing. Beneath his wrinkled cheeks his jaws convulsed. The gamblers returned to their game. They did not believe Lanphier, but each of them stowed away in a dark corner of his brain these "people as foolish as crocodiles, swindlers, and swine."

VI.

Craning his neck, Bekeko looked up. A monkey was hanging from its tail below a patch of sky; its round, childlike yet old eyes quickly took in the figure of the idiot, sometimes getting distracted and pondering the distance to the next tree.

Bekeko gave an amicable nod, winked, and with his hands invited the animal to climb down, but the experienced capuchin began screeching incredulously and with alarm, at times pulling hideous faces. Bekeko laughed. A painful, euphoric feeling tore through his mangy little body, and he began to choke with ludicrous delight, shaking from the unbearable excitement. The capuchin, like all living things, he placed above himself, and with polite perseverance, fearing to offend the furry acrobat, he continued his exhortations.

Then, looking more carefully at the monkey's wrinkled face, he shuddered and winced; a vague apprehension shook his gaiety. There could be no doubt about it: the capuchin was getting ready to crack Bekeko's skull open with its teeth and perhaps even sink them into his lean stomach.

"Now, now . . ." the agitated man muttered in fright, taking a step back.

He could no longer bring himself to look up and looked around anxiously, in the hope of finding a branch with which he might defend himself. Under the sky hung a beast of enormous proportions, which for a time had been pretending to be small, but now Bekeko saw it all: a trap had been set for him, and he had fallen into it in the most foolish way. Not yet certain on which side danger lurked (but for the old fellow with a tail), he began to back off, stumbling and trembling with fear. But his enemies lost no time; invisible, they silently crawled through the grass, pricking Bekeko's bare feet with thorns that painfully stung his skin. The sudden suspicion that an ambush lay in wait behind him brought him out in a sweat. Unsure of what to do, he shifted from one foot to the other, afraid to move, filled with the mad terror of the forest's excruciating silence and the green giants covering their faces.

When the enemy did appear, inquisitively examining Bekeko's puny figure, the idiot screamed, hurled a heavy yellow pellet at this adversary, and slumped to the ground, swooning in the dismal expectation of death. Horn hesitated. Almost frightened, though not by ghosts, he turned over in his hands the little nugget that Bekeko had launched at him. A powerful excitement gripped him; his eyes glittering with surprise, his throat dry from the sudden onset of exhilaration, without thinking, the hunter threw down this dull, dirty lump, forgetting all about Bekeko, the forest, and time.

The capuchin was still there, swinging; puffing out its cheeks, it pulled an angry face and, having spotted the rifle, wrathfully gritted its teeth. Then with a noise, it jumped to the neighboring tree, began to hiss, tossed a large walnut at Horn, and dashed headlong away, diving into a thicket.

Horn looked around. He was pale, enrapt, and finding it difficult to order his thoughts. Despite himself, they flew quicker than grapeshot. The dark seething of his soul demanded release, action; the forest had to be filled with sounds capable of drowning out the screaming silence. Yet its old, indolent splendor dozed all around, indifferently enfolding a confused, pale man in its solemn embraces.

"Bekeko!" said Horn. "Bekeko!"

The idiot stuck his head out fearfully from behind a tree trunk. Horn softened his voice, which was almost imbued with a tenderness for the exhausted freak, and he carefully examined this strange being that reminded him of a gnome.

"Bekeko," said Horn, "don't you recognize me?"

The idiot raised his eyes, unsure whether to say a word. The hunter gently touched his arm, but he immediately jerked it away: a piercing shriek rent the forest. Bekeko was like a frightened hedgehog that had rolled itself into a ball.

"Very well, then," Horn continued, as if agreeing with Bekeko on some point. "I'm really not your enemy. I'll go now, only tell me, my youngling, wherever did you find that glittering little nugget? I need it. Do you understand? For me and Esther. We need a good few of these little nuggets. If you're good and tell me, Esther will give you some sugar."

He reached out his hand and immediately clenched his fist, as if the dim glimmer of gold burnt his skin.

"Esther . . ." the idiot muttered indecisively, lifting his head, "will give . . . sugar!"

He began blinking plaintively and was again lost in the hazy void of madness. Horn sighed impatiently.

"Esther," he quietly repeated, leaning into Bekeko. "You understand, don't you? Esther!"

Bekeko's face broadened as his wide, protruding lips formed a smile. The arduous work of association had been accomplished within him. His dark mind had managed to link together sugar, a name, a man with a rifle, and a woman's image that floated like a bright, indistinct blur. All of a sudden, Bekeko blossomed with an almost comprehending grimace, one of whining, convulsive laughter.

"Esther," he slowly pronounced, scrutinizing the hunter with a frown.

"Yes," Horn sighed. His whole body was being torn away, to a feverish intoxication, by his searches. "Esther needs little nuggets like this. Where did you find them?"

"There!" Bekeko cried, waving his hand and clearly coming to his senses. "Little blue river."

"The stream?" Horn asked.

"Water." The idiot nodded affirmatively.

"Water," Horn repeated insistently.

"Water," Bekeko answered, like an echo.

Horn fell silent. The north, a little blue river, and a little nugget of gold, no bigger than a bullet.

"Bekeko," he said, as he began to move off. "Remember: Esther will give sugar."

He was already far away from the spot where the frightened half-man sat squirming, and he himself did not notice this. He walked hurriedly, taking great strides, suffused by an unbearable anxiety, as if he were afraid of being late, of losing something of incredible importance. Later Horn would remember everything, starting with Bekeko and ending with that night, as though it were the vague memory of a dream, full of soundless music, one that had swept past in the blink of an eye. A sense of life's unreality enveloped him: remembering fragments of the past, like a dream about a flock of clouds, and linking this with his present, he experienced the rapture of a seafarer who, in the midst of a fog, spies the virgin shore of an uncharted continent, and the anxiety of a man faced with a stranger lying in wait for him. His body grew stronger and somehow lighter; his face, softened by daydreaming, became engrossed in thought and smiled, as though he were reading an interesting, compelling book, in which grief and rapture, humor and tenderness had been interwoven in a subtle pattern. Tree trunks with the thickness of a well-proportioned hut reached up to the sky like pillars, and he felt like a small child, entrusted to the dependable, mysterious care of the forest, the green depths of the thicket, which recalled the disquieting twilight of rooms engulfed in a deep silence. A little blue river flowed before his eyes, and in its damp sand gold slept innocently, a mighty power, young, like shoots of grass, never yet having known the trembling of human fingers or the lascivious gaze of bourgeois people possessed of an insatiable hunger. He walked in one direction, grudging every step that diverted him whenever he had to pass a tree trunk or a knoll. Gradually, with frowns and smiles, he reached a glittering jungle of the imagination, a thicket of dreams that were no less intoxicating than wine. He was like one who, on the verge of sleep, hears voices in a neighboring room, which mingle with the blossoming of fairy tale episodes, inspiring in his liberated mind his own outlandish prologues. It was everything and nothing, doubt in success and a fierce confidence in it, the feeling of a criminal who leaves prison with empty hands only to find a seven-shot revolver, the impetuous course of desires; his breathless soul was in a hurry to touch the future, while his body, insensible to fatigue, quickened his steps.

It was that hour of day when, lazily meditating, the evening draws its attentive eyes toward the earth, and the noise of the cicadas rings out more softly, sensing the wary gaze of the Unseen, at work lengthening the shadows of the tree trunks. The forest thinned out, yawning vistas ended in the purple of cliffs, glittering in the blood of the sun, wounded by Diana. Shards of quartz, traces of past earthquakes, flashed yellow as they reflected the light of dawn, and the brief cawing of a cockatoo rang out obstinately and with angry satisfaction. Horn pressed on, his legs moving of their own accord.

Half an hour later, he caught sight of the water. Of course, it was that same little blue river, a narrow stream with the sky at its bottom and the brilliance of sandbanks as pure as gray faience. From a distance it looked like a blue ribbon among a nymph's green tresses. Its line, cut by the sprawling peaks of individual groups of trees, trailed off toward a rocky grotto black with vines, inwrought crevices, and overhangs, like the folds of green rugs falling down toward the water. Hardly able to move his legs in the damp clutch of clinging grass, Horn made his way toward the blue ribbon and stopped to inhale the sweet, musty aroma of seaweed.

Here, for the first time, he realized that thirst was relentlessly tormenting his body, and he very nearly fell to his knees, cupping in his palm the warm liquid, like boiling water that had cooled. The limpid drops streamed down his chin and fingers like rainwater. He would gulp down as much as he could, catch his breath, exhale, and again dip his hand into the warm depths.

The gratification filled him with a weakness that came on suddenly, a heavy lethargy in each of his limbs, a reluctance to move. He gazed at the riverbed, but his eyes were pained by the sun playing on the submerged sand. Gazing more intently, Horn brought his face closer to the very surface of the water, almost touching it with his eyelashes. He spent about two minutes like this; his body shuddered with a momentary, fleeting tremor, and the blood flowed back to his blanched cheeks faster than the shadows of clouds encompassing the plain.

Yellow scintillations, gently glimmering in the water's refraction, dappled the untainted riverbed, and the more Horn looked, the more difficult it became to distinguish pebble from gold. It rested mysteriously in the water's depths, and from its dim kernels little invisible, tinkling fountains struck Horn's pupils, ringing in his ears like the rapid influx of blood. He broke into peals of laughter and cried out loudly. The trembling sound of his voice echoed in the heart of the forest with a faint rumble before fading away. Horn stood up.

Everything seemed to him unspeakably beautiful, imbued with the triumph of joy. The bridge of air stretching across to the bank of the future led him to the glittering gates of life, henceforth accessible, where earlier there had stood fortresses impregnable to desire. The earth seemed to have shrunk in volume and become like a large globe on top of which stood an agitated man with burning cheeks. And foremost, Horn thought of the power of gold, capable of bringing back a woman. He journeyed to her on board a thousand trains, their wheels fusing into solid discs, and the rails shuddering from the mass of iron carrying him. He would tell her everything a person could, and be with her.

Then he imagined he heard the word "no," but already he felt not the insulted party but the avenger, and with grim avarice he sketched scenes of shrewd commercial cruelty, a vast circle of ruin, which drew into its spinning vortex the well-being of the man who had knocked on the door. Horn would flood the world market with undervalued goods. And with each passing day the woman's face would grow dimmer, because, one by one, her husband's factories were falling silent, and cobwebs were covering the stagnant nest where his machines had once thundered.

Scarcely had two minutes passed, but during that time Horn had relived several years with painful clarity. He looked around, his face drawn from the rush of emotion. The sun had dipped behind the cliffs, the light evening shadows now enveloped the cooling earth, and the river glimmered silently.

He cut out a patch of turf and, setting it at an angle, heaped several fistfuls of sand from the riverbank onto the green surface of the makeshift cradle. He proceeded to cut a piece of bark and, having fashioned from it a sort of ladle, scooped up some water.

This first moment of labor excited the hunter more than the sand on the riverbed. He kept pouring and pouring the water until a thin, heavy layer of gold glittered amid the grass of the turf. Strength momentarily deserted Horn; he sat down beside his spoils with his hand on the wet surface of the contraption, whereupon a frenzied dance of thoughts instantly quit his wearied mind, leaving behind a stupor like rapture mixed with anguish.

VII.

Horn returned sans shirt or smock, with a leather bag full of little nuggets of the aforementioned items, which weighed down his shoulder so much that he found it painful to move his arms. Half-naked and sunburned, he brought to the lake the aroma of the woodland swamp and a sweet, importunate exhaustion.

A new sensation struck him as he reached his home—that of his own body, as if he were touching it with hands that were weak from the heat—and he gave out a wanton, spasmodic yawn. He shut the door and dug a pit in the earthen floor, carefully burying there the tightly packed, weighty nuggets. There were a great many of them, each one a decent size.

He slumped down onto his bed of dry grass, sat there for a long while, dejected and unable to explain to himself his sudden melancholy indifference to the newly trampled-down patch of earth in his cabin. Clasping his left wrist, he listened to the mute rush of blood, while his teeth chattered, these little drums beating a tattoo, and his body shivered, as though snowflakes were falling from the ceiling and melting on his perspiring skin.

Without undressing, Horn lay down with his eyes wide open, in a state of sensual languor that was interrupted by periodic convulsions of his body, after which profuse perspiration would run down his face. Convinced that he was ill, Horn began to reckon the number of days for which he would have to stop work and how much he would stand to lose because of this. Swamp fever could cost him a good few acres of land, for, as he had been told and knew well, this illness ordinarily lasted at least ten days.

Clenching his jaws and writhing, Horn gradually succumbed to euphoria—a sign that the fever was intensifying. The shivering left him, and he smiled mockingly at the bare walls of the house, which were hiding something that would have given Lanphier cause to deal him a direct blow, without the military tactics of a commander plotting an ambush.

Horn lay there until sunset, when the heat temporarily forsakes man only to return the next day at a strictly appointed hour—with the accuracy of a German who lunches at 12:56 precisely. Weak, his head spinning and with a revolver in his pocket, Horn put on a new smock and went out into the open air. His thoughts had taken a calm direction; he carefully weighed his chances of success and decided that there was no mistake—excepting for some unforeseen eventuality, the chances of which were marginally greater than he deemed strictly necessary. Refreshed by the cold air, he lingered there, examining the starry atlas of the sky and the Southern Cross, which shone with great contempt for the affairs of the earth's inhabitants. Yet this did not depress Horn, for his eyes, in turn, recalled a fine pair of stars—such did they shine out into the darkness—and he felt neither pitiful nor lonely, for he was not dead planetary matter.

There was a gust of wind, which abated after having drowned out the faint clatter of hooves carried from a distance. Horn unconsciously pricked up his ears; after a minute he could already tell that the horseshoe was hitting against stone, and the next moment against friable soil. He then went back inside and lit the little lamp that he had bought in the colony. Its wavering light shone through the window onto the nearby stalks of bamboo. Horn opened the door and stood there at the threshold, lit dimly from one side.

The unknown figure was continuing on his way. He was riding a little more gently now, from which Horn concluded that the stranger must have been coming to pay him a visit, since there was no sense in galloping to the lake only to slow the pace for the pleasure of the return journey. He waited until he could hear the horse's snorting nearby.

"Who is it?" asked Horn, handling his revolver. "Esther!" he said after a pause, stepping back in surprise. "Why aren't you asleep?"

"Why aren't you?" she asked with a merry laugh, breathless from the brisk ride. "What matters is that you're still alive."

"I am," said Horn, buoyed by the sound of her voice, which was loud, like the peal of a modest bell. "Your father may sleep quite easily now."

She made no reply and, silently walking over to the table, sat down on a stool. The expression on her face changed continually, as though taking place within her were a mental conversation with someone known only to her. Horn said:

"You can see that I'm alive. I have nothing to offer you by way of refreshment. I usually dispose of any scraps; they spoil so quickly."

"You say that because you don't know why I've come," said Esther, her voice sounding a semitone lower. "You see, it's a holiday today. The men have been on the go since the early morning, but now they can barely hold themselves up. Everywhere has run out of alcohol. You can see torches burning all over the place; our home has been decorated with lanterns. It's very pretty. Those who don't begrudge the gunpowder are going about in packs, shooting blank cartridges. They've cleared away all the tables and benches at The Green Conch and people won't stop dancing."

She looked at Horn's face expectantly. He noticed that Esther had on a yellow silk dress and a blue kerchief; her swarthy neck was adorned with pearl beads.

"I fell behind as they were passing the little bay, when I remembered you. Then I spotted young Dribb turn around, looking for me. King set off at a gallop, and I treated him mercilessly to my heels. You'll enjoy yourself, I'm sure. You can't go sitting around alone with your own thoughts for so long. We can be there in half an hour if you like."

"Esther," said Horn. "Why is it a holiday?"

"It's the colony's founding day." Esther blushed; a silent smile opened her mouth, dewy with excitement. "Oh, just think how lovely it will be, Horn! We'll be together and you can tell me whether people celebrate things like this where you're from."

"Thank you, Esther," said Horn, who was very touched by this. "I don't think I'll go, but still, I feel as though I was as good as there."

"Hang on a minute." The girl cast a sly look at the hunter, and her voice began to drawl, like a shepherd's horn in the morning. "Bekeko keeps asking for sugar."

"Bekeko!" repeated Horn, deeply perplexed. "Asking for sugar?"

The memory put him on his guard. It occurred to him that everyone would know about the little blue river. An unpleasant sensation made his chest tighten; he got up and stretched his legs before taking up the conversation.

"He came creeping up to me and said ever so many incomprehensible things," the girl continued, looking out the window. "I didn't understand any of it, except for one thing: 'Your man (he calls you my man) said that he and Esther need a lot of yellow stones.' After which he made out that you promised him sugar from me. Oh, I'm sure he wouldn't have understood a word of what you said to him. In any case, I gave him a handful."

Horn listened, trying not to miss a single word. His face now blanched, now blushed, and finally reacquired its natural hue. The girl was still wide of the mark.

"Yes," he said, "I met the simpleton in a fit of panicked, inexplicable terror. He would doubtless have been more forthcoming with you. I managed to calm him down, without getting a single word out of him. Yellow stones! Only the mind of a madman could splice ravings with reality. And the sugar, too . . . But weren't you at all angry?"

"Not in the slightest." Esther looked down pensively. "'Esther and I need it,' he said." She laughed. "Do you need what I do? It's time to go, Horn. I've given a lot of thought to these words, though I doubt you gave them much. But then you didn't know that they'd reach me."

Her quickened breathing touched Horn's soul, and he, as though awake but not daring to understand the truth, stopped with a cry of puzzled astonishment frozen on his lips.

"Esther," he said longingly, "look at me, otherwise I fear I'll misunderstand you."

Esther looked him straight in the eye, and not a hint of shyness or embarrassment could be discerned in her subtle features, which were, unexpectedly even for her, in thrall to her female emotions. She stood up; a distance of less than a yard separated her and Horn, but already he felt an invisible wall being planted at his feet. He was alone; the girl's presence unnerved him and filled him with an alarm similar to pity.

"I could be your wife, Horn," Esther said slowly, smiling with her mouth, while her eyes grew tensely serious, as if a shadow had been cast over the upper part of her face. "Maybe you wouldn't have spoken the straightforward words of a man for some time yet. But you already mean a great deal to me, Horn. And I won't dishonor you like *she* did."

Horn walked up to her and firmly clutched her limp hand. A great weight was crushing him, and he dreadfully wanted his voice to utter more pitiful human words. Sensing that there could be nothing more offensive at this moment than silence, he said loudly and tenderly:

"Esther! If I could die right now, it would be easier for me. I don't love you as you might expect. Cast me out of your proud head; to be your husband, to turn life into sheer toil—this isn't what I want. I want another life, one that is perhaps unattainable, but the thought of it alone makes my head spin. Are you listening to me? I'm speaking honestly, as you are."

The girl tossed her head and grew paler than snow. Horn let go of her hand. Esther wiggled her fingers, as if shaking off a lingering touch.

"Well, yes," she said caustically, in full possession of herself. "If you cannot understand a joke, so much the worse for you. You're probably looking for a wealthy bride in any case. I always thought it was the man who earned the money."

Each of her words struck Horn painfully. It was as if she held a whip in her hand and was lashing him with it.

"Esther," said Horn. "Have pity on me. It isn't me who's to blame, but life, which twists and turns us both. Would you have me pretend that I love you? Would you have me take your body because it's beautiful and—truly, I mean it—attracts me? Only then to part from you?"

"Farewell," the girl said.

Her entire body seemed to exude the affront she had just borne and shuddered with hatred. Horn threw himself at her, full of keen, tender pity.

"Esther!" softly, almost imploringly, he said. "Dear girl, forgive me!"

"I forgive you!" Esther cried, choking with tears of rage, and truly she forgave him with her gaze, which was filled with indescribable pride. "But never, do you hear, Horn, never will Esther rue her mistakes! I'm not like that!"

Horn went over to the window, reeling from weakness. By the window a horse was neighing quietly. "King!" the girl called out calmly. She mounted the horse, her silk skirt rustling. Horn listened. "King!" Esther said again, "will you forgive me my heels in your side? I'll never do it again."

King's easy gallop filled the darkness with an even, fading clatter of hooves.

VIII.

There was no reason to be thinking of dogs. The little blue river had never seen their ilk, and, if it had, then it was a long time ago, long before the first locomotive crossed the plain two hundred miles from the spot where Horn, on his knees, had imbibed the water and the golden brilliance.

And yet, as he shook out a handful of the metal onto a kerchief, the fruit of a three-hour labor, he unexpectedly caught himself thinking of all the different sorts of dogs he had seen before. As it turned out, he was thinking of mastiffs more often than of grey-hounds, and of beagles more often than of pugs. He put an end to all this with a brief sigh. Horn's face took on a concentrated expression, and he straightened up, fixing his gaze on the green vistas of the forest, which was shrouded in radiance.

The sounds were so faint that only unconsciously were they able to turn his thoughts from gold to domestic quadrupeds. They sooner resembled an echo of wood-chopping than of barking muffled by the thickets and the distance separating them. And there were so few of them, far fewer than the exclamation marks that cover two pages of a dramatic script.

The time it took for them to grow, to acquire the characteristic inflections of a dog's voice and the angry assurance of a hound panting after a long search, was for Horn a time of abstracted reverie and cold alarm. He waited for the men to draw nearer, comforting himself with the hope that the dog's path lay out of his way. The valley of the river delivered him from this fallacy. It stretched out in a curve toward the forest, and from every point along the edge of the forest Horn could be seen. There was no reason to think that the stranger would turn back.

Horn hurriedly hid the groaning kerchief in his pocket, threw the patch of turf that had served as a cradle into the water, and, holding his rifle horizontally, retreated about a hundred paces from the spot where he had been washing the sand. A restrained, gruff barking emanated from the nearby bushes.

Horn took up his position behind a tree, listening intently. Invisible, he saw in the distance a little figure on horseback crossing the meadow at a round trot, while a diminutive bloodhound weaved in and out under the horse's hooves, zigzagging among the grass. Enraged somewhat, Horn went out to meet them. He felt it to be beneath his dignity to hide from a single man, whatever his purpose in approaching Horn. He resented the interference and the fact that he, Horn, was being sought out.

There could be no doubt about it. The dog performed two loops on the spot that Horn had just left and, with a whine, rushed over to the hunter, jumping almost as high as his head with a bewildered yelp. The dog could have started barking or biting; it all depended on the behavior of its master. But its master betrayed no excitement; only to Horn, at a distance of seven feet, did his eyes seem fixed and sharp.

Horn stood there, holding his rifle, both barrels loaded, under his arm—like an umbrella one wants to forget when the weather is fine. Young Dribb stayed the horse. His own rifle lay across the saddle, vibrating from the impatient movements of the horse as it beat it hooves. The farmer's absurd silence drove the blood from Horn's face, who was first to raise his hat and bow.

"Hello, Mr Horn," said the giant with a heavy sigh. "It's very hot. My horse is lathering. I had to travel at a fair pace, you see."

"I pity the horse," ventured Horn softly. "You must be on an important journey."

"More important than were I bearing news of my own mother's death," said Dribb quietly. "You'll forgive me for the intrusion," he added without smiling, staring at the horse's trimmed withers. "I would rather have spoken with you at your home than disturb you out on one of your walks. But you haven't been there for three days, that's just the thing."

"Three days," Horn repeated.

Dribb cleared his throat and wiped his mouth, even though it was as dry and dusty as the manager of a boarding house. His little eyes looked anxious and inflamed. Horn waited.

"You see," Dribb began, pronouncing each word with difficulty, "I can't explain it to you all at once. I'll have to start from the beginning, telling you how it all began and leading up to the present day."

There was a point when Horn had wanted to stop him. "I know, so there," he had wanted to say. "What's the use?" the other half of his soul replied. "If he's wrong, there's no need to alarm him."

The dog darted off and, with its tongue hanging out, lay down in the shade of an oak tree. Dribb chewed his lips indecisively; it seemed to be unspeakably difficult for him. At last he began, looking off into the distance.

"You aren't saying anything, but of course I haven't asked you anything yet." He sniffed loudly, agitated. "About five days ago, sir—that is, roughly seven or eight days after our festival—I was at Astis's house. 'Esther!' I said, and, even then, I was only joking, since she refused to say anything. 'Esther,' I say, 'you're like Winter's child these days.' And since she didn't answer me, I filled my pipe, for if a woman is out of sorts, you mustn't anger her. That evening

I met her in the square. 'You won't cut through me,' I said. 'Or do you think I'm like the air?' Then she was the one who stopped, otherwise our foreheads would have banged together. 'I'm sorry,' she says, 'I was lost in thought.' Seeing as I was in a rush, I kissed her and went on my way. She caught up with me. 'Dribb,' she says, 'it's painful for both of us, but it's best to come out with it. There will be no wedding.' "

He took a deep breath, and a big apple seemed to leap up in his throat. Horn observed his drawn face in silence; Dribb's eyes were fixed on the cliffs, as though he were protesting to them and to heaven.

"At that point," he continued, "I began to laugh, thinking that it was a joke. 'Dribb,' she says, 'nothing's going to come of laughing. Do you think you can forget me? If you can, then use all your strength to forget.' 'Esther,' I said with sorrow in my heart, because she was as pale as flour, 'don't you love me anymore?' For a long time she said nothing, sir. She felt sorry for me. 'No,' she says. It was as if I'd been cut asunder. She walked off without looking back. I began to weep like a child. I won't find another girl like her upon this earth."

The giant was breathing like a steam engine and perspiring all over. Upset by his own story, he stood stock-still, watching Horn.

"Go on," said Horn.

Dribb's hand rested convulsively on the barrel of his rifle.

"Well," he continued. "You know that vodka's the stuff in such circumstances. I drank four bottles, but that wasn't enough. He was drunk, too, the old man."

"Lanphier," Horn hazarded.

"Yes, although we call him the Red Father, because he's spilled blood, sir. He kept looking at me and smirking. It was a nasty sight, so I raised my hand, but he said: 'Dribb, where do girls go at night?' 'If you know, tell me,' I replied. 'Listen,' he says, 'don't wrack your brains over it. The valley was covered in darkness; on the night of the festival, I'd gone to keep an eye out for that fellow who's settled by the lake. If he's a curious sort, I tell myself, he'll come to the colony. I tied the muzzle of the rifle with a white rag so as not to miss and sat down on my hunkers. Half an hour later a girl leaves the colony; I couldn't make out who she was, but there was something familiar about the clatter of hooves.' My heart clenched, sir, as I listened to him. 'I very nearly fell asleep,' he says, 'waiting for her to come back. She rode back at a walk. It was different from an hour ago.' 'Esther!' I shouted. 'She sat up in the saddle and galloped off. Was it not her, my dear fellow?' he said."

Frowning, Horn bit his lip.

"Go on—and be done with this!"

"Well," Dribb seethed, while his chest heaved like the deck of a ship during a monsoon, "I didn't know why Esther wasn't by my side or why she'd been gone so long . . . I thought she might have needed to go home. Now the ball is in your court, Mr. Horn. If she loves you, let's take our positions ten paces from one another and let fate decide what it pleases. I came to see you the other day, but you weren't at home. I searched all the forest paths, the seashore, and all those places where it's easier to get around. Then I spent two days in your home, but you didn't come back. Afterward, I took Sigma with me—she's a fine dog, sir—and all it took was a little over four hours for her to lead me here."

"What of it?" said Horn resolutely. "Every word of it's true, Dribb. Esther did indeed come to see me. I won't lie to you; maybe it'll help you. She wanted me to marry her. But I don't love her, and I told her this, just as I'm telling you."

The giant buckled over, as though he were being crushed by a roof. His face turned a dirty white. Choked with anger and grief, he threw himself awkwardly on the ground and, rocking there, gritted his teeth.

"You weren't thinking of me," he cried, "when you were stealing the girl away. And woe betide you if you're lying to me!"

"No, Dribb," said Horn quietly, with the indifferent smile of a man in possession of himself. "You're wrong. I wasn't thinking of you in particular, I'll grant you that, but I was thinking about you. It occurred to me that it would be nice if this beautiful forest sparkled with shady canals and flowering banks, and if elegant bamboo houses stood on these banks, full of carefree happiness, like a lone cloud drifting in the sky. What's more, I wanted to populate this forest with swarthy little people, beautiful, like Esther, with doe eyes and limbs that are unsullied by dirty labor. How and on what these people would live, I don't know. But they're what I should have liked to see, not some unwieldy torso like yours, Dribb, befouled by the sweat of work and decorated with a button instead of a nose."

"Just try saying one more word!" With a menacing look, Dribb marched straight up to Horn. "And I'll kill you on the spot. I'll leave you swinging from this rubber tree, you scoundrel!"

"Oh, enough!" Horn turned pale. He was shaking with rage. The valley and the forest fused for a moment into a single circle of green before his very eyes. "It isn't a case of you or me, Dribb, there's only me. I'll kill you, remember that well. Then it'll be too late for you to see whether I'm lying."

"Ten paces," Dribb barked in a hoarse voice.

Horn turned and counted out ten, holding a finger on the trigger. A little patch of grass separated them. Their eyes were drawn to one another. Horn jerked up his rifle.

"No commands," he said. "Shoot at will."

As the word "will" ended, he quickly turned his side towards Dribb, and just in time, for Dribb had pulled the trigger. The bullet grazed Horn's chest and struck a tree.

Keeping his nerve, he took aim at the middle of the farmer's hairy chest and fired without hesitating. A new cartridge had jammed in

Dribb's magazine on its way to the barrel. Dribb staggered back, opened his mouth and fell on his side, without taking his round, vacant eyes off Horn.

Horn walked up to the wounded man. Dribb was wheezing slowly and heavily, while his enormous body twitched as it lay awkwardly on the ground. His eyes were closed. Horn trembled as he walked away; the sight of the dying man was as unpleasant as any act of destruction. The horse, which had run off a little to the side, had started neighing in alarm. Horn looked at the horse, then at the dog whining beside Dribb, and walked off, loading a fresh cartridge as he went. His thoughts leaped; suddenly he felt profound fatigue and weakness. The flesh on his chest, grazed by Dribb's bullet, was swollen, oozing with thick blood that trickled in burning drops down his stomach. Squatting down, he tore his shirt into several broad strips, and, having fashioned a bandage from them, tightly bound his ribs. The dressing quickly soaked through and turned red, but there was nothing more to be done.

While Horn was busying himself, Dribb, who had been lying motionless with a bullet hole through his chest, opened his eyes and spat out a thick wad of blood. The approach of death was bringing him to despair. He stirred himself; his body moved like a sack, replete with sharp pain and weakness. Dribb began crawling toward his horse, groaning as he picked his way through the wet grass, like a puppy that has lost its box. The horse was standing still with its head turned. The nine-yard journey seemed to Dribb to last a thousand years. Choking on blood, he crawled toward the stirrup.

Spinning around and jumping, Sigma watched the man's efforts as he tried to get into the saddle, having lost half his blood. He fell five times, but on the sixth attempt he succeeded, yet because of the incredible strain, the forest and sky were dancing before his eyes quicker than flies on carrion. As he sat there with his arms around the horse's neck, one of his legs slipped out of the stirrup, though he did not attempt to put it back in its place. The horse, with a shake of its mane, set off at a trot.

Hearing the clatter of hooves, Horn rushed headlong to the spot where Dribb had fallen. A bloody trail led toward the forest—red on green, like liquid, scattered corals.

"Too late," said Horn, paling from this unexpected revelation.

Gripped by alarm, he entered the forest and headed in the direction of the lake as quickly as he could. The golden vistas had disappeared and an even twilight shadow was cast over the tree trunks and the earth. His chest ached as if it had been stabbed. Almost running, hurriedly jumping over trunks that had been felled by a storm, Horn pressed on and saw Dribb's body, which had fallen from a horse ridden almost to the point of death, surrounded by a crowd of colonists.

"If that corpse finds the strength to utter just one word, I'll have to answer to them all," thought Horn.

He was already running, gasping from nervous tension. The forest, like a crowd of impotent friends, parted thoughtfully before him, revealing shady depressions, filled with the noise of blood and fanciful green waves.

IX.

The door, locked from inside, shuddered from the impatient blows but held fast. Horn quickly shifted his gaze from the undefended window to the door and back again, externally calm but filled with mute frenzy and alarm. This was one of those moments when life stumbles in the darkness over an abyss.

He found himself in the midst of a crowd that had dismounted in order to spare the horses. The beasts were neighing nearby, anxiously snorting in anticipation of the impending battle. The ground, which had been dug up in the middle of the floor, gaped with a small pit, along the edges of which lay dirty bundles and homemade leather purses, swollen with the fine gold that filled them. Dull, wrapped in damp skins still smelling of dried meat, the gold was as unattractive as a live red lump in the arms of a midwife who was yawning from a sleepless night. But there was enough of it that a man of average strength, having loaded all the little purses and bundles onto his back, could not walk even one hundred paces.

Horn thought of the gold as much as he thought of himself, though he was penned in by four walls. Everything depended on how events played out. He almost ached at the idea that the accidental trajectory of a bullet could level him with the unexpected gift of fate lying at his feet.

Fresh blows from the butt of a rifle drummed on the door so frequently and weightily that Horn automatically reached out his hand, expecting it to cave in. A voice said:

"If you can't appreciate civility, we'll have to think of something else. What would you say, for instance, if—"

"Nothing," Horn interrupted, without raising his voice, because the thin walls let the words out distinctly. "Even if there were a thousand of you, you could kill only one man. Whereas I can kill many."

A gunshot rang out, and simultaneously a bullet pierced through the door and struck the upper part of the window. Horn changed position.

"Right," he said, "I'm not going to talk to you, because you'll be able to aim for the sound and shoot at my vocal cords. So far you've been missing by only four feet or so."

He turned to the window and discharged his rifle into a head that appeared there, before loading a new cartridge.

"Don't you think," the same voice said, emphasizing certain words with the butt of a rifle, "that death under the open sky would be better than dying in a mousetrap?"

"Dribb's dead," said Horn. "Nothing can bring him back. He was hot-tempered and conceited; I had to cool the fellow down. I'm the obliging sort until I myself am threatened with death. Now he's dead, so what's to be done about it?! The dog Sigma is more to blame than I: it's a dangerous thing having such a keen sense of smell."

A wild roar and the crack of boards pierced by new bullets stopped him.

"What perseverance!" said Horn. The chill exhilaration of despair pushed him to make caustic jokes. "Won't you give it a rest? One would need the patience of a saint to listen to your incoherent threats."

Talk continued outside. Hushed exclamations and footfalls would die away and then begin to circle around the house again, closer then farther away, closer then farther away, first in one and then in all directions. A pale rectangle of the moon's glassy dust fell by the window; there was a persistent crackling of reeds, as if a great beast were settling down to sleep but could not get comfortable. Horn was losing sensation in his body, which was trembling from this excess of excitement; now all ears, he mechanically turned his head in every direction, the rifle's hammer cocked, and each second remembering the revolver weighing his pocket down.

A sudden burst of shots made Horn's hands tremble and his ears ring. Myriad little wood chips, knocked out by the bullets, hit his face and neck, scratching his skin in places.

After a moment's silence a voice behind the door dryly inquired: "Are you alive?"

Horn discharged both barrels, aiming for the voice. Behind the door, which shuddered from the impact of a bullet, something soft thudded.

"I am," he said, cracking the hot bolt. "And how are you getting on?"

In response came cursing and an explosive new round of shots. Around the corner, another voice shouted haltingly:

"Do you like wasting bullets?"

"I do it for fun," said Horn, dispatching another round.

The noise grew.

"Hey, you!" someone shouted. "I swear by your liver, which I'll see today with my own eyes, it's useless to resist. We'll just hang you; it's nothing to be afraid of—much better than being burnt alive! Think on this!"

These words would have sounded perfectly good-natured were it not for the deathly silent pauses that punctuated each phrase. Horn grinned with loathing in his soul; the company that had assembled to roast him was provoking in him a persistent desire to crush the heads of his attackers one by one. He was not afraid; his loneliness in the midst of these talking walls, under this roof, was much too bleak and too much like a dream for him to feel any fear.

"You don't recognize me," continued the halting voice. "Dribb's the name. I haven't even seen your face; you're too proud to find yourself under another man's roof. And back then, in the bay, it was too dark. But patience has its limits."

"A pity that it's you," said Horn dryly. "You oughtn't to have come, out of a sense of impartiality. What did your son say as he fell from his horse?"

"As he fell from his horse? You weren't there for that, I hope. He said: 'Ho—' and choked. That's what he said, and you shall answer to me for this half a word."

"You should treat life with a philosophical composure," said Horn mockingly. "I'm not responsible for the actions of young whelps. I should have aimed for his forehead, then he would have died in the firm certainty that I'd been killed by his first shot. Isn't Guppy here?"

"I am," a husky voice called out. It sounded farther away than the spot where Horn imagined Dribb to be.

"Guppy," said Horn after a pause, "you should go and get drunk on the sacrificial blood of your pigs!"

His cheeks twitched with nervous laughter. The colonist's shrill profanities lodged in his ears with a piercing screech. He went on, as if trying to reason with himself:

"Guppy is a good man."

An unexpected, melancholy joy straightened the hunter's back; he already regretted it, for this joy extended two hands, giving with one and taking away with the other. But there was no way out. A grotesque death troubled him to the depths of his soul, he had decided.

"Wait!" cried Horn. "Just a minute!" Quickly, with several blows of an axe he hacked out the upper part of a board in the very top corner of the door and jumped back, fearing a shot. But the sound of iron cutting into the door, it seemed, had somewhat quelled the attackers—as though it were a man peacefully chopping wood. In the jagged hole a piece of misty sky loomed black.

"Guppy," said Horn, catching his breath and pricking up his ears. "Guppy, come closer, from whichever side you like. Upon my honor, I won't shoot. I need to tell you something."

A man stationed by the window emerged and, hurriedly taking aim, fired into the darkness of the room. Horn recoiled as the bullet scorched his cheek. Gripped by the searing rage of one being hunted, Horn remained silent for several seconds, aiming the muzzle toward the window with everything inside him shaking, like a factory in full swing—all because of his anger and fury.

Recollecting himself, he thought that Guppy might already have come close enough. Then, taking a pouch filled with gold dust weighing two or three pounds, he flung it through the hole in the door.

"This is for you," Horn said loudly. "And another one . . . and another."

Almost without realizing what he was doing, he tossed the gold into the darkness with a feverish rapidity, listening vacantly to the dull thud of the little bags falling rhythmically on the other side of the door. Tears choked him. The little blue river flowed innocently before his eyes.

Rapid, confused conversation erupted outside, individual voices sounded now rushing, now muffled, like a somnolent babbling. Horn looked out of the window and listened.

"Hang on, Guppy!"

"What do you want?"

"Put it down!"

"Leave it!"

"Hey, where are you going?"

"What, you too? Damn and blast!"

"What's it got to do with you?"

"Where did he get it all?"

"There's so much!"

"I'll tear your hands off!"

"For one thing, you're all fools!"

The distinctive sound of a slap cut through Horn's tension. For a moment, the sound abated before bursting forth again with tenfold strength. Footsteps, hurried exclamations, profanities, Dribb's wrathful cry, and the heavy breathing of people struggling blended, each drowning the other out, and turned into a howling roar. Almost frightened, not quite trusting himself, Horn wheezed, resting his head against the door. He sensed a tussle turning into a brawl, the sudden onset of avarice that in the imagination amplified what was there to grandiose proportions. He also sensed a sharp shift in mood.

A long, sonorous cry escaped the general fray. And suddenly a shot rang out, after which it seemed to Horn that somewhere off to the side of his home, a dense crowd was thrashing around in some enormous quadrille without lights or music. One after the other, he knocked out the bolts securing the door, quietly opened it, and at once all thought vanished, leaving only the instinctive, unconscious semireflexes of a cornered animal.

The tumult was coming from Horn's right, just around the corner. There was no one to be seen, since they were busily finishing their counting. It was unlikely that they would rush to burn down the house in a bid to find there even more of what Horn had tossed out. Cruel and impatient, like children, they preferred what they could already see to what they could not. Horn exited through the door.

The shadows cast by the moon looked like strips of black velvet on grass awash with milk. The still air smoldered with a thick light, like chalk dust. The darkness trapped on the edge of the forest dappled it with dark-green cutouts.

Horn stood there for a moment, listening to the beating heart of the night, silent, like a melody being performed in the mind, and suddenly, hunching over, he made a break for the forest. The air whistled in his ears, his body suddenly began to ache all at once from the quick movements, everything lost its stillness and rushed headlong beside him, gasping, deafeningly loud, like water in the ears of a man who has dived from a great height. Even the horse tied by the edge of the forest seemed to hurry to him, as it stood there side-on, lazily kicking its legs. He gripped its mane; the saddle slowly rocked beneath him. Having hastily cut the tether with a knife almost the moment he discovered it, Horn discharged all six bullets from the revolver into three or four of the nearest horses, which bolted at the sound of the shots. He set off at a gallop, while the darkness, like an invisible deluge of air, rushed to meet him.

Somewhere high up above his head, moving from a falsetto to an alto, a stray bullet sang out before fading, describing an arc and harmlessly falling in the sand beside a harassed ant, which was in the process of dragging a twig that was somehow very essential to it.

■ □ ■

Horn rode, without stopping, for a distance of around six or seven miles. He cut across the plain, descended into the scrub of the marine plateau, and came out onto the road leading to the town.

At that point he paused, saving the animal's strength for a likely chase. To the left, from the depths of the nocturnal abyss, coming from the direction of the lake, he heard an indeterminate thudding, as though someone were drumming his fingers on a table, losing the rhythm and then picking it up again. Horn pricked up his ears, shuddered, and struck the horse with great force.

He was consumed by the mechanical, impetuous numbness of the galloping, where the horse's mane, the dark nocturnal earth, the fleeing silhouettes of hills, and the rhythmic convulsions of his whole body comingled in an eroding sense of space and dizzying motion. They were coming after him, it was plain to see, and he swayed from weakness. Fatigue was beginning to grip him. Crouching down, he pressed on without a sense of dread or alarm, with the painful calm of a man who is mechanically performing what others did consciously in similar situations; saving his life seemed a futile, horribly tedious business.

And at that moment when, exhausted by everything he had gone through, he was ready to give up the reins, letting the horse go as it pleased, Horn distinctly saw in the air the pale light of a candle and a little hand encircled by lace. It looked like a reflection in the dark glass of a window. He smiled—to die in the middle of the road would be a droll, monstrous injustice, death by thirst.

Esther's pensive face flashed somewhere in a corner of his consciousness and paled, vanishing along with the hand dressed in lace, as if it were an invisible, firm link between the girl from the colony and the woman with the capricious face, for whom he would do anything.

"Hello!" said Horn, sitting up in the saddle. "The poor thing's begun to quiver!"

And he jumped off to the side before the falling horse had time to crush him under its violently heaving flanks.

Then, calmed by the silence, he paused for a moment, casting one last glance in the direction of a life that he did not need, one that was reaching out its arms to him, before moving on.

THE DEVIL OF THE ORANGE WATERS

"Hear me," the devil said amid the midnight still.
"Hear me! And I shall tell you of a land where sorrows dwell."

Edgar Allan Poe

PROLOGUE

Inger was lying in bed, coughing more than he ought. His right hand, dangling limply from the bedstead, wearily wiggled its pale fingers, the heat of a fever flashed in his half-closed eyes, and from under his arm protruded a clinical thermometer, which had been preheated sufficiently under a lamp.

This sight, intended to inspire sympathy, reduced the forty-year-old man who entered the room to peals of laughter. The man's movements were sharp, quick, and angular; his broad, pale face might have seemed inconspicuous were it not for the harsh curvature of his high, arched eyebrows. He had on an ill-fitting, baggy black suit and heavy boots, while his right hand, adorned with antique signet rings, clutched a top hat.

"It's only me, not the doctor," the man said. "The doctor wasn't on my train. And so, my dear Inger, you may save the thermometer for another occasion."

Inger began blinking intensively, blushing and squinting.

"Now listen here, Bangok," he said, "if you so much as dare—"

"Oh, but I do," Bangok cut in. "I was watching through the keyhole. For starters, I saw my pipe, which so mysteriously vanished. You were holding it between your teeth. Ignorant of how to use it, you filled the room with smoke and dropped the light on the bedsheets, burning a hole in them. That hole is currently under the most delicate part of your body. Then you took out that cheap, vile little mirror and had a turn admiring your face as you grimaced imperiously. After that you carried out your fraud with the thermometer and, finally, when you heard the door creak, you sprawled out in the pose of a dying gladiator."

"If I recover tomorrow," Inger said despairingly, "they'll send me back to the city. We love each other so very much."

"Do you indeed?" Bangok fixed his gaze upon the boy, sneezed, and blew his nose. "Curious," he said. "And where do you plan to live after the wedding?"

"On the Canaries, or the Maluku Islands."

"A true bucolic idyll," observed Bangok. "How do you manage to see each other?"

"She comes to my window."

"Inger," said Bangok, "I won't ask whether you kiss or not, I won't ask whether you eat up all those sweet pies that your beloved steals for you. But I will ask whether you intend to give me back my pipe, you little rascal."

Inger thrust his hand under the covers to extract the pipe and silently handed it over to Bangok.

"In exchange for this," he said, "you have to tell me something."

"So that's how it is!" said Bangok. "Indeed," he added, as though to himself. "The ways of a bandit and a Don Juan . . . The boy will go far . . . Tell you something, eh?" Bangok repeated slowly. "What would you like to hear about, young hope of the nation? Say, I'll tell you about the reconstruction of the naval academy building."

"Not interested," said Inger.

"About suffrage for the lower classes . . ."

"Not that."

"About the law against gypsies . . ."

"Oh, please!"

"About the taxation of luxuries . . ."

"No."

"About the excavation of an ancient Roman aqueduct . . ."

Inger maintained an affronted silence.

"Well," Bangok continued with a chuckle, "how about something to do with *the lives of the people*? About the psychologies of sorrel and dappled horses, the history of the bridle, the power of black earth and the despotism of loam, about labor pains, weavers' looms and boiled potatoes? Why are you shaking your head? Don't you want to know anything about these things?"

"I don't," Inger snapped furiously.

"Even sailors like to chat," said Bangok, "on gloomy autumnal days like this. I enjoy reminiscing about what used to be. What shall I tell you about, strange creature that are not interested in feminism or social psychology? What will you?"

"I want to hear about all the things you've seen," said Inger. "About chasms, caves, volcanoes, cyclones and cannibals . . . you know. Remember how you used to tell me about negroes, gold, a white girl, and yellow fever?"

"I do," said Bangok, no longer smiling.

"Well, something like that then."

"Something like that! Very well, listen to me, Inger, and I'll tell you about the devil of the Orange Waters."

Inger's eyes came greedily ablaze.

"Is it something very sensational?" he exclaimed.

"No, it's a true story," said Bangok.

"And the devil?"

"Listen and judge for yourself."

I. AN ENCOUNTER WITH THE DEVIL

This happened, Inger, long before I was made captain of your father's yacht, back when I wasn't even a sailor. Young, nimble, and daring, I looked upon everything under the sun from the vantage of luck and curiosity.

In 1892, I had stowed away on board the *Cassiopeia*, which was owned by Fitz & Co. and making the voyage from Australia to China. Being of a truthful disposition, I replied to all the first mate's questions and openly admitted to having no ticket. This conversation took place a full day after the *Cassiopeia* put out to sea. Until then, I had managed to dodge the ticket check. Of course, I was traveling in steerage. The conversation took place in the evening—knowing that I would be ejected at the nearest port of call, I ceased dwelling on it and went out on deck for a smoke while I gazed up at the starry sky.

As I was standing there, pondering whether to steal the diamond eyes of the Buddha of Bogor, to become a card sharp, or to enlist in the volunteers, a man, leaning over the side of the ship some distance from me, straightened up and approached me with the words:

"What are we to do?"

Without replying, I looked him over carefully, from head to toe, to establish just with whom I was dealing. On this occasion, however, my eye and experience failed me: the stranger's identity remained a mystery. He wore a soiled suit; instead of a waistcoat, he had on a garish calico shirt; and he wore tall boots—and his fair hair, the color of rotten hemp, was covered by a black fedora. I must add to this description that the calico shirt was not tucked into his breeches but belted by a cord with raspberry-colored tassels. The man's gaunt face, with its protruding cheekbones, his snub nose covered in freckles, his scraggly little beard and moustache, and his sunken colorless eyes, all left an indelible impression on me. His long, greasy hair, trimmed haphazardly behind the ears, spread out like a fan over the collar of his jacket. The stranger was tall, thin, hunched, and his voice was piercing.

"What are *you* to do?" I said. "In all likelihood, you know the answer to that better than I. As for me, I'll think of something."

"No," he hastily replied, gesticulating and smiling officiously. "You must have misunderstood me. I mean to say that I, too, have no ticket, that we're fellow travelers, as it were. I suggest that we discuss our situation collectively. Allow me to introduce myself: I am Ivan Baranov, a Russian political exile."

"Very well," I said. "My name is Bangok, I'm a nobody."

He winked, mistaking my answer for a joke, and laughed.

After a pause, Baranov asked: "Are they going to disembark us?"

"Of course they are."

"Where?"

"At the first port of call."

He fell silent. I did not stoke the conversation, and so we parted, having wished each other a pleasant night. I settled on top of some crates; I was calm, I felt fine, cheerful even; I knew that life would fall into my tenacious paws sooner or later and that I would squeeze everything I could out of it. I fell asleep. I was awoken by something touching my head. "Go to hell!" I cried, half-awake. There was somebody sitting beside me on the crate; with a heavy sigh, he woke me up definitively. I lifted my head.

A weak matinal light glimmered in the far reaches of the ocean, and after several minutes the sun would begin to rise. Irritated, I asked rudely:

"What do you want?"

"Come now . . . don't be angry," Baranov began quietly. "I feel wretched, I'm afraid, and I can't sleep . . . I need to talk to somebody . . ."

He was smoking a cigarette. I watched him in amazement. Baranov's face twitched, his voice cracked, and his hands were trembling . . .

"Are you unwell?" I asked.

"No . . . that is . . . I'm in a strange way. Just now I wanted to go up on deck and jump overboard."

"Why?"

"Listen," he began quickly. "Don't you feel it? You're sailing somewhere aboard a great, strange ship, across a strange sea, surrounded by night, silence, and the stars, and everybody's asleep. Do you see? Man is tragically alone. Nobody cares about anybody else. All they care about is their own affairs. Life in all its complexity, greatness, mystery, absurdity, and cruelty is leading you—but where? In the name of what? To what end? I felt it just now amid the silence of the sleeping ship. Who am I? Why am I here? Why am I alive?"

I listened without the faintest idea what this man wanted from me. But he went on talking, lighting one cigarette after another— talking of humanity, class struggle, idealism, the soul and matter, religion and machines, all in that same devastatingly hopeless tone, and I noticed that all his pontifications lacked a center, a basic idea, and conviction. He spoke as though he relished the sound of his own voice; the sense of what he said could be laid out in three words: despondency, bewilderment, trepidation. Indifferent at first, I listened with occasional interjections of "yes," "no," and "maybe."

I even found Baranov's vehemence amusing. Then I experienced a particular sort of impatience, which expressed itself in the desire to whistle, to box someone about the ears, or to scream, when suddenly, apropos of nothing, I began to feel so very sad and my back began to ache. As I listened, I was powerless to break this strange stupor, like a drowsiness caused by a vampire, a drowsiness as sweet-smelling and repellent as the aroma of nightshade.

Baranov fell silent. His last words were: "Yes, everything sours, everything is repulsive, one goes around as though wading through water."

He got to his feet. In terror I awaited the continuation.

"We'll talk again," he said by way of consolation, taking my hand and shaking it limply. I pretended to sleep. He left, while over the horizon, gilding the ship and the ripples on the water, the sun's disc blazed.

II. TERRA FIRMA

I did not see him again until we disembarked. At ten o'clock in the morning, Port Mel came into view—it was the spot where, as one sailor explained to me, the rails for a branch line of the Sinnigham railway were to be unloaded.

The *Cassiopeia* approached the shoreline. Along the muddy bank stood a small crowd of natives and about five Europeans. A few wooden posts with boards nailed to them constituted the dock. Farther along were a newly constructed embankment, piles of railway sleepers, and several wooden structures.

Naturally, I didn't wait to be told, in more or less crude terms, that my sea voyage was at an end. Nonchalantly hooking the thumbs of my idle hands into the top pockets of my vest, I began whistling a sailor's farewell tune, "Cursed Be the Shore without Food or Water," and descended onto terra firma.

You're too young, Inger, to know what it means to feel isolation, but when I went ashore, I felt it again for the umpteenth time as I cast a glance back at the ship. Its smokestack puffed away indifferently. I felt too independent, alien to everything around me. I had known better days, so to speak. All I could do was to rely on my own skill, my luck and cunning; I had just enough money to pull a long face when I thrust my hand into my pocket.

It was exceedingly and unbearably hot. Drenched in sweat, I walked slowly along the embankment, determined to purge my mind of all thoughts and cursing Fulton, the inventor of the first steamship. Just then, someone called out to me. I turned and saw Baranov.

I do not know why, but as I scrutinized his awkward, lanky figure, I experienced something almost akin to a superstitious malaise. He hurried up to me, obviously in a rush and happy about something, since the shadow of a sour smile glinted in his nervous eyes. As he drew near to me, he asked:

"Where are you going?"

"I need to press on," I replied dryly. "Shanghai's still a ways off."

"Listen," said the Russian, assuming a businesslike air. "We have to think of something. I'm glad that I found you," he added after a pause.

A man in a white hat was walking in our direction along the rails; he was bared to the waist and dark in the European way (that is to say, the color of weak coffee). I stopped him to ask when the next ship would arrive.

The man, having looked me over thoroughly, uttered a few phrases that offered no consolation whatsoever. A ship might call in, but then again it might not. If one were to call in, then it would be no sooner than a week hence.

The railway had not yet been completed, although they were already putting locomotives on the line. If we so desired, however, we could walk thirty-odd miles to a railway bridge that was being built across the river; there, we could knock together a raft and sail down to San Riol, where ships made scheduled stops at the estuary.

We stood there facing each other for some time. Then the man in the white hat nodded and, without looking back, continued on his way.

I considered my options. This man was the so-called track foreman; he was, of course, well informed about the state of the railway. There was little sense in waiting for a ship, though I didn't much relish the idea of walking. On the other hand, I cannot abide inaction; I had no choice but to walk, even if it meant walking on the spot, which, as soldiers know full well, is easier than sitting with one's arms crossed.

Thus, my mind was made up. I looked at Baranov. Naturally, the manpower of two was better than one, and a strong pair of hands could well come in handy when it came to building the raft. Besides, there was something about this strange Russian that inspired a vague pity. Stretching out my hand to him, I said:

"We're in quite a pickle, you and I. We'll very likely need each other, so I propose making the journey to San Riol together."

We were standing on the edge of a forest that was drenched in heat. Deep therein, birds called to one another with their sharp, melodious snatches of song. Baranov's face, when he lifted his head in response to what I had said, took on a calm, attentive, impassive aspect; he looked at me as if my words had lulled him into a state of boredom.

"Listen," Baranov said in a muffled, changed voice. Taking off his hat, he ran his fingers through his hair, looked at his feet, and continued: "I have an alternative proposal for you."

I waited silently to hear what he would say.

III. THE DEVIL'S FIRST TEMPTATION

"You know," the Russian began, smiling ambiguously into the distance, "while you were talking with the native, I had the following thought. In our country, when political criminals, for instance, justly demand some action from the prison administration, but the administration won't do it, they declare a so-called hunger strike. They refuse to eat, threatening to starve themselves to death. The administration is left with a choice: either to yield or to watch a man slowly die."

I had indeed heard and read about this strange means of resistance, and so I nodded, giving Baranov to know that I was waiting for him to go on, although, by my ears and beard, I swear I hadn't the faintest idea where the Russian was going with this.

"Now then," he rubbed his hands, as if speaking before an audience, "I shall refer to our situation and compare our life with prison, and us with prisoners. You and I are prisoners of life. I am a weary, broken intellectual, torn from my dear homeland, a man without a future, without money, without anything to tie him down, a man who knows not for what purpose he lives. But I should like to know. I'm a prisoner—and so are you. You're a wanderer, Life's stepson. She will lure you with false promises, scatterings of the wealth of others, beautiful love, bold flights of fancy—everything that beckons through a prison window looking out over sun and sea. But it's a fraud. Just like any proletarian, you have but one chance in your favor, one versus the many millions that are against you, for the world teems with proletarians. Surely you must feel the shackles of our current situation, those with which we have been fettered since birth, those that jangle especially painfully? We have been cast out, like whelps, just because we have no money. We're lost in a strange land. Life is trying to force us to make a thousand efforts: to go on foot, then to find a boat, or perhaps to build a raft, to starve, to get drenched in the rain, to suffer torments—and after all this, only then to arrive at our destination and ask ourselves: 'What awaited us here?' You, a man of an old and cultured race, know what I mean. We are people, human beings from head to toe, with all the inherent right to life that people have, the right to health, love, and food. But we have nothing, because we are life's prisoners. And so here, under the open sky, on the edge of this wonderful enchanted forest, within the walls of this splendid prison, I propose that we declare a hunger strike—to life. We'll lie down right here and not move an inch—come what may."

I was ready to tap his forehead with my finger, but there was no madness or irony on the Russian's face. Baranov's deep-sunken eyes gazed at me searchingly while he stroked his beard, clearly expecting an earnest response from me.

Intrigued, even somewhat stunned by the fervor in his voice and the outlandishness of his suggestions, I said:

"All right, we'll lie down. Then what?"

"Nothing," he declared simply, as though talking of the most ordinary thing. "Day will become night, and night—day. We shall grow weak and be visited by morbid, famished hallucinations. Then, there will be either a miracle, or else . . ."

"Death," I said. "You are proposing death."

"Yes."

I said nothing while I considered the most emphatic but inoffensive answer possible. And again, as I had done that night on board the ship, when Baranov first appeared, I felt a revolting, sweet, stupefying sensation, one of stupor and alarm. But then, the usual thoughts of the day's goings-on rose to the surface, and Baranov began to disgust me, like a slippery mushroom one finds in a cellar when you reach out for a hammer and instead your fingers graze the mushroom's moist cap. Evidently my companion took me for the same sort of person as he—an archetype of some rare and freakish race of people.

"Look here," I said, "you lie down here and snuff it. But I can see something better up ahead: a handcar. Do you see it? It's standing in the siding next to the signal. Everyone is on a break right now, and there's nobody about on the line. How about we get on and travel down to the river?"

I confess, pride wouldn't allow me to do this alone, leaving the Russian behind. I wanted to show him how cheerfully and swiftly an unfortunate life flowed in the right hands.

"Regarding what you said," I added, "know this: that I, Bangok, shall come up trumps."

"And if you don't?" he countered, clearly enlivened by my derisive tone.

"Over my dead body. But so long as there's air in my lungs . . ." And there I remembered that I truly was alive, and that I held all the cards in my hand. "No, my dear fellow," I added, "to me you're nothing but a catalyst. Now I'm beginning to sputter. Come on!"

With a listless smile, the Russian followed me. The gleaming, well-oiled handcar had taken my fancy from the moment I laid eyes on it. Besides, after all that had been said, it was too late to go back now.

I took the handle and pressed down, remembering that we had to get away from there as quickly as possible, while Baranov sat there with his head bowed. We thundered across the points at the signal, gaining speed, and, gliding along the brand-new rails, our purloined chariot rounded the corner.

IV. THE DEVIL'S SECOND TEMPTATION

I.

I was working the handcar's lever so furiously that I lost my hat. The wind plucked it from my head, and it went tumbling down the embankment before vanishing for good. Rails, sleepers, the dark-blue horizon with its forest-covered hills, it all came rushing toward us. Baranov got to his feet. With that same expression of dumb indifference, typical of him during moments requiring the greatest effort, the Russian, gripping the other handle and facing me, inclined his head like a bull and set to work.

"The fellow has bucked up!" I thought. He displayed remarkable strength. His gnarled fingers firmly clenched the lever's wooden beam. We pumped away with abandon. Not a word was spoken between us. The platform of the handcar, rattling over the points, shook my whole body. Sweat poured over my eyes, and I was as wet as a fish.

We must have covered around twenty miles, since the nature of our surroundings changed several times before our very eyes. We were now racing through a valley in full bloom, just like the face of a country beauty, while up ahead, scattered about in islets, a marvelous forest of ibexes hurtled toward us, all rare patterns and outlines.

"A horn!" said the Russian. Wiping his face with the palm of his hand, he looked at me inquiringly and listened. I looked around: a locomotive—ahead or behind, it didn't matter—would have knocked us off the rails. The claxon sounded again; its piercing shriek echoed through the surrounding area. We had already entered the forest; suffering from the heat, I extracted a handkerchief from my pocket and tied it around my head.

"If the train's coming from behind and not head on," I said, "we can still travel another half-mile or so. Come on, put some elbow into it!"

We began pumping so energetically that we risked dislocating our shoulders. The track began on an incline before making an enormous turn, and finally we came onto a section of track that was as straight as a needle, revealing a long stretch of forest and embankment. At the very end, puffing out little white clouds of steam, loomed a long train resembling a smoking pile of coals.

We hurtled past a quarry where black-skinned diggers, who were busily plying their shovels, turned to look at us in astonishment. I stopped pumping and shouted:

"Brake!"

The Russian applied the brake. The handcar, its axle screeching, traveled a further thirty-odd yards before coming to a halt. We jumped off about forty paces from the locomotive and the astonished face of the driver, and legged it in the direction of the forest. Glancing back as I ran, I saw a row of open wagons loaded with soil and clouds of steam as the train backed up. Baranov, breathing heavily, came running behind me. Understanding full well what we could expect if we were captured, I did not spare myself. The damp, wild undergrowth, the twilight, and the sprawling treetops crowded around us; my sprinting turned into a brawl amid a crowd—invisible enemies struck me in the face, arms, and whole body with fleshy green knots of vines, sabre-sharp leaves, and hard brushwood. A chorus of exclamations, dampened by the forest, came from the embankment; shots immediately rang out, and a shriek of bullets cut through the foliage above our heads, providing additional impetus to our legs.

Staggering with exhaustion, I came to a standstill. Baranov was right there; as pale as glass, he leaned his shoulder against a tree trunk, closed his eyes, and lowered his head. First I sat down, then

I lay down. My head started spinning; the forest, the greenery, and I myself seemed like a great spinning top that had been set in motion with murderous speed. However, we must have made it quite far, since we were surrounded by total, gloomy silence. After sufficient rest, I got to my feet.

Baranov was sitting by a tree, rolling a cigarette with his fingers, which were still trembling from fright.

"We can't be far from the river," I said. "Our daring has paid off! Get up, we must get going."

He silently rose. Evidently, even from his fantastical point of view, it would have been absurd to remain in the forest. For a moment we stood rooted to the spot—partly to give ourselves the necessary time to realize what had just happened and what yet lay in store, and partly because our legs were still unresponsive to our will. Then the Russian and I set off, keeping the railway track to our right lest we lose our way, and after about ten minutes, we saw, through the dark gaps between the tree trunks, which were entangled with the lacy patterns of creeping stalks, the sunlit mound of the embankment.

I do not recall for how long we walked. Keeping the track in sight to guide me, with Baranov following behind, I moved mechanically, without irritation or impatience. I walked because I had no alternative. Fatigue rendered us speechless; strange, magnificently plumed birds flew through the air, and the living coil of a serpent, hidden in the grass, slithered away at the sound of our footsteps; sounds recalling a strangled scream, a sigh, a muffled whistle, a distant trampling skimmed along on either side of us in the mysterious depths of the dark-green wooded groves, while we, numb and exhausted, listlessly made our way toward the river, our weary attention dully noting the forest animal's hidden, solemn feast of life filled with enchantment. The sun's golden tresses, falling on the shady thicket, glinted red, stretching out and cooling—a sign of the approaching evening.

From time to time, experiencing pangs of hunger, I would smoke, but this was of little and very dubious help: gulps of smoke intensified my weakness. I was hounded by the steady, persistent thought of food; yesterday had come and gone without sustenance, and today promised more of the same. Aside from the revolver weighing heavily in my pocket, we had no other weapons; it was ludicrous to hope for a successful hunt with only seven bullets. I asked:

"Are you hungry?"

"Yes," replied Baranov, "and that's the worst part. I haven't eaten for three days, and even then it was a light, dainty meal."

He paused, raising his hand to shade his eyes, a look of certainty flashing across his face.

"The river, Bangok," he calmly pronounced. "It's the river."

Cheered by this, I looked in the direction of his gaze. We were standing very close to the embankment; on the other side of the track, through the gaps in the opposite wall of forest, which was evidently no more than a small, narrow promontory, water glittered in the low light of sunset.

I heaved a sigh of relief. The river—a direct route to civilization, the city, the ocean, and a ship.

II.

The shoreline was low, empty, and covered in tall grass, sand, and seashells. Looking downstream, I saw that the forest now extended as far as the river, now withdrew in a semicircle to reveal sandbanks, glades, and snaking pools of water. The rainy season had ended about five days prior to this, and the Adara, laden with water, lazily eddied, flowing darkly in its calm splendor, with drowning reflections of the steep bank on the opposing shore. White-headed birds fluttered their wings over the surface of the water, pecking at it, and the quicksilver of fish thrashed about in their beaks, shedding droplets of limpid water.

"If we're to sail," said Baranov, perching on a rock, "then we'll need a boat. Or, as you said, a raft."

With this in mind, I examined the shore carefully. My penknife would have been useful for building a child's water mill, but even before I pulled it out, I knew that it would never fell a tree. I was counting on there being tree trunks carried away by the river and washed ashore, but there were none to be seen. We would have to keep looking; this was, after all, a common occurrence in wooded areas.

I wanted to keep going but couldn't: my stomach was in knots with hunger. I dreamed of impossible things—edible sand, branches made of dough, the prospect of finding bread. Of course, all this was ridiculous. Whistling as he went, Baranov chewed on a stalk of grass.

All of a sudden, as though conforming to our foul mood, the river ceased glittering. The sun, ready to go to sleep, enswathed itself in the clouds; the great airborne chrysanthemums they formed, saturated with red and pink light, accumulated fancifully on the horizon, while the color of the water turned wan and grey.

"In half an hour," I said, "darkness will fall. We need to think about shelter for the night."

"What about food?" he asked wearily.

"That too. Why don't you collect some brushwood and get a fire going, while I try my luck."

Weakened and tortured by hunger, I saw in my mind's eye the seven bullets of my revolver and the accidental but inescapable fate awaiting some unfortunate bird. Baranov set off in one direction picking up branches while I headed in the other.

In the fading light of the semidark, almost sleeping forest, I extracted my revolver and cocked it as I looked around. It was quiet; every now and then, the shadow of a bird would flicker against the backdrop of a deep-blue evening sky; and an invisible cockatoo would mutter away in the branches, like a monk reading vespers. Carefully, trying not to frighten my impending victims, I moved through the brush. I was not having much luck. Nothing alive caught my eyes; sometimes, mistaking a tangle of branches or oddly shaped leaves for a living creature, I would stop, with my heart pounding, raise the revolver and lower it again, realizing the illusion. Suddenly, I spotted a bird.

It was resting quite nearby, whistling melodically between two branches that stretched out in parallel; a round eye glinted on the side of a head turned toward me. My eyes, having grown accustomed to the darkness, could make it out rather well. It was the size of a hen, dirty pearl in color, with gray wings that turned to red and a white plume on its head. A gently curving feather stretched down from its tail.

I raised my revolver, took aim, and, with the target in my sights, fired. The bird flitted up to a higher branch. Anxious, I fired a second shot and, lowering my trembling hand, saw the gently curving tail feather flicker through the leaves and fall. The bird beat its wings against the ground; I made a dash for it, but just as my hands were about to seize my prey, it began to thrash about noisily before taking off and disappearing.

Having run a few paces in the direction of its flight, I stopped, spotting a squirrel. Clinging to a tree trunk, the squirrel flexed, ready to race to the top of the tree. Enraged by the bird's escape, I began shooting at the squirrel from where I stood; the first bullet forced it to make a bewildered upside-down turn around the tree; the second made him corkscrew up; and after the third, with all the energy of a steel spring, it jumped over to a neighboring tree with its tail outspread, vanishing. I searched for it for a long time but was unable to find it.

I had two bullets left. I didn't dare waste them. They might prove useful for something far more important than squirrel fricassee. My anxiety and excitement evaporated as soon as I realized this. I wanted to drop to the earth and scream or let out a long, lingering howl. Tears of rage welled up in my throat; clutching the revolver in my hand, I made for the shore. In a passage running between two tall bushes that were as tangled as a skein of wool, I noticed pear-shaped blackberries hanging under each leaf, and so I popped one into my mouth. I had an irresistible urge to swallow it without chewing; fearing that it might be poisonous, however, I slowly rolled the berry around in my mouth with my tongue; the stale, bitter taste of the fruit made me spit the filthy thing out.

The sun vanished and darkness fell. Before me, slashed by the branches' black claws, Baranov's fire glowed. I stepped out of the forest. The flames' reflections stretched out across little puddles and the sand, which was damp from the dew; my companion's moving figure was silhouetted against the background of a flickering, fiery, red crown.

"Bad news," I said, approaching the fire. "But there's nothing to be done about it."

"I see-e . . ." he drawled, glancing at my hands. A strange look of satisfaction and mockery appeared on his face; he seemed to rejoice in the power of the circumstances supporting his icy despair.

My heart sank. I sat down, but in full view of the nocturnal river, the wilderness, and the silence of the starry sky, I wanted to rise up, to stand tall and hold my head high. The silence oppressed me. Baranov lay down and closed his eyes; as the light of the fire fell onto his drawn face, it cast shadows over the sockets of his eyes and the hollows of his cheeks, sharpening his features; the man lying before me resembled a corpse.

I, too, lay down and closed my eyes, feeling as though I were sinking into the earth, descending into its very depths—and I fell asleep. I was tormented by hungry dreams. I saw warm, freshly baked loaves, chunks of fried meat, dishes of fruit, game pies, sumptuous hors d'oeuvres aplenty, and wine. With the great zeal of a cannibal, I devoured all these marvels, unable to sate myself. The Russian and I awoke at dawn, our teeth chattering from the cold.

The fire had gone out. Black embers smoked feebly amid the gray sand. The river, white with a gauze of mist, slowly eddied, while the army of morning clouds was brightened by the pale fire of the stirring sun.

I leaped up, hopping from one foot to the other and waving my arms to get warm. Propping himself up on his elbow, the Russian said:

"We're done for . . ."

"We cannot be certain of that," I retorted.

"Damned will to live," he continued, while I scrutinized him and saw the face of a man who was totally deranged and on the verge of madness. He was not even pale but a bluish gray; his wide-open eyes glittered nervously. "Yes, dying . . . is necessary . . . but the moment you begin to suffer, your body revolts. Do you believe in God?" he asked unexpectedly.

"Yes, I believe in God."

"I do not," said the Russian. "But I, you see—I need there to be someone higher, cleverer, stronger, and better than me. I'm prepared to pray . . . but to whom? I don't know. Pray for bread? No. Pray that my strength is returned to me, that my life becomes orderly . . . and you?"

I was amazed by his ability to speak everything that came into his head. I felt ill at ease. I was waiting for something like yesterday— that peculiar soul-baring to which I myself am not inclined. And so it happened.

"Say," said the Russian without a smile, apparently quite inspired by the mood that had taken him, "perhaps it'll be easier, better for us . . . Let's pray—without any gestures, words, or bowing. When all else fails, autosuggestion—"

"Stop," I interrupted him. "You aren't a believer. Go ahead and pray—split your head open for all I care. But I, a believer, won't stand for it. God must be respected. You can't go crawling to him like a beaten dog only when you're up against a wall. It smacks of the nephew who remembers his rich uncle only because the dear nephew has signed a false promissory note. I dare say He doesn't enjoy seeing his creation numbed with fear either. My attitude toward these things differs from yours; and so, my dear chap, gather your arms and legs . . . we're going to try and find ourselves a bite to eat."

He thought about it and laughed. We set off side by side, and I noticed that he was looking at me out of the corner of his eye, as if trying to fathom something—just as I in turn pondered the makeup of his awkward, effeminate soul.

V. THE THIRD TEMPTATION AND THE CHARITY OF A BULLET

I.

What with the way we were walking, we must have looked like drunken workmen. But we were in no mood to laugh. As we walked along the water's edge, I pondered the need for food—the thought singularly possessed me. Baranov's look of dejection was taking a toll on my nerves. I purposely marched on ahead of him so as not to see my disheveled, unkempt companion.

Having now passed the sandy depressions full of muddied water along the shoreline, we continued to make our way through the forest. It stretched all the way to the water's edge and was relatively sparse. The electric shock of sudden hope struck me; I crouched down, peering up at a tree from which I was being showered with bits of branches. Drawing my revolver, I approached the trunk and made a sign to Baranov to halt and leave me to it.

In the tree, swinging its tail, pulling faces, showing off, and puffing out its cheeks, sat a sizable monkey, throwing all sorts of rubbish at us. I took aim. The monkey, thinking I was playing with it, gave out a piercing screech, wrapped its tail around the branch on which it was sitting, and dropped down, head first, swinging back and forth, like an acrobat about to let go of a trapeze. I fired and hit it square in the forehead; its tail unwound and the furry body with its red behind fell before my feet.

I went up to it, squatted down, opened the animal's clenched teeth with my penknife and, running my hand in its cheek pouches, pulled out a handful of barely chewed walnut pulp. I swallowed this on the spot without thinking. Lifting my head, I saw Baranov leaning over; his face, now red with excitement and nervous laughter, beamed with joy and hungry longing. He giggled almost hysterically, seizing the monkey by the paw. Pulling out my handkerchief, I spread it on the ground, split open the animal's skin and, having hastily and haphazardly chopped the still-warm red meat into little pieces, I piled it onto the cloth.

We ate, grunting with pleasure and morbid greed . . . I remember—I was in such a rush to chew that I bit my finger. Just then the sun rose, shedding its light on us, our repast, and the dead monkey; its fiery splendor dappled the forest with smoky bands of light, and the day began. The triumphant foray of the dew-bathed luminary captured the Earth and made Her its mistress, delighting her with caresses.

Feeling the weight of my brazen stomach, I lowered my hand clutching a half-eaten morsel and saw the Russian watching me with the heavy, dull gaze of a man who has gorged himself to the point of disgust. He must have thought the same of me. With a contented sigh, we lay down, stretched out, and diligently applied ourselves, as it were, to digestion.

Our strength slowly returned to us. I began to feel the density, weight, and musculature of my body. The movement of my hands and fingers acquired a lively elasticity, my legs felt as though they had recovered from a fainting fit, every organ, so to speak, heaved a sigh of relief. Only now, sated, did we start exchanging lazy, good-humored phrases about food and drink.

"Do you like steak tartare?" Baranov asked, picking at his teeth.

"What is that?"

"Ah . . . it's what we just ate. Raw meat."

"Yes, it's delicious. I like," I added thoughtfully, "cold strawberry jelly and pies served with sago."

"I love chicken and rice. It's a pity we have nothing to drink. Take our Russian vodka . . . it's a marvel."

I knew the miraculous qualities of this truly enchanting beverage and licked my lips.

"Come on," I said. "We aren't there yet." The Russian got to his feet and so did I; the forest, enchanted by the sun, hummed with the life of myriad woodland critters, the deep blue sky exhaled the loveliness of a southern day, and life didn't seem at all bad. Having bundled what was left of the monkey into the handkerchief and tied the bundle to a stick that I placed over my shoulder, I set off at a brisk pace, examining the shoreline.

Life is a true patchwork, Inger, like the shadows cast by leaves on a mountain spring with its golden shimmer and many-colored stones on the bottom; joy and woe, lucky and unlucky incidents rush by, smiling and frowning like a noisy crowd before avid eyes; true wisdom lies in not being surprised by it all. I wasn't surprised when, after several hours of difficult woodland terrain, I saw, from a low ledge overhanging the river, two tree trunks bobbing there in the water. These were enormous trees that had been born away in a flood; their roots looked like a witch's tangle of hair.

The work fell largely to me. Baranov assisted wearily and lackadaisically. Having flayed off about forty long strips of bark, we used them to tie the trees together; then, having covered them with a mass of branches, we carved two rather unwieldy poles, dulling the knife and finally breaking it in the process. Using the poles as levers, the Russian and I heaved the ends of the trees out of the sand and into the water, whereupon we went aboard and pushed off.

The raft sank deep into the water, but the incredible thickness of the trunks maintained a dry surface to sit on. And so, on this narrow structure that resembled a drowning hay bale, we sailed quietly downstream, sitting nearer to the roots, which spread out their enormous claws over and into the water. At first, as though debating whether or not to receive us into its flow, the river pulled the raft along the shore; then, turning at a rapid whirlpool, the raft moved smoothly toward the middle of the river and was carried with the flow, bobbing up and down like the back of a horse going at a walking pace.

II.

It was night: darkness and silence stood all around. Ahead of us, bringing joy to my heart, countless lights outlined the darkness; from behind a promontory, the amphitheater that was San Riol came into view—the city, the battle of people.

Setting down our poles, we stood shoulder to shoulder, watching the approaching fiery pattern of the dark. I felt calm and quietly cheerful; even my irritation with Baranov had subsided and was replaced by a warm amicability—one way or another, we had made this journey together.

I placed my hand on his shoulder and said:

"It would seem we're almost there. Everything's going well."

"I feel wretched," he retorted. "Ah, Bangok, somehow you've bound me to you. The city frightens me. It's the same all over again: sleeping rough, looking for crumbs of bread and work, fatigue, a life half-starved . . . loneliness. It's as though my thirty years count for nothing, as though I'm only just beginning to fight for my existence . . . It's dull. Let's turn back . . ." he added quietly. "Back, to the forest. People are terrible, man is inhumane. Countless cruel jokers await us in this wicked life. Let's turn back. We'll buy or steal rifles, and, at the first possibility, we'll leave these people. The years will pass in quiet savagery, and those times we spent among people, fearing them, loving or hating them, will be erased from our memories; we'll even forget their faces. We shall immerse ourselves in all that surrounds us—the grass, trees, flowers, and animals. Within the stern wisdom of nature, the soul, free of man, feels at ease, and heaven will bless us—the pure heaven of the wilderness."

"You've reverted to childishness again," I said, touched by his despair. "I am a warrior, a fighter, a stubborn man, cock of the walk. No. I'm raring to go. The poisonous air of the city excites me."

Our talk was halted by a small island that appeared out of the darkness. I wanted to go around it and even picked up my pole in order to set the raft on the necessary course, but suddenly a useful thought struck me.

"We have nowhere to spend the night in the city," I said. "Let's go ashore and spend the night there."

The Russian nodded. Soon we were sitting in front of a fire, roasting the monkey's hindquarters on sticks, smoking and thinking.

III.

"Look," said the Russian. "Look at the water."

The fire, on which we had lavished wood, illuminated the river for some distance, blazing like a burning barn. Red-orange water surrounded the shore, and the light of the fire, tangled in the currents, painted changeable, iridescent patterns on them in carmine, blue, and gold.

"Yes, it's beautiful," I said.

"Doesn't it seem to you," the Russian began, gazing at the water, "that I'll be gone before long?"

"Gone where?" I coolly asked, already inured to the eccentricities of my companion.

He gazed fixedly at me, before closing his eyes and continuing:

"I'm not sure that I exist. Perhaps I'm but a mere interweaving of light and shadow upon this phantom-red expanse of water before you."

"Whatever do you mean?"

"Give me your revolver for a moment."

With a shrug, I extracted the weapon from my pocket and handed it to him. There was only one bullet left—I remembered this by chance, far from suspecting anything.

Still sitting there, Baranov pressed the muzzle to his temple and turned away. I saw the back of his head, the sudden shudder of his shoulders and, frozen, realized what was happening. It had come about so unexpectedly that I opened my mouth several times before I cried out:

"What's wrong with you?"

"I'm tired . . ." he said, bending down toward the earth. "It's all stuff and nonsense."

Covering my face with my hands, I awaited the shot.

"I cannot," Baranov cried in anger, gripping my by the arms. "Better you do it . . . I beg you!"

For a long while, I looked at his deathly face, mulling over this much too solemn request and . . . Inger . . . I found that it would indeed be better for him.

We walked over to a precipice. I led him by the hand. And there, feeling for the soft skin of his forehead with the muzzle, I turned away and carried out what my companion had asked of me, having grown too weary to go on.

The shot was deafening. Doubling over, the Russian's body fell into the water, its pale hands moving, illumined by the fire, and vanished in the streaming depths. But for a long time it seemed to me as I stood there, head bowed, that I could see his face serenely smiling back from the red, iridescent ripples as they flickered with the fire's reflections.

■ □ ■

Two days later, I enlisted on the *Southern Cross* and set sail for Shanghai.

Life is fascinating, Inger, so very fascinating. So much fear and beauty! One can sometimes die laughing! But it's a sin to cry.

My pipe has gone out, my dear fellow . . .

THE POISONED ISLAND

I.

According to the tale told by Captain Tart, who arrived in Ahuan Skap from New Zealand, and his statement to the local authorities, which was corroborated by evidence provided by the ship's crew, on the little island of Farfont in the South Pacific, there was an episode wherein by general consensus the entire population of islanders committed mass suicide—with the exception of two children, aged three and seven, who were left in the care of the ship *Viola*, in the command of Captain Tart.

The island of Farfont lies at 41° 17' South, well clear of any shipping lanes. It was discovered in 1869 by Van Lott, the master of a whaler, and is often unmarked on maps, even on the official ones. It has no commercial or political significance, and John Webster, in his *History of Merchant Shipping Navigation*, disdainfully classifies such islands as "useless trifles," noting of Farfont in particular that the island is exceptionally small and rocky.

The following was recorded in the logbook of the *Viola*:

June 14, 1920. Strong southwesterly wind. Thrown off course all day,
stormy toward evening. Three sails lost.

June 15, 1920. Mainsail and foresail torn by wind. Mainsail replaced,
heading south. Seaman Nock fell overboard and perished.

June 16, 1920. Moderate wind. Land sighted at noon. Farfont Island.
Dropped anchor. Captain Tart, First Mate Insar, and five seamen
gone ashore.

These five seamen were Haverney, Drokis, Bikan, Gabster, and
Strock.

The captain revealed that before the boat was launched, he
had observed someone through his telescope—a figure standing
on the shore. That person had quickly vanished into the forest.
Reckoning on the basis of this that the little island was populated,
the captain—though he noted no traces of habitation when the
boat arrived ashore—nevertheless found it necessary to replenish
supplies and set out in search of the islanders. Indeed, they soon
came upon five thatched log cabins set amid picturesque and lush
vegetation in a small valley of astonishing beauty. There was no
one to be seen. Nobody appeared even when the captain fired his
revolver into the air to attract the natives' attention. No smoke was
coming from any of the chimneys, and, on the whole, the curious
marked silence of the community struck Tart forcefully. He began
to make a tour of the structures, whose doors he found unlocked,
but inside the first three houses he inspected, he found nobody,
either asleep or awake. In the fifth house he visited, there was
also no one, but in the fourth, the seafarers found a man who was
dying or in an unconscious state; he was lying on the floor with
only the whites of his eyes showing, his face pale and damp
with sweat. A feeble groan burst convulsively from his throat.

A young boy and a girl of six or seven were standing beside him, very frightened and crying.

The captain began to question the boy but, getting nowhere with him, turned instead to the young girl. From her disjointed and obviously confused idea of what had gone on, he learned only that "everyone went away"—where exactly, she did not know; "Uncle Scorrey," the man who was now lying senseless, had remained with her and little Philip. The girl, who was called Liv (short for Livia), also said that only half an hour previously, Scorrey had been joking with her and saying that there were people coming to take her and Philip away to the "mainland," where life would be good for them. Scorrey himself had drunk something from a mug that was still standing on the table. After this, he had said that he was dying, lay down on the floor, and began to groan. He had then said to Liv: "Give the letter to the man with the gold buttons." And that was all the children knew.

There was a strong fragrance emanating from the blossoming shrubbery by the window, which set the sailors' heads spinning. Despite this, the captain, sniffing what remained of the murky liquid at the bottom of the mug, deemed it necessary to take immediate measures in order to save Scorrey. It was presumed that he had taken poison. The liquid had an unpleasant, pungent, bitter smell. Tart opened the unfortunate man's clenched teeth with a pocket knife and, with nothing better to hand, began pouring vodka into Scorrey's mouth, little by little, lest the unconscious man choke. Half an hour later he had emptied his own flask, as well as Haverney's and Drokis's. Meanwhile, the mariners boiled water in a clay pot and placed bunches of grass that had been soaked in the boiling water around the naked Scorrey—thus creating a semblance of a bathhouse. Tart acted more out of inspiration than out of adherence to any medical guidelines, but at any rate, the patient stopped wheezing. Next, they applied poultices, massaged him, and, finally, the patient opened his eyes. He had the look of a madman. He said nothing and understood nothing; he began to speak only as they were arriving at Ahuan Skap, but the intelligibility of his speech was scarcely that of a rational being.

The children, completely pacified by Drokis's pocket watch, which had been entrusted to their care, were sent aboard the *Viola* on stretchers along with the revived Scorrey, while the captain set about investigating the sorry incident. Scorrey's letter, since submitted to the judicial authorities, was written on the title page of a Bible that had yellowed with age. Instead of ink, the quick-darkening juice of a plant seemed to have been used. Tart read the semiliterate but enigmatic and terrible lines. The following is what was written (it was undated):

> We, the inhabitants of Farfont, declare and bear witness before others that we, finding it no longer possible to go on living, since we are all insane, or else have been possessed by demons, voluntarily and by mutual agreement, commit suicide. The present letter has been entrusted to Joseph Scorrey until such a time that he is able to deliver it to a boat or ship. By common consent and with his good agreement, Scorrey does not have the right to commit suicide until it is possible to send away the children, Philip and Livia, who have been left alive in view of their tender age.

Thereafter followed twenty-four signatures along with the respective ages of each suicide. The eldest was 111 and the youngest 14. Not far from the village, Tart discovered a tall, freshly raised mound—a mass grave. The withered flowers on the wooden cross were removed by the crew of the *Viola* and replaced with fresh wreaths.

"The general impression of all this," concluded Captain Tart, "was such, as if a bound man had been slaughtered before our very eyes. We hurried, as fast as we could, to fix the rigging, and on the following morning we left the terrible island of Farfont."

II.

Thus the *Viola* dropped anchor in Ahuan Skap, in possession of the following evidence that an entire populace had committed suicide: the remnants of a poisonous liquid, which had been poured into a carefully stoppered bottle; the crazed Scorrey; an open letter signed by twenty-four people who were now dead; and two children, a boy and a girl, who were, by our standards, completely feral.

Further questioning of the children added very little to the testimonies of the sailors and the captain. The boy could offer nothing at all, since he scarcely knew how to speak, while the girl, evidently confusing her memories of life on the island with her impressions of the voyage and the city, uttered patent absurdities:

"Father said they'd kill us all."

"Who would?"

"Some people. There were a lot of them."

"Did you see them?"

"No."

"Did ships come to the island?"

"A very big one came, taller than me."

"Try to remember, Liv, when was this? A long time ago?"

"Yes, a long time ago."

"Or perhaps not so long ago?"

"Not so long ago."

She could not orient herself in time, and her subsequent remarks about the ship, the people who visited the island, and their number bore the mark of a dark, half-forgotten dream. She then began to tell how everyone had feared they would be killed, and how at night, many ships arrived and fired at the houses. Several ships were airborne. The investigator put this down to a child's fantasy, adulterated by the sailors' tales, and also attributed it to the children's marked disposition toward mystification. Still, he wrote down everything, but only as a formality.

And yet, a peculiar and rare circumstance emerged from the girl's account—one that virtually eliminated the possibility of any outside interference in the affair. The six-year-old child recalled only one visit to Farfont by a single ship; assuming that lasting impressions on the memory begin at the age of three, then, for the duration of three years, the island had been cut off from all contact with the outside world, which naturally gave rise to the question: How often did ships visit the shores of Farfont, and did these visits not constitute a sort of legend in the years that followed? Put plainly, was Farfont not such an out-of-the-way place, where ships stopped but a few times in a century, and even then by accident, like the *Viola*?

In view of Farfont's near-total obscurity as far as administrative authorities were concerned, and owing to its almost perfect nonexistence for all major and minor shipping lanes, the answer to this question was, self-evidently, affirmative. In that case, there could not have been any outside criminal interference in the affair of the natives of Farfont, and the isolation of the settlement was confirmed by the testimony of the crew of the *Viola*. Domestic utensils, implements, clothing, and other items that the sailors had swiftly examined bore traces of local manufacture, with the exception of several old rifles, books, and trinkets such as a shard of a mirror and a piece of fabric that had at one time ended up on Farfont. As for the island's ecology, everyone concurred that it was "a very pretty spot." More impressionable than others, Gabster declared that the island was a veritable paradise. Captain Tart expatiated on the island in more detail but, being a practical man, noted the richness and fertility of the soil, as well as the abundance of excellent springwater.

Below we shall encounter a detailed description of the island, and so let us return to an examination of the facts. On the basis of the testimony, the investigator fixed upon two versions of events: (1) the inhabitants of Farfont, under the pressure of strange and inescapable circumstances, reasons, and motives—of a local and not external origin—voluntarily, by consensus, committed suicide; (2) they were killed for reasons not uncovered during the investigation by the only person left alive, the now insane Scorrey, who, in an attempt to divert suspicion, confected a spurious letter containing the forged signatures of the Farfont inhabitants attesting to their suicide.

The second version, corresponding better to the simplicity of the criminal investigator's mind and to the irresistible gravitation of the authorities toward the unmasking of malicious intent, even in cases where a person has simply fallen and cracked open his head, was unfortunately picked up on too eagerly by certain newspapers, whose publishers thus saved the public any exasperating puzzlement, while the reporters maintained the facile position of "common sense"—the very one that should be avoided like the plague with regard to certain phenomena.

The *Morning Herald* wrote:

> Ha! We are asked to believe that an entire village of healthy people, raised in the bosom of nature, people who knew no excess, who were unaffected and half-savage, experienced some kind of common tragedy. It is of course possible that the men might have quarreled over a native beauty. But what of the women? Yet in this case we are supposed to assume a general disillusionment with life, a collapse of ideals and so forth! However, Scorrey is alive, as are two of the children, and they, more than anything, convince us of the villain's cunning foresight. He knew that a ship might call at Farfont, and he was prepared for this unlikely event. Now he stands before us as

the savior of these children, who have supposedly been entrusted to his, Scorrey's, care. The children could quite conceivably have slept while this diabolical murderer poisoned his fellow villagers. Note that he also drank the poison but did not die. Clearly the dose had been calculated through experiment . . .

And so it continued.

The *Observer*, which insisted on mass suicide, stuck primarily to the testimony of the *Viola*'s captain. "Besides the gravity of the poisoning," wrote the *Observer*,

a poisoning that very nearly dispatched Scorrey to the hereafter, his innocence is supported by the sighting of a mass grave. According to Captain Tart, a mound was discovered in the vicinity of the village; it had been dug and filled conscientiously, covered over with topsoil and topped with a durable cross. It constitutes the surest evidence that Scorrey executed with respect the lamentable duty thrust upon him by fate. Several rowboats were at his disposal; had he been the murderer, he could have thrown the corpses into the sea without haste or hindrance and proclaimed that all the inhabitants had drowned on a fishing expedition. These are merely possible scenarios. Naturally, the reasons for the suicide are inscrutable, since the text of the letter, which is written quite lucidly, suggests neither madness nor "possession by demons," but only the consequences of certain factors that have not yet come to light. The authors of the letter clearly harbored strong doubts as to the possibility of its being made public; otherwise, we might perhaps be dealing with a lengthier document outlining the situation in detail. The letter's brevity also indicates the haste with which these unfortunate souls rushed to do away with themselves. All we can do is await Scorrey's recovery, for which, according to Doctor Nessar, there is now hope.

The analysis of the liquid recovered by Captain Tart established the presence of a strong poison.

Scorrey, assigned to Professor Arno Nessar's clinic, was declared to be suffering from a mild form of temporary insanity. Scorrey spent four months at Nessar's clinic, during which previously unknown circumstances came to light owing to an expedition and a publication by the psychiatrist De Maistre.

III.

De Maistre, who had devoted a significant part of his life to the study of suicide, was for some considerable time besieged by journalists, ladies, officials, and undercover policemen; to each of them he pointed out the obvious intricacy of the affair, although he himself was inclined toward the hypothesis of suicide.

On August 11, subsidized by the magazine *Union* and hoping to obtain new leads through a private visit to the island, he sailed from Ahuan Skap aboard the *Terentius*, a steamer that had been chartered for this very purpose, and returned on September 24 to astound the world with what he had uncovered, facts that cast strong doubt on the view that the deaths of the Farfontese had come about independently of outside factors. Namely: not far from the sea, in a rocky hollow by the shore, De Maistre found forty-four wine bottles (a product foreign to Farfont), a white safety pin, and an aged, half-disintegrated issue of the *Guard Ship*, dated May 18, 1920. It was this last article that finally convinced De Maistre that another ship had visited the island not long before the *Viola*.

Meanwhile, thanks to the publication of De Maistre's findings and, more generally, the wave of publicity accorded the affair, the editorial board of the *Observer* received a letter from Bombay that was signed by a Captain Brahms and witnessed by a notary. Brahms had served in the Sidney Transport Company aboard the steamer *Rickshaw*. His report constituted, as it were, a gateway to the truth, whose melancholy visage appeared in full only on the day of Scorrey's recovery. Here is Brahms's letter:

On April 5, 1920, the *Rickshaw*, in search of the lost ship *Vendôme*, was thrown off course by a cyclone and, having sustained significant damage, carried far to the south. On the morning of April 20, we spotted a small island that was not shown on the map; none of my crew had visited it, nor had they heard of its existence. The inhabitants, who had interbred, explained that they were descended from two families of emigrants that had been put ashore in this secluded corner of the world in 1870 by the military cruiser *Brobdingnag*, for reasons of a political nature. Because of this, only two families lived on Farfont: the Scorreys and the Gonzálezes. Their pursuits were farming, hunting, and fishing. Placed in exceptional circumstances, they manufactured or obtained all of life's necessities with their own hands and resources, with the exception of a small number of things that had been brought by the first settlers or sold to the island subsequently by ships that happened to pass by.

The last ship to visit them was the mutinous *Scarab*, which dropped anchor off the shore of Farfont six years ago. You can imagine with what fatiguing attention and excitement we were met. The inhabitants spilled out onto the shore, surrounding these miraculous visitors. Everything, right down to the buttons on our clothing, became the subject of endless disputes, questions, and explanations. It transpired that we had arrived on the wedding day of the young Antonio González and the no less young Johanna Scorrey. Feasting, unceasing questions about life in the outside world, and a primitive but quite charming spectacle lay in store for us.

The bridegroom, dressed in clothing of a fairly good cut and an enormous straw hat, left everyone in agreement about his looks: he was a well-built, swarthy young man with a slightly foolish smile and large, serious eyes, in which one could espy an awareness of the moment's importance and solemnity. However, at the crucial moment, the bride hid herself around the corner of the house— embarrassed, of course, by our presence—and we wasted no little patience before we were able to see her charming visage. Finally, blushing crimson, she came out of her hiding place. The skipper Polladiou, a master of the compliment, began vociferously extolling her virtues, whereupon she became markedly more cheerful and deigned to look at him with one eye that was as black as a walnut and as naive as a week-old chick. Her simple dress of coarse home-spun cloth fitted her pretty, slender, still awkward figure well.

The wedding ceremony was a simple and dignified affair. We stood on the shore of a stream that glittered blue and white in the fissures of the granite that formed an intricate deep-red arc across the stream in front of us. Along the arc stretched velvet clusters of creeping plants. The sun's rays, which scattered over the arc, made the air look like a blazing bonfire or a golden curtain, through which the contours of the shore shone in pale-blue shadows. The shore was dappled with colorful flowers. On the horizon, a narrow sickle of ocean glinted.

Grandfather Scorrey read several prayers and excerpts from the Bible, and with his aged hand, he joined the burning hands of the young couple, whereafter we returned to the village. There, in a rocky hollow by the ocean shore, a feast began, which we irrigated with two crates of wine and rum. I began to tell stories of the momentous world affairs of the day, the inventions and the titanic struggle of our times, relishing the effect my tale would have on these people.

Indeed, they were shaken. I painted for them as complete a picture of the gigantic struggle of nine nations as I could, describing all its major events, its timeline, its movement and tempo, the technical and moral resources deployed by the antagonists. There were those who expressed doubt as to the veracity of my words, so I gave them an old edition of the *Guard Ship* that we happened to have. If people from Mars or the Moon were to land on Earth, it would not have drawn such murderous interest as we, with our *Guard Ship* and our tales of battles between million-strong armies: they asked us so many questions that it would have taken half a lifetime to answer them all in any detail.

I confess that in spite of the gravity of the events that blighted the last decade, I experienced an involuntary sense of pride or, rather, of superiority over these half-Robinsons when I began to tell them of man's ingenious achievements in the fields of aeronautics, radio, chemistry, naval design, and ordnance. I described to them the appearance of dreadnaughts, Zeppelins, airplanes, concrete bunkers, and armored fortifications, setting my audience atremble with the weight of a sixteen-inch shell or the dimensions of a crater following the explosion of a bomb capable of sweeping away a village.

We talked throughout the night. On the following day, toward evening, the *Rickshaw* finished repairing the damage and weighed anchor, arriving in Melbourne on May 3. All the circumstances of our sojourn on Farfont are set forth in this letter; I consider it necessary to add that news of the tragic and unusual death of our former hosts has produced an indescribably painful impression on all of us who met them. If my report, which ostensibly has no direct bearing on the matter, can shed light on the mystery of the death of these cheerful and hospitable people, I shall experience the bitter gladness of a man who has enabled the discovery of a terrible truth.

IV.

On September 20, Scorrey finally gave his testimony. The stenographic record of Scorrey's account is greatly confused, replete with repetitions and digressions; moreover, the speaker's very language is so unlike our modes of thought and expression—modes developed through continual association with a multitude of people, present and absent, via letters, telegrams, books, and newspapers—that we have found it necessary to imbue his testimony with a common literary form, omitting neither the facts nor the impressions produced by them. "It was very hard for us," said Scorrey,

> to believe the words of Captain Brahms, who told us that Europe had suffered a terrible war while we, suspecting nothing of the sort, had heard only the lapping of waves and the rustle of blossoming branches. However, Brahms showed us a newspaper, which, though old, convincingly relayed the self-same story.
>
> Throughout the night the captain and his crew talked with us, initiating us fearful, shaken, and spellbound people into the terrible scale of the events. We learned that hundreds of millions of people had found themselves in the grip of war. We learned that many cities and whole countries had been destroyed. We learned that man now flew in flocks on winged machines, dropping bombs on ships, houses, and forests. We learned that by means of a special asphyxiating wind, the lungs of tens of thousands of soldiers were burned, and much else. And also that no one knew whether there would be another such war again.
>
> In the morning, the captain and his crew returned to their ship to repair the damage, while we carried on discussing what we had heard. None of us even thought of working that day. Each appraised the goings-on in his own way. Some averred that Brahms had not told us the whole truth and that the war was probably still raging. Others maintained that it was a propitious time for pirates and that soon we would very likely come under attack. On the whole, we were gripped by a mood of suspicion and melancholy; each of us became obsessed with forebodings, making predictions left and right about events in the Europe we so vaguely imagined.

Somebody—I do not remember who exactly—said that it was quite possible that in a year or two, we would be the only inhabitants left on earth, because the belligerents would undoubtedly destroy one another with their monstrous inventions. Leon Scorrey, my nephew, said that the danger lay elsewhere, in a mass exodus of millions of people from the heavily populated continents—people who would scatter to the farthest corners of the earth in search of safety. A great number of outsiders, well armed, could, of course, conquer us, taking our property, cultivated lands, and boats. It was even proposed that we ask the *Rickshaw* to take us with it, lest we be left alone in fear and ignorance, but the coward who suggested this was intimidated and brought to his senses after it was explained to him that ignorance was better than what was then taking place in the great nations. That evening, however, as the *Rickshaw* was weighing anchor, two of our elders went aboard with a request that they tell everyone about us and send a ship back for those who want to leave, if any so decided. Brahms calmed them with a promise to do just that. At sunset, the *Rickshaw* got under way and departed.

Like many others, I passed that night in a heavy half-slumber, getting up from time to time to help my wife, who had fallen ill from all this unrest. Two days after the *Rickshaw*'s departure, Juan González, who had gone fishing with Johanna's husband, Antonio, came back early and announced that half a mile from shore, they had spotted a shiny round object that was studded with nails and bobbing on the waves. Before long Antonio arrived and confirmed this. "We very nearly sailed into it," he said, turning pale. Apparently this was one of those floating mines that Brahms had mentioned.

At noon a powerful crackling rumble resounded above our heads, and everyone came running out of their houses. Terrified workers rushed from the fields. Up above, skirting a tree, an enormous dark object with changing contours flew as fast as a gull; after altering its course by the forest, it plunged down and vanished.

We were so frightened that everyone cried out at once without understanding each other. Now there could be no doubt, even among the most skeptical, that all around the island, unseen by us, sea battles were raging and scouts were flying over us, reconnoitering the vicinity. A short while later, the sound of muffled hits or explosions came from the western horizon. Everyone rushed to the shore. At the line where the water met the sky, a great deal of smoke was curling up; from there, dulled by the distance, the slow, heavy sound of gunfire reached us, and the earth seemed to tremble beneath our feet. So it went on for an hour or more; then it all stopped.

That evening, three of the Gonzálezes, who had gone to the forest to fetch firewood, came back out of breath. They had heard the clatter of many hooves, shouts, the clash of sabers, and moaning, though they had seen no one. Alain Scorrey, who had at that time been with his wife by the waterfall, returned a little later; they had seen on the cliff an armed rider looking in the direction of the forest, shading his eyes with his hand. Having spotted Scorrey, he gave a slight tug on the reins and disappeared.

"There's been a landing on the island," Alain said after he had told his story and heard González's. "We don't know what kind of war this is; danger, perhaps death, is hanging over us. We'd better search the island."

Antonio González and I volunteered to do this. We spent half of the following day scouring Farfont. Though we failed to detect any traces, we did hear ringing and clattering noises accompanied by shouting. After we returned, we found the others greatly depressed. The women were crying. Our tale surprised and frightened them even further.

"Perhaps," said old man Ransom, shaking his head, "Perhaps, people have found a way to make themselves invisible. This is, they say, a time of wondrous inventions."

"What about the corpses?" I asked.

But he did not answer me.

"Look, look!" my sister then shouted, and, tracing the line of her horrified gaze, we observed that the entire sky was covered in mysterious, darting ships with strange riggings that none of us had ever before seen; they recalled sailing ships and had what appeared to be a reflection beneath them, in the air. A roaring and whistling came from them, as did percussive sounds and the ringing of bells, and soon everything was obscured in the smoke of gunfire, which echoed in our ears like a death sentence. Women fainted, ran indoors, and wept. We men stood there as if bound and powerless to move. Finally the last sterns of these monsters vanished beyond the cliffs, and after we had gathered together again, we were able to admit to one another, in fear and terror, our general despair. Nobody could explain what had happened. That night, only the children slept . . .

A month and a further two weeks passed with the same incessant, oppressive, merciless, threatening phenomena, and ultimately we became half-crazed and utterly pitiful. We feared to stray far from our homes, lest we find ourselves alone; all work was abandoned; disturbing, oppressive dreams haunted those who threw themselves into bed seeking repose; the children, who were frightened most of all by the threat that had rent our quiet way of life, cried like their mothers, who had grown thin from the constant terror; we men, resolving to cast off the tyranny of these warring forces, made rounds of the island, in order to convince ourselves that we were its sole masters, and every time we convinced ourselves we fell prey to ever more acute despair. A dull rumbling resounded above our heads day and night; the sound of faraway explosions stopped people in their tracks, midsentence, and a groaning and howling, now quiet and plaintive, now loud and replete with rage and pain, filled the air. At night a powerful cannonade could be heard, as if an endless battle were being fought there: people who would go out to watch the ocean would see colossal dark ships of unknown nationality pursuing one another. We no longer knew any peace. What was happening to us? What was going on around us? We wearied of asking each other questions. Finally we assembled at the house of my second cousin, Alain Scorrey, one evening, and he told us that he saw no way out of our hopeless situation other than death: "We can neither stay awake nor sleep. We have fallen under the spell of some diabolical nightmare, or, rather, some horrific reality, which, by means unknown to us, has attained a perfect incomprehensibility. We are cut off from the world, knowing nothing, innocent, losing our reason, and soon we shall go mad and fill the air with savage howls. And why? We cannot know. I propose that we die voluntarily."

There was nobody who wanted or could bring himself to object. In the profound silence of those present, Alain prepared lots, equal in number to the men: whoever pulled out the shortest straw was to remain alive in order to bury the others. That misfortune fell to me. Thereupon my sister, the widow Alice Scorrey, said: "So be it, but I won't take my Philip and Livia with me." And so she entrusted them to my care, begging me to wait until a ship arrived and not to kill myself until an opportunity arose to take the children off the island.

I resisted as much as I could but eventually had to yield to her pleadings; besides, there was a real necessity for someone to take care of the burials. I began to weep, however, once I had envisaged clearly the great burden of my future. Alone, full of dark memories, with two children on my hands, I had to bear and endure suffering worse than death by torture. Perhaps because my reason was clouded and I did not fully understand what was taking place, I agreed.

At this point in his tale, Scorrey lost consciousness. When he revived, he was clearly hurrying to finish telling the remainder. Here the stenograph is muddled, disconnected, and brief.

> A veritable fever of impatience seized everyone. They wrote the note, then Alain brought the poison. I left, taking the children away and telling them that the others would soon follow. Not for all the world would I have returned there, to Alain's house. I lay semiconscious. What happened there, I do not know. The sun was setting by the time I decided to open that fateful door.
> And I saw . . .

Scorrey refused to tell how he buried these unfortunates. The rest of his testimony—a bleak tale of a sickly man with two young children, whom he had to feed and comfort by thinking up all sorts of stories to explain the general disappearance—may be found in the *Ahuan Skap Monthly*, a magazine that carried the most detailed account of the Farfont affair. Its author, quoting Miller, Quincey, and Ribot, advances the hypothesis of mass hallucination, and also "a fear of life"—a particular psychological aberration, which is the subject of a detailed study by Krafft.

In conclusion, the author describes the island's beautiful vegetation, its mild climate, and the unique enchantments of its unpretentious, harmless seclusion; he ends the article with the following observation:

> These were the happiest people on earth, killed by the echo of long-silenced salvoes that are unparalleled in history.

THE HEART OF THE WILDERNESS

I.

The discovery of diamond deposits at Cordon Brun brought with it a taste for all things civilized. But the only discovery that interests us is that of a splendid café there. Among its miscellaneous patrons let us now single out three skeptical minds, three artistic temperaments, three lost souls—talented men, to be sure, but who could no longer perceive the *kernel* of things. In their various ways they had come to see only the *shell*.

This outlook of theirs directed their talents toward the art of deception. They made of it both their vocation and their religion. And each in his own way achieved perfection in it. Thus, for instance, the legend of an eighteen-hundred-carat diamond (maliciously and subtly devised by them between glasses of champagne and arias from *Jocelyn*) had caused an almighty commotion, launching thousands of rogues in quest of a miracle, bound for the waterfall at Alpetri, where, it was said, the monstrous gem glittered in the rocks above the water. Et cetera, et cetera. Thanks to them, Stella Dijon was convinced that Harry Evans, who was hopelessly in love with her (which he was not), had married the O'Neal girl out of despair. Drama ensued, the shameful outcome of which did credit to no one: Evans got Stella *on his mind* and put a bullet through his brain.

Hart, Weber, and Conseil liked to amuse themselves. The visions they espied in the patterns of smoke rising up from their strong cigars governed their wily, carefree lives. One morning they were sitting in comfortable rocking chairs in the café, smiling silently like seers: pale despite the heat, affable and pensive, men without hearts or futures.

Their yacht was still anchored at Cordon Rouge, and they were reluctant to leave, savoring as they were their impressions of the diamond fever amid all the filth and the avarice glittering in men's eyes.

The morning's heat was already abating in the shade of the banana trees. Through the open doors of the café Congo, across the alleyway, dusty mounds of earth could be glimpsed, and every now and then a pickaxe would fly up into the air above them. Throughout the digs, cork helmets flashed white and straw hats showed red under the sun. A wagon was being drawn by buffaloes.

The café was one of the few wooden structures in Cordon Brun. It had mirrors, a piano, and a mahogany bar.

Hart, Weber, and Conseil were drinking when Emmanuel Steel strode in.

II.

The man who had just walked in brought a sharp contrast to these three African snobs: he was handsome, powerfully built, and possessed of a childlike faith, betrayed by his serious eyes, that no one would ever wish to do him any harm. He had great, heavy hands, the physique of a soldier, and the face of a simpleton. He had on a cheap cotton suit and splendid boots, and the butt of a revolver bulged beneath his shirt. His hat, which had a white kerchief sewn onto the wide brim at the back, looked like a tent fit for a giant. He said little and would nod in a charming manner, as though bowing his head along with all the world, which would mark his favor. In short, when Steel walked into a room, you made way.

With a gentle nod, Conseil glanced at Hart's weathered face with its evasive smile; Hart peered back at Conseil's marble brow and his pale-blue eyes; then they both winked at the truculent, bilious, dark Weber, while Weber in turn shot them the sharpest of looks from behind his spectacles; whereupon they all struck up a conversation.

Several days prior to this, Steel had been sitting with them, drinking and talking, and they came to *know* the man. The conversation, from beginning to end, had been replete with arid inner laughter— yet Steel had rather naively believed in everything that impressed him and captivated his attention, and never so much as suspected that the wool was being pulled over his eyes.

"It's him," said Conseil.

"The man from the fog," Hart chimed in.

"In a fog, you mean," corrected Weber.

"In search of a hidden spot."

"Or a fourth dimension."

"No, he's a seeker of rarities," declared Hart.

"What was he saying about a jungle the other day?" asked Weber.

Mimicking Steel, Conseil said in a rapid patter:

"This enormous jungle that stretches out thousands of miles into the heart of the mainland must conceal King Solomon's mines, the tales of Scheherazade, and thousands upon thousands of other things just waiting to be discovered."

"Let's suppose," said Hart as he doused a fly in cognac (it was already drunk in a little puddle of wine that had been spilled on the table). "Let's suppose that he didn't quite mean it like that. That he was just thinking aloud, distractedly. The heart of the matter is this: that somewhere in this ocean of jungle there's a place that would produce the greatest, most astonishing effect on a man, an unending Himalaya of impressions scattered all over. And if he only knew how to find that *summit*, he'd set off there."

"That's a strange sort of chap to find in Cordon Brun," noted Conseil, "and rich pickings for a bit of sport. Shall we have a go?"

"What do you have in mind?"

"I've concocted a little plan—just as we've done many a time before. I think I can set it out in a fairly *credible* fashion. All you have to do is say 'yes' whenever the *pickings* gives you a questioning look."

"All right," said Weber and Hart.

"Steel! Well, I never . . ." drawled Conseil. "Come and join us."

Steel, who had been talking with the barman, turned around and made his way over to the group. They offered him a chair.

III.

The conversation was unremarkable at first, but later it turned to more interesting matters.

"You're idle, Steel," said Conseil. "You've raked in thousands of pounds from a single pit and now you're kicking your heels. Have you sold all your diamonds?"

"Long ago," Steel replied measuredly, "but I wouldn't relish taking up anything like that again. I liked the mines because they were a novelty."

"So what now?"

"I'm a novice in these parts. The land is beautiful and awe-inspiring. I'm waiting for something to take my fancy."

"I noticed this quirk of yours the last time we spoke," said Conseil. "Incidentally, the very next day I happened to talk to Pelegrin, the hunter. He picked up a lot of ivory across the river, about five hundred miles from here, in the jungles that so captivate your soul. He told me of a curious phenomenon. Deep in the jungle there's small plateau with a charming human settlement, which you happen upon quite unexpectedly; the jungle, in all its sumptuous twilight, is suddenly broken by high log walls that form the rear of a building, the exterior facades of which give onto a lush inner garden, full of flowers. He spent a day there after he came across this little colony just before evening. He thought he heard the sounds of a guitar. Amazed—for nothing but jungle, only jungle, stretched out in every direction, and there wasn't a single native village within less than a fortnight's journey on foot—Pelegrin followed the sound and was given a warm welcome. There were seven families living there, bound by the same tastes and a love for the flourishing remoteness of their surroundings. And it's true, you know, it is difficult to imagine anywhere more remote than this almost inaccessible heartland. The livelihood of these Robinsons of the wilderness presented an interesting contrast to their completely civilized mode of living: they were hunters. They lived on hunting alone, sending off what they caught by boat to Tankos, where the manufacturers' agents are, and trading it for everything they required, right down to electric lightbulbs.

"How they wound up there, how they had established and sustained themselves, Pelegrin never found out. A single day is little more than a magnesium flare above a wreck—but perhaps it's enough to understand and forget what's essential. But the labor had been immense: beautiful carved balconies, a winding tangle of flowers around the windows with blue and violet awnings, a lion's skin, a piano with a rifle propped up beside it, swarthy, carefree children with the fearless eyes of fairy tale heroes, beautiful, slender girls with revolvers in their pockets and books by their bedsides, and hunters as sharp-sighted as an eagle. What more could you ask for? The people seemed to have got together *to sing*.

Pelegrin remembered his first impression particularly vividly, like some outlandish drawing: a narrow passage between two log walls, to his left a little hand beckoning him from a balcony, ahead of him sunlight and paradise.

"You will, of course, have spent a night with a strange family. Their life goes on around you, appearing to you as a *fragment*, full of charm, torn from the pages of some *unknown* book. You glimpse the face of a young girl or an old woman, which never again appears amid the evening's scene; you hear snatches of conversation concerning some private matter you don't understand; you surrender your senses to all manner of things, and all you know is that these people have given you shelter; you *haven't* stepped into their lives, and that's why it remains steeped in a strange poetry. That's how it was with Pelegrin."

Steel listened closely, looking Conseil straight in the eye.

"I can see it all," he said simply. "Quite *something*, isn't it?"

"Yes," said Weber. "Yes."

"Yes," affirmed Hart.

"Words can't express how you'd feel," Steel continued thoughtfully and full of emotion, "but how right I was! Where's Pelegrin now?"

"Oh, he left with the caravan for Ogo."

Steel drew a straight line on the table with his finger, gingerly at first but then quickly, as though brushing something aside.

"What was the name of this place?" he asked. "How did Pelegrin find it?"

"The Heart of the Wilderness," said Conseil. "He came across it somewhere directly between Cordon Brun and Lake Ban. Isn't that right, Hart?"

"Oh, yes."

"There was another detail," said Weber, chewing his lips. "Pelegrin mentioned the approach: there was a steep slope running north, covered in trees, that cut diagonally across his path. He came across one of the hunters, who was looking for his own kind. (They believed him to be dead, while in actual fact he had just been knocked senseless by a falling tree.) He had been heading in the opposite direction the whole time."

"Does the slope lead up to the plateau?" asked Steel, turning his whole body toward Weber.

Weber proceeded to list several topographical details, so specific that Conseil shot him an admonishing glance, whistling 'Whither do you rush, my beauty, the sun is not yet risen . . .' But Steel was none the wiser.

Nodding with characteristic warmth throughout, Steel listened to all that Weber had to say. He then got to his feet with sudden haste, and, as he bid the men farewell, the look in his eyes was that of a man who has just woken up. He failed to mark how attentively the six piercing eyes of these cold men were taking in his every move. Then again, it was hard to tell his thoughts by looking at him—this was a man of dynamic complexity.

"How is it," Conseil asked Weber, "that you're so sure of the unknown? How did you come by this knowledge of the region?"

"From the account of Penn's expedition. And from *my* memory."

"Well, then. What now?"

"That's his business," said Weber with a laugh. "But if I know what men are like . . . In any case, we sail at the week's end."

A shadow blocked the light streaming in through the door. It was Steel.

"I'm back, but I won't come in," he said quickly. "I read the name of your home port on the stern of your yacht, Conseil. Melbourne. But I'd . . ."

"Number Two, Flag Street," replied Conseil. "And—"

"Thank you, that's all."

Steel disappeared.

"This could end badly," Hart noted coolly, once the silence had spoken to each of them in turn. "He'll *find* you."

"What's that?"

"People like that never forgive."

"Bah!" retorted Conseil with a toss of the head. "Life is short: the world, large."

IV.

Two years passed, during which Conseil turned up in a great many other places, observing the variety of life with his eternal attempts to make a mockery of its dizzying flight; but at last, of this, too, he grew weary. And so he returned home, taking a caustic delight in his solitude—without the aesthetic convulsions of des Esseintes, though with the acrimony of a chill desolation that he found impossible to comprehend.

Meanwhile, hearts had gone on being broken and patched together again, the world trundled on, and amid this trundling came the sound of even footsteps. They fell silent at Conseil's doorstep. That was when he received a visiting card reminding him of Cordon Brun.

"I'll see him," said Conseil after a brief pause, experiencing in the exquisite unpleasantness of his situation a vivifying and acute curiosity. "Show Steel in."

They met at a distance of twenty yards across a vast hall. The silvery light, in all its translucent array, seemed to halt Steel when he appeared at the threshold. Thus he stood awhile, peering at the inscrutable face of his host. In this moment, both men felt that their meeting had been inevitable; then they quickly approached each other.

"Cordon Brun," said Conseil amiably. "You vanished, and I left without giving you that engraving by Morad, as I'd planned. It's to your taste—by which I mean to say that the fantastic landscape of Saturn that it depicts evokes the mysteries of the universe."

"Yes," said Steel, smiling. "As you can see, I remembered your address. I made a note of it. I've come to tell you that I made it to the Heart of the Wilderness, and I saw just what Pelegrin did— more even, for I live there now."

"I am to blame," said Conseil drily, "but my words are my business, and I'll answer for them. At your service, Steel."

Laughing, Steel took Conseil's limp hand, raised it, and gave it a smack.

"Good heavens, no!" he cried. "That's not what I mean. I made the Heart of the Wilderness. I tell you, I did! I didn't actually find it, because it wasn't there, of course, and then I realized that you'd been joking. But what a splendid joke! There was a time when I, too, used to dream of such things. Yes, I've always loved discoveries that stir the heart like a beautiful song. They called me an eccentric— but what of it? I admit, I was deathly envious of Pelegrin, but that's why I set off alone, to see what he had seen. Yes, a month's journey showed me *what* the jungle is. Hunger . . . and thirst . . . alone. A fever that lasted ten days. I had no tent. I thought the flames of the campfire were many-colored, like a rainbow. White horses would come charging out of the forest. My late brother turned up and sat watching me; he kept whispering, beckoning me somewhere. I would take quinine and drink. All this delayed me, of course. A snake bit my hand. How the prospect of death enraged me! But I took myself in hand and listened to what my body was telling me. Then, like a dog, I felt drawn to a patch of grass and ate it; that's how I saved myself, but I broke into a sweat and had to sleep. I suppose I was lucky. It was all like a dream: the wild animals, the fatigue, the hunger, the still. I killed the animals. But there was nothing at all in that place you'd mentioned. I scoured the whole plateau; it descends to a small tributary where the slope widens out. Of course, I saw it all so clearly. But there I'd found true beauty. There are things that words strike like hail on a windowpane—just pinging . . ."

"Go on," said Conseil softly.

"It just *had* to be there," Steel continued gently. "That's why I sailed downriver on a raft toward the fort and hired all the men and materials I needed at the trading post. I built it, just as it was in your tale and just as it pleased me. Seven houses. It took a year. After that, I scoured thousands of people, thousands of souls, traveling here and there, looking high and low. Of course I was *bound* to find them, given the sort of man I am—that much was obvious. Now then, shall we go and take a look? It's clear you have the gift of artistic imagination, and I want to know whether *you* pictured it *as it is.*"

He related all this with the horrifying simplicity of a boy telling a story from world history.

Conseil blushed. Long-forgotten music resounded in his soul, and he worked out this unexpected agitation, pacing the diagonals of the hall. Then he froze, as though rooted to the spot.

"You're a dynamo," he said, his voice choked. "You know something, you're a real dynamo. I mean that as a compliment."

"When you can see something so clearly—" Steel began.

"I've been asleep for so long," said Conseil severely, interrupting him. "So then . . . But how like a dream it all is! Perhaps I ought to live again, eh?"

"Not a bad idea," said Steel.

"But *it* didn't exist. It just didn't."

"It did," said Steel, raising his head without intending to make an impression. But from this gesture the impression reeled and thundered in every corner. "It did, because I carried it in my own heart."

From this meeting and this conversation there came a conclusion, which strongly recalled the arid delirium of a sophisticated mind back in Cordon Brun. Two men, their eyes still full of the great, wild expanse they had just left behind, were propping themselves up against a log wall hidden by the jungle. A ray of evening light met them, and from a balcony overlooking the natural orangery that constituted the garden came the gentle voice of a woman singing.

Steel smiled, and Conseil knew why.

THE RAT-CATCHER

In the water's bosom stands Chillon
There, in a dungeon, seven columns
Decked in the gloomy moss of years . . .

Byron, tr. Vasily Zhukovsky

I.

In the spring of 1920, more specifically in March, more specifically on the twenty-second of the month—let us make these offerings of precision so as to buy a welcome into the bosom of the arbiters of documentary evidence, without which the inquisitive reader of our time would likely question the editorial staff—I went to market. I went to market on March 22, and, I repeat, in the year 1920. It was the one at Haymarket Square. I cannot tell you at which corner I was standing, however, and I do not recall what was in the newspapers that day. Since I was walking back and forth along the pavement near the ruins of the market building, I was not really standing at any corner. I was selling some books—the last of what I had.

The bitter cold and the sleet falling like clouds of white sparks upon the heads of the crowd in the distance added a foul look to the spectacle. Fatigue and a feeling of being chilled to the bone showed in every face. My luck was out. For more than two hours I wandered, meeting only three people who asked what I would take for my books, but even they found the price—five pounds of bread—exorbitant. Meanwhile, darkness was falling—the least propitious condition for bookselling. I stepped onto the sidewalk and leaned against a wall.

To my right stood an old woman garbed in a burnouse and an old black hat with glass beading. Tossing her head mechanically, she proffered with her gnarled fingers a pair of children's bonnets, some ribbons, and a bundle of yellowed shirt collars. To my left, pinching with her free hand a warm gray head scarf snugly beneath her chin, stood a young, rather independent-look-ing girl, carrying the same merchandise as I—books. Her smart little slippers, her skirt that draped leisurely all the way down to her ankles (quite unlike those frivolous little dresses cut at the knees, which even old women had begun to wear in those days), her cloth jacket, her warm, antiquated mittens, the bare cushions of her fingers peeping out from the holes in them, and also the manner in which she looked at passers-by—without smiling or inviting, at times thoughtfully lowering her eyelashes toward the books—how she held them, these books, and how she would groan, letting out a restrained sigh, whenever a passer-by, having cast a glance at her hands and then at her face, would walk off, as though astonished by something and popping some sunflower seeds into his mouth—all this pleased me no end, and the market even seemed to me a little warmer.

We take an interest in those who correspond to our notion of an individual in a given circumstance, and so I asked the girl whether her little trade was going well. With a slight cough, she turned her head, ran her attentive blue-gray eyes over me, and said: "Much as yours."

We exchanged a few comments on trading in general. At first she kept her remarks to the bare minimum, but then, after a man in blue spectacles and riding breeches bought her copy of *Don Quixote*, she seemed to perk up.

"Nobody knows I'm selling these," she said, credulously showing me a counterfeited note that the canny citizen had placed among the rest and brandishing it absentmindedly. "I'm not saying that I steal them, exactly; I just take them from the shelf while my father's asleep. My mother's dead, you see . . . We had to sell everything back then, or almost everything. We had no bread, no firewood, no kerosene. You know how it is. But my father would be furious if he found out that I come here. But I do, and bring a few books on the sly. It's a pity about the books, but what can you do? Thank God we have so many of them. Do you have many?"

"N-no," I said, my teeth chattering (I had already caught a chill and was a little hoarse). "Not many, as far as I remember. At least, these are all I have left now."

She looked at me with naive attention—thus, crowding into a woodland cabin, do young village boys gawp at a passing civil servant taking tea—and, reaching out her hand, touched my shirt collar with the naked tip of her finger. My shirt, just like the collar of my summer coat, had no buttons; I had lost them and not yet bothered to sew on replacements, for I had long since stopped taking care over my appearance, having waved goodbye to both my past and my future.

"You'll catch your death," she said, pinching her kerchief that little bit more tightly out of habit. It was then that I realized the girl's father loved her, that she was cosseted and mischievous, but a good sort. "You'll catch your death, going about with an open collar. Come here a second, citizen."

She gathered up the books under her arm and walked over to an archway. Lifting my head with an inane smile, I gave her access to my throat. The girl was well proportioned but rather shorter than me, and so, as she reached for what she needed with that enigmatic, vacant expression that women have when they fiddle around with a safety pin, the girl set the books on top of a bollard, made the briefest of efforts under her jacket, and, standing on tiptoe, breathing with concentration and purpose, tightly fastened the edge of my shirt to my coat with a white safety pin.

"Lovey-doveys," said a thickset woman who was passing by.

"There now." Critically appraising her handiwork, the girl chuckled. "All done. Now be off with you."

I laughed in astonishment. Seldom had I encountered such guilelessness. We either do not see it or do not believe it; we see it, alas, only when we are ill.

Taking her hand, I shook it, thanked her, and asked her name.

"I could tell you in a jiffy," she replied, regarding me with pity, "only why do you want to know? It's neither here nor there. But come to think of it, why don't you write down our telephone number; perhaps I'll ask you to sell some books."

I jotted it down, watching with a smile as she led her index finger through the air, the others having been clenched into a fist, and pronounced one number after another in a pedagogical tone. We were subsequently surrounded and separated from one another by a crowd fleeing a mounted police raid. I dropped my books, and by the time I had picked them up, the girl had vanished. The panic proved insufficient for people to leave the market entirely, and several minutes later an old-timer with a goatee and round spectacles, straight out of a work by Andreyev, bought the books from me. He offered me very little, but I was glad to have even that. Only as I was going home did I realize that I had sold the book in which I had written down the telephone number, and that I had forgotten it irrevocably.

II.

My initial reaction to this was the negligible shock of any minor loss. However, as yet unsated hunger forestalled this impression. Lost in thought, I boiled a potato in a room with a window that had begun to rot from damp. I had a little iron stove. For firewood . . . In those days many people would go up to the attic—and I, too, would go there, stepping through the oblique half-light of the roofs, feeling like a thief, listening to the wind playing the pipes, and examining through the smashed dormer window a pale patch of sky that scattered down snowflakes onto the rubbish. There I would find wood shavings left over from cutting the rafters to size, as well as old window frames and dilapidated curtain rails, which I would bring back to my cellar by night, pricking up my ears on the landing for the creak of a door letting out some late visitor. A laundress lived in the neighboring room; for days on end I would listen to the powerful motions of her hands in the washtub, which produced a sound like a horse chewing rhythmically. The ticking of a sewing machine also emanated from there, often in the dead of night—like a clock gone mad. A bare table, a bare bed, a stool, a cup with no saucer, a frying pan, and the teapot in which I boiled my potato . . . But enough of these reminders! The spirit of everyday life often turns away from the mirror that is assiduously held up to it by immaculately literate people, those who curse in the new orthography with just the same degree of success as they had with the old.*

As night fell, I remembered the market and vividly replayed everything in my head as I examined my pin. Carmen did very little—all she did was throw a flower at an idle soldier. Nothing more had been done here. For a long time I reflected on chance meetings, initial glances, first words. They become so deeply etched in one's memory so long as there is nothing *extraneous* about them. There is an irreproachable purity that belongs to these characteristic moments, which wholly lends itself to poetry or drawing—this is an aspect of life that lays down the foundation of art. An authentic experience, bound up in the serene simplicity of an unaffected tone, the sort for which we thirst with our heart at every step, is always full of charm. So faintly, but so fully does its melody convey the impression.

That is why I returned repeatedly to the pin, hammering into my memory what the girl and I had said to each other. Then I grew tired and lay down to sleep; upon waking, I stood up but immediately lost consciousness and fell to the ground. This was the onset of typhus, and in the morning I was borne to a hospital. I managed to retain sufficient memory and reason, however, to stash away my pin in a tin that had been serving as a snuffbox, and I held onto it right to the very end.

III.

With a temperature of almost one hundred and six degrees, my delirium took on the form of visitations. I was visited by people

---

* *in the new orthography . . . old*: Russian orthography underwent a major reform in 1918, which saw, among other things, the elimination of four letters from the alphabet. Although the reforms had been prepared by the Academy of Sciences before the events of October 1917, their implementation after the revolution brought an immediate association with the new political regime.

from whom I had not heard in many years. I talked with them at length and asked all of them to bring me soured milk. But, as though in cahoots with one another, they all insisted that soured milk had been forbidden me by the doctor. Meanwhile, I was secretly waiting to see whether a new nurse would appear among the gallery of faces I glimpsed as if through the steam in a sauna—she would surely be none other than the girl with the safety pin. From time to time she would pass by outside, among the tall flowers, wearing a green garland, against a backdrop of golden sky. So meekly, so gaily did her eyes shine! Even when she failed to appear, the ward's flickering, dim light was imbued with her invisible presence, and every now and then I would finger the pin in the box. By morning five people had died; ruddy orderlies bore them away on stretchers, while my thermometer showed a fraction over ninety-six. Now a languid, sober state of recovery set in. I was discharged from the hospital once I was able to walk around, albeit with a pain in my legs, three months after I fell ill; when I left I had no fixed abode. My former room had been requisitioned for an invalid, and I lacked the moral fortitude to go about the various institutions, petitioning for another one.

Now, perhaps it would be appropriate to introduce a few details about my appearance, availing myself for this purpose of an extract from a letter written by my friend Repin to the journalist Fingal. I do this not because I have a vested interest in seeing my features imprinted in the lines of a book, but merely to impart some visual impression. "He is of swarthy complexion," writes Repin, "and the regular features of his face express a reluctance for everything. His hair is cropped short, and he speaks slowly and with difficulty." This is true, although my manner of speaking is not a consequence of my illness but, rather, results from the melancholy feeling—of which we are rarely even aware—that our inner world is of interest to few others. I, myself, however, was fascinated by every other soul, which is why I say little, preferring instead to listen. Hence, when several people congregate, vigorously rushing to cut each other off as often as possible, so as to draw the maximum attention to themselves, I usually sit on the sidelines.

For three weeks I spent the night with friends and friends of friends—on the basis of compassionate referral. I slept on floors and sofas, on stoves and empty crates, on chairs pushed together, and once even on an ironing board. During this time I saw my fill of a great many interesting things, to the glory of life, which fights so staunchly for warmth, family, and food. I saw a stove fueled by a sideboard, a kettle boiled on a lamp, horsemeat fried in coconut oil, and wooden beams stolen from dilapidated buildings. But all this—and much, much more—has already been described by quills that have torn these new topics to shreds, and so we will not touch the scrap that has been thrown our way. Something else is leading me—what happened to me next.

IV.

By the end of the third week I was blighted by acute insomnia. It is difficult to say how it began; I remember only that it required great efforts to fall asleep, and that I would awaken earlier and earlier. During this time a chance meeting led me to a dubious refuge. Wandering along the Moika and taking pleasure in the spectacle of some fishing—a peasant with a net attached to a long pole was walking slowly around the granite banks, occasionally lowering his tackle into the water and pulling out a handful of little fish— I met the shopkeeper from whom I used to purchase groceries on account several years previously; this man now appeared to be doing something official. He was received well in a great many buildings on fiscal and economic matters. I did not recognize him at once: now without an apron, without his calico shirt (which had looked as though it came straight out of a Turkish painting), without his beard and moustache, the shopkeeper was dressed in strict military pleats, cleanly shaven, and reminded me of an Englishman, albeit with shades of Yaroslavl. Although he carried a fat briefcase, he did not have the authority to lodge me just wherever he pleased, and so he suggested the empty chambers of the Central Bank,[*] where 260 rooms were standing like water in a pond, quiet and stagnant.

"The Vatican," I said, shuddering slightly at the thought of such a lodging. "What, is there really nobody living there? And what if people show up? And, if they do, won't the caretaker hand me over to the militia?"

"Ach!" was all that the former shopkeeper had to say. "The building isn't far from here. Go and take a look."

He led me into a large courtyard partitioned by archways that led into other courtyards, looked around, and, since we met no one there, strode over purposefully to a dark corner that had a servants' staircase leading up. He paused on the third landing in front of an ordinary apartment door; rubbish was spilling out of the small gap at the bottom. The landing was littered densely with grimy papers. The uninhabited silence lurking behind the door seemed to seep out through the keyhole like a vast emptiness. Here the shopkeeper explained to me how to open the door without a key: while pulling the handle, just give it a shake and press it up, then both halves would come apart, since there was no bolt.

"There is a key," the shopkeeper said, "only I don't have it. But if you have the method, you can come and go as you please. Just be sure not to let anyone in on the secret. You can lock it from within and without—all you have to do is slam it. If you need to go out, take a peek at the staircase first. There's a little window that you can

---

[*] *the Central Bank*: The building in question is the Chicherin House at 15 Nevsky Prospect. It was converted into the House of Arts in 1919 (see Introduction).

use for this." (Truly, in the wall by the door, around eye level, there was a dark little window, the glass of which was broken.) "I won't go in with you. You're an educated man and you'll see for yourself how best to install yourself; just know that you could hide a whole company of soldiers here. You can stay here for a couple of days; as soon as I find you a place, I'll let you know. Consequently—and do forgive the indelicacy, but every man has to eat and drink—please be so kind as to accept a loan until circumstances improve."

He laid out a fat wallet, thrust into my tacitly drooping hand (as one would pay a doctor for a home visit) several paper notes, repeated his instructions, and left, while I, having closed the door, sat down on a crate. Meanwhile, the silence that we always hear inside us—like memories of the sounds of life—was already enticing me, like a forest. It was hiding behind the half-open door that led to the neighboring room. I got up and began to explore.

I walked from one door to the next, through large, high-ceilinged rooms, feeling like a man taking his first steps on the ice. It was spacious and echoed throughout. Scarcely had I left behind one door than more would appear ahead of me and off to the side, leading into the dim light of the distance with its even darker doorways. Paper lay scattered around on the parquet like the grimy snow of spring roads. Its abundance recalled a scene of snowdrifts being cleared away. In several rooms, from the very threshold, I was forced to wade knee-deep through this clutter.

Paper of every kind, of every calling and color, spread out here in a ubiquitous jumble on a truly prodigious scale. It washed up in screes against the walls and hung from the window ledges, its white deluge flowing from one parquet floor to the next, streaming from open cupboards, filling corners, in places forming hedgerows and ploughed fields. Notebooks, letterheads, ledgers, binder labels, numbered pages, ruled pages, typescripts, and manuscripts—the contents of thousands of cupboards had been turned out before my very eyes, and my gaze ran over everything, overwhelmed by the magnitude of the scene. All the rustling, the echo of footsteps, even my own breathing, sounded as if they were happening right beside my ears—so great, so spectacularly stark was the bleak silence. The whole time I was plagued by the stale smell of dust; the windows were double framed. Looking at their vespertine glass, I could see now the trees lining the canal, now the roofs of the courtyard or the facade giving onto Nevsky Prospect. This meant that the premises took up an entire block, but the dimensions, thanks to the frequent and tiresome palpability of the space, which was partitioned by never-ending walls and doors, seemed to entail a journey of many days on foot—a feeling that is the antithesis of what we call "a little street" or "a little square." Having scarcely begun my tour, I was already comparing this place to a labyrinth. Everything looked the same—heaps of clutter, voids here and there, indicated by windows or a door, and the expectation of many other doors that had been robbed of a crowd. Thus a man might move, supposing he could move, inside the reflection of a mirror, when two mirrors replicate ad nauseam the space they enclose, and the only thing missing is his own face, peeping out of a doorway, as though enframed.

I had passed through no more than twenty rooms, but already I was disoriented and had begun to take note of distinguishing features, lest I should lose my bearings: a layer of lime on the floor; over there a broken bureau; a door that had been pulled off and placed against a wall; a window ledge littered with pots of lilac ink; a wire basket; reams of used blotting paper; a fireplace; every now and then a cupboard or a forlorn-looking chair. But these features, too, began to repeat themselves: there were times when, looking around, I would think in astonishment that I had already been there, establishing my error only by contrasting the sequence of other objects. Sometimes I would come across a steel safe with a heavy, gaping door, like an empty stove; a telephone apparatus that looked like a post box or a fungus on a birch tree amid the desolation; a stepladder; I even found a little black hat block that had at some unknown time and by some miracle added itself to the inventory.

Twilight had already penetrated the depths of the hall, and mounds of paper gave off a white glow in its farthest reaches. The contours and corridors merged with the haze, and a dim light cut rhombus-like across the parquet and through the doors, but the walls flanking the windows still shone here and there with the dramatic brilliance of the sunset. As soon as new doorways appeared in front of me, the memories of what in passing I was leaving behind curdled like milk, and really I was conscious only of traversing an array of walls through rubbish and paper. In one spot I had to climb and wade through piles of slippery files; it made such a noise, as if I were making my way through bushes. As I walked on, I kept looking back in anguish: the slightest noise amid the silence clung to me so inextricably that I felt as though I were dragging bundles of dry brushwood with my feet, and I listened to see whether someone else might not have heard my steps. To begin with, I walked about the nervous entity that was the bank, trampling over the black grain of figures with the sense that I was disrupting a sequence of orchestral notes that could be heard all the way from Alaska to Niagara. I was not seeking comparisons: provoked by the unforgettable spectacle, they appeared and disappeared, like a chain of nebulous figures. I felt as if I were traversing the bed of an aquarium that had been drained of water, or in an ice field, or even—to put it in the most precise and sinister terms—as if I were wandering through past centuries that had been perverted by the present day. I passed through an inner corridor, so tortuously long that you could have ridden a bicycle along it. At the end of it there was a staircase; I walked up to the next floor and came down again by another staircase, passing a hall of average size, its floor covered with electrical components. I could see globes of frosted glass, lampshades in the shapes of tulips and bells, serpentine bronze chandeliers, bundles of wires, piles of ceramics and copper.

The next tortuous passage led me to an archive, where, amid the dark squeeze of shelves running in parallel athwart the room, from floor to ceiling, passage was unthinkable. A medley of copybooks swelled up higher than my chest; I could not even survey the area, so densely was everything jumbled up.

Exiting by a side door, I proceeded in the half-light of the white walls, until I saw a large archway that connected the corridors to a central hall with a double row of black columns. The rail of an ala-baster gallery stretched along the tops of these columns, forming an impressive rectangle; the ceiling was barely visible. Sufferers of agoraphobia would have left, covering their faces—so great was the distance to the other end of this receptacle for crowds that the doors looming there were but the size of playing cards. A thousand people could dance here. In the center of the hall stood a fountain: its gargoyles, with their gaping mouths, comic and tragic, looked like a cluster of human heads. Abutting the columns, a long counter stretched out like an arena, surmounted by a frosted-glass screen that announced in gold lettering cashiers and accounts depart-ments. The broken partitions, the collapsed booths, the tables that had been moved over to the walls were scarcely visible on account of the room's size. My gaze hardly registered these tokens of a life-less desolation equal to that which reigned everywhere else. I stood motionless, taking in the view. I began to develop a taste for this spectacle, absorbing its style. The exultation experienced by some-one watching a great conflagration became apparent to me once again. The allure of destruction grew like poetic inspiration—before me unfurled a unique landscape, a region, a country even. Its colors naturally transformed the impression into suggestion, like a musical extemporization on an original theme. It was hard to imag-ine that there had once been a crowd here, carrying thousands of business affairs in heads and briefcases. Everything bore the stamp of decay and silence. A breath of incredible audacity had passed here from door to door—one of elemental, irresistible destruction, which had played out just as easily as crushing eggshells under foot. These impressions provoked a kind of cerebral itch that made the very notion of catastrophe fascinating, just as the heart's magnetism draws one to stare into an abyss. It was as if here a single thought echoed in every possible form and, like a ringing in one's ears, importunately recalled the motto:

"It is done, and now there is only silence."

V.

Fatigue came at last. It was difficult now to distinguish the passageways and staircases. I was hungry. There was no hope of finding an exit in order to go out and buy something to eat at the corner. In one of the kitchens I slaked my thirst by turning on the tap. To my surprise, the water still flowed, albeit a trickle, and this insignificant sign of life buoyed me after a fashion. I then set about choosing a room. This took several more minutes, until I stumbled upon an office with a single door, a fireplace, and a telephone. There was hardly any furniture; the only thing to sit or lie down on was a sofa that had been scalped and deprived of its legs; fragments of its slashed leather, springs, and hair were sticking out all over. In an alcove stood a tall walnut cupboard: it was locked. I lit a cigarette, then another, while I restored myself to a point of relative equilibrium, and set about installing myself for the night.

For quite some time I had not known the pleasure of fatigue, the joys of deep and pleasant sleep. While there was still daylight, I pondered the approaching night with the caution of a man carrying a pail full of water, trying not to work myself up, almost certain that this time exhaustion would overcome the oppressive vigor of consciousness. Yet as soon as evening came, the fear of *not falling asleep* gripped me with the full force of obsessive thought, and I yearned for the night's coming, to know whether I would fall asleep or not. Yet the closer it came to midnight, the more distinctly I was prevailed upon by my emotions in their unnatural, heightened state; at the slightest agitation, a disquieting excitement, like the brilliance of magnesium in the dark, wrought my nerves into a taut, reverberating string, and it was as if, the day being over, I would awaken only to begin a long nocturnal journey through my restless heart. The feeling of fatigue lifted; my eyes stung, as though grains of sand were in them. The embryo of any thought would mature immediately in all its complexity and ramifications, and the impending long, languid hours, full of memories, raised in me nothing more than impotent indignation, like the prospect of a labor that is fruitless, obligatory, and inescapable. I tried to summon sleep as best I could. In the morning, feeling as though my body had been drenched in hot water, I drew in the illusory presence of sleep with an artificial yawn, but when I closed my eyes, I felt that same sense of absurdity as we do when we close our eyes for no good reason during the day. I tried everything: examining marks on the wall, counting, lying still, repeating the same phrase over and over again—all without success.

I was in possession of a candle end, an item of absolute necessity when there was no light in the staircase. Dim though its light was, it illuminated the frigid heights of the room. Next I stuffed the pits of the sofa with paper and constructed a headboard of books. My overcoat served as a blanket. I then thought it would be a good idea to light the stove, so as to watch the flames. More to the point, though it was summer, the place lacked warmth. In any case, I had concocted a pastime and was glad of it. Before long, the bundles of accounts and books were ablaze in the grand fireplace, spilling as ash into the grate. The flame shook the shadows of the open doors in the darkness before vanishing into the distance with a gentle phosphorescence.

Yet this fortuitous fire burned in sterile secrecy. It did not illuminate the customary objects, those we examine against the fantastic glare of red and golden coals while we probe the inner warmth and light of the soul. It was comfortless, like the fire of a thief. I lay there, propping up my head with a numb arm, without any desire to drift off. All my efforts in this regard had been equal to the acting of a player who lies down in bed, yawning, before a crowd. What was more, I was hungry, and, in order to stay my hunger, I chain-smoked.

I lay there, lazily observing the fire and the cupboard. Just then the thought struck me that the cupboard would not have been locked without good reason. What, though, could be hidden there, if not those same bundles of obsolete dossiers? What could yet remain to be pillaged? A woeful experience with burned-out electric bulbs, of which I had found a pile in one of those same cupboards, led me to suspect that the cupboard had been locked without any particular intention and only because the key had matched the lock so well. Nevertheless, I beheld the massive, solid doors—like those of a porte-cochère—with food in mind. I did not seriously hope to find anything edible there, but I was being led blindly by my stomach, which always forced me to think only of it, according to its summary logic—that same logic that produces hungry saliva at the mere sight of food. In order to distract myself I wandered through several of the nearest rooms, but, fumbling there by candlelight, I failed to find so much as a crust, and so I returned, even more enticed by the cupboard. In the fireplace the embers were giving out a dusky light. My thoughts were like those of a vagrant. Might not one of those people have locked away a loaf of bread in this cupboard, or perhaps a teapot, tea, and sugar? The diamonds and gold were kept elsewhere; that much was obvious. I considered it within my rights to open the cupboard, for it was not my intention to pilfer anything that might be locked up there. But as for food—ah, as for food!—whatever the letter of the law might say, I had the right.

Candle in hand, I was slow, however, to challenge this rationale, lest I should lose my moral fortitude. Therefore, taking a steel ruler, I inserted the end into the gap opposite the lock and, applying a little bit of pressure, pulled it away. With a tinkle, the latch came flying off, and, creaking stiffly, the cupboard opened. I recoiled, for what I saw was extraordinary. With a shudder, I flung the ruler away in a nervous gesture. The only reason that I did not cry out was that I hadn't the strength. It was as if I had been floored by a rush of water from a barrel.

VI.

The first shudder of the discovery was also one of momentary though terrifying doubt. This was not a sensory illusion, however. I saw a store of costly provisions—six deep shelves, heavily laden and overflowing. Their contents included items that had become rarities—the choicest produce, fit for a wealthy table, the tastes and smells of which were in those days nothing but a vague memory. Having dragged a table over, I set about my inspection.

I began by closing the doors, fearing open spaces as I do suspicious eyes; I even went out into the corridor to listen for the sounds of somebody walking about within those walls, just as I was doing. The silence gave me my cue.

I started with the top. The upper shelves (that is, the fifth and sixth) were occupied by four panniers, from one of which, as soon as I moved it, an enormous ginger rat jumped out and tumbled to the floor with a nauseating squeak. I snatched my hand away convulsively and froze with disgust. My next movement caused the flight of two more vermin, which darted between my legs like giant lizards. I then shook the pannier and tapped it against the cupboard, standing back in case there should be a deluge of these dismal, devious creatures, their tails flitting about. But the rats (supposing there had been others) must have slipped away through the back of the cupboard into the cracks in the walls—the cupboard was silent.

Naturally, I was surprised by the notion of storing foodstuffs in a place where only mice (*Murinæ*) and rats (*Mus decumanus*) would feel at home. But a feeling of elation outstripped any of my thoughts, which, instead, like water behind a dam, barely filtered through this whirling apotheosis. Let no one say that emotions related to food are base, that appetite lays equal man and amphibian. In times such as these, our whole being takes wings, and joy shines no less brightly than the rising sun viewed from the summit of a mountain. The soul moves to the strains of a march. I was already drunk on the sight of this treasure, especially since each pannier offered a varied assortment of delights. One contained cheeses, an array of cheese—from dry green to Rochester and brie. The second, no less heavy, smelled of a delicatessen; its hams, sausages, cured tongues, and minced turkey sat snugly beside another basket that was tightly packed with conserves. The fourth groaned under the weight of a pyramid of eggs. I got onto my knees to take a look at the lower shelves. Here I discovered eight sugar loaves and a tea caddy, a little oak barrel with brass hoops containing coffee, and baskets filled with biscuits, cakes, and crackers. The two lowest shelves reminded me of a bar, for they offered exclusively bottles of wine that were neatly and tightly packed, like firewood. Their labels described every taste, every estate, every glory and guile of the winemaker.

I had, if not to hurry, then, at any rate, to set about eating, since plainly this treasure trove, bearing the fresh look of a well-thought-out store, could not have been left by someone with the aim of giving some chance visitor to these parts the pleasure of an enormous boon. Be it in the light of day or the dead of night, a person could show up with a scream and raised arms, if not with something worse—a knife, for instance. Everything bespoke the dark urgency of the situation. I had much to fear in these spaces, for I had arrived at the unknown. Meanwhile, hunger had begun to talk in its own language, and I, having closed the cupboard door, settled myself on what was left of the divan, surrounding myself with morsels placed on, instead of plates, large sheets of paper. I ate what was most substantial—that is, crackers, ham, eggs, and cheese, chasing it down with biscuits and port wine, each sip imparting a sense of marvel. At first I could not cope with the chills and nervous, heavy laughter, but once I had calmed down a little, adjusted a little to the dumbfounded wonder of these tasty treats, which no more than fifteen minutes ago had been the stuff of dreams, I mastered my thoughts and actions. I was soon sated, far sooner than I had expected when I began eating, because of my anxiety, which wore even upon my appetite. However, I had been famished too much to sit idly, and I was utterly delighted by the satiety, without that drowsy mental torpor that accompanies the daily ingestion of handsome dishes. Having eaten all that I took and then carefully destroyed all trace of my feast, I felt that this had been a *good* evening.

Meanwhile, no matter how I strained my mind, my guesses, like a blunt knife, of course only scratched the surface of the episode, leaving its true essence hidden to the uninitiated gaze. As I paced among the bank's sleeping heaps, I perhaps quite rightly conceived how my shopkeeper was involved with this Klondike of stationery: from here one could extract and transport hundreds of cartloads of wrapping paper, so valued by merchants for the purposes of selling the customer short; moreover, the electric cords and the fittings would amount to more than a stack of banknotes; it was not for nothing that the cords and plugs here had been stolen from almost every wall that I set eyes on. Accordingly, I surmised that the shopkeeper was not the owner of these clandestine provisions;

he was likely putting them to use elsewhere. However, I did not stray further than this: all my subsequent conjectures were vague and anonymous, as is the case after any discovery. The evidence of rats demonstrated that it had not been touched for some time; their teeth had left vast caverns in the hams and cheeses.

Satisfied, I set about carefully examining the cupboard, noticing much that I had missed in those first moments of discovery. Among the baskets lay bundles of knives, forks, and napkins; a silver samovar was hiding behind the sugar loaves; in a box a multitude of patterned glassware of various types clinked together. Apparently some society gathered here, one that pursued rakish or clandestine aims, seeking isolation and secrecy, perhaps some powerful organization with the knowledge and participation of the housing committees. If that was so, I had to remain on my guard. I carefully tidied up the cupboard as best I could, figuring that the insignificant quantity I had devoured for supper would hardly be noticed. However, without the slightest sense of guilt I selected a few other little provisions, together with another bottle of wine, which I wrapped up securely and stashed under a heap of papers at a bend in the corridor.

It goes without saying that in these moments I was in no mood to lie down, let alone sleep. In a long holder I lit a white cigarette whose fibrous tobacco gave off a subtle aroma. This was the only find that I truly appreciated as I stuffed all my pockets full of these glorious cigarettes. I was in a state of intoxicating, melodious excitement, and I believed I was destined to meet a string of resounding improbabilities. Amid such glittering confusion, I recalled the girl in the gray head scarf who had fastened my collar with the safety pin— could I forget that action? She was the only person about whom I thought in beautiful, touching terms. It would be pointless to list them, since, barely having been uttered, they would lose their captivating aroma. This girl—even her name was a mystery to me—had, in disappearing, left a trace like a trail of shimmering water, flowing into the sunset. All it had taken for her to produce this delicate effect was a simple safety pin and the sound of her concentrated breathing as she stood on her tiptoes. It was the truest form of white magic. Since the girl had also been in need, I longed to pamper her with my dazzling discovery. But I had no idea where she was, and I could not call her. Even a blessing of memory, were it to cry out the forgotten number, would not have helped me here with this great multitude of telephones, one of which inadvertently drew the attention of my eye: they did not work, could not work for obvious reasons. Yet I gazed at the instrument with a certain inquisitive doubt, in which rational thought played no part whatever. I reached out to it, feeling playful. The desire to do something foolish gave me no rest; like all nocturnal nonsense, it was embellished by the ephemera of sleepless fantasy. I convinced myself that the number would come to me if I physically placed myself in the situation of speaking over the telephone. Besides, I have long held these mysterious wall mushrooms with rubber mouths and metallic ears to be ambiguous objects—a type of superstition that has been inspired by, among many other things, *L'Atmosphère* by Flammarion and his story about lightning. I heartily recommend everyone reread this book and to ponder again the peculiarities of an electrical storm, particularly the behavior of ball lightning, which can, for example, plant a knife in a wall and hang a frying pan or a shoe from it, or turn over a tiled roof, so that the tiles are stacked in the reverse order with the accuracy of a schematic drawing, which is to say nothing of the photographs that lightning imprints on the bodies of its victims, photographs of the circumstances in which the misfortune occurred. They are always darkish-blue in color, like old daguerreotypes. Kilowatts and amperes say little to me. In my case, the instrument came not without the presentiment, the strange languor, the confusion of consciousness that accompany the majority of our absurd creations. I can explain this now, but back then I was merely like iron before a magnet.

I picked up the receiver. Mute against the indifferent wall, it seemed colder than it really was. With no more hope than a broken clock inspires, I lifted it to my ear and pressed the button. Was it a ringing in my head or an auditory memory? With a shudder, I heard a fly buzzing, that vibration of wires like the drone of an insect. This was the very absurdity of which I dreamed.

The particular effort required to *understand* how a worm can bore its way through even a marble sculpture undermines every illusion with a hidden source. The will to fathom the unfathomable did not number among my virtues. However, I checked myself. Moving the receiver away, I reproduced this characteristic noise in my imagination and heard it for a second time only after I began listening to the receiver again. The noise did not skip and did not break off, nor did it weaken or intensify; in the receiver, as it should, an invisible expanse vibrated, awaiting contact. I was possessed by vague, strange notions, as strange as was the buzzing of this wire, in use in a dead building. I saw a jumble of wires that had been severed by a gust of wind and were establishing connections in untraceable points of their chaos: bundles of electric sparks, flying from the arched backs of cats bounding along the roofs, the magnetic flashes of streetcar cables, the weave and soul of a material imprinted with an angular futurist design. Such thoughts and visions did not exceed in duration a palpitation of my rearing heart; it was beating, tapping out in its untranslatable language the experience of nocturnal forces.

Then, rising up from beyond the walls, as luminous as a new moon, the image of that young girl appeared. Could I have imagined that the impression she made would be so vivid and implacable? A hundred-strong force tore through me, spinning and buzzing, when, as I stared at the number that had been effaced from the instrument, I led my memory through a tempest of figures, vainly trying to establish what combination of them reproduced the missing number. O false, fickle memory! It swears never to forget numbers, days, details, or dear faces, and answers doubt with a look of innocence. But the time will come when the credulous man will see that he has made a deal with a shameless monkey, who will give away a diamond ring in exchange for a handful of nuts. The features of a recollected face are vague and incomplete, the number is missing a digit, circumstances become jumbled, and a man, clutching his head in vain, is tormented by the slipperiness of memory. But if we remembered, if we could recollect *everything*, what kind of mind could endure with impunity a whole life in a single moment, and especially the recollections of emotions?

Like a madman, I kept repeating numbers, moving my lips to test their authenticity. At last a sequence matching my impression of the forgotten number flashed before me: 107—21. "One—zero—seven. Two—one," I said aloud, listening to it, but not knowing for sure that I was not mistaken again. A sudden doubt blinded me when I pressed the button for a second time, but it was already too late— the buzzing echoed, and in the depths of the telephone there was a click, a change, and directly against the skin of my cheek a weary female contralto intoned dryly: "Switchboard." "Switchboard! . . ." the voice impatiently repeated, but even then I did not speak straightaway, for my throat was choked from the cold, and in the depths of my heart I was still merely *playing*.

Whatever it was, my invocation of the spirits (ascribe them to *L'Atmosphère* or to the *Kilowatts* of the 1886 Company) was heard: I spoke, and they answered. The gears of the dilapidated clock had begun to turn. Above my ear the steel rays of hands resumed their movement. Someone had pushed the pendulum; the mechanism began to tick rhythmically. "One—zero—seven—two—one," I said flatly, watching the candle burning amid the rubbish. "Group A," came the irritated reply, whereupon the buzzing was severed by the distant movement of a weary hand.

I experienced a *mental fever* during these moments. I pressed the button with the letter A; as a result, not only was the telephone spurred into action, but this astonishing reality was further substantiated by the fact that the wires were crossed—a striking detail for an impatient soul. In an attempt to get A on the line, I pressed B. Then, crackling voices, like the prattle of a gramophone, burst forth into the rushing current, as though from a door that had been flung open—mysterious orators pulsating in my hand that clutched the receiver. They cut each other off with the haste and fierceness of people who have dashed out into the street. The medley of phrases recalled a chorus of rooks—"A-la-la-la-la!"—some invisible creature shrieked in the background of another person's slow, sober baritone, whose words were broken by pauses and mellifluously expressed punctuation. "I cannot give . . ."—"If you look . . ."—"One of these days . . ."—"I'm saying that . . ."—"Are you listening? . . ."—"Thirty by five . . ."—"The all-clear . . ."—"The car has been packed off . . ."—"I don't understand a thing . . ."—"Hang up . . ." Like the humming of a mosquito, groans, distant lamentations, laughter, sobbing, the strains of a violin, the sound of unhurried steps, rustling and whispering faintly crept into this hypnotic bazaar. Where, in which streets, were these words of care, these cries, these exhortations and complaints being heard? At last there came a matter-of-fact click, the voices disappeared, and through the din of the line appeared that same voice, saying: "Group B."

"A! Give me A!" I said. "The lines are crossed."

After a silence, during which twice the din abated, a new voice announced in a softer and more signsong tone: "Group A."

"One—zero—seven—two—one," I enunciated as clearly as I could.

"One—zero—eight—zero—one," the operator vacantly repeated in an attentive tone of voice. I scarcely managed to hold back the ready, ruinous correction, yet this error had undoubtedly restored the forgotten number; no sooner had I heard it than I recognized it, remembered it, just as we recognize a familiar face.

"Yes, yes," I said in a state of extreme excitement, as though I were running high up along the edge of a dizzying cliff. "Yes, that's it exactly. One—zero—eight—zero—one."

Hereupon everything stopped dead in and around me. The sound of the transmission clenched around my heart like a rush of cold waves; I didn't even hear the usual "I'll try now" or "I've connected you"—I do not recall what was said. I heard the intense trilling of birds. Feeling faint, I leaned against the wall. Then, after a chilling pause, a sober little voice, as fresh as fresh air, said warily:

"Let me check. I know it's out of order, but didn't you just hear it ring? Hello, who's speaking?" she said, apparently not expecting a reply and, just to be on the safe side, in a frivolously severe tone of voice.

Nearly shouting, I said:

"We spoke at the market. I went off with your safety pin. I was selling books. I beg you, try to remember. I don't know your name— tell me that it's you."

"It's a miracle," the pensive voice replied with a cough. "Wait, don't hang up. Let me think. Did you ever see the likes of it, Father?"

This last phrase was not directed at me. A man's voice replied to her indistinctly, evidently from another room.

"I remember meeting you," she once again addressed my ear. "But I don't remember any safety pin. Ah, yes! I didn't know you had such a formidable memory. But how odd it is that I'm talking to you—our telephone is out of order. What's going on? Where are you calling from?"

"Can you hear me well enough?" I replied, dodging the question, as though I had failed to understand what she was asking, and, having received her confirmation, I continued: "I don't know whether we'll be able to talk for long. I have my reasons for not dwelling on this. Like you, there are a lot of things I don't understand. That's why you must give me your address at once; I don't have it."

For some short while the current hummed monotonously, as though my last words had interrupted the connection. Again a distance fell between us like a blind wall—a repugnant feeling of frustration and shameful yearning almost abashed me enough to launch into an unseemly diatribe on the nature of telephone conversations, which do not allow one to express freely all the shades of the simplest, most innate feelings. In some instances a face and words are inseparable. Perhaps this is the very thing that she, too, was pondering as the silence continued, after which I heard:

"Why do you want to know? Oh, very well. Take it down then." She said this not without cunning. "The address is: apartment eleven, number ninety-seven on the Fifth Line.* Only why, why do you need my address? Frankly, I don't understand. I'm at home in the evenings . . ."

I continued to hear the unhurried music of the voice, but suddenly it rang out, quiet and muffled, as though it were in a box. I could hear her talking, apparently telling me something, but I could no longer make out the words. Her speech flowed farther and farther away, growing ever more indistinct, until it became like the patter of raindrops—at last the barely audible pulsing of the current led me to understand that the apparatus had stopped working. The connection disappeared and the instrument fell obtusely silent. Before me stood the wall, the box, and the receiver. The nocturnal rain drummed against the glass pane of the window. I pressed the button; it gave out a jangle and stopped. The receiver was dead. The spell was broken.

---

* *the Fifth Line*: The street is located on Vasilyevsky Island; however, the numbering in the street runs only as far as 70.

But I had heard and I had *spoken*; what had been could not be denied. My impressions of these minutes had come and gone in a whirlwind; I was filled with its echoes still, and I sat down, suddenly exhausted, as though from climbing a steep staircase. What was more, I was only at the start of my adventure. Its progress began with the sound of distant footsteps.

VII.

Still a long way off—was it not from the very point where I had begun my journey? or perhaps from the opposite direction?—either way, at the significant distance from which one first catches these sounds, I could hear the approach of unknown footsteps. Insofar as I could ascertain, someone was walking alone, treading nimbly and lightly, along a familiar path, through the darkness and possibly lighting the way with a lamp or a candle. In my mind's eye, however, I saw *him* carefully scurrying about in the darkness, on the alert and looking around as he went. I do not know why I imagined this. I sat there, frozen and alarmed, as though gripped from afar by the tips of giant pincers. I became flooded with anticipation, which caused my temples to ache; I was in a state of fear that stripped me of any ability to resist. I would have been calm, or at least have begun to calm down, had the footsteps been receding, but I could hear them getting more and more distinct, drawing closer. My ears tormented, I was lost in conjecture, wondering about the purpose of this long, agonizing peregrination through the deserted building. Already the presentiment that I would not manage to avoid an encounter grazed my consciousness, horrifying me; I stood up and sat down again, not knowing what to do. My pulse followed the articulation or pauses of the steps exactly; however, having at last mastered the gloomy inertia of my body, my heart began beating violently, so that I could feel my condition with every throb. My impulses were contradictory.

I hesitated: should I snuff out the candle or leave it burning? Lacking any rational indication, it was the very notion of taking action that seemed to provide a reasonable means of escaping this dangerous encounter. I did not doubt that this encounter would be dangerous or distressing. I groped for solace among the uninhabited walls and longed to retain the nocturnal illusion. At one point, endeavoring to tread noiselessly, I passed through a door so as to see in which of the adjoining rooms I could hide, as though the room in which I had been sitting, with my back shielding the candle, were already scheduled for a visit and somebody knew that I was there. I abandoned this, realizing that in making these transitions I was acting like a gambler at the roulette wheel, who, having changed his numbers, sees in exasperation that he has lost only because he changed his bet. The most prudent option would be to sit and wait with the candle extinguished. And that is what I did. I began to wait in the dark.

However, there could be no doubt that the distance between me and the unknown newcomer was diminishing with every throb of my pulse. Now no more than five or six walls separated us; he was going from door to door with the assured speed of a slight body. Cowering, riveted by his steps, everything tending toward the moment when our eyes would meet (this moment was speeding toward me like a motorcar), I prayed to God that these were not pupils with a crazed band of white around their central glimmer. I no longer expected, rather I knew that I should see him; my instinct, having replaced reason in these moments, spoke the truth, offering its blind face to the sharp blade of fear. The darkness was crowded with phantoms. I saw the gremlin that haunted a dark corner of the nursery, a phantom of the twilight, and, most horrible of all, more terrifying than a fall from a great height, was the obsessive fear that those footsteps would fall silent right at my door, that no one would be there, and that this absence of anyone at all would skim my face in a puff of air. I already found it impossible to imagine this being as a person, like me. The encounter was imminent; I had nowhere to hide. Suddenly the steps fell silent, stopping near the door, and for so long I heard nothing but the bustle of mice scurrying among the heaps of papers that I almost let out a scream. Someone hunched over seemed to be creeping noiselessly though the door with the intention of seizing me. The shock of a mad exclamation filling the darkness suddenly thrust me forward, arms outstretched— I staggered back, covering my face. A dancing torch revealed to me the whole chain of doors as far as I could see. It grew as light as day. I received a sort of nervous shock, but after a brief hesitation I pressed on. Then, from beyond the nearest wall a woman's voice said: "Come here." There followed a quiet, teasing laughter.

For all my amazement, I did not expect such an end to the torture I had just endured over what may have been an hour. "Who's there?" I asked quietly, carefully approaching the door, behind which some unknown woman had revealed her presence with a beautiful and tender voice. Hearing her, I imagined her appearance to be commensurate with the pleasure of hearing her, and I trustingly drew nearer, listening to her repeating the words: "Come here, come here." But I saw nobody behind the wall. The frosted-glass balls of the chandelier glittered below the ceiling, disseminating a nocturnal day among the black windows. Thus, asking, and each time receiving a response invariably from behind the wall of an adjacent room—"Come, oh, come on, quickly!"—I toured five or six rooms, in one of them catching my reflection in a mirror, watching as I carefully transferred my gaze from one void to another. It then seemed as if the shadows in the mirror's depths were full of hunched, creeping women, one after another, in cloaks or veils that they pressed to their faces, concealing their features, and only their black eyes, lit by a smile under schemingly knit brows, flashed elusively. But I was wrong, for I turned around with such speed as would not allow even the most agile of creatures to escape the building. Weary and dreading, what with the excitement that was overwhelming me, something truly terrible amid these silently illuminated voids, I said at last in a sharp tone of voice:

"Show yourself, or I shan't go any farther. Who are you and why are you calling me?"

Before any answer could come, an echo enveloped my exclamation in a vague and muffled reverberation. I detected a troubled alarm in the words of the mysterious woman when she beckoned me uneasily from an unknown corner: "Hurry, don't stop! Come on, come on, don't argue." These words seemed to have come from somewhere alongside me—as quick as the splashing of water, and so clear in their half-whisper, as if they had been spoken directly into my ear. Yet in vain I rushed impetuously from one door to the next, throwing them open or else making a complex detour to try to catch the woman unawares as she made her slippery movements— everywhere I met only emptiness, doors, and light. This continued, like a game of hide-and-seek, and several times I let out an exasperated sigh, not knowing whether to go farther or to stop, to stop resolutely, until I saw the woman with whom I had been conducting this hopeless dialogue at a distance. If I fell silent, the voice would seek me out; it sounded ever more affectionate and anxious, always indicating the way and quietly exclaiming ahead of me, behind the very next wall:

"This way, hurry!"

Sensitive though I was to the tenor of a voice in general— particularly so in such states of extreme tension—I perceived neither mockery nor dissimulation in the elusive woman's calls, in her importunate beckoning; although her conduct was more than astonishing, I had no reason to suspect anything ominous or malign, since I was ignorant of the circumstances causing this behavior. Rather, I might have suspected an insistent desire to communicate or show something to me in haste, with time pressing on. If I made a false move, landing in the wrong room, a musical interjection, accompanied by a rustling and rapid breathing, would pursue me: a soft and gentle "This way!" would put me back on track. I had already gone too far to turn back. I was drawn anxiously by the unknown, rushing across vast parquets, my eyes fixed in the direction of the voice.

"I'm here," the voice said at last, in a tone that suggested the end of this adventure. This was at a point where the corridor crossed a staircase and there were several steps leading up to another corridor.

"Very well, but this is the last time," I warned. She was waiting for me at the start of the corridor, on the right, where the light was at its weakest; I could hear her breathing and, climbing the staircase, I angrily surveyed the semidarkness. Both walls of the corridor were littered with piles of books, leaving only a narrow path between them. By the light of the solitary lamp dimly illuminating the staircase and the end of the passage, I could not make anyone out at a distance.

"Where are you?" I said, straining my eyes. "Stop, you're going too quickly. Come here."

"I can't," the voice replied quietly. "Can you really not see me? I'm here. I'm tired, so I sat down. Come closer."

It really did sound as if she were nearby. I would have to turn the corner. Beyond lay darkness, underscored by the bright light of a door at the end. Stumbling over books, I tripped, staggered, and, falling to the floor, toppled over a shaky pile of ledgers. They went tumbling down, far below. As I fell, my hands met a void, and I almost disappeared entirely over the edge of this sheer drop, from where, to my involuntary shriek, the sound of an avalanche of books soared up. I saved myself only because I happened to fall before I reached the edge. If terrified awe at this moment stopped me from drawing conclusions, then laughter, that cold, merry snicker on the far side of the trap, immediately clarified my role. The laughter retreated, abated, to the point where I could no longer hear its cruel intonations.

I took care not to make any sudden movement, any noise that could cast doubt on my supposed disappearance; understanding the game, I remained absolutely still, meaning to confirm the assumption of the desired outcome. I could not resist peering, however, into the bed that had been prepared for me. Nothing for the moment indicated that I was being observed, and, taking great care, I lit a match. I saw the rectangle of a gaping hole in the floor. The light did not reach to the bottom, but, recalling the time it had taken for the books to plummet before crashing below, I estimated a drop of forty feet. Which meant that there must have been a hole in the floor directly below, identical to this one, forming a double aperture. I was disturbing somebody. I understood this, in possession now of substantial evidence, but what I did not understand was how this airiest of women could have flown across the vast aperture, whose walls had no border along them that allowed one to circumvent it; it reached six *arshins* in width.[*]

Waiting for the incident to lose its perilous freshness, I crawled back to the spot where the distant light allowed me to distinguish the walls, and there I stopped. I did not dare return to those lit places. Nor, however, was I capable now of leaving the stage where I had scarcely finished playing out the finale of the fifth act. I had touched on things much too serious to prevent my going. Not knowing where to begin, I trod gingerly in the opposite direction, hiding at times in the recesses of the walls so as to be sure that there was nobody coming. In one of these recesses I found a washbasin, with water dripping from the tap; beside it there hung a towel

---

[*]   *six arshins in width*: The *arshin* is an old Russian unit of measurement, equivalent to two and one-third feet; the width of the aperture is thus fourteen feet.

bearing the damp traces of just-wiped hands. The towel was still *swaying*; somebody was absconding, perhaps ten paces away from me, and only by chance had he escaped unseen, just as I had. I did not want to risk tempting this place any longer. Petrified by sight of the just-touched towel before me, I finally set off, breath bated, spotting in the shadow of a recess a narrow side door that was almost blocked up by papers. With no little effort, I was able to force the door open a fraction in order to squeeze through. I exited through the door, as though through a wall, and found myself in a quiet, well-lit, deserted passageway, very narrow, with a turning not far ahead. I did not want to risk peering around it, however, preferring to stand there, propping myself up against the wall, in the niche of a boarded-up door.

No sound, no phenomenon intelligible to the senses could have escaped me during those moments, since I was strained, on edge. My whole being was centered in my hearing and breathing. Life on earth seemed to have vanished—such was the silence that met my eye in the light of the white, desolate passageway. Apparently every living creature had forsaken this place or else was in hiding. Exhaustion overwhelmed me; with the impatience of despair I began to reach out for any sound at all, if only to banish the torpid light that clenched my heart in its silent vice. All of a sudden there were more than sufficient sounds to *calm* me—if I can employ the phrase "calm amid a storm"—an abundance of steps rang out behind the wall, coming from the lower floors. I could hear voices, exclamations. To the sounds of this nascent, unseen animation were added those of instruments being tuned: a violin squeaked, a cello, a flute, and a double bass strung out a few disparate measures, only to be drowned out by the racket of furniture being moved.

In the middle of the night—I did not know the hour—these signs of life three floors below, after the episode with the gaping hole, sounded like a new threat. Perhaps tireless peregrinations would have eventually led me to an exit from this labyrinthine building, but not now, now that I knew what could be lying in wait for me behind the very next door. I could establish my position only if I determined what was going on downstairs. Listening carefully, I ascertained the distance between myself and the sounds. It was significant, reaching up from beyond the wall facing me.

I stood for so long in the doorway, but in the end I managed to muster the strength to leave, with the aim of seeing whether I could do something. After a few furtive steps, I noticed to the right of me a glazed aperture in the wall, no bigger than a ventilation window; it was within reach just above my head. A little farther on I discovered a portable folding ladder of the sort used by decorators to treat the afflictions of ceilings. Having dragged over the ladder as carefully as I could, without knocking it, without hitting the walls, I placed it beside the aperture. Despite how dusty the glass was on both sides, after wiping it with the palm of my hand as best I could, I was able to see, but still as if through smoke. My hypothesis, founded on the basis of my hearing, was confirmed: I was looking at that same central hall of the bank where I had been earlier that evening, but I could not see the lower half of it, since my little window looked onto the gallery. The vast stucco ceiling hung very low over my head; the balustrade right before my eyes obscured the depths of the hall, and I could see only the upper portion of the faraway columns on the opposite side. Throughout the length of the gallery there was not a soul present, while downstairs, tormenting me with its invisibility, a merry crowd thronged. I could hear laughter, cheers, chairs being moved, unintelligible snippets of conversation, and the calm clatter of the downstairs doors. The chink of crockery rang out with conviction; people coughing, clearing their noses, a chain of light and heavy footsteps, melodic, malicious intonations: yes, it was a banquet, a ball, a gathering, guests, a celebration—you name it—anything but the vast, cold emptiness of old, with its stagnant echo amid the dust. The chandeliers discharged their brilliance in a fiery pattern below, and although there was light in my dungeon, too, the brighter light of the hall fell across my hand.

Almost certain that nobody would come here, to my nook, which had more in common with a cramped attic than it did with the sumptuous expanse of the chamber below, I ventured to remove the glass. The frame, held in place by two crooked nails, was slightly loose. I extracted the nails and got rid of the barrier. The noise now became palpable, like the wind in one's face; while I was attempting to unravel its particularities, the band struck up a music-hall number, but their playing was so strangely muted, as if they could not or did not want to let the music grow. The orchestra was playing *con sordino*, as if by order. However, the voices that were being drowned out by the band began to grow louder, making a natural effort to overcome the music, and the general sense of their words carried up to my refuge. Insofar as I could understand, the interest of various groups in the hall revolved around suspicious deals, although I caught only incoherent snatches of conversation. Certain phrases resembled neighing, others a dreadful scream; the ponderous laughter of business mixed with a hissing. Women's voices rang out with a tense and gloomy timbre, crossing from time to time into tempting playfulness with the depraved intonations of camellias. Occasionally someone's solemn remarks would lead the conversation to the prices of gold and precious jewels; other words would make you shudder, alluding to a murder or some crime of a no less conclusive nature. Prison slang, the shamelessness of nocturnal streets, the false luster of reckless adventure, and the nervous prolixity of hunted souls mixed with the strains of *another* orchestra, to which the first was making subtle, playful replies.

There was a lull; several doors opened down in the faraway depths below, and it seemed as if new faces were making their entrance. This impression was immediately confirmed by the solemn exclamations I heard. After indistinct negotiations came the thunder of exhortations and invitations to listen. Somebody's speech was already trickling there quietly, spattering like raindrops, making its way like a beetle among pine needles in a forest.

"All hail our Savior!" roared the assembly. "Death to the Rat-Catcher!"

"Death!" the women's lugubrious voices rang out.

The echoes passed in a long howl before dying down. I do not know why, despite the dread attention I paid to what I heard, but at that moment I turned around, as if I were being watched; only I heaved a deep sigh of relief, for there was nobody standing behind me. I had time yet to think of a way to conceal myself: two individuals had clearly passed around the corner without the slightest suspicion of my presence. They paused. Their gentle shadow fell across my dungeon, but I examined it in vain, seeing in it only an indistinct mass. They struck up a conversation with the assurance of confidants who believe themselves to be alone. They were clearly continuing a conversation begun earlier. En route here their narrative had come to a halt at some unknown question, to which I now heard the answer. I remembered this dark, rasping promise word for word.

"He will die," said one of them, "but not right away. Here is the address: apartment eleven, number ninety-seven on the Fifth Line. He has his daughter with him. This will be a great feat for the Liberator. The Liberator has come here from a faraway land. His journey was wearying, and he is expected in a great many cities yet. Tonight everything shall be accomplished. Go and inspect the passage. So long as nothing threatens the Liberator, the Rat-Catcher is a dead man, and we shall see his vacant eyes!"

VIII.

I listened to this vengeful tirade, with one foot already on the floor, for no sooner had I heard the address of the girl repeated to the letter—the girl whose name I had not managed to learn today—than a blind force pulled me down, impelling me to flee, to hide, and to fly as a messenger to the Fifth Line. Even under the most reasonable scrutiny, these numbers and the street name could not tell me whether another family lived in the apartment—yet it was enough that I was thinking about *her* and the fact that she was there. In my terror, my infernal haste, as if a fire had broken out within me, I missed the last step; the ladder slipped with a clatter, my presence was revealed. I froze at first, like a fallen sack. The lights went out instantly; the music instantly faded, and a cry of fury outstripped my blind escape through the narrow passageway, where, I do not recall how, I crashed into the door by which I had entered. With inexplicable strength, in a single burst of effort I pushed away the rubbish blocking it and ran out into that unforgettable corridor with the aperture. I was saved! The dawn was breaking with its first glimmers of gray light, outlining the doorframes; I could have run until I was out of breath. But instinctively I sought ways up, not down, bounding up the little steps and along the empty passageways. Sometimes I thrashed around, spinning on the spot, taking doors I had already tried for new ones or finding myself at a dead end. It was terrible, like a nightmare, especially since I was being pursued—I could hear them scurrying back and forth, the sound of the chase, which was driving me mad and from which there was no escape. The noise rose and fell with the irregularity of traffic in the street, sometimes coming so close that I jumped behind a door, or else it tracked me in a parallel race, as though promising to broadside me at any moment. I grew weak, paralyzed by fear and the never-ceasing tumult of the floors echoing. But now I was running through the top floor. The final stairway I spotted led up through the ceiling via a square opening; I threw myself up it, feeling as though I was being struck in the back—so quickly had my assailants closed in on me. I found myself in the suffocating dark of an attic, immediately toppling over everything that dimly showed white about either side of the hatch; these proved to be a stacks of window frames, which only the strength of my despair allowed me to move in a single stroke. They lay there, scattered in all directions, their sashes an impassable thicket. This being done, I ran over to a far-off dormer window, in the gray light of which I espied barrels and boards. The way was incredibly cluttered. I leaped over a forest of beams, boxes, brickwork, pits, and piping. At last I made it to the window. The freshness of the open air exuded the calm of deep sleep. Beyond the far roof, an indistinct, rose-colored shadow loomed; there was no smoke coming from the chimneys, nor could I hear any passers-by. I climbed out and made my way over to the funnel of a drainpipe. It was loose; its fixings rattled when I began to climb down it; halfway down its cold iron acquired a coat of dew, and I slid fitfully down, barely able to maintain my grip. Finally, my feet touched the sidewalk; I hastened toward the river, fearing to find the bridge raised, and so, as soon as I caught my breath, I made a dash for it.

IX.

As soon as I turned the corner, I was compelled to stop when I saw a handsome lad of around seven crying, his little face blanched from the tears; he was rubbing his eyes with his fists and sobbing. Moved by a pity that would have been natural for anyone upon meeting this sight, I leaned down and asked him: "Where have you come from, little boy? Have you been abandoned? How did you get here?"

Without a word, he went on sobbing, peering up at me mistrustfully. The sight of him was heartrending. There was nobody around. His thin little frame shivered, his little feet were filthy and bare. Despite my rush to get to the place of danger, I could not abandon this child, all the more so because he was meekly silent, from either fright or exhaustion, trembling and squirming at my every question, as though it were a threat. Stroking his head and looking into his eyes full of tears, I achieved nothing; he could only hang his head and cry. "Little one," I said, having resolved to knock on some door in order to deposit the child, "sit here. I'll be back soon, and we'll find that unfit mother of yours." To my astonishment, however, he clung to my arm and refused to let it go. There was something absurd and wild about his efforts; he even followed me along the sidewalk, screwing up his eyes, while I, with a sudden pang of suspicion, snatched my hand away. His beautiful little face was contorted, straining with effort. "Hey, there!" I cried, trying to free my hand. "Stop that!" I pushed him away. No longer crying and also silent, he fixed his enormous black eyes on me. Then he recovered and, chuckling, ran off so quickly that I flinched, dumbstruck. "Who are you?" I shouted menacingly. He giggled and, quickening his pace, vanished around a corner, but for some while I kept looking in that direction, feeling as though I'd been bitten, before I came to my senses and broke into a run with the speed of someone trying to catch a tram. I was out of breath. Twice I had to stop before continuing on as fast as I could, running again and, again losing my breath, having to content myself with a mad dash, a fitful sprint.

I was already on Horse Guards Parade when I was overtaken by a girl who fleetingly glanced at me with the expression of someone trying to recall a face she had seen before. She was about to run on, but I recognized her instantly with such a violent internal jolt equal to the ecstasy of salvation. As I called to her, she let out a soft exclamation and stopped with a shadow of annoyance on her sweet face.

"It really is you!" she said. "How could I not have recognized you? To think I would have gone straight past you, were it not for the look of shock on your face. How haggard you look, how pale!"

Great bewilderment and yet the greatest calm swept over me. Overwhelmed by a radiant and violent confusion, I looked at this face that I might well have lost, with a faith in the complex significance of this happy accident. I was so stunned, so internally arrested, for in my pursuit of her my galloping imagination had envisaged the end of my journey in such different circumstances that I now felt a sense of frustration—it would have been nicer had I met her *there*, where she lived.

"Listen," I said, unable to break away from her trusting gaze. "I was running on my way to see you. It's still not too late . . ."

She stopped me, taking me aside by the sleeve.

"It's too soon," she said significantly, "or too late, as you will. It's light, but it is still night. You will come to me this evening, do you hear? I'll tell you everything then. I've been thinking a lot about us. Know this: I love you."

It was like stopping a clock. That moment my soul separated from hers. She couldn't, wouldn't talk like that. With a sigh, I let go of her fresh little hand that was clasping mine and took a step back. She looked at me with a face that was ready to twitch with impatience. The expression distorted her features—her tenderness gave way to obtuseness, her eyes darted about sharply, and, with a dreadful laugh, I shook my finger.

"No, you can't deceive me," I said. "She's there. She's sleeping now, and I'm going to wake her up. Avaunt, foul specter, whoever you are."

With a quick sleight of the hand she covered her face with a kerchief, and that was the last I clearly saw of her, two paces away from me. Then the narrow strips of light filtering through the trees began to flicker, now recalling the silhouette of a woman dashing through them, now reminding me that I was running at full pelt. I could already see the clock on the square. The bridge was already barricaded by *chevaux de frise*. In the distance, on the opposite side of the embankment, a black tug was puffing out plumes of smoke, towing a barge by a rope. I jumped over a *cheval* and made it across the bridge at the last possible moment, just as the midsection was beginning to rise up, splitting apart the tramlines. My flying jump was met by the guards' cry of frantic obscenities; however, with a mere glance at the gap of water glittering below, I was already far away from them, and so I ran until I reached the gates.

X.

Then—or, rather, presently—there came a moment, subsequent to which I can reconstruct only part of the fleeting, obscure events in reverse order. To begin with, I saw the girl, standing by the door, listening, with her hand stretched out as people do when they are asking or silently bidding you to sit down quietly. She had on a summer coat; her face wore a worried, sad expression. She had been asleep when I arrived. This I knew, but the circumstances of my arrival slipped away, like water in a clenched fist, as soon as I made an immediate, conscious effort to link everything together. Obeying her gesture, which was pregnant with anxiety, I sat there, stock-still, waiting to see how this listening for something would end. I tried to understand its meaning but in vain. A little longer and I would have made a concerted effort to master my extreme weakness; I wanted to ask what was going on in the main room, when, as if divining my movement, the girl turned her head, frowning and threatening me with a finger. Now I remembered that her name was Suzy, that someone had given her this name—the man who had gone out, with the words: "There must be absolute silence." Was I asleep, or was I simply befuddled? In an attempt to answer this,

I instinctively lowered my gaze and saw that the flap of my overcoat was torn. It had been intact while I was running here. I passed from bewilderment to surprise. Suddenly everything began to tremble and seemed to dart away, blocking the light; blood rushed to my head, there came a deafening crash, similar to a shot above the ear, and then a cry. "Halt!" somebody shouted behind the door. Taking a deep breath, I leaped to my feet. A man in a gray dressing gown appeared from the doorway, holding out to the recoiling girl a little board, on which, trapped in an arc of wire, hung an enormous black rat that had been broken in two. Its teeth were bared and its tail hung down.

Then, rent out of my truly dreadful condition by the shock and the cry, my memory crossed a dark precipice. In an instant I grasped a number of things and refused to let them go. My feelings were moved to speak. My inner vision turned to the opening of the scene, going over the chain of exploits. I remembered how I had climbed the gate, fearing to knock, lest I invite new dangers; how I had bypassed the door and pulled the third-floor bell. But the conversation through the door—a long and anxious conversation, during the course of which a man's and a woman's voices argued over whether to let me in—I forgot irrevocably. This I recalled only later.

All these details that were not yet quite aligned came to me in the blink of an eye. The old man who had brought in the rat trap had a head of thick gray hair that was cut evenly all round, recalling the cup of an acorn. His sharp nose, his thin, clean-shaven lips with their complex, stubborn expression, his bright, colorless eyes, and the wispy gray whiskers on his rosy face, which ended with his little protruding chin, which nestled in his pale-blue scarf, might have been of interest to the portrait painter or an amateur of typologies.

He said:

"You see before you the so-called black Guinean rat. Its bite is very dangerous. It causes a slow living decay, turning the victim into a collection of tumors and abscesses. This type of rodent is rare in Europe, but they occasionally arrive on ships. The 'free passage' you heard mentioned last night is an artificial hole that I made near the kitchen so that I could experiment with all different manner of traps. For the past two days the passage really was free, for I was absorbed in reading Hert Hertrus: *The Storehouse of the Rat King*, a book that is a rarity *par excellence*. It was published in Germany four centuries ago. Its author was burned at the stake as a heretic in Bremen. Your story . . ."

Consequently, I had already said everything that I had come to say. But I still had doubts. I asked:

"Have you taken measures? Do you know the nature of this danger? I do not understand it myself entirely."

"Measures?" said Suzy. "What measures do you mean?"

"The danger . . ." the old man began, but paused, looking at his daughter. "I don't understand."

There was a moment of confusion. All three of us exchanged expectant glances.

"I mean," I began uncertainly, "that you should beware. I must have told you already, but, forgive me, I don't quite recall what I said. I feel as though I must have fainted."

The girl looked at her father, then at me, before smiling embarrassedly: "How can this be?"

"He is tired, Suzy," the old man said. "I know what insomnia is. *Everything* has been said, and the measures have been taken. If I name this rat"—he set down the trap at my feet with the satisfied look of a hunter—" 'the Liberator,' you shall have something of an idea."

"This is a joke," I objected, "the joke of a rat-catcher, of course."
As I said this, I remembered having seen a bell, below which hung
the modest sign bearing the words:

> RAT-CATCHER
> Extermination of rats and mice
> O. Jensen
> Tel. 1–08–01.

■ □ ■

I had seen it at the entrance.

"You must be joking, for I don't believe that *this* 'Liberator' could
have caused you so much trouble."

"He isn't joking," said Suzy. "He knows." I compared these two
gazes, to which I then replied with a disconcerted smile—the
gaze of youth, full of genuine conviction, and the gaze of aged but
bright eyes, doubting whether to continue the conversation as it
had begun.

"I prefer to let Hert Hertrus speak for me on these matters."
The rat-catcher left and came back carrying an old book bound in
leather and with red edging. "Here is the part you may laugh at or
ponder, as you please."

> This black and artful creature possesses the powers of the human
> mind. It is further master of the secrets of the underworld, where it
> hides. It is within its power to alter its appearance, to take on human
> form, with arms and legs, to wear clothing and to adopt the face,
> eyes, and movements resembling those of a human, and its impos-
> ture, in its perfection, is in no way inferior to the very image of a
> human. Rats may also cause incurable disease, using to this end
> means known only to them.

They are beloved of pestilence, famine, war, flood, and invasion. Then they gather under the sign of mysterious metamorphoses, acting like people, and you will talk to them, not knowing who they are. They steal and sell at a profit inconceivable to the honest worker, and they deceive with the splendor of their garments and the meekness of their speech. They murder and destroy by fire, swindle, and lay traps; surrounded by luxury, they eat and drink their fill and have everything in abundance. Gold and silver is their most beloved loot, and precious jewels too, which they store underground.

"But enough of this," said the rat-catcher. "You have guessed, of course, why I translated specifically this passage. *You were surrounded by rats.*"

But I had already understood. In certain cases we prefer to say nothing, so that our impression, wavering and being rent by other considerations, find a sure haven. Meanwhile, the furniture covers had begun to glint in the intensifying light streaming in through the window. The first voices in the street rang out as clearly as if they were in the room itself. Again I plunged into oblivion. The faces of the girl and her father receded, becoming a vague mirage, shrouded in a transparent mist. "Suzy, what's wrong with him?" came the booming question. The girl approached me, standing somewhere near me, but where exactly I did not see, for I was in no state to turn my head. All of a sudden my forehead grew warm from the touch of a woman's hand, while my surroundings, full of distorted, crossed perspectives, were engulfed in the chaos of my psyche. A wild, heavy dream carried me off. I heard her voice: "He's asleep"—the words to which I awoke after thirty hours of nonbeing. I was taken to a cramped neighboring room and transferred onto a real bed, after which I learned that "for a man" I was "very light." They took pity on me; the very next day, a room in the neighboring apartment was placed entirely at my disposal. What happens next is of no consequence. But it falls to me to ensure that it be just like that moment when I felt a warm hand on my head. I must win trust . . .

And not another word about this.

FANDANGO

I.

In winter—when faces pale from the cold, when a person will run about a room wildly, hands thrust in sleeves, casting longing glances at the cold stove—how pleasant it is to think of summer, for in summer it's warm.

I saw before me a burning glass and the sun overhead. Let us imagine that it's July. A harsh, blinding spot, caught by the glaring lens, begins to smoke at the tip of a cigarette placed under it. The heat is fierce. It makes you unbutton your collar, wipe your damp neck and forehead, down a glass of water. But spring is a long way off, and a tropical pattern on the frosty window absurdly unfolds a transparent palm leaf.

Frozen stiff, trembling, I couldn't make up my mind to leave, even though it was an unequivocal necessity. I do not like the snow, the frost, the ice—the pleasures of the Eskimo are foreign to my heart. Moreover, my clothing and footwear were simply no good at all. My old summer coat, an old cap, boots with worn-out soles—these were all I had to see out December and its twenty-seven degrees of frost.

S. T. had entrusted me to buy a painting by Gorshkov from the artist Brock. This was a kindly favor on S. T.'s part, since he could easily have bought the painting himself. As an act of pity, he meant to give me the commission. I was pondering this just now, as I was whistling the "Fandango."

In those days I had no aversion to earning money by any means. I had discovered this little picture the week before, when I stopped off at Brock's to collect some belongings, for until only recently I had occupied the room that was now his. I didn't care for Gorshkov, much as people don't care for cold, clammy, or limp handshakes; still, knowing that for S. T. the "who" was more important that the "what," I informed him of my discovery. I added further that I doubted whether Brock's acquisition of the painting had been entirely aboveboard.

Corpulent, wearing his dressing gown, S. T. thoughtfully scratched his beard and yawned, saying: "Well, well . . ."—and began drumming his red fingers on the table. Meanwhile, I drank his genuine Chinese tea, ate his ham, his bread and butter, his eggs; I was hungry and gauche, and I spoke with my mouth full.

S. T. stirred his glass with an engraved gilt teaspoon. He lifted the spoon out, took a sip, and said:

"Why don't you get it for me? I'll give you fifteen percent, and if it comes in at under two hundred, the difference is yours."

I am relaying the figures in today's money, for I should now find it difficult to reckon the chain of zeroes that would have been placed after the two hundred back then.

In those days, thirty gold rubles were the equivalent of a thousand today in real terms. With thirty rubles in your pocket, you understood the line, "Man! How proud the word rings!"*

---

* *Man! How proud the word rings*: A line, now proverbial in Russia, from Satine's monologue in Act IV of Maxim Gorky's (1868–1936) play *The Lower Depths* (*Na dne*, 1902).

They turned the scale at a quarter-ton of bread—half a year of life. What was more, I could haggle lower still, get it for less than two hundred, and in so doing earn more than thirty rubles.

I was spurred to action by a glance in the cupboard, where there were empty saucepans, a griddle, and a pot. (I lived like Robinson Crusoe.) They reeked of hunger. There was a little rust-colored salt, some cowberry tea bearing the endorsement "tea-lovers' choice," some dry crusts and potato peelings.

I fear hunger—loathe it and fear it. It is the corruption of man. This tragic but most banal of feelings spares not even the soul's tenderest roots. Hunger supplants *true* thought with false thought— while retaining the same outward form, it acquires a different quality within. "I'll stay honest," says a man, starved so cruelly and for so long, "because I love honesty. But I'll kill (or steal, or lie) just this once, because I must if I'm to stay honest in the future." Public opinion, self-respect, the suffering of those dear to us—it all exists, but it's like a lost coin: it is there, and yet it isn't. Cunning, slyness, tenacity—it all aids the digestion. Children will eat up half the kasha they are given at a canteen on the way home; the canteen administration steals, the hospital administration steals, the warehouse administration steals. The head of the household secretly cuts into a loaf of bread in the pantry and devours it, trying not to make a sound. The friend who shows up, having followed the pathetically steaming trail of some measly spread that has been procured with heroic efforts, is met with hatred.

But that isn't the worst of it, for all that is done out in the open: worse still is when some outrageously painted doll, the spitting image of me (or you, or him . . .), unashamedly drives our soul from its weakened body and joyfully runs after some crust in the firm and sudden belief that it is the very same person whom it has just laid hands on. *That* person has already corrupted everything: taste, desire, thought, and *his own* truth. Every man has his own truth. And he keeps saying "I, I, I," meaning the doll, which repeats the same thing and with the same connotations. When looking at cheeses, cold cuts, or bread, I've often experienced an almost spiritual transfiguration of these "calories": they seem to be written all over with paradoxes, metaphors, the subtlest arguments in the brightest and gayest of tones; their logical weight is equal to the number of pounds. And there is even an ethical aroma—which is to say, a particular hungry lust.

"How plain it is to see," I would say, "the path from counter to stomach is so natural, so sensible, so *simple.*"

Yes, that was the way of it, with all the false sincerity of such ravings, and that is why I cannot, as I said, abide hunger. Even now I meet strangers with such vivid memories of two ounces of oats. Their recollections have been drastically altered by the introduction of a romantic note, and this musical vibration is beyond my comprehension. It may be regarded as an original form of cynicism. For example: a man standing before a looking glass may give himself a gentle slap in the face. This is disrespect toward oneself. However, if such an experiment were to be conducted publicly, it would denote disrespect both toward oneself and toward others.

II.

I overcame the frost by lighting a cigarette, warming my fingers as I cupped the lit match between my palms, and whistled a tune from a Spanish dance. For several days already I had been haunted by this melody. I had begun hearing it whenever I lapsed into thought.

I'm seldom morose, least of all in restaurants. Of course, I'm talking of the past as though it were the present. It would happen that I'd arrive at a restaurant in high spirits, *simply* in high spirits, without any notion that "Here, now, it's a good thing to be in high spirits, because . . .", and so on. No, I was in high spirits, just as it is a man's right to be in any mood. I would sit there, listening to "Autumn Violins," "Have Pity, My Love," "What Do You Want? I Want Nothing" and other such talentless, hysterical nonsense, with which a Russian typically rides roughshod over his merriment. When I had wearied of this, I would give the conductor a nod, and, running his fingers over his silky moustache, the Romanian would acknowledge this, accepting in his other hand, like a doctor, a folded banknote. Turning back his head ever so slightly, he would say to the orchestra in a hushed voice:

"Fandango!"

With this short, energetic word, a tender hand in a glove of armor was placed upon my head—the hand of a dance as impetuous as the wind, as reverberant as hail, as melodious as a deep contralto. A slight chill passed from my feet to my throat. Some drunken Germans, banging away with their fists, vociferously demanded "Haff Pity, Meine Liebe," which had brought tears to their eyes, but a tap of the baton against the music stand informed them that their number was over.

The "Fandango" is the rhythmic hypnosis of passion, of a passionate and strange exultation. In all likelihood, it is the transcribed warbling of a nightingale, raised to the highest degree of musical articulation.

I put on my things and left; it was eleven o'clock in the morning, cold, and hopelessly light.

Along the road a long trail of officeworkers was hurrying to the various commissariats. The "Fandango" grew muffled; it retreated into my pulse, into my breathing, yet the impetuous passage of the measures was still distinct—even in the scarcely audible humming through my teeth, which had become a habit of mine.

The passers-by were dressed in overcoats refashioned from soldiers' greatcoats, sheepskin coats, elkskin jackets, gray trench coats, service jackets, and black leather peacoats. If one came across a civilian coat, it was sure to be old and narrow-fitting. A pretty young lady in a head scarf came tramping through the snow in enormous felt boots, emitting puffs of blue and white steam from her mouth. With a hand encumbered by a mitten, she awkwardly clasped a briefcase to herself. Weathered, like limestone—down to the pores of her wanton cheeks—briskly trotted an old woman smoking a fat Zephyr and wearing a bowl haircut and yellow high-heeled boots. Gloomy young men shuffled along with a strange, alien look. I was interested in everything and had often asked why pedestrians avoided walking on the sidewalk. The answers I received were various. One man said: "Because it's easier on the shoes." Another replied: "On the sidewalk you have to step aside, judge when to give way and when to press on." A third explained simply and wisely: "Because there aren't any horses" (which is to say, no coaches would get in the way). "Everyone else does it," declared a fourth, "so I do, too."

Amid this scene I marked a certain confusion created by the appearance of a group that was sharply distinguished from the rest. They were gypsies. A great many of them had turned up in the city that year, and one would come across them every day. Their itinerant troupe came to a halt around ten paces from me, chattering away among themselves. There was a stooping old man with bushy eyebrows wearing a tall felt hat; two other men wore new dark-blue peaked caps. The old man had on an old tobacco-colored wadded jacket, and there glittered upon his wrinkled ear a fine gold earring. In spite of the frost, he wore his coat open, revealing a mottled velvet waistcoat with a buttoned collar and crimson braiding, plush pantaloons, and high, well-polished boots. One of the other gypsies, who was around thirty, wore a quilted plaid kaftan adorned at the back with huge mother-of-pearl buttons; he had a rounded beard and splendid, luxuriant moustaches the color of pitch; they were of such proportions that they recalled a blacksmith's tongs, gripping him across the face. The youngest gypsy, well built and with a thin, thievish face, looked like a highlander—a Circassian or a Hutsul. He had fiery eyes, with blue marks about the bridge of his aquiline nose, and carried under his arm a guitar wrapped in a gray kerchief; he had on a new sheepskin jacket trimmed with lambskin.

The old man was carrying a hammer dulcimer.

A brass clarinet was protruding from the middle gypsy's bosom.

Apart from the men, there were two women: one young and one old.

The old woman was carrying a tambourine. She was enswathed in two tattered shawls: one green, the other brown; the edge of a soiled red jacket stood out beneath their corners. Enormous gold bracelets glittered whenever she waved her hand, which resembled a bird's claw. Her dark, ugly face betrayed a mixture of thievery and arrogance, impudence and equipoise. Perhaps in her youth she had looked no worse than the young gypsy woman who stood beside her, exuding warmth and health. But it would have been very difficult to be certain of this now.

The beautiful young girl had few gypsy features. Her lips were not thick, only a little plump. Her fresh, well-proportioned face, with its searching gimlet eyes, seemed to peer out from the shadows of leaves—so shaded was it by the length and luster of her eyelashes. Atop a warm fur jacket hung a fringed shawl, creased in the crook of her arms; atop the shawl flowered a silken Turkish kerchief. Heavy turquoise earrings dangled from her diminutive ears, and an austere black braiding with rubles and gold coins draped below the fringe of her shawl. A long skirt—the color of nasturtiums—almost concealed her new booties.

There is a reason for describing these people in such detail. When I caught sight of the gypsies, I involuntarily tried to detect a trace of that unfathomable ancient path, along which they strolled past automobiles and gas lamps, like Kipling's cat, who walked by his wild lone, called all places alike and never told anybody. What is history to them? Eras? Evils? Upheavals? I saw those same magic-eyed travelers, the kind this very city will see in the year 2021, when our progeny, decked out in India rubber and synthetic silk, will alight the cabin of his electric airmobile onto the surface of an aluminum aerial causeway.

After speaking awhile in their barbarous dialect, of which I know only that it is one of the world's most ancient tongues, the gypsies retreated into a back alley, while I set off straight ahead, pondering this encounter with them and calling to mind suchlike former encounters. They were always *at odds* with any mood and *cut right through* it. These encounters bore a resemblance to a strong-colored thread that can be seen invariably on the border of a certain fabric, the name of which I have forgotten. Fashion alters the design of the fabric, its splendor, thickness, and breadth; the market sets an arbitrary price, and it is worn now in spring, now in autumn, in a variety of cuts, yet in every instance the border retains that same many-colored thread. So, too, the gypsies—in and of themselves—remain the same, just as yesterday: throaty raven-haired creatures who inspire vague envy and an impression of wild flowers.

I raked all this over again and again in my mind, until at last the frost squeezed the south out of me, which, out of season, had retreated to the southernmost corner of my soul. My cheeks seemed to be pricked with ice; my nose, too, was far from ablaze, and there was snow packed betwixt a torn sole and my little toe, which was now frozen numb. I hurried as fast as I could, arrived at Brock's apartment, and started knocking on the door, where there was a notice inscribed in chalk: "Bell out of order. Pls. knock loudly."

III.

Diminutive, sharp features, a goatee belonging to one of Chekhov's characters, prominent shoulder blades and long arms, with a lean build and spectacles that made his lusterless, sunken eyes sparkle unnaturally—such was the figure that opened the door to me. Brock was dressed in a long gray coat, black trousers, and a brown waistcoat worn over a sweater. His thin hair had been smoothed down, but not everywhere did it follow the declivities of his skull; in places it stood out horizontally, as though he had stuck dirty feathers in it. He spoke slowly and in a deep voice, like a deacon, peered out mistrustfully over his spectacles, tilting his head to the side, and now and then he rubbed his flaccid hands.

"It's you I've come to see," I said (there were others who lived in the apartment). "But let me warm up a bit first."

"Cold, is it?"

"Yes, bitterly . . ."

While talking on that subject, we passed through a dark corridor toward the bright rhombus of a door that was ajar, and, having gone in, Brock closed it carefully behind him. He proceeded to toss some firewood into a blazing iron stove and, nonchalantly twirling a cigarette, slumped down onto a dusty ottoman, where, leaning on his elbow and crossing his outstretched legs, he hitched up his trousers a little.

I sat down, directing my palms toward the stove, and as I watched my rosy fingers in the light of the flames, I imbibed the blissful warmth.

"At your service," said Brock, removing his spectacles and wiping his eyes with the end of a snotty handkerchief.

Glancing to the left, I saw the painting by Gorshkov hanging where it ought to be. It was a landscape of a swamp, with smoke, snow, and the obligatory dismal light between a spruce and a pair of crows flying away from the viewer.

Paintings of this kind, following Levitan's airy example, suggest an intended "idea."* Of old have I feared these depictions, whose purpose is, naturally, none other than to provoke a deadening feeling of emptiness, submission, and indolence—which suggests, nonetheless, some *impetus*.

"*Twilight*," said Brock, seeing the object of my gaze. "A magnificent work!"

"That is subjective. All the same, what would you take for it?"

"What? You mean to buy it?"

"That's the idea."

He jumped up and, standing in front of the picture, stroked his beard with the tips of his fingers.

"Ehh . . ." said Brock, casting a sidelong glance at me over his shoulder. "You don't have that kind of money. I'm not sure, two hundred would be giving it way, but then again I do need the money. But you haven't got that money!"

"I can find it," I said. "That's why I came—to cut a deal."

A faraway knocking reached us from the front entrance.

"Ah, that'll be for me."

Brock rushed to the door, thrust his small beard through the chink out into the corridor, and shouted:

"Just a minute, I'll be right with you."

While he was gone, I surveyed my surroundings, as was my wont, to while away the time rather with things than with people. Again I caught myself whistling the "Fandango," unconsciously fencing myself off from Gorshkov and Brock with the melody. Now the tune corresponded perfectly to my mood. I was right there, and yet I saw everything around me as though at a distance.

---

* *Levitan's . . . suggest an intended "idea"*: Isaac Ilyich Levitan (1860–1900) was an influential Russian landscape painter, whose "mood landscapes" sought to capture the lyrical qualities of the Russian countryside.

I found myself in a rather large sitting room, with windows looking out onto the street. When I lived there, there had been none of this abundance of things that Brock had introduced since my time. Cluttering the passage between the chairs, which had been arranged haphazardly, were easels, gypsum, and boxes and baskets with clothing and underwear strewn all over them. On the piano stood a stack of plates; on top of them, amid cucumber peels, lay a little knife and fork. The dusty window curtains were parted at an angle, in a most slovenly fashion. By the stove, an old rug covered in holes, footprints, and wood chippings was smoking where a red-hot coal had fallen on it. An electric bulb burned in the middle of the ceiling; in the light of day it looked like a scrap of yellow paper.

There were numerous paintings on the walls, some of which were by Brock himself. I did not examine those, however. Now warm and breathing calmly and evenly, I thought about an elusive musical idea, a firm sense of which always appeared whenever I heard this tune, the "Fandango." Knowing full well that the soul of music is beyond comprehension, I nevertheless reeled this *idea* intently in, and the more I reeled it in, the more distant it became. The impetus for a new sensation was provided by a temporary dimming of the bulb; that is, within its gray glass there appeared a red filament—a phenomenon familiar to all. After flickering a few times, the bulb lit up once again.

In order to understand the strange moment that then followed, it is necessary to call to mind our normal sense of optical equilibrium. I mean to say that, finding oneself in any room, we customarily perceive a center of gravity in the space surrounding us, subject to its shape, the quantity, size, and configuration of objects, and also the direction of light. All this can be schematized in a linear fashion. I term such perception "the center of optical gravity."

While I was sitting there, I felt—perhaps for a millionth fraction of a second—that the space before me, into which I was looking, simultaneously flashed both within me and without. It was in part like the movement of air and was accompanied by the immediate and unsettling feeling that the optical center had shifted. Thus thinking, I determined at last the change in mood. The center had vanished. I stood up, mopping my brow and looking about in the hope of comprehending what had just happened. I felt that absolutely inexpressible determinacy of the visual, while the center, that sense of optical equilibrium, fell beyond its limits, vanishing.

Hearing that Brock was on his way back, I sat down again, unable to drive away the feeling that everything had altered while at the same time remaining exactly the same.

"You must be tired of waiting," said Brock. "Not to worry, warm yourself up, have a smoke."

He came in, dragging a painting of considerable dimensions, but with the back turned toward me so that I could not see what the painting looked like; he placed it behind the cupboard, saying:

"Just bought it. That was the third time this chap has been to see me, so I took it just to get rid of him."

"What kind of painting is it?"

"Oh, it's worthless! A daub, done in very poor taste!" said Brock. "Better take a look at mine. There are two I did just recently."

I walked over to the spot he indicated on the wall. Yes, that's what was in his soul! . . . One was a pea-green landscape. The vague outline of a road and the steppes with an unpleasant dusty hue; with a nod, I moved on to the second "article." It, too, was a landscape, consisting of two horizontal strips of differing shades of gray (lead and slate) with green tufts dotted around it. Both paintings, talentless as they were, evoked a cold, dull tension.

Without a word I stepped away from the paintings. Brock peered at me, coughed, and lit a cigarette.

"You work quickly," I remarked, so as not to draw out the silence. "So, what about the Gorshkov?"

"As I said. Two hundred."

"Two hundred for a Gorshkov?" I exclaimed. "That's a lot of money, Brock!"

"Permit me to inquire about the tone in which you just said that. Gorshkov... What exactly is your opinion of him?"

"The subject under discussion is a painting," I said. "A painting I intend to buy."

"No," objected Brock, who was now irritated both by my words and by my indifference toward his paintings. "For this disrespect to a great national painter of ours, the price for you is now three hundred!"

As often happens with nervous people, in the heat of the moment I couldn't resist a caustic question:

"And what would you take for this cabbage if I were to tell you that Gorshkov is simply a bad artist?"

Brock let the cigarette fall from his lips and gazed at me lingeringly and malevolently. It was a sharp, piercing look of quivering hatred.

"You're a fine judge... You cynic!"

"Why this quarrelling?" I said. "What's bad is bad."

"Well, fine then," he declared, frowning and looking at the floor. "Two hundred it was, so two hundred it shall be."

"It won't be two hundred; it'll be one hundred."

"Now *you're* the one who's starting..."

"Very well, one hundred and twenty-five?"

Still more offended, he gloomily walked up to the cupboard and dragged out from behind it the painting he had just brought.

"I'll make a gift of this one," he said, brandishing the painting. "It's to your taste, it could be yours for twenty rubles."

Now turning the painting the right way around, what he brought level with my eyes was something staggering.

IV.

What I saw was a long room, flooded with light, with a glass wall to the left, grown over with entwining ivy and flowers. To the right, above a row of antique chairs upholstered in green plush, hung several small etchings in a horizontal line. A door stood ajar in the distance. Closer to the foreground, on the left, atop a round walnut table with a gleaming surface, stood a tall glass vase with flowers that were shedding their petals; these were scattered across the table and on the floor, whose surface was of polished stone. Through the glass of the wall, which was made up of hexagonal panes, the flat roofs of an unknown eastern city could be glimpsed.

The words "something staggering" may thus seem like an expositional whim, for the subject was commonplace enough, and its execution here lacked not only great originality but any originality whatsoever. Yes, indeed! And yet, the painting's simplicity was replete with the immediate suggestion of a persistent summer heat. The light was hot. The shadows were limpid and somnolent. The hush—that special hush of a sultry day, filled with the silence of a secluded, sated life—was conveyed through an intangible expressiveness; the sun burned my hand when, grasping the frame, I looked ahead, straining to make out the *brushstrokes*—that disenchanting mathematics of paints, which, upon bringing a work closer to ourselves, we see in place of faces and objects.

The room depicted in the painting stood empty. To varying degrees of success, hundreds of artists have used this device. However, the greatest talent has never yet attained the psychological effect that immediately asserted itself in the given instance. The effect was that of the viewer's unexpected abduction into the depths of the perspective, so that I felt as if I were standing in *that* room.

It was as though I had stopped by and seen that there was nobody there but me. Thus, the emptiness of the room compelled me to regard it from the vantage of my individual presence. Moreover, the distinctness, the *materiality* of the depiction was greater than anything of the kind I had ever seen.

"Indeed," said Brock, seeing that I was silent. "A most commonplace daub. And yet you say . . ."

I could hear my heart pounding, but I didn't want to argue.

"Well, then," I said, laying the painting aside, "I'll get those twenty rubles and, if you wish, I'll stop by this evening. Who's the artist?"

"I don't know," said Brock in vexation. "Paintings like this aren't exactly a rarity. Anyhow, Gorshkov . . . Let's discuss the matter."

By now I was afraid of angering him, lest I lose the painting of the sunny room. I was more than a little stunned; I had become vacant and forbearing.

"Yes, I'll buy the Gorshkov," I said. "I'll definitely buy it. So that's your final price—two hundred? Very well then. What am I to do with you? As I said, I'll bring the money this evening. Two hundred and twenty. When can I find you at home?"

"If you're serious, I'll expect you at seven o'clock," said Brock, placing the painting he had shown me on top of the piano, and with a smile he rubbed his hands. "That's what I like: one, two—and it's in the bag. Just like the Americans do it."

Had S. T. been at home then, I should have set off for his apartment immediately to collect the money, but at that hour he would himself be puttering about the city in search of antique porcelain. That is why, in spite of my great impatience, I headed from Brock's apartment to the House of Scholars—or KUBU, as its Russian acronym went—to find out whether I had been granted the rations for which I had filed a request.

V.

To a warmly dressed man with a cold soul, the frost may seem an exquisite pleasure. Indeed, everything had grown numb and turned blue. Was this not truly a delight? Beneath the white sky the crowded city froze. The air was unpleasant, nakedly transparent, as in a cold hospital. The windows of the gray buildings were blinded by hoarfrost. The frost imparted a fanciful sense to everything: boarded-up shops with snowdrifts on the entrance steps and smashed plate glass windows; a deathly silence at the front doors; kiosks that had fallen in on themselves; inns that lacked windows and roofs, with floors that had been ripped up; a dearth of cab drivers—thus, so cruelly, it seemed, the frost had dealt with everything. A motorcar that had been running fairly well but had suddenly got stuck because its engine had been damaged—that, too, had apparently fallen into the jaws of the frost. The movement of people headed for warmth called the frost to mind even more. Along the road and sidewalks, carried in hands, on sledges, and on carts, with the rasping slowness of habitual despair, the firewood crept. Wagons creaked, as snow crunched into frost: piercingly and terribly. Ice-covered logs were being dragged along the sidewalk by the hands of exhausted women and adolescents of the kind who know all the unacceptable playground vocabulary and ask for "a light" in a deep bass. Incidentally, among the businesses the likes of which the city had never seen, in addition to "domestic husbandry" (hay strewn about a room, like grass for goats) and "new-old" (the glittering illusion of newness imparted to "footwear" found in a dump), about which de Régnier speaks in his curious book *The Backstreets of Paris*, one was now compelled to note the profession of "kindling salesmen," too. These tattered figures sold bundles of kindling weighing no more than five pounds, which they carried under their arms for those who could permit themselves that most prudent of luxuries: holding them under the base of a teapot or a saucepan, burning them one after the other, until the water in it boiled. Moreover, firewood was being sold from sledges in little bundles or whole armfuls—to each according to his means. Carts, heavily laden with firewood, went by, and the driver, walking alongside, whipped the thieves as he passed—children who were pinching logs on the run. Occasionally, passions were inflamed by a log that had fallen from the cart of its own accord: passers-by would dash to it headlong, but usually the bounty would be obtained by some moustachioed villain—the sort who in the military can make soup out of an axe.

I walked quickly, almost at a run, seeing off one block after another, the snow crunching underfoot, and mopping my face. In one courtyard I spotted a crowd of good-natured people. They were breaking the wooden parts off a brick outbuilding. Involuntarily I paused—there was an expansive, businesslike tone to this spectacle, something of what in the laconic language of our psychology is termed: "That's the spirit, lads! . . ." A double door flew open, and a floor beam came crashing down with one end sticking out of the snow. In one corner of the yard, two men were furiously knocking into each other as they sawed the end off a log as thick as a barrel. I entered the courtyard with a sense of human solidarity and said to a sleepy chap in a dark-blue coat who was looking on:

"Citizen, won't you give me a couple of boards?"

"What's that?" he said after a long, affected silence. "Can't. We're collecting the wood for an artel;* it's an institutional matter."

---

* *an artel*: Artels were cooperative workshops that existed throughout the Russian Empire and the Soviet Union, generally operating in the areas of art, crafts, and light industry.

Though I had no idea what he meant, I understood nevertheless that I would get no boards from them, and so, without pressing the matter, I withdrew.

"How can it be? We've hardly met, and already we part," I thought, recalling the words of a certain interesting man: "We meet without joy and part without sorrow..."

Meanwhile, that picture of the sunny room, which had been banished temporarily by the frost, once again excited me so much that I directed all my thoughts toward it and S. T. The bounty was alluring. I had made a discovery. At the same time, my cheeks had begun to burn, and shooting pains had appeared in my nose and ears. I looked at my fingers: their tips had turned white and become almost numb. The same thing had happened to my cheeks and nose, and so I began to rub the frostbitten parts until sensation returned to them. I was not chilled to the marrow, as I would have been in the damp, but my whole body ached and felt unbearably contorted. Growing numb, I ran off in the direction of Millionnaya Street. Here, at the gates of KUBU, an odd sense of space flitted before my eyes for a second time, yet in my agonies I was not so surprised by this as I had been at Brock's—and so I only rubbed my forehead.

Standing by those very gates, among the cab drivers and automobiles, was a group that I would have paid greater attention to, had it been a little warmer. The central figure of the group was a tall man in a black beret with a white ostrich feather; he wore a gold chain about his neck, over a black velvet cloak lined with ermine. He had an angular face, a ginger moustache parted in an ironic arrow, a golden beard worn in a narrow spiral, and a smooth and authoritative way of gesturing...

At this point my attention faltered. It seemed that a covered sedan chair with feathers and a fringe had drawn to a slightly rocking halt behind this angular, glittering figure. Three swarthy, strapping young men with cloaks thrown back over their shoulders, covering half their mouths, silently watched on as out of the gates walked the professors, dragging behind them sacks of bread. These three men seemed to constitute a retinue. But in a frost such as this there was no time for any more curiosity. Lest I delay myself further, I crossed through to the courtyard, while behind me a conversation as quiet as the strumming of strings took place:

"This is the very building, Señor Professor! We've arrived!"

"Excellent, Señor Caballero! I'll go to the main clerical office, while you, Señor Euterp, and you, Señor Arumito, prepare the gifts."

"Right away, Señor."

VI.

Idlers in the street, heralds of the "indisputable" and the "reliable," as well as the merely curious, would have flayed me upon learning that I didn't linger around the mysterious foreigners, didn't so much as sniff the air they breathed in the narrow passageway of the entrance, beneath the red signboard of the House of Scholars. Yet I have long since taught myself to be surprised at nothing.

The above conversation was held in the pure Castilian dialect, and since I know the Romance languages rather well, I had no difficulty understanding what these people were talking about. From time to time the House of Scholars received goods and provisions from various countries. Hence, a delegation from Spain had arrived. No sooner had I entered the courtyard than this deduction was confirmed.

"Have you seen the Spaniards?" said a paunchy professor to his emaciated colleague, who was thoughtfully chewing on a cigarette while standing at the tail end of a queue for salted bream, which was being distributed from a wooden hut in the courtyard. "They say they've brought a lot of everything and it'll be given out next week."

"What will we get?"

"Chocolate, canned foods, sugar, and macaroni."

The large courtyard of KUBU was taken up, almost as far as the main entrance, by a long series of outbuildings that had been built by the grand duchess to whom this palace had formerly belonged. To the left and right of the outbuildings were narrow, poorly cobbled passageways with staircases and storerooms, where, from time to time, they distributed rations of fish, potato, meat, candied fruit, sugar, cabbage, salt, and other such kitchen supplies. In the yard's storerooms they tended to distribute things that would have impeded the distribution of other foodstuffs from the central storehouse, which was located on the ground floor of the former palace. There, at the appointed hour on the appointed day of the week (both had been appointed once and for all), each member of KUBU received his basic weekly ration: portions of cereal, bread, tea, butter, and sugar. This curious, powerful, and active organization still awaits its historian, and so we shall not sketch out in meager strokes what shall one day be unrolled as a finished painting.

The point of these observations of mine is that there were many people in the courtyard who came primarily from the ranks of the intelligentsia. These people, if not passing through the courtyard, stood queuing by the doors of several storehouses, where shop assistants were cleaving meat bones with axes or dumping piles of sopping herring off scales into buckets. In one shop they were dishing out bream, about ten pounds per person, and I noticed the rusty tin-colored tail of a fish poking out of a torn sack that had been placed onto a little sledge. The load's owner, an old man with abundantly bushy gray whiskers and matching long hair, held the sledge's rope crooked in his elbow; he was intending to hand over a slip of paper to a downcast woman no longer in the first flush of youth, but was searching for it vainly among the bundle of documents he had extracted from the side pocket of his overcoat.

"Wait, Lucy," he was saying with incipient annoyance, "let's look again. Hmm . . . hmm . . . The pink one is the card for the bath-house, the white, the one for the co-op, the yellow's the one for the basic ration, the brown, the one for the family, this is a coupon for sugar, this one's for the bread I haven't yet received, and—what do we have here?—certificates from the housing committee, a questionnaire from the institute, an old, out-of-date coupon for herring, a receipt for the repair of my watch, a coupon for the laundry, and a coupon . . . Good Heavens!" he cried, "I've lost my other white card, and today's the last day I can get the sugar ration!"

With that exclamation—a bitter one, for this was the fifth time he had leafed through his papers—he was forced to admit defeat and hurriedly shoved the whole volume back into his pocket, adding:

"Perhaps I left it the kitchen, when I was cleaning my boots! . . . I still have time! I can run home! I'll be back in an hour, wait for me!"

They agreed where to meet, and the old man, wrapping the rope around his mitten, began mincing toward the gate, hauling the sledge behind him. A sharp jolt dislodged the bream from the hole, and the fish dropped onto the snow. Picking it up, I shouted:

"A fish! A fish! You've lost a fish!"

But the old man had already vanished through the gate, and the woman was nowhere to be seen. Then, owing to the pained feeling of finding something edible, without any particular practical idea or burning joy, I picked up the bream, simply because it was lying at my feet, and thrust it into my pocket. I then began to cut across various queues, stumbling now and again over creeping sledges. I made my way through the thronging crowd in the first corridor toward the clerical office, intending to inquire about my application.

A secretary with a gloomy face, whose desk was surrounded by women, children, old men, artists, actors, writers, and scholars, each on his or her own dreary business (that peculiar breed—ration adventurists—was also present), finally rifled through a heap of papers, in which he found a note against my name.

"Your case has yet to be decided," he said. "The next committee session will take place on Tuesday—that is to say, in four days' time."

The hopes with which I had fought my way over to the desk having somewhat chilled, I removed upstairs, to the canteen, where for my last *thousand* I could have a glass of tea and a slice of bread. The commotion around me was so great that it recalled a ball or a banquet, the sole difference being that everyone was in hats and overcoats and dragging sacks behind them. Doors slammed throughout the entire building, above and below. The rumor about the foreign delegation bringing gifts was sweeping through; people were talking about it at every turn, in the canteen, and in the lobby.

"Have you heard about the delegation from Argentina?"

"Not from Argentina, but Spain."

"From Spain, yes."

"Oh, it's all the same—but tell me, what have they brought? Oil, butter, lard? And are there any fabrics?"

"They say there's a lot of everything and they'll be giving it out next week."

"But what exactly?"

Someone authoritative and pompous, with a condescending arch of his brows, asserted that the delegation had arrived from the island of Cuba.

"And not from Salamanca?"

"No, from Cuba, Cuba," said omniscient actresses who were passing.

"What do you mean, from Cuba?"

A pun had already been born, and I heard it twice: "To KUBU from Cuba." Two young girls, running down the stairs as girls do—that is, two at a time—stopped their acquaintances with a shout:

"Chocolate! Yes, sir!"

Even the old women had livened up, and so, too, those hunched-over, shortsighted, bespectacled folk who lack any obvious facial hair and always seem insensate in their forever narrow overcoats. A mark of inner equilibrium had appeared in their gaze. Hungry faces, with intense worry about food in their tired eyes, hurried to repeat the news, while some headed directly for the clerical office with the intention of finding out everything.

A certain time passed in this way, while I loitered on a marble staircase adorned with statues and drank tea in the canteen, sitting at a glass table under a palm tree—there had once been a winter garden in this room. Wondering why the bread smelled of fish, I looked at my hand, saw the scales sticking to it, and remembered the bream that was poking out of my pocket. Having stuffed the bream down more snugly, lest its tail chafe my elbow, I raised my head and saw Afanasy Terpugov, a cook from the Madrid restaurant, whom I had known for a long time. He was a dry, dispirited person with a wandering gaze and a certain affectation in his facial expression; his thin, tightly pursed lips were shaven, and he peered over his spectacles.

He had on an overcoat that was as long as a chimney and a tight-fitting lambskin hat. Jokingly, this man tugged at the tail of my bream.

"My congratulations on your supplies!" said Terpugov. "And there was me thinking it was a hatchet. I was afraid I might cut myself, ha-ha!"

"Oh, hello, Terpugov," I replied. "What are you doing here?"

"Well, now, a friend of mine has been pulling some strings to try to find me a job here in the kitchen or in one of the shops. I've stopped by to tell him I'm not interested."

"Where have you found work?"

"What do you mean, where?" said Terpugov. "But of course, you haven't heard. I'll let you in on a secret—come to the Madrid tomorrow. I've leased the restaurant and I'm opening it. The cooking is top-notch! Well, don't you remember the time when you were a bit tipsy, you took some of my little *rasstegai* home with you as a keepsake? And you said to me: 'I'll frame them and mount them on the wall!' Ha-ha! Those were the days! And those Polish *kolduny* with butter . . . Well, I won't keep ragging you like this. In any case, there'll be an orchestra—the finest you'll find anywhere. The prices are reasonable, and, what the hell, we'll play some Spanish dances for you at the grand opening."

"But, Terpugov," I said, choked with amazement, "do you realize what you're saying? That you alone, against all the rules, have been allowed an undertaking like the Madrid? This, in nineteen twenty-one?"

Thereupon something happened to me—something like that universally known moment of double vision, when you see two of everything. Something was preventing me from seeing clearly, preventing me from looking directly ahead. Terpugov drifted off, then appeared even farther away, and, although he was standing right beside me, across from the window, I saw him against the background of the window, as though he were in the distance, taking snuff with a thoughtful look about him. He spoke as though addressing not me, but someone off to the side:

"As you like, but come all the same. Anyway, do give me the bream. I'll soak it and clean it—I'll serve it with a little buckwheat and dress it in horseradish and sour cream, you'll love it! I don't imagine you even have the firewood."

Still enraptured, I rubbed my eyes and regained control over my vision.

"You're talking nonsense," I said in vexation. "But even so, take the bream, I myself can't cook it. Here, take it!" I repeated, handing over the fish.

Terpugov examined it carefully, patting its tail and even looking in its mouth.

"A good fish, nice and plump," he said, secreting it under his overcoat. "Rest assured. Terpugov knows his business—I'll be sure to get rid of all the bones. Well, till we meet again! So don't forget, tomorrow at the Madrid. We open at eight."

He doffed his cap, shuffled his feet, and cast me a serious look before disappearing behind the glass door.

"The poor fellow's gone crackers!" I said as I left via the staircase, making for the carved doors of the Rose Hall. I had warmed up and was no longer so tormented by hunger. Remembering Terpugov, I smiled and thought: "So the bream has ended up with Terpugov. What a strange fate it's had!"

VII.

The hall's enormous double door stood half-open. No sooner had I reached it than several members of the senior administration, both with and without briefcases, rushed past me through the door, one after another, peering over the heads of those in front—such was the hurry they were in, doubtless to see something in connection with the Spaniards. I recalled the conversation at the gate, and so I, too, peered in and saw that the great hall was full of people. With a shrug of the shoulders, a sign of my equality, I dignifiedly walked in; as it was rather crowded, I stood somewhat off to the side, observing the goings-on.

The hall was usually used for clerical work, but now the tables had been moved over to the walls, while the typewriters had vanished. One large table, dressed in a dark-blue cloth, stood closer to the wall farthest from the door, between plate glass windows with a view of the snow-covered river. The praesidium of KUBU sat solemnly along the right end of the table, while along the left was that same ginger-haired man whom I had seen at the gate in a beret and a cloak with a turned-down ermine collar. He sat bolt upright, leaning slightly on the firm back of the chair and taking in the scene with his gaze. His right hand lay directly in front of him on the table, atop some papers, while with his left he casually fingered a golden neck chain adorned with a single pearl. His three traveling companions stood behind him, exuding patience and attention in their bearing and expression. Before the table towered a barricade of leathern and canvas bales, and I was astonished that the administration had allowed them to bring in so many goods.

Meanwhile, with the utmost attention, I listened to what was being said and whispered in various quarters. The crowd was the usual *ration*-seeking crowd: doctors, engineers, solicitors, professors, journalists, and a multitude of women. As I soon learned, they had all crowded in, gradually though quickly, attracted by the outlandishness of the delegates.

The quiddity of "rumor" is the subtlest emanation of a fact that is always true in essence, no matter which monstrous form has been devised for it by our apparatus of perception and dissemination—that is, the mind and its cunning servant, language. And so it was not without a certain curiosity that I listened in. Breathing down the back of my neck, someone said to his neighbor:

"This Spanish professor is a queer fellow. They say he's a real character and a most terrific eccentric: he goes about the city in a sedan chair, as though it were the Middle Ages!"

"But is he really a professor? Do you know what I heard? They say he isn't quite what he seems!"

"Well, I never!"

"What's one to think?!"

An old woman in front of me was elbowing her way back so that she could listen to the speakers and take part directly in the discussion.

"Now, what's all this? How are we to understand it?" she mumbled with her frog-like mouth, her gray, avaricious eyes glittering mysteriously. She lowered her voice:

"But listen to me, do you hear? I was told that their documents were checked but the stamp wasn't the right one . . ."

I realized that the public nose was at work. But there was no time to listen to the other whisperings, for the committee had demanded the removal of all unauthorized persons.

Rising to his feet, the Spaniard made a brief movement with his hand.

"We ask," he said in a loud, commanding voice, "that everyone be permitted to remain here, since we are glad to be in the company of those for whom we have brought our modest gifts."

The interpreter (a writer, who had published several volumes of Spanish lore) proved not to be completely fluent in the language. He translated "we are glad to be" incorrectly as "we *ought* to be," which, after elbowing my way to the front, I immediately pointed out.

"Does the señor know Spanish?" The visitor turned to me with a seductive, serpentine smile, and all of a sudden he stared at me so intently that I began to feel ill at ease. His black and green eyes, with their piercing, steely pupils, fixed me with a look that was reminiscent of an arm with the sleeve coolly rolled up, thrust to the very bottom of a sack by a man implacably groping for a sought-after object.

"Do you know Spanish?" the foreigner repeated. "Would you care to interpret?"

"Señor," I rejoined, "I know Spanish as well as I know Russian, though I have never been to Spain. I know, moreover, English, French, and Dutch; but don't you already have an interpreter?"

General crosstalk ensued between me, the Spaniard, the interpreter, and members of the committee, during which it came to light that the interpreter admitted an imperfect knowledge of the language and so willingly yielded his role to me. The Spaniard never once looked at him. Evidently, he wanted me to interpret. The committee, wearying of the commotion, raised no objection. Then, turning to me, the Spaniard introduced himself:

"Professor Miguel Anna María Pedro Esteban Alonso Bam Gran." To which I replied in the correct fashion:

"Alexander Kaur" (my name), after which the meeting resumed its official character.

At this point I translated in turn the usual exchange of greetings expressed by the committee and the Spaniard, which were composed in the spirit of those times and do not merit a detailed retelling now. Bam Gran then read aloud a list of gifts sent by scholars from the island of Cuba. This inventory elicited general delight. Two wagons of sugar, five thousand kilos of coffee and chocolate, twelve thousand of maize, fifty casks of olive oil, twenty of marmalade, ten of sherry, and one hundred boxes of Manila cigars. Everything had already been weighed and deposited in the storehouses. However, those bales, which lay before the table, contained objects concerning which Bam Gran said only that, with the permission of the rationing committee, he "would have the honor to show the assembly their contents forthwith."

No sooner had I translated these words than there came a roar of approval in the hall: they promised a spectacle, or, rather, the continuation of the spectacle that the delegation's presence had already provided. Everyone, myself included, was overjoyed. We were witnesses to a generous and picturesque *gesture*, ostentatiously made, as in drawings depicting the arrival of travelers in far-distant lands.

The Spaniards exchanged glances and began to talk quietly among themselves. One of them, extending a hand toward the bales, suddenly smiled and looked at the crowd amiably.

"All adults are children," Bam Gran said to him quite distinctly, so that I caught the words; then, understanding from my face that I had heard him, he leaned in toward me and, gazing into my eyes with the blade of his glittering pupils, whispered:

In northern wilds, above the sea,
There stands alone a pine.
It slumbers there midst snow and ice
And plaintively it cries.

It dreams: down on the even plains,
A land of endless spring;
A bright-green palm forever now
Its one and only dream.

VIII.

The joke was so mild and subtle—he had only been joking, of course—but I felt as though I had been given a firm handshake, and, with my heart now beating violently, and without even paying attention to how boldly and effortlessly he had imparted in this strange allusion a special meaning to Heine's poem—a work of infinite meanings—I managed to say only:

"Is that so? What was it you were trying to express?"

"We know a thing or two," he said in his usual tone of voice. "So then, to work, Señor!"

No sooner had this mood, this moment—like the unexpected plucking of a string—died away amid the hubbub that had arisen around the bales than I was plunged again into my duties, listening intently to Bam Gran's fitful speech. He spoke of the haste of his departure, apologizing for having brought less than he might otherwise have done. Meanwhile, the Spaniards' hands, with the sureness of feline paws, flew out from under their cloaks, clutching glittering, narrow knives; having turned over the bales, they cut the ropes, then quickly tore open the leather and canvas. A silence fell. Onlookers crowded around in anticipation of what was to come. The only sound came from behind the door of an adjoining room, where a typewriter clattered telegraphically under an indifferent, dismal hand.

By now the hall was so tightly crowded with patrons and workers of KUBU that only those standing at the very front could see what was going on. Already the Spaniards had pulled out from one bale a box of short dark candles.

"Behold!" said Bam Gran, seizing a candle and deftly lighting it. "These are scented candles for freshening the air!"

He raised the light with his dry, pale hand, and the subtle perfume, which recalled the fragrance of a warm garden, passed through the hall, which was filled with foul-smelling tobacco. Many began to laugh, but a shadow of bewilderment settled on the faces of several scholars. Having failed to hear my translation, these people said:

"Ah, candles, how lovely! Doubtless there'll be soap as well!"

However, disappointment flitted across the majority of faces.

"If all the gifts are going to be like this . . ." said a gray-haired man with a ruddy nose to a young lad, who had grown crimson from his overflowing gloom and crossed his arms on his chest, " . . . what on earth is going on?"

The young lad screwed up his eyes scornfully and said:

"Mmm, quite . . ."

Meanwhile, the work continued apace. Another three bales had come apart under the direction of the sharp knives. There appeared lengths of wonderfully colored silks, patterned muslin, white Panama hats, broadcloth and flannel, stockings, gloves, lace, and many other fabrics, on seeing the color and shimmer of which I could only surmise that they were of the finest quality. Cutting open a bale, the Spaniards would extract a piece or a sample, unwrap it, and set it down at their feet. One after another, fabrics rustled as they poured from the Spaniards' swarthy hands; soon a mountain had formed, as in a shop when the assistants throw down onto the counter all the newest goods and latest patterns. At long last, they were done with the fabrics. The ropes of a new bale were snapped off, and I watched on as seashells spilled out with a dry rattle—red and white corals cascading behind them.

I stepped back, so vivid were these colors from the seabed among the folds of silks and linens—they had retained the luster of an underwater ray penetrating the green depths. As dusk had begun to set in, the hall was now illuminated with electricity, which set the heaps of gifts even more aglitter.

"These are very rare shells," said Bam Gran, "and we would be greatly pleased if you would accept them as a souvenir of our visit and of the far-distant ocean!..."

He turned to his assistants, hurrying them on with a gesture:

"Step lively, *caballeros*! Don't delay the effect! Señor Kaur, please tell the congregation that we have brought fifty guitars and as many mandolins; we shall show you examples of them presently."

Now six of the largest and longest bales came to rest before us upon a dais; unwrapping them, the Spaniards laid bare the palm wood of the strong, narrow crates and cautiously forced them open. There, wrapped in cotton wool, lay the new instruments. Taking out the guitars, one after the other, carefully, like sleeping children, the Spaniards wiped them down with silk handkerchiefs and stood them against the table or else laid them on top of the piles of brightly colored fabric. Soon, however, there was nowhere to put them, save for on top of one another, and so the onlookers had to be asked to make way. The neck and soundboard of the guitars were the color of a dark cigar and were decorated with mother-of-pearl inlay—and in places with fine gold engraving.

A vague clanging accompanied the fuss over the guitars; sometimes the knock of a guitar against wood would elevate the disorderly clangor to a tender harmony.

Soon the mandolins, also adorned with mother-of-pearl and gold, appeared. Giving off a sharp, metallic ring when people inadvertently touched or knocked into them, these mandolins took up an entire table and all the space underneath it. The business of unpacking them was completed comparatively slowly, and so I had time to scrutinize the faces of the committee members and apprehend their exceedingly tense state.

Indeed, the proceedings had come to resemble a dramatic scene with a strong decorative aspect. The clerical office, the round loaves of bread, the guitars, the sherry, the telephones, the oranges, the typewriters, the perfumes and silks, the felt boots and velvet cloaks, the vegetable oil and corals formed a strikingly odd mixture, which flouted the institution's gray tone with the reverberation of strings and the sounds of a foreign tongue that recalled a tropical land. The delegation had entered KUBU, like a comb through hair, forming an admittedly short-lived but vivid and unusual excenter, while the administrative and rationing centers involuntarily yielded to the newcomers in precedence and the nature of their gesture. Now these swarthy, ceremonious eccentrics were masters of the situation, and hospitality did not permit even the slightest hint of a desire to end the scene, which had become the apotheosis of the spontaneity that had pitched its motley camp in a clerical office devoted to "public supply." Contrary to custom, the business day had come to a halt. The staff had assembled from every direction—from shops, bureaus, agencies, storerooms, the fuel department, the bathhouse, the hairdresser's, the laundry, from the canteen and duty rooms, from the library and the medical station—and if some did not come, that was only because not even a single leaf of paper could move without them. The would-be recipients, who had come for their rations, delayed getting their supplies, not wanting to miss a rare spectacle for what they saw every day. Several of the sort who were well seasoned and always sniffing around everywhere had by now run off to the various departments to inquire about their chocolate and sherry; this was done in the hope that, having already received their coupons, they would avoid the impending lines.

Though I had penetrated the mood of the committee members, I also had to take into consideration that now only one bale— the longest, which had been sewn up more painstakingly than all the others—remained untouched. It was going on four o'clock in the afternoon, and so the deputation could stay in the hall for only another half hour. The hall, naturally, was then to be locked in order to take stock and put away the goods, while the Spaniards withdrew to a meeting room to conclude the business side of their visit to KUBU. Because of all this, I was convinced there would be no trouble.

The Spaniards seized the long bale and stood it on end. With their knives they cut at the ropes obliquely, so that they frayed and burst, falling around the bale like snakes. The bale had been sewn up in several layers of cloth. A pile of white ribbons heaped up as they unwrapped it. Then, glittering and glinting gold, an enormous roll of silk, around fifteen feet wide and almost the length of the entire hall, emerged from its huge cocoon. As they fanned and unfurled it, the Spaniards dispersed among the parted crowd to opposite corners of the hall; one of them, hunching over, unrolled the bundle, while two others, on arms that reached higher and higher, bore the end of the material as far as the wall and there, hopped on top of two chairs and nailed it beneath the ceiling. Thus were all the disorderly piles of goods covered by a splendidly skillful pattern, which sloped down across the distance; the design was embroidered on gold silk with carmine flamingo feathers and the feathers of a white heron— the precious feathers of South America. The pearl, silver, and gold sequins, the rose and dark-green beading against the other material imparted a savage and striking beauty, steeped in the tenderness of the composition whose essential motif may have been borrowed from lace patterns.

With noise and gasps, multiplying the noise with yet more noise, and amid the noise becoming noisier still, the onlookers mingled with the committee as they drew nearer to the glittering article. There arose the disorder of satisfaction—our true order of being. The hanging began to flutter in the dozens of hands that touched it from all sides. I withstood an attack from enthusiastic women, who demanded that I immediately ask Bam Gran where and by whom such rare luxury had been crafted.

Looking at me, Bam Gran slowly and imposingly pronounced:

"This is the work of young girls from the island of Cuba. It was made by twelve of the most beautiful girls in the capital. They spent half a year embroidering this design. You are right to look on it with deserved favor. Read the names of the seamstresses!"

He lifted the edge of the silk for all to see a little wreath embroidered in Latin letters; I translated what was embroidered: "Laura, Mercedes, Nina, Pepita, Conchita, Paula, Vincenta, Carmen, Inés, Dolores, Anna, and Clara."

"This is what they have asked me to tell you," I continued loudly, accepting a sheet of paper from the Spanish professor: "Our faraway sisters! We, twelve young Spanish girls, embrace you from afar and press you to our hearts! May you affix this hanging we have embroidered on your cold wall. May you look upon it and think of our country. May you have thoughtful bridegrooms, faithful husbands, and dear friends, among whom every one of us ranks! We further wish you happiness, happiness, and still more happiness! That is all. Please excuse us, unlearned and uncultured Spanish girls, who are growing up on the shores of Cuba!"

I finished translating, and for a while complete silence reigned. Such silence occurs when something within us seeks to escape, something we wish to say that cannot be translated into any language. It flows in silence . . .

"Our faraway sisters . . ." These words contained the graceful purity of those swarthy maidens' fingers that pierced the silk with needles for those northern women whom they did not know, so that in their snowy country weary eyes would smile at their fantastical and ardent embroidery. Twelve pairs of black eyes lowered over the Rose Hall from afar. With a gentle laugh, the south greeted the north. It outstretched its warm hand to those frostbitten fingers. This hand, fragranced with rose and vanilla pod—an airy hand of a creature bearing twelve names, as jittery as a goat—has brought to this tale of potatoes and cold apartments a naive design, like those Thompson Seton makes in the margins of his books: an arabesque of petals and rays of light.

IX.

When the effect of this had reached a climax, there was a noise at the doors—the insistent words of someone wanting to break through to the middle of the hall.

"Let me through!" the man was saying somberly and portentously.

I couldn't yet see him. He would cry out loudly and raise a voice that cut the ear whenever somebody tried to stop him:

"Let me through, I say! Citizen! Why won't you listen to me? Citizen, let me through, I beg you! This is the second time I'm telling you, and all you do is pretend it doesn't concern you. Let me through! Let me—" But already the onlookers had parted hastily, so used were they to making way for any angry oaf with a high opinion of himself.

Then, two paces from me, an elbow forced its way through, pushing aside the last professor blocking his way, and onto the very edge of the precious hanging stepped a man of indeterminate age with thick lips and a bushy red moustache. He was small in stature and looked puffed up—he held his diminutive figure very erect and wore a half-length fur coat, felt boots, and a bowler hat. He stood there, chest thrust out, head thrown back, arms outstretched, and legs astride. His spectacles glittered boldly; a briefcase poked out from under his arm.

It seemed as if that ineffable, womanish principle that ordinarily accompanies hysterics had passed into the face of this man. His nose resembled a three-dimensional ace of clubs, his puffed-out cheeks pinched toward the nostrils, while his eyes glinted mysteriously and haughtily.

"Well, now," he said in the same disgruntled tone that he had used as he elbowed his way through the crowd, "you must know who I am. I am the statistician Ershov! I saw and heard everything! This is some kind of madness! It's stuff and nonsense, an outrageous scene! This cannot be! I don't . . . I don't believe any of it! None of this exists, and never did! These are phantoms, phantoms!" he cried. "We're hallucinating or being poisoned by the fumes from the iron stove! There are no Spaniards! The hanging doesn't exist! There are no mackintoshes or ermines! Nothing! It's all hocus-pocus! I see it, but I disavow it! I hear it, but I reject it! Come to your senses! Pinch yourselves, citizens! I'll pinch myself! You can throw me out, curse me, beat me, bribe me, or hang me— it's all the same—but I still say: none of this exists! It's not real! It's a fiction! Smoke and mirrors!"

The members of the committee jumped up one after another and ran out from behind the table. The Spaniards exchanged glances. Bam Gran also stood up. Head thrown back, eyebrows raised, and arms akimbo, he smiled menacingly; this smile was as enigmatic as a rebus. The statistician Ershov was breathing heavily, as though in a delirium, and staring everyone in the eye defiantly.

"What's the meaning of this? What's wrong with him? Who is he?!" the exclamations resounded.

Begun, the secretary of KUBU, placed his hand on Ershov's shoulder.

"You've taken leave of your senses!" he said. "Get a grip of yourself and explain the meaning of this outburst."

"It means that I cannot take any more of this!" the statistician, whose face was becoming covered in red blotches, screamed in his face. "I'm hysterical, I'm shouting and making a scene, because I've reached my limit! I'm seething! That hanging! What the devil do I want with that wall hanging? Does it even really exist? I'm telling you: this is psychosis, an apparition, the devil knows what! But they're no Spaniards—they're no more Spanish than I am!"

Standing closer to Bam Gran, I translated, insofar as I could, quickly and accurately.

"Yes, this man's no child," said Bam Gran mockingly. He began to speak slowly—so that I could interpret—with a somewhat malicious smile, bearing his white teeth. "I ask Caballero Ershov, what does he have against me?"

"What do I have against you?" exclaimed Ershov. "This is what: I come home at six o'clock in the evening, I have to break up my cupboard just to warm up my shoebox of a room, I bake a potato in the stove, wash the dishes, and clean the linen! I don't have a servant. My wife is dead. The children have turned gray with filth. They bawl. There isn't much butter, there's no meat at all—ugh! And you're telling me that I should accept some shell from the ocean and ogle Spanish embroidery! I spit in your ocean! I'll roll a cigarette from your rose petals! I'll caulk the window frames with your silk! I'll sell your guitars and buy myself boots! I'll put you, you exotic birds, on a turnspit and roast you without bothering to pluck you. I . . . oh! You don't exist, because I won't allow it! Avaunt, apparition, and, amen, disappear!"

He flew into a rage, began to thunder and stamp his feet. This consternation went on for a minute, after which, with a sigh, Bam Gran straightened himself, quietly shaking his head.

"You're a madman!" he said. "A madman! So be it, keep those things that have rent your heart: firewood and potatoes, butter and meat, linen and your wife—but nothing else! The matter is closed. The damage is done, and so we shall leave—leave, Caballero Ershov, for the country you shall never see! You, however, Señor Kaur, may come whensoever you wish, and I shall repay you for your work as an interpreter with anything you desire. Ask the gypsies, and any one of them will tell you how to find Bam Gran, who has no reason to conceal himself any longer. Farewell, learned world, and hail to the pale-blue sea!"

Thus he spoke. Scarcely had I managed to utter a dozen words of the translation, when he bent over and seized a guitar; his fellow travelers did likewise. Laughing quietly and haughtily, they withdrew to the walls, standing in a row, each with one leg to the side and his head held high. Their hands touched the strings . . . With a chill, I heard those rapid, muffled chords, the rude beat of a melody so familiar to me: the "Fandango" began to ring out. Like a kiss to the heart, those robust strings burst forth, and to the gathering tempo was added the dry clacking of castanets. Suddenly the electricity cut out. A powerful blow to the shoulder caused me to lose my balance. I cried out because of a sharp pain in my temple, fell, and—amid the roaring din, the shouts, the frenzy of darkness glittering with the thunder of guitars—I lost consciousness.

X.

I came to with a heavy feeling, as though fettered. I was lying on my back. From the ceiling hung an electric light, shining beneath a green lampshade.

There was an unpleasant numbness in my right temple. When I turned my head, the numbness developed into a dull ache.

I began to survey my surroundings. A narrow room, all in white, the floor of which was covered with a white oilcloth, appeared to be an ambulatory care clinic. There was a narrow glass cabinet with instruments and medicines, two stools, and an empty white desk.

I had not been undressed and therefore concluded that nothing serious had happened. My cap was lying on a stool. There was no one in the room. Feeling my head, I found that it had been bandaged, so I must have cut myself on the corner of a table or some other hard object. I removed the bandage. Behind my ear blazed a terrible bruise that gave me intermittent shooting pain.

The hands on the round wall clock showed half-past four. Well then. I must have been in this room for around ten or fifteen minutes.

They had brought me here, bandaged me, and left me alone—most likely by accident, which was no great inconvenience, since I was free to leave whenever I wished. I was in a rush. Recalling everything that had happened, I experienced an acute, agonizing worry and the irrepressible urge to get moving. But I was still weak, as I soon learned when I got up to button my coat. However, where there is medicine, help is at hand. There was a set of keys dangling in the lock of the glass cabinet, and, having quickly sought out the alcohol, I filled a large beaker and drank it with a sense of relief and great satisfaction, for in those days vodka was a rarity.

I covered up the traces of having taken the law into my own hands before heading down the narrow corridor; there I reached an empty canteen, and so I proceeded down the stairwell. Passing the doors to the Rose Hall, I tried one but found that it was locked.

I stood there for a moment, listening. The staff had already left the building. I didn't come across a single soul as I made my way toward the exit; only in the foyer, the caretaker was sweeping up litter. I was wary of asking him about the Spaniards, since I didn't know exactly how the affair had ended, but the caretaker took it upon himself to strike up a conversation.

"Going out through a door," he said, "is the right way to do things. Not like ghosts or evil spirits!"

"Through a door or through a window," I replied, "what's the difference?!"

"Through a window . . ." said the caretaker thoughtfully. "I'll tell you, it's a different matter if somebody goes out through a window. But after that scene the Spaniards went right through the wall. Straight onto the Neva, they say, and, hear this, where they came down, the ice broke, they say. They all ran out to look."

"What's one to make of it all?" I said, hoping to learn something further.

"They'll know what to make of it up there!" The caretaker spat on his palms and began sweeping. "It's a wonder."

Leaving him to prevail over the unfathomable, I stepped out into the courtyard. The guard sitting by the gate, wearing an enormous sheepskin coat, took his time getting up off the bench, clutching a set of keys, and—not before scrutinizing me—went over to open the gate.

"What are you looking at?" I shouted, seeing that he kept following me with his eyes.

"It's my job," he declared. "I've got my eye out because I've been ordered not to let any suspicious characters pass. Haven't you heard?"

"I have," I said, and the gate slammed behind me with a rattle.

I paused, weighing up how and where to find the gypsies. I wanted to see Bam Gran. It was a burning and implacable desire— one that a gambler might understand as he searches for his hat, which his wife has hidden.

Alas, my poor head! It had been set a task in the ill-befitting conditions of the street, the frost, and the emptiness intersected by the lights of automobiles. Perplexed, I ought to have sat down by a fireplace in a deep, restful armchair—that would have been conducive to the flow of my thoughts. I ought to have surrendered to the furtive footfalls of inspiration and, sipping a century-old cherry-hued wine, listened to the slow striking of the clock as I gazed upon the golden coals. As I walked, an unpleasant residue formed, no longer allowing me to brush aside questions as they arose. Who was the man in the velvet cloak, with the gold chain? Why had he recited a poem to me, imparting a special meaning in the tone of his whisper? And finally, there was the "Fandango," played by this scholarly deputation in the midst of a ruckus, the sudden darkness, and the disappearing act, and my being carried to a bed in the sick bay. What explanation could quench reason's thirst, when the super-rational went on unconcernedly imbibing a copious diamond-like liquid, without putting itself to the trouble of imparting to the thinking apparatus even the slightest notion of the pleasure it was experiencing illicitly and absolutely—the pleasure of that very incoherence and inexplicability that constitutes the bitterest agony to every Ershov—and, just as there is an Ershov in everyone (albeit suppressed), I, too, was in this sense most inquisitively inclined.

I paused, trying to work out where I was now, having rushed ahead half-unconsciously, without a thought for the direction. Judging by several of the buildings, I gathered that I was not far from the railway station. I thrust my hand into my pocket for a cigarette and touched a mysterious solid object; I took it out and, by the light of one of the few illuminated windows, discerned a little yellow leather bag that had been tied very tightly. It weighed at least two pounds, and only my feverishness could explain why I had not noticed this heavy weight in my pocket until now. I could feel the edges of coins through the leather. "Lost in conjecture . . ." they used to say in such cases. I cannot recall whether I was lost in conjecture back then. I believe my mood was more inclined than ever before to expect the inexplicable. I hastened to untie the little bag, thinking more of its contents than of the reasons behind its appearance. Examining it on the street as one might at home, however, left one open to danger. I espied some ruins off to one side and headed for their snowy breaches along a mound of packed snow and debris. Inside this chaos a multitude of muddy tracks headed off in all directions. Here rags and frozen waste lay scattered; apertures alternated with pillars and collapsed beams. Moonlight wove the pits and shadows into one gloomy pattern. Picking my way deeper still, I sat down on some bricks and, untying the yellow bag, shook out some of the coins onto my palm and immediately recognized them as gold piastres. Having counted them and recounted them, I found that there were in all two hundred coins—no more, no fewer—and, feeling somewhat feeble, I lapsed into thought.

The coins lay between my knees, on the hem of my coat; I turned them over, listening carefully to the distinct, transparent clink of metal, which rings only in the imagination or when you place two coins on the tips of your fingers and touch their edges together. And so, in my unconscious state, some benevolent hand had sought me out, depositing in my pocket this small capital. I was not yet in any condition to make mental purchases. I merely gazed at the money, heeding, perhaps unconsciously, the admonition of some remarkable person, who had taught me the art of looking. In his view, it was possible to comprehend the soul of an object only when the gaze is deprived of impatience and effort, when he, serenely becoming one with the object, gradually becomes aware of the complexity and character concealed in the apparent simplicity of the commonplace.

I became so engrossed in my task—inspecting and sorting through the gold coins—that it was some time before I first sensed some interference, the presence of some extraneous force, one that was subtle and precise, as if the wind were exerting the slightest of pressures from one direction. I lifted my head, wondering what it could be and whether some vagrant or bandit were watching me from behind, inadvertently transmitting to me the intensity of his covetousness. I slowly surveyed the ruins from left to right and failed to discover anything suspicious; but although it was quiet, and the fragile, lingering silence would have been abruptly shattered by the slightest crunch of snow or clatter of debris, I did not dare to turn around for so long that I finally rebelled against myself. I turned around *suddenly*. The pounding of blood resounded in my heart and head. I jumped to my feet, scattering the coins, but was already prepared to defend them and seized a stone . . .

Around a dozen paces away, among the jumbled and deceptive shadows, stood a tall, thin man, hatless, and with drawn, smiling face. Head bent and arms by his sides, he was watching me silently. His teeth gleamed. His gaze was directed over my head, and he wore the look of a man trying to think of something to say in a difficult situation. From the back of his head a straight black line rose up, the end of which was hidden from me by the upper edge of the embrasure through which I was looking. A backward surge of blood, rushing now toward my heart, revived my breathing, and, stepping closer, I examined the body. It was difficult to decide what it was—murder or suicide. The dead man was wearing a black satin shirt, a decent overcoat, and new boots, while not far away lay a leather cap. He looked about thirty. His feet were dangling a foot off the ground, and the rope was tied around a ceiling beam. The fact that he had not been undressed, as well as a certain fastidiousness in the fixing of the rope to the beam, and, moreover, the diminutive, feeble features of the face, which was encircled by a tawny beard around the hollows of the cheeks, inclined one to a verdict of suicide.

I proceeded to gather up the coins, stuffed them into the purse, and hid the purse in my jacket's inner pocket; then I put several questions to the void and the silence that surrounded me in this remote corner of the city. Who was this joyless and sorrowless witness to my reckoning with the inexplicable? Had he pricked himself on a thorn while trying to pluck a rose? Or was he a desperate deserter? Who knows what brings a man to a pile of ruins with a length of rope in his pocket? Perhaps it was an unsuccessful administrator who hung before me, an apostate, someone disillusioned, a merchant who had lost four wagons of sugar, or the inventor of perpetual motion, who accidentally beheld his own face in the mirror as he was testing the device. Or was he a predator, whose relatives had zealously shaken him by the beard, saying over and over: "That's what you get, you vulture, for this thieving life of yours!"[*]—and, unable to take it, did away with himself?

This and more was possible, but I could not bear to sit there any longer, and, after walking only one block, I came across just the thing I had been looking for—a secluded tearoom.

A yellowing sign hung in the basement of an old, gloomy building; part of the sidewalk was illuminated from below by the misted windows. I descended the steep, narrow steps and entered the comparative warmth of a spacious room. In the midst of it a brick stove crackled warmly, while its iron chimney led off into the semidark depths beneath the ceiling, and light radiated from the

---

[*] *That's . . . life of yours*: A gloss on the final lines of Nikolai Nekrasov's (1821–1878) poem of 1855 "The Secret" (*"Sekret"*), which in ballad form tells of two brothers who stand by their father's deathbed and quarrel over their inheritance.

dim electric lamps, which glowed wanly and with a reddish hue in the damp air. Yawning and scratching under her arm, a bareheaded woman in felt boots dozed by the stove, while the barman, sitting behind the counter, read a tattered book. In the kitchen somebody was heaping on firewood. The place was almost empty—only in the second room, where the tables had no tablecloths, were there half a dozen shabbily dressed men, who looked like travelers, sitting in a corner; under the table, their bags lay at their feet. The men ate and conversed, holding their faces in the steam that rose from the saucers of hot chicory.

The barman was a young fellow of the modern type, with a lean soldier's face and a look of intelligence about him. He looked at me, licked his finger to turn the page, while with the other hand tore a tea coupon out of a green booklet and rummaged around in a tin box of candies, tossing me the coupon and the candy together.

"Take a seat. You'll be served," he said as he engrossed himself once more in his reading.

Meanwhile, the woman, tucking her hair behind her ear, sighed and went through to the kitchen to fetch some boiling water.

"What are you reading?" I asked the barman, having glimpsed the words "my bright-eyed princess . . ." on the page.

"He-he!" he said. "Nothing much, a play. *The Princess Far-Away*, by Rostand. Care to take a look?"

"No, thanks. I've read it. Do you like it?"

"Yes," he said indecisively, as though embarrassed by his impression. "It's a fantasy . . . about love. Take a seat," he added, "you'll be served right away."

I did not leave the counter, however, and began to talk about another matter.

"Do many gypsies come this way?" I asked.

"Gypsies?" the barman repeated. He evidently found this abrupt transition—from his extraordinary book to the ordinary—odd.

"They do." He automatically directed his gaze to my hand, and I guessed what his next words would be:

"Why do you ask? Are you looking to have your fortune told?"

"I want to do a drawing for a magazine."

"I see . . . An illustration. So you're an artist, citizen? Pleased to meet you!"

But I was still disturbing him, and, smiling as broadly as he could, he added:

"Two bands of them come here regularly. For whatever reason, one of them hasn't yet come today. I'd imagine they'll be here soon . . . Your tea is ready!" With that, he pointed to a table behind the stove, where the woman was laying out crockery.

I was gripping one of the gold coins, and now I liberated its hidden power.

"Citizen," I said mysteriously, as the circumstances demanded, "I'd like to have a little something to eat and drink, to perk myself up. Take this roundel, from which you can't even make a button since it has no holes, and reimburse my paltry loss with a bottle of real spirits. I'll have some meat or fish to go with it. And a decent amount of bread, pickled cucumbers, and some ham or cold cuts with vinegar and mustard."

The barman lay down his book, stood up, stretched himself out, and dissected me into my constituent parts with a gaze as sharp as a saw.

"Hmm . . ." he said. "What an awful lot you're wanting . . . But what sort of coin is this?"

"It's a Spanish coin, a gold piastre," I explained. "My grandfather brought it over"—here I was only half-lying, for my maternal grandfather lived and died in Toledo—"but, you know, these aren't the times to prize such trinkets."

"That's true enough," agreed the barman. "Wait here while I step out for just a moment."

He left, and when he returned two or three minutes later, his face was much brightened.

"Step this way," the barman announced, leading me behind a partition that separated the bar from the first room. "Sit yourself down. Everything will be here shortly."

As I examined the cubicle into which he had led me—a narrow room with yellow and pink wallpaper, stools, and a table with a grease-stained tablecloth—the barman appeared, closing the door behind him with his foot and carrying a tray of lacquered iron, decorated in the middle with a bouquet of fantastically colored flowers. Atop the tray was a large teapot of the kind found in taverns—dark blue with a gold relief—with a matching cup and saucer. A dish of bread, cucumbers, salt, and a large piece of meat surrounded by potatoes was brought in separately. As I had surmised, the teapot contained spirits. I poured and took a drink.

"There won't be any change," said the barman. "And, please, keep it quiet and proper."

"Quiet and proper," I assured the barman, pouring a second helping.

At that moment the creaky entrance door slammed, and a low, guttural voice sounded a strange note among the basement hush of the Russian tearoom. Heels banged, shaking off the snow; several people immediately began talking loudly, rapidly, and incomprehensibly.

"Pharaoh's tribe has arrived," said the barman. "Take a look at them if you like; perhaps they won't do!"

I went out. The same group of five gypsies that I had seen that morning was standing in the middle of the room, looking around and trying to decide where to sit and with what to begin. Noticing that I was staring at them intently, the young gypsy girl trotted up to me with a brazen and shameless look about her, like a cat catching the smell of fish.

"Come, I'll tell your fortune," she said in a firm, low voice. "Happiness will be yours, I'll tell you whatever you want, you'll discover your true thoughts, you'll live well!"

Just as before, I would soon have put an end to this banal recitative before with a sign of the left hand—the so-called *jettatura*, a conventional sign using two fingers, the index and little finger, to depict the horns of a snail—so now I hastily and willingly replied:

"My fortune? You want to tell my fortune?" I said. "But how much will you want for that?"

While the gypsy men, their blackest of eyes glittering, had taken their seats around a table to await their tea, the barman and an old gypsy woman came over to us.

"Pay us," said the old woman, "pay us, citizen, what you can, as much as your heart's desire. If you give a little, so be it; if you give a lot, I'll thank you kindly!"

"All right, tell me my fortune," I said. "But first I'll tell yours. Come here."

I took the young gypsy girl by—yea, gods!—her little but oh-so filthy, hand, of which I could have made a copy just by pressing it against a clean sheet of paper, and dragged her into my lair. She came willingly, laughing and saying something in her gypsy tongue to the old woman, who evidently sensed a profit. They quickly exchanged glances as they walked in, and I sat them down.

"Give me a crust of bread," my swarthy Pythia said at once, and, without waiting for my reply, she deftly grabbed a piece of bread, breaking off half a cucumber with it there and then. She proceeded to eat with the characteristic and natural shamelessness of her wild steppe nature. She chewed, while the old woman repeatedly intoned:

"Cross my palm, and happiness will be yours!" Having extracted a deck of cards, black with grime, she licked her thumb.

The barman peered through the door, but when he saw the cards he shrugged and disappeared.

"Gypsies!" I said. "You'll tell my fortune after I tell yours. I'll go first."

I took the hand of the young gypsy girl and began a feigned scrutiny of the lines on her swarthy palm.

"Here's what I'll tell you: you've seen me before, but you don't know what you're just about to do."

"Tell me, then, and you'll be a gypsy!" she said with a laugh.

I went on:

"You're going to tell me . . ."—and I quietly added—"how to find a man who goes by the name of Bam Gran."

I did not expect this name to have such a powerful effect. The gypsies' faces suddenly altered. Whipping off her head scarf, the old woman covered her face, which was convulsed with fear; buckling over, she looked as though she wanted to be swallowed up by the earth. With a bold, savage look, the young gypsy girl snatched her hand from mine and pressed it to her cheek. Her face blanched. She cried out, shot up, overturning the chair in the process, and, after rapidly whispering to the old woman, hurriedly led her off, looking back several times, as though fearing I might give chase. Seeing the smile on my face, she recollected herself and—with a nod to me, now standing in the doorway, gasping heavily for breath—said in a changed voice:

"Hold your tongue! I'll tell you everything. Wait here. We don't know you, so we'll have to talk it over!"

I do not know whether I lost my nerve when the power of this strange name was confirmed to me in so sudden and drastic a manner, but my thoughts came to a crashing halt; it was as if in the dead of night a trumpet blared into my ear, accustomed as it was to silence. Nervously hunched up, I drank another cup of the concoction and bit off a good chunk of the meat—though I did it abstentmindedly, unconscious of hunger through the fog of feelings silently bubbling up inside me. Worried by the uncertainty of the situation, I inclined my head toward the partition, listening to the enigmatic timbre of the gypsies' talk. They conferred among themselves for a long time, arguing, sometimes shouting or lowering their voices to a barely audible whisper. This went on for some while, during which I managed to calm down a little. Three of them then entered—the two women and the old gypsy man, who cast me a sharp, ambivalent look from the doorway. By now everyone was standing. They stood there as they went on talking, so animatedly that they broke into a sweat; beads of it glistened on the forehead of the old man and at the girls' temples, and, pausing for breath, the women wiped it off with the ends of their fringed head scarves. Only the old man, paying them no heed, kept staring right at me in silence, as though trying to divine at once, in a hurry, what my face had to tell him.

"How do you possess this word?" he said. "What do you know? Tell me, brother, don't be afraid, you're among friends. Tell us, and we'll tell you; if you don't, we won't believe you."

Assuming that this was for some reason a part of their plan to deal with me, I told them, insofar as I could, plainly and intelligibly, the story of the Spanish professor, omitting much but naming the place and enumerating all the accessories. At the mention of each curious thing, the gypsies exchanged glances, uttering a few words and nodding; getting carried away, they no longer paid me any notice, but once they had finished talking among themselves, they all together trained their alarmed eyes upon my face.

"Everything you say is correct," the old woman told me. "You've told the undeniable truth. Listen to what I have to tell you. We gypsies know *him*, only we cannot go where he is. Go yourself—as for how, I'll tell you presently. The cards will show you, and you'll see what you need to do. I cannot speak Russian well; it's impossible to tell you everything; my daughter will explain to you!"

She took out the cards and, after shuffling them, fixed my gaze in hers; she proceeded to lay out four rows of cards, one on top of the other, then mixed them up again and bade me cut them with my left hand. Thereupon she extracted seven cards and spread them out across the table, leading her finger about them while speaking to the young girl in their gypsy tongue.

The girl, having cleared her throat, leaned over the table, wearing an exceedingly serious expression as she listened to what the old woman was saying.

"Now," she said, raising her finger and evidently finding it difficult to choose her words. "That place where you were today, go there again, and from there you will get to *him*. What place it is, I don't know, only there your heart was touched. Your heart glowed," she emphasized. "It's for you to know what you saw there. You promised money and wanted to come again. When you go there, let it be alone, let no one in. Am I saying this right? You yourself know I am. Now, think on what you've heard from me and what you've seen."

Naturally, in these instructions I could see only Brock and his painting of the sunny room; I nodded in agreement.

"It's true," I said. "What you say did happen today. Please, go on."

"You'll get there . . ." she paused to hear out the old woman and fell into contemplation as she wiped her nose with her hand. "But you cannot get there just like that. Don't talk with anyone when you're doing the deed, no matter whom you meet along the way. Whatever you see, fear not; whatever you hear, say nothing—as if you don't exist. Extinguish the light when you go in, unwrap the tool we will give you and set it aside, then lock the doors so that nobody else can enter. You yourself will understand what happens, and you'll find the way. Now give me some money, place it on top of the cards, give to a poor gypsy; don't begrudge it, brother, happiness will be yours."

The old woman began to beg, too.

"How much should I give you?" I asked, not because I was hesitant but to test this force of habit that does not betray them under any circumstances.

"If you give a little, so be it; if you give a lot, I'll thank you kindly!" both women repeated forcefully and insistently.

Placing my hand into my pocket, I clutched a handful of eight or nine piastres—as many as I could hold at once.

"Here, take this," I said to the beauty.

With a servile and greedy look, she grabbed the coins. One fell to the floor, and the old man nimbly apprehended it; the old woman rushed from her seat, thrusting her cupped hand at me.

"Cross it, cross my palm, don't begrudge an old woman!" she began to wail, peppering her Russian words with exclamations in her gypsy tongue. All three of them were aquiver, now examining the coins, now outstretching their hands toward me.

"I won't give you any more," I said, though I added a further five pieces to my donation. "Hold your peace, or else I'll tell Bam Gran!"

This word seemed to have a universal effect. The excitement died down; only the old woman sighed heavily, as though she had lost a child. Quickly hiding the coins in the recesses of her shawls, the young girl, demanding something, stretched out her hand to the old man, palm facing upward. He began arguing, but the old woman shouted at him, and, after slowly unbuttoning his waistcoat, the old man extracted a sharp cone made of white metal. When it glinted in the light, a green line flashed inside it. He immediately wrapped it in a dark-blue handkerchief and gave it to me.

"Don't uncover this in the open air," the man said. "Uncover it when you arrive and set it on the table. When you leave, wrap it up again, but don't take it with you. It will find its way back to me, all right. Well, farewell, brother—if we've said something wrong, don't bear us any ill will."

He retreated toward the door, beckoning the women to leave.

"But tell me, who is Bam Gran?" I asked. But he only shrugged.

"Ask him," said the old woman, "we won't tell you any more."

The gypsies anxiously and cautiously left, talking quietly with one another. I had startled them. I saw that their amazement was great; their bewilderment and haste to please mixed with the fear that their lives had been marked by some *event*. I myself was so greatly agitated that the spirits had no effect on me. As I was leaving, I collided with the barman, who had peered in at the door several times already, though never interrupting us—a fact for which I was most grateful to him. The gypsies usually take a profitable client behind a door or into some other secluded corner, where they make him look into water while they repeat some simple incantation; so the barman might well have thought that I had changed my mind about drawing them and succumbed to the temptation of knowing the future.

"Pharaoh's tribe has run off!" he said, looking at me with gloomy interest. "They were served tea, but they didn't drink it. They just made a bit of a ruckus and left. Were they afraid of you or something?"

I supported this conjecture by telling him that gypsies are very superstitious and that it is difficult to convince them to let a stranger draw them. With that, we parted, and I stepped out into the street, which was wrenched out of obscurity by an array of shadows. The moon was not visible, but a bright fog adorned the sky, imparting a sleepy whiteness that passed into gloom.

I walked on and paused to extract from my inside coat pocket the dark-blue handkerchief. I could feel the cone within it. I still had to find out why the gypsies forbid me to uncover this object before arriving at my destination—that is, at Brock's—for their instructions in this regard had been quite explicit. By "had to" I infer a degree of skepticism, which lingered in me despite the day's strange occurrences. Besides, a striking surprise that presents itself and in so doing refutes doubt is always sweeter than barefaced certainty. This I knew for sure. But I did not know *what* was going to happen, otherwise I should have been patient for many an hour yet.

Stopping at a corner, I undid the handkerchief and saw that the glint of green in the cone had the strange appearance of a distant light—just as if the cone were an aperture through which I could observe the approach of a lamp. The line would vanish, leaving behind a bright spot, or else appear on the very surface, glaring so brightly that I could see my own fingers as though by the light of a green coal. The cone was rather heavy, about four inches tall, and with a base like a cross-section of an apple, perfectly smooth and regular. Its color—old silver with an olive hue—was remarkable in that with the intensification of the greenish light, it appeared a dark lilac.

Fascinated and enchanted, I watched the cone, noticing a vague pattern forming around its greenish radiance, a movement of parts and shadows, similar to the papery black ash that flutters about a stove against the light of its coals. Inside the cone there was a depth, a gloom in which a hand-held lantern with a green flame was distinctly moving. As it approached the surface, the lamp seemed to be emerging from a third dimension. Its movements were capricious and magnetic, as if it were searching for a hidden way out, lighting its own way above and below. At last the lantern undeniably began to increase in size, rushing forward, and, as on the silver screen, its contours grew to such proportions that they fell beyond the confines of the cone itself. A brilliant green ray of light shone directly and piercingly into my eyes. The lantern disappeared. The whole cone lit up with the most intense brightness; no sooner had a second gone by than a terrible green glow, surging out of my fingers, spilled over the roofs of the city, turning night into a blinding brilliance of walls, snow, and air—a green day dawned, in whose light there was not a single shadow.

This silent blow lasted only a moment, the length of time it took for my fingers to clench convulsively and conceal the surface of this amazing object. And still, this moment was fraught with incident.

The all-rending brilliance was still flickering in my startled eyes, full of blind spots, but, like an enormous wall, darkness came crashing down on me—it was so dark, because of the momentary transition from maximal radiance to dense gloom, that I lost my balance and very nearly fell over. I reeled but remained standing. Trembling all over, I wrapped the cone back in the handkerchief, feeling like someone who has just thrown a bomb and managed to hide around a corner. Scarcely had my numbing hands achieved this, than a commotion of alarm arose in various parts of the city. I could but imagine that everyone who was in the streets at this hour was shouting, since from every quarter a distant "ahhh" could be heard, followed by the rapping sound of gunfire. The previously rare barking of dogs now rose to a frenzy, as if all the dogs had come together to chase some rare, lone beast that had wearied of its narrow warrens. Frightened passers-by ran past me, filling the street with frantic, pathetic cries. Breaking into a nervous sweat, I somehow walked on. A red light blazed amid the darkness; a din and ringing leaped out from around the corner as a fire engine cut across the road, racing willy-nilly to where it was needed. Along with smoke and sparks, the disturbing blaze of fire flew from the torches, reflected with an infernal quivering in the glittering helmets. The little bells on the shaft bow beat a shrill tocsin, the carts thundered, the horses tore along, and everything galloped past and vanished, like a blistering attack.

I never did find out what else befell the frightened populace that evening, for I was nearing the building where Brock lived.

As I walked up the stairs with my heart beating violently, it was only with an extreme effort of will that I forced my legs to obey me. Eventually I reached the landing and recovered my breath. Amid total darkness I groped for the door, knocked, and entered, without a word to the fellow who let me in. He was one of the tenants who knew me from before, when I lived in this apartment.

"Have you come to see Brock?" he asked. "I think he's gone out. He was here just a moment ago and was expecting you."

I said nothing, fearing to utter so much as a single word, since I had no idea what would happen if I did. I chanced upon a happy idea: I placed my hand to my cheek and began to roll my tongue and groan.

"Ah, toothache!" said the tenant. "I myself have a bad filling that often has me climbing the walls. Perhaps you'll wait for him?"

I nodded, thereby solving a difficulty that, though trifling, might have dashed all my further doings. Brock never locked the room, since with his many commercial dealings he was interested in the notes left for him on his desk. Thus, nothing stood in my way, but, on the off chance that I found Brock at home, I had already come up with a good way out: without a word, I would give him a gold coin and signal to him that I should like some wine.

Cradling my cheek, I entered the room, thanked the man who let me in with a nod and a sour smile, as befits a person in the throes of pain, and carefully closed the door behind me. Once the footsteps in the corridor had died away, I turned the key, so that no one should disturb me. As soon as I turned on the lights in Brock's quarters, I ascertained that the painting of the sunny room was standing on the floor between two chairs, by a pillar beyond which lay the nocturnal street. This detail bears an undoubted significance.

I walked up to the painting and examined it, trying to fathom the connection between this object and my visit to Bam Gran. Despite the forceful jolt to my mind caused by my terrible experience out-side, even a brain three times as stimulated as mine would not have arrived at any reasonable hypothesis. Once again I marveled at the grand though delicate exuberance of the beautiful painting. It was replete with a summer air that diffused an elegant midday somnolence; its details, impossible under even the most stringent mastery, were now especially striking. Thus, on one of the window ledges lay a woman's glove—not in plain sight, as one seeking cheap effects might have placed it, but behind the wooden frame of an open window; through the glass I could see it: diminutive, with a distinction of its own, just as every object on this wondrous canvas had a distinction of its own. Moreover, casting my view along the window with the glove, I marked a bronze hinge of the sort used to hold window frames in place, and the heads of screws in the hinge; what was more, you could see that the slots of the heads contained the vestiges of dried-out white paint. The detail of the image was no less than in those colored reflections of the mirror-like balls that are placed in gardens. I had already begun to reflect on this level of detail and wonder whether my eyes were not deceiving me; recol-lecting myself, however, I took out the cone from the handkerchief and, rooted to the spot, began scrutinizing its surface.

The green line was hardly showing now, as if waiting for the moment to blind me again with its emerald brilliance, the power and beauty of which were such that even lightning could not com-pare. The line flared up, and the green lantern raced out from the darkness of the cone. Entrusting myself to fate, I then set the cone in the middle of the table and sat down to wait.

After a little time the cone began to emit a light that grew with the force and speed of a reflector shone in one's face. I seemed to be inside the green lantern. Everything, with the exception of the electric lamp, appeared green. Bright green corridors stretched through the windows to the farthest roofs. It was an illumination of such intensity that it seemed the building would collapse and burn. A strange business! A yellow mass emitting golden steam began to condense about the electric lamp; it appeared to penetrate through the glass, eddying like boiling oil. The incandescent wire loop was no longer visible; the whole lamp looked like a glowing golden pear. Suddenly it shattered with the noise of a shot; shards of glass went flying in all directions. One of the shards landed in my hair, while fiery yellow clots rained down onto the floor, as though seething egg yolks had jumped out of a frying pan. They went out instantly, and alone the green light, which had scarcely flickered throughout all this, now surrounded me like a flood.

Needless to say, my thoughts and emotions but remotely resembled ordinary human consciousness. Any comparison, even the most fanciful, would give an idea only of my efforts to compare, but essentially it would reveal nothing. One has to endure such moments oneself in order to have the right to talk of things that have never been experienced. But perhaps you will appreciate my intense, all-embracing bewilderment if I tell you that when I accidentally brushed the chair with my hand, I did not feel its touch, as though I were disembodied. Hence, my nervous system had been shocked to the point of physical insensibility. The memory of my *psychological* experience therefore ends here—anyone who has charged with a bayonet will know what I mean: you forget *yourself* but still act as the perilous battle demands.

What happened next, I shall lay out in *my* sequence of events, without vouching for its authenticity.

"Open up!" shouted a voice from an unintelligible world—as though over the telephone, at a distance.

Someone was trying to force his way through the door. I recognized Brock's voice. A knock followed. I stood stock-still. When I examined the door, the section of wall seemed unfamiliar. It had been raised higher and now had the appearance of an arch with locked iron gates, through the openwork of which I glimpsed a deep vault. I no longer heard knocks or voices. Now I saw dramatic changes wherever I looked. A massive bronze chandelier hung from the ceiling. A part of the wall giving onto the street had seemingly been destroyed by the light, and in the expanse that opened up I saw a vista of tall trees, beyond which the waters of a bay glittered. To my right a marble balcony rose up with flowers around the railing; from under it a matador appeared, sword drawn, and raced down through the floor, chasing a bull that was running away. Artwork glinted about the chandelier. This mixture of incongruent phenomena bore a resemblance to sketches left through laziness or reverie on paper, where profiles, landscapes, and arabesques are mixed arbitrarily, according to the mood of the moment. What was left of the room was hardly visible and had altered in essence. Thus, for instance, a number of paintings hanging on the wall to the right of the entrance had shed their figures; likenesses of dolls and objects had tumbled out of the frames, leaving a profound void. I reached into the painting by Gorshkov, which looked like a tea caddy from within, and ascertained that the fir trees in the painting had been joined to the wooden base with carpenter's glue. I broke them off with ease, destroying along the way a wooden hut with a little light in the window, which turned out to be merely red paper. The snow was ordinary cotton wool dusted with naphthalene, and sticking out of it were two dried-out flies, which earlier I had taken for the classical "pair of crows." In the very depths of the chest were a tin of shoe polish and handful of walnut shells.

I turned around, uncertain of what to do, since my instructions had been to wait.

A dynamic chaos of light sparkled all around. Beneath the piano stood a crude stone and a wooden stump grown over with grass. Everything was in flux, appearing and disappearing, metamorphosing. A donkey laden with wineskins trotted past me along a stony path; its driver—a dark, hefty, barefooted lad with a red cotton bandana tied about his head—ran along behind it. Opposite me a window with an iron grille opened into a room, and a woman's hand splashed out slop from a dish. Unfamiliar people of a southern type, disappearing in an abyss of green brilliance, passed by in the air, at an angle, horizontally, vertically, in front of me, and from behind; all this was distinct yet transparent, like stained glass. There was no sound: just movement and silence. Amid this spectacle, the corner of the table with the glittering cone was barely noticeable. Having seen enough, and also fearing for the integrity of my reason, I threw my pocket handkerchief over the cone. But darkness did not descend, as I had expected; instead, only the green brilliance vanished, while my surroundings appeared again as they did before. The painting of the sunny room, which had become incomparably larger, now resembled an open door. It emitted the clear light of day, while the windows of Brock's lodgings were as black as night.

I say it emitted a light because a light truly did come from there, from the tall open windows in the painting. *There* it was day, and the day communicated its bright illumination to my domain. There also seemed to be a path. I took a coin and threw it into the background of what I continued to call a painting; I saw the coin roll across the entire floor toward a half-opened glass door at the end of the room. It only remained for me to pick it up. I stepped through the frame with a feeling as though I were meeting resistance from a headwind that silently stunned me as I drew even with the frame; day seemed to become night. I found myself standing on a solid floor and automatically took several petals from the round lacquered table, feeling their silky moistness. At this point exhaustion overwhelmed me. I sat down on a plush chair, looking back at where I had come from. *Over there* was an ordinary blank wall covered in lilac-striped wallpaper, and on it, in a thin black frame, hung a small painting that related—though I was unconscious of it—to my feelings. Having mastered the weakness natural for anyone in my position, I hurried to my feet in order to see what was depicted on the painting. What I saw was an exceptionally executed rendering: a view of a shabby, shabbily furnished room, immersed in a twilight that was barely pierced by a ray of light from the burning stove; it was the iron stove in *that* room, the very one from which I had come *here*.

I rank among those people who are not stunned by the enigmatic, those for whom it does not provoke wild excitement or distraught gestures mixed with cries. That winter's day, with the icy knife of frost stuck into its throat, had already yielded a sufficient quota of the enigmatic, yet nothing was so eloquently enigmatic as this phenomenon of a room vanished without trace and reflected in a painting. I finished by tying a small knot in my memory: I calmly went over to the window and with a firm hand flung it open to look at the city. It is not hard to imagine my *calm*, if now I get incredibly excited at its mere recollection. But *then* it was a *calm*—a state in which I was able to move and look.

As you may have gathered from my previous descriptions, the room, bathed in a glaring golden light, was a wide gallery with large windows along one side that overlooked some buildings. I inhaled the cheerful air of the south. It was warm, as at midday in June. The silence came to an end. I began to hear noises, the sounds of a city. Wheels clattered, cocks crowed, and passers-by cried discordantly beyond the ledges of the roofs scattered beneath this building, as far down as ships' masts and a sea that glittered with the toreutic blue of waves.

A terrace, surrounded by an orchard whose green tips reached as high as the windows, lay below the gallery, jutting out from under it. I was in a real but unknown place, and in such a season or at such a latitude where January is scorching hot.

A flock of pigeons flew back and forth from roof to roof. A cannon went off, and the slow tolling of a bell rang twelve o'clock.

It was then that I understood everything. My understanding derived neither from calculation nor from proof, and my brain had no part in it. It appeared like an ardent handshake and struck me no less than my former amazement. This understanding contained so complex an essence that it could be clear only for an instant, like the feeling of harmony that precedes an epileptic fit. At the time I could have described my condition only in muddled, inarticulate terms. But within me a perfect understanding arose in and of itself, in sharp, clear lines that formed an unprecedented pattern.

Then it began to recede into the depths, nodding and smiling like a woman bidding farewell from the steps of a staircase that gradually conceals her from view.

I was again at the threshold of ordinary emotions. They had returned from the fiery sphere scorched but assembled securely and precisely. My state now differed little from the usual reserve one feels during any dramatic episode.

I passed through a door and cut across the twilight of a room that I did not have time to examine. Carpeted steps led downstairs. I descended into a large and very bright room that had a low ceiling and was filled with beautiful furniture, divans, and flowers. Its walls were covered in an array of colored silks. Halfway I was stopped by Bam Gran's gaze; he was sitting on a divan holding a cane and a hat in his hand; with a biscuit he was teasing a fox terrier, which was jumping about and barking amusingly, ecstatic at both his failure and anticipation.

Bam Gran had on a suit the color of seawater. His gaze recalled the end of a whip lashing the air.

"I knew I would see you," he said, "and though I had intended to take a stroll, I place myself entirely at your disposal. If you wish,

I'll give you the name of the town. It's Zurbagan, Zurbagan in May, when the orange trees are in blossom—the pleasant Zurbagan of jokers like myself."

With these words he let go of the biscuit and, standing up, shook my hand.

"You are a brave man, Don Kaur," he exclaimed, "and I like that, just as I like all things extraordinary. What do you feel, having conquered thousands of miles?"

"Thirst," I said. "I feel a difference in air pressure, and I feel terribly unnerved!"

"I understand."

He squeezed the dog's muzzle with his elegant fingers and, peering into its ecstatic eyes with a smile, ordered:

"Go and tell Remm that we have a guest. Have him bring some wine and ice."

With a yap, the dog sped off.

"No, no," said Bam Gran, noticing my involuntary movement. "It's only a matter of first-rate training. The word 'Remm' means 'fetch Remm.' Remm himself knows what to do when he sees Pli-Pli. Meanwhile, Señor Kaur, treasure what time you have, for you can stay here for only half an hour. I should not want you to have cause for regret. In any case, we'll each have time for a glass of wine. Remm, your alacrity is touching!"

The servant entered. He was wearing white pyjamas and his head was shaved. Having set down on the table a tray bearing a colored-glass carafe of wine and a decanter filled with pomegranate juice, as well as ice in a silver vase and some straws, he retreated and looked at Bam Gran with adoration.

"We've run out of ice, Señor!"

"Take some from a Norwegian fjord or a river in Siberia!"

"I took Remm from Tristan da Cunha," said Bam Gran after the servant had left. "I removed him from the terrible mystery of a looking glass, by which he became transfixed during a *particular* moment in his life. Let's have a drink!"

He dipped a straw into a mixture of ice and wine and thoughtfully sipped it, while I, tortured by thirst, simply emptied the glass into my mouth.

"Well then," he said. "The 'Fandango'! Such wonderful music, and we'll hear it presently from Barcelona, in a rendition by Van Herd's orchestra."

I looked at him in astonishment, for truly at that moment I had been thinking of the guitars that broke into that remarkable dance as Bam Gran disappeared. I had been silently humming it to myself.

"Barcelona is not Zurbagan," I said. "I'd like to know what *radio* you'll use to produce this orchestra."

"Oh, you simpleton!" said Bam Gran, standing up with a rather haughty air. "Van Herd, play us Walter's arrangement of the 'Fandango.'"

A rich bass answered politely and succinctly out of the void:

"Very well! Right away."

I heard a cough, some noise, the rustle of sheet music, and the clatter of instruments. Biting his lip, Bam Gran listened. A dry tap of the conductor's baton put an abrupt end to the squeaking of a violin string; I looked around, trying to figure out the trick, but, recalling everything that had already taken place, I sat back and began to wait.

Then, as if the orchestra were truly there, the one and only "Fandango" surged forth in all its glory. I can say that I was hearing it with greatly heightened emotions, but nevertheless it raised them higher still, to heights from which the earth is scarcely visible. The exceptional purity and plasticity of this music, in combination with the perfection of the orchestration, caused my legs to grow numb. I myself reverberated, like a pane of glass that vibrates when it thunders. Spinning in the rapid, circular movements of the glittering rhythm, I watched Bam Gran vacantly and found it difficult to understand what he was saying. "It bears everything away," said the man who had led me there, in the way a firm hand guides a diamond on glass to score a whimsical, wonderful pattern. "It bears it away, scatters it, rends it," he was saying. "It stirs the wind and inspires love. It strikes at the strongest bonds. It holds the heart in its ardent hand and kisses it. Instead of calling you, it gathers whirlwinds of gold discs around you, spinning them among a frenzy of color. Long live the dazzling 'Fandango'!"

The orchestra slowed and paused silently for the final transition. It broke into a nerve-rattling explosion of ultimate triumph. The music soared to its captivating zenith, being borne from summit to summit, and descended touchingly and proudly, with a restraint of expressiveness. Silence fell, like a train that comes to a standstill at a station—a silence that puts an abrupt end to the melody that plays out to the rhythmic clatter of turning wheels.

I came to my senses, like a stopped clock when its pendulum is given a push.

"You see," said Bam Gran, "Van Herd really does have the world's finest orchestra. He gave us his best. Let's go now, for time is slipping away. If you stay here another ten minutes, you may have cause to regret Bam Gran's hospitality!"

He stood up; I, too, got to my feet, my head full of smoke and the flying, impetuous rhythms of the fantastic orchestra. We passed through a blue-glass door and found ourselves on the landing of a grimy stone staircase.

"Now it is I who mustn't remain here," said Bam Gran, retreating into the shadows, where he became a design on the wall's crumbling limestone, a design that bore, it was true, a vague resemblance to his angular figure. "Farewell!"

The voice came either from the courtyard or from a door that slammed shut below, and so I was alone again . . .

The staircase led down a narrow seven-story well.

The pale-blue summer air was shining through the open window on the landing. Below was a very familiar courtyard—that of the building in which I lived.

I inspected the three doors that led onto the landing. On one of them, below a number seven, was a brass plate bearing my landlady's name: Maria Stepanovna Kuznetsova.

Beneath this plate, affixed with tacks, was my visiting card. It was where it ought to be, but the card itself had changed.

I read: "Alexander Kaur" and after it an "and" written in ink. It was placed between the upper and lower lines. The lower line, whose meaning was connected to the top line by this *conjunction*, was also written in ink. It read: "and Elizaveta Antonovna Kaur." Well! Behind this door where I stood, my wife Liza was waiting for me in a small, out-of-the-way room. Remembering this, I seemed to receive a mighty blow to the forehead. But I did not *come to*, for the sequence of events that had only just relinquished its power over me came flowing back to me vividly. At that moment I *fell*; it was as if I had leaped on top of a creature that had begun to shriek in the darkness. With the horror of an exhausted mind, I came to life through a life that had vanished without trace. My strength deserted me, while two years, emerging from the void, rushed into my consciousness, like water through a burst dam. My fists hammered on the door, and I went on pounding until Liza's quick steps and the sound of a key confirmed the validity of my violence in the face of my own life.

I leaped inside and embraced my wife.

"Is it you?" I asked. "Is it really, truly you?"

I pressed her close, repeating:

"You, you, you?"

"Whatever's the matter with you?" she said, freeing herself, her face pale and startled. "Don't you feel well? Why have you come back so soon?"

"Soon?!"

"Let's go," she said with the determination of sudden, extreme agitation brought on by fear.

The faces of curious residents appeared in the doorways. Ordinariness was regaining its lost strength; I went in and sat down in an armchair.

I sat there, perfectly still. Liza took off my cap and turned it over in her hands.

"Tell me, what's happened?" she said blankly, in growing fear. "Your hair is matted. Are you hurt? Did you bang into something?"

"Liza, tell me," I began, taking her by the hand, "and please don't be afraid of my questions: when did I leave the house?"

She grew pale but immediately surrendered to the mysterious internal transmission of my state. Her voice was unnaturally clear; she fixed my eyes in hers. Her words were rapid and submissive.

"You left to go to the post office about twenty minutes, maybe half an hour ago."

"Did I say anything to you as I left?"

"I don't remember. You slammed the door a little, and as you left I heard you whistling the 'Fandango.'"

My memory performed an about-face, and I recalled having gone out to send a registered letter.

"What year is it?"

"Nineteen twenty-three." Saying this, she began to cry but did not wipe away the tears; very likely she did not realize she was crying. The intensity of her gaze was extraordinary.

"The month?"

"May."

"The date?"

"May twenty-third, nineteen twenty-three. I'll go to the pharmacy."

She stood up and quickly put on her hat. Then she took some small change from the table. I did not stop her. Looking at me peculiarly, my wife left, and I heard her quick steps in the direction of the front door.

While she was gone, I reconstructed the past; it did not surprise me, for it was *my* past, and I saw clearly all the minute details that constituted this moment. However, I was faced with the problem of reconciling a certain parallel existence with the past. The parallel's physical essence was expressed in a yellow leather purse, which weighed the same two pounds in my hand now that it had also done *some* time ago. I surveyed the room, making a complete connection between the individual moments of the two years that had flashed by and the history of each object that had knotted its loop in the lacework of my existence. And so I grew weary, reliving the past, which seemed as though it had never been.

"Sasha!" Liza stood before me, holding out a phial. "You're to take twenty-five of these drops. Please, take them . . ."

But at last the time had come to give vent to everything. I sat her down beside me and said:

"Listen and think. It wasn't *this room* that I left this morning. I left the room I lived in before I met you, in *January, nineteen twenty-one.*"

With these words I took out the yellow purse and poured the glittering piastres into my wife's lap.

Only by means of repeating the conversation under those same circumstances could I convey both it and our agitation following such a demonstration of the truth.

We sat down, stood up, sat down again, and interrupted each other until I had related what had happened to me from beginning to end. Several times my wife cried:

"You're raving! You're frightening me! You want me to believe that?"

Then I pointed to the gold coins.

"Yes, I know," she kept saying, her head spinning so much from the hopelessness of the situation that all she could say was: "Ugh, I'll die if I can't understand this."

Finally, in profound exhaustion, she began to ask questions over and again, almost mechanically, now laughing, now dropping her head onto her arms, tears streaming. I was calmer. My composure gradually rubbed off on her. It had already begun to grow dark by the time she lifted her head with a distraught and meaningful look lit up by a smile.

"I'm such a fool!" she said, sighing fitfully and attending to her hair—a sign that the psychological turmoil was at an end. "It's really quite clear! Everything has gone topsy-turvy, and in this topsy-turviness turned out in its rightful place!"

I marveled at woman's ability to define a situation in a few words, and had to agree that the accuracy of her definition left nothing to be desired.

After this she began to cry again; I asked what was wrong.

"But you were gone for two years!" she said, horrified and angrily twisting the button on my vest.

"You know yourself that I was gone for thirty minutes."

"All the same . . ."

I agreed and, having talked a little longer, Liza, like one over-whelmed, fell into the deepest sleep. I left quickly and quietly, hot on the trail of life—or of a vision? Feeling the gold roundels in my vest pocket, I could not—and still cannot—give a positive answer.

I reached the Madrid almost at a run. Terpugov was pacing up and down the half-empty hall; spotting me, he rushed toward me, shaking my hand with the vigor of a gracious, cordial meeting.

"There you are," he said. "Take a seat, you'll be served right away. Vanya! His bream! Go and ask Nefedin whether it's ready."

We sat down and began to talk of various things, while I pretended that there was nothing to explain. It was perfectly simple, like any other day. The waiter brought the food and opened a bottle of Madeira. A fried bream sizzled on the dish; I was sure it was the same fish I had given Terpugov, for I recall that its gill had been torn lengthwise.

"Well, Terpugov," I said, unable to restrain myself, "you've kept your word after two years."

He gave me a sly look.

"He-he!" said the former cook. "What's this you're remembering? I saw you just yesterday—you were bringing a bream from the market, whereas I was drunk and began pestering you, I admit, in order to drag you here."

He was right. I remembered it now with the annoying unassailability of fact. But I, too, was right, and, leaning into Terpugov's ear, I whispered:

Over the sea, in the plains,
Full of the heat and the snow,
Dreaming, and in fluid motion,
An evergreen palm bends down low.

"He-he!" he said, filling the glass with more Madeira. "You do like to joke."

It was evening. A drizzle was falling.

RUSSIAN LIBRARY